THE WOMAN IN THE MIRROR

THE WOMAN
IN THE MIRROR

REBECCA JAMES

THORNDIKE PRESS
A part of Gale, a Cengage Company

Copyright © 2018 by Rebecca James.
Thorndike Press, a part of Gale, a Cengage Company.

ALL RIGHTS RESERVED
This is a work of fiction. All of the characters, organizations, and events portrayed in this novel are either products of the author's imagination or are used fictitiously.
Thorndike Press® Large Print Basic.
The text of this Large Print edition is unabridged.
Other aspects of the book may vary from the original edition.
Set in 16 pt. Plantin.

LIBRARY OF CONGRESS CIP DATA ON FILE.
CATALOGUING IN PUBLICATION FOR THIS BOOK
IS AVAILABLE FROM THE LIBRARY OF CONGRESS

ISBN-13: 978-1-4328-8046-0 (hardcover alk. paper)

Published in 2020 by arrangement with Macmillan Publishing Group, LLC/St. Martin's Publishing Group

Printed in Mexico
Print Number: 01   Print Year: 2020

For the little soul
who wrote this book with me.

Shade of a shadow in the glass,
O set the crystal surface free!
Pass — as the fairer visions pass —
Nor ever more return, to be
The ghost of a distracted hour,
That heard me whisper, "I am shew!"
— MARY ELIZABETH COLERIDGE

PROLOGUE
CORNWALL, WINTER 1806

Listen! Can you hear it?

There, right there. Listen. You are not listening. Listen hard.

Listen harder.

I hear them before I see them. Their shouts come from across the hill, calling my name, calling me Witch. They come with their spikes and flames, their red mouths and their black intent. They say I am the one to fear, but the fear is with them. Fear is in them. It has no need of me. Their fear will catch them at the final hour.

Shadows crawl over the moors, spreading dark against dark. Their torches dance, lit from the fire at the barn. Burn her! Drown her! Smoke her from her hole!

Witch.

It is not safe for me here. They will touch their fires to my home and I will perish inside. So I escape into the night, their steps bleeding close on the wind like a dread gal-

9

lop. Down the cliffs, low to the ground, the sky watches, patient and indifferent. Stars are frozen. Moon observes. I cannot turn back: my home is lost.

At the end I will put myself there again, sitting by my hearth and staring at the painting on the wall. It is the painting I did for him but never gave him, a likeness of my house for he had admired it so; he had said what a perfect spot it held, high on the cliffs, a sweet little cottage circled by hay and firs. Oh, for those first days of innocence! For those days of blind hope, before he turned me away. On the night I planned to bestow the painting on him, he broke my heart. The gift I had meant for him remained with me, just as did every other part I imagined I would share.

I never thought I would be a woman for love, or a woman to be loved.

A woman should always trust herself.

What will remain at my home, after I am gone? What will he keep and what will he burn? I fear for my looking glass, my beloved mirror. I pray that it survives, for I wonder if a piece of me, however small, might survive with it.

Ivan. My love. How could you?

I shall never know. I will never understand. What is the point, now, in any case? Ivan de

Grey betrayed me. I believed that he worshipped me, I swallowed his deceits and oh, it hurts, it hurts, to think of his arms around me . . .

Now they have built their case against me. They have shaped their fight and honed their resolve. There is nothing I can say or do; to protest confirms my fate.

I spill down the cliff path. I know it well enough in the dark. Brambles tear my skin and eyes; blood tastes sour in my mouth. I stumble, holding mud and air. My head hits a rock, sharp, hard, and I fall until a pain pulls me back, my hair caught on a stalk. For a moment, I lie still. *Thunder, thunder, thunder.* I gaze up at the night, the cool white pearl of the moon. I wish I were an animal. I wish I were a wolf. I wish I would transform, and be waiting for them when they come over the edge. I would leap at them with my jaws thrown wide.

But I am a woman. Not a wolf. Perhaps I am something in between.

Run.

I meet the sea, which has swallowed the sand completely. It foams around my ankles and I wade through it, salt burning the cuts on my legs. Ivan long ago decided I was marked. He saw the red on my body and the rest was easy. He told his friends and

11

those friends told their enemies, and all are united in the crusade. *Witch.*

All he had to do was to make her believe in his love.

Love.

Rotten, stinking, hated love. Love is for fools, bound for hell.

I detest its creeping treacheries. I resent the shell it made of me. My weakness to be wanted, my pathetic, throbbing heart . . .

There is comfort in knowing that while I die, my hatred lives on. My hatred remains here, on this coast, in this sea and under this sky. My hatred remains.

I trust it with my vengeance, for vengeance I will take.

The water pulls me to my knees, black and thrashing and soaking my dress.

I turn to shore. High on the hill is a bright, living blaze. The men stride toward me, stride through the sea. I will not go with them. I will go on my own, willingly. I will swim to the deep and deeper still. I will picture my home as I drown.

I crawl into the wild dark.

A hand grabs my ankle and pulls me down.

CHAPTER 1
LONDON, 1947

"Alice Miller — for heaven's sake, wake up."

It might be Mrs. Wilson's uppity remark that jolts me out of my eleven o'clock reverie, or else it's the warm muzzle of the Quakers Oatley & Sons' resident Red Setter as it nudges hotly against my lap, for it's hard to know which happens first.

"I'm awake," I tell her, finding the dog's warm ears under my desk and working them through my fingers; Jasper breathes contentedly through his nose and his tail bangs on the floor. "Can't you see my eyes are open?"

Mrs. Wilson, the firm's stuffy administrator, draws deeply on her cigarette, sucking in her cheeks. She dispels a plume of smoke before grinding the cigarette out in an ashtray. She pushes her glasses on to the bridge of her nose.

"I wouldn't suggest for a moment, Miss Miller, that your eyes being open has the slightest thing to do with it." Her fingers

13

clack-clack on the typewriter. "It doesn't take a fool to see that you're miles away. As usual."

If I were able to dispute the accusation, I would. But she's right. There is little about being a solicitor's secretary that I find stimulating, and my memories too often call me back. This is not living, as I have known living. Haven't we all known living — and dying — in ways impossible to articulate? But to look in Jean Wilson's eyes, just two years after wartime, as flat and gray as the city streets seem to me now, it's as if that world might never have existed; as if it had been just one of my daydreams. I wonder what Mrs. Wilson lost during those years. It is easy for one to feel as though one's own loss overtakes all others' — but then one remembers: mine is a lone story, a single note in a piece of music that, if played back many years from now, would be obscured by the orchestra that surrounds it.

Jasper pads out from under the desk and settles on a rug by the window. Through it, I hear the noisy brakes of a bus and a car tooting its horn.

The telephone rings. "Good morning, Quakers Oatley?"

We are expecting a call from an irksome client but to my surprise it is not he. For a

14

moment, I hear the crackle of the line and the faint echo of another exchange, before a smart voice introduces itself. My grip tightens. I'm quiet for long enough that Mrs. Wilson's interest is aroused. She glances at me over the top of her spectacles.

"Of course," I say, once I've taken in all that he's said. "I'll be with you right away."

I replace the telephone, retrieve my coat and open the door.

"Where are you going?"

"Goodbye, Mrs. Wilson." I put on my coat. "Goodbye, Jasper."

It is the last time I will see either of them.

The Tube still smells as it did in the war — fusty, sour, hot with bodies. Next to me on the platform is a woman with her children; she smacks one of them on the hand and tells him off, then pulls both to her when the train comes in. I imagine her down here during the Blitz, when they were babies, holding them close while the sky fell down.

I take the train to Marble Arch, repeating the address as I go. The building is closer than I think and I'm here early, so I step into a café next door and order a mug of tea. I drink it slowly, still wearing my hat. A man at the table next to me slices his fried egg on toast so that the yolk bursts over his plate and an orange bead lands on the greasy, checkered oilcloth. He dabs it with his finger.

I've kept the advertisement in my handbag for a month. I didn't think anything would come of it; the opportunity seemed too niche, too unlikely, too convenient. GOVERNESS REQUIRED, FAMILY HALL NR. POLCREATH, IMMEDIATE APPOINTMENT. I spied it during a sandwich break, in the back of the county paper Mrs. Wilson brought home from a long weekend in the South West.

I unfold it and read it again. There really isn't any other information, nothing about the people I would be working for or for how long the position might be. I question if this isn't what drew me toward the prospect in the first place. My life used to be full of uncertainties: each day was uncertain, each sunrise and sunset one that we didn't expect to see; each night, while we waited for the bombs to drop and the gunfire to start, was extra time we had somehow stumbled into. Uncertainty kept me alive, knowing that the moment I was in couldn't possibly last forever and the next would soon be here, a moment of change, of newness, the ground shifting beneath my feet and moving me forward. At Quakers Oat-

16

ley, the ground sticks fast, so fast I feel myself drowning.

The tea turns tepid, the deep cracked brown of a terracotta pot, and a fleck of milk powder floats depressingly on its surface. The man next to me grins, flips out his newspaper: *India Wins Independence: British Rule Ends.* I sense him about to speak and so stand before he can, buttoning my coat and checking my reflection in the smeared window. I pull open the café door, its chime offering a weak ring.

There it is, then. No. 46. Across the road, the genteel townhouse bears down, its glossy black door and polished copper bell push like a delicately wrapped present that my fumbling fingers are desperate, yet fearful, to open. Before we begin, it has me on the back foot. I need it more than it needs me. This job is my ticket out of London, away from the past, away from my secrets. This job is escape.

"Welcome, Miss Miller. Do please sit down."

I peel off my gloves and set them neatly on the desk before changing my mind and scooping them into my bag. I set the bag on my lap, then have nowhere to put my hands, so I place the bag on the floor, next to my ankles.

He doesn't appear to notice this display, or perhaps he is too polite to acknowledge it. Instead, he takes a file from the drawer and flicks through it for several moments. The top of his head, as he bends, is bald, and clean as a marble.

"Thank you for meeting us at short notice," he says, with a quick smile. "My client, as you'll understand, prefers to be discreet, and often that means securing results swiftly. We would prefer to resolve the appointment as soon as possible."

"Of course."

"You have experience with children?"

"I used to nanny our neighbors' infants, before the war."

He nods. "My client's children require tutelage as well as pastoral care. We are concerned with the curriculum but also with a comprehensive education in nature, the arts, sports and games — and, naturally, refinement of etiquette and propriety."

I sit straighter. "Naturally."

"The twins are eight years old." His eyes meet mine for the first time, sharp and glassy as a crow's.

"Very good."

"I'm afraid this isn't the sort of position

you can abandon after a month," he says. "If you find it a challenge, you can begin your instruction by teaching these children the knack of perseverance." He puts his fingers together. "I mention this because my client lost his last governess suddenly and without warning."

"Oh."

"As a widower, he has understandably struggled. These are difficult times."

I'm surprised. "Did his wife die recently?"

Immediately I know I have spoken out of turn. I am not here to question this man; he is here to question me. My interest is unwelcome.

"Tell me, Miss Miller," he says, bypassing my inquiry with ease, "what occupation did you hold during the war?"

"I volunteered with the WVS."

The man teases the end of his mustache. "Nurturing yet capable: would that be a fair assessment?"

"I'd suggest the two aren't mutually exclusive."

He writes something down.

"Have you always lived in London?"

"I grew up in Surrey."

"And attended which school . . . ?"

"Burstead."

His eyebrow snags, impressed but not liking to show it. I know my education was among the finest in the country. My mother was schooled at Burstead, and my grandmother before that. There was never any question that my parents would send me there. I tighten my fists in my lap, remembering my father's face over that Sunday lunch in 1940. The ticking of the mantel clock, the shaft of winter sunlight that bounced off the table, the smell of burned fruit crumble . . . His rage when I told him what I had done. That the education they had bought for me had instead brought a nightmare to their door. The sound of smashing glass as my mother walked in, letting the tumbler fall, shattering into a thousand splinters on the treacle-colored carpet.

He clears his throat, tapping the page with his pen. I see my own handwriting.

"In your letter," he says, "you say you are keen to move away from the city. Why?"

"Aren't we all?" I answer a little indecorously, because this is easy, this is what he expects to hear. "I would never care to repeat the things I have seen or done over the past six years. The city holds no magic for me any more."

He sees my automatic answer for what it is.

"But you, personally," he presses, those eyes training into me again. "I am interested in what makes you want to leave."

A moment passes, an open door, the person on each side questioning if the other will walk through — before it closes. The man sits forward.

"You might deem me improper," he says, "but my inquests are made purely on my client's behalf. We understand that the setting of your new appointment is a far cry from the capital. Are you used to isolation, Miss Miller? Are you accustomed to being on your own?"

"I am very comfortable on my own."

"My client needs to know if you have the vigor for it. As I said previously, he does not wish to be hiring a third governess in a few weeks' time."

"I've no doubt."

"Therefore, if you will forgive my impudence, could you reassure us that you have no medical history of mental disturbances?"

"Disturbances?"

"Depressive episodes, attacks of anxiety, that sort of thing."

I pause. "No."

"You cannot reassure us, or you can that you haven't?"

For the first time, there is the trace of a

smile. I am almost there. Almost. I don't have to tell him the truth. I don't have to tell him anything.

"I can reassure you that I am perfectly well," I say, and it trips off my tongue as smoothly as my name.

The man assesses me, then squares the paper in front of him and replaces it in its folder. When he leans back in his chair, I hear the creak of leather.

"Very well, Miss Miller," he says. "My client entrusts me with the authority to hire at will in light of my appraisal of an applicant's suitability, and I am pleased to offer you the position of governess at the Polcreath estate with immediate effect."

I rein in my delight. "Thank you."

"Before you accept, is there anything you would like to ask us?"

"Your client's name, and the name of the house."

"Then I must insist on your signature."

He slides a piece of paper across the desk, a contract of sorts, listing my start date as this coming week, the broad terms of my responsibilities toward the children, and that my bed and board will be provided. There is a dotted line at the foot, awaiting my pen. "I understand it is unorthodox," he says, "but my client is a private man. We need assurance of your allegiance before I'm permitted to give details."

"But until I have details I have little idea what I am signing."

The man holds his hands up, as if helpless. I wait a moment, but there is never any hesitation in my mind. I collect the pen and sign my name.

CHAPTER 2

My train pulls into Polcreath Station at four o'clock on Sunday. The warmth has gone out of the day and a rich, autumn sun sits low on the horizon, casting the land in a burned harvest glow. I'm quick to see the car, but then it's hard to miss, a smart, black Rolls-Royce whose white wheels gleam like bones in the fading light.

A man greets me, short, middle-aged, fair. "Miss Miller?"

"How do you do."

He lifts my bags into the car then opens the rear door for me. Up close, the Rolls is more decayed than it first appeared. Its paintwork is peeling and inside the upholstery is fissured and coming away from the seat frames. There is the smell of old cigarettes and petrol. It takes the chauffeur a moment to start the engine.

"I'm Tom, Winterbourne's houseman," he says, when I ask him: not a chauffeur after

all, then. "I'll turn my hand to anything."
He has a gentle Northern accent and a
friendly, easy manner. "There's not many of
us — just me and Cook. And you, now, of
course. The house can't afford anyone else,
though goodness knows we need it. We're
mighty excited to have you joining us, miss.
Winterbourne always seems darker at this
time of year, when the evenings draw in and
the light starts to go. The more company
the better, I say."

"Please, call me Alice."

"Right you are, miss."

I smile. "Is it far to Winterbourne?"

"Not far. Over the bluff. The sea makes it
seem further — there's a lot of sea. Are you
used to the sea, miss?"

"Not very. One or two holidays as a child."

"The sea's as much a part of Winterbourne as its roof and walls. I expect that
sounds daft to a city lady like yourself, but
there it is. You can see the sea from every
window, did they tell you that?"

"They didn't tell me much about anything."

Tom crunches the gears. "This car's a bad
lot. The captain would never part with it,
but really we'd be better off with a horse
and cart, at the rate this thing goes."

"More comfortable, though, I'd wager."

Although I'm being generous: with every bump and rut in the road the car squeaks in protest, and the springs in my seat dig painfully into my thighs. The short distance Tom promised is ever lengthening. In time we come off the road and on to a track, on either side of which the countryside spreads, a swathe of dark green that eventually gives way, if I squint into the distance, to a flat sheet of gray water.

"The moors look tame from here," says Tom, with a quick glance over his shoulder, "but wait till we reach the cliffs. It's a sheer drop there — ground beneath your feet one moment, then nothing. You've got to be careful, miss. The mists that come in off the sea are solid. Some days you can't see more than a foot or two in front, you can't see a thing. All you've got to go on is the sound of the sea, but if you lose your bearings with that, one wrong step and you're gone. Winterbourne's right on the bluff. Some people say it's the second lighthouse at Polcreath."

"How long have you worked for the captain?"

"Since before the war. I knew him when he was a . . . different sort of person. The war changed people, didn't it? Just because you have a title, or a place like Winterbourne, it doesn't spare you. He was hurt

26

in France; it's been hard for him, an able-bodied man like that suddenly made a cripple. Did the war change you, miss?"

I focus on the horizon, an expanse of steel coming ever closer, and concentrate on the clean line of it so intently that I can't think of anything else. "Of course."

"Between you and me, I could likely find better-paid employment elsewhere, but I've got loyalty for Winterbourne, and for the captain. My mother used to say that you're nothing without your friends. The captain would never say I was a friend, but he doesn't say a lot of things that he might really mean."

"How tragic that he lost his wife."

"Indeed, miss." There's a laden silence. "But we don't speak about that."

I sit back. I had hoped that Tom's loquaciousness might lend itself to a confidence, but seemingly not on this matter. Two people now have refused to speak to me about the former woman of the house. What happened to her?

I am expecting us to come across the Hall suddenly, to catch a quick glimpse of it between trees or to swing abruptly through the park gates, but instead I spot it first as a ragged smudge on the hill. That's how it appears — as an inkblot the size of my thumb, spilled in water, its edges seeming to fall away or dissolve into air. There is something about its position, elevated and alone, that reminds me of a fortress in a storybook, or of a drawing of a haunted house, its black silhouette set starkly against the deepening orange of the sky. As we approach, I begin to make out its features. To say that Winterbourne is an extreme-looking house would be an understatement.

It's hard to imagine a more dramatic façade. The place instantly brings to mind an imposing religious house — a Parisian cathedral, perhaps, decorated with gaping arches and delicate spires. Turrets thrust skyward, and to the east the blunt teeth of a battlement crown remind me of a game of chess. Plunging gargoyles are laced around its many necks, long and thin, jutting, as if leaping from the building's skin. Lancet windows, too many to count, adorn the exterior, and set on the western front is what appears to be a chapel. I was scarcely aware of having entered the park, and it strikes me that we must have crossed into it a while ago; that the land we've been driving on all this time belongs to Winterbourne.

Gnarled trees creep out of the drowning afternoon. To our left, away from the sea, spreads a wild, dark wood, dense with firs and the soft black mystery of how it feels to be lost, away from home, when you are a child and the night draws close. On the other, the sea is a wide-eyed stare, lighter and smoother now we are near, like pearls held in a cold hand. I see what Tom meant about the drop from the cliffs: the land sweeps up and away from the hall, a brief sharp lip like the crest of a wave, and then it is a four-hundred-foot plummet to the rocks. Further still into that unblinking spread I detect Polcreath Point, the tower light, a mile or so from the shore.

"Here we are, miss." Tom turns the Rolls a final time and we embark up the final stretch toward the house, a narrow track between overgrown topiary. Leafy fingers drag against the windows, and the car rocks over a series of potholes that propels my vanity case into the foothold. At last we emerge into an oval of gravel, at the center of which is an unkempt planter, tangled with weeds.

"Winterbourne Hall."

I gaze up at my new lodgings, and imagine how my arrival must look. A throbbing engine, a lonely car — and a woman, peering skyward, her hand poised to open the door, and some slight switch of nameless apprehension that makes her pause.

The first thing I notice is the smell. It isn't unpleasant, merely unusual, a liturgical smell like the inside of a church: wood, stone and burning candles.

There are no candles burning. The entrance is gloomy, lit by a flickering candelabrum. "Ticky generator," explains Tom, taking off his cap. "We use fires, mostly." I look up at the chandelier, its bulbs bruised with dust and casting an uncertain glow that sends tapered shadows across the walls. The ceiling is ribbed and vaulted, like the roof of a basilica, but its decorations are bleached and crumbled. A staircase climbs ahead of me, a faded scarlet runner up its center, bolted in place by gold pins. Some of the pins are missing and the carpet frays up against the wood like a rabbit's tail. On the upper walls, a trio of hangings in red and bronze sits alongside twisting metal sconces, better suited to a Transylvanian castle than to a declining Cornish home. There is a large stone fireplace, coated in soot, and several items of heavy Elizabethan furniture positioned in alcoves: elaborate dark-wood chairs, an occasional table, and a hulking chest with edges wreathed in nail heads.

On the landing above, I see closed doors,

set with Gothic forging. The windows are heavily draped in velvet, with tasseled tiebacks. Dozens of eyes watch me watching. Paintings of the captain's ancestors bear down from every facet.

For a moment I have the uncanny sense of having been here before — then I place the connection. The headmaster's study at Burstead. How, when a girl was called in for a flogging, she would be surrounded by an army of onlookers — those men, tyrants past, with their shining eyes and satisfied smirks, their portraits as immovable as the headmaster's intention, and she would stand in the red punitive glow of the stained-glass window and bite her lip while the first lash came . . .

Afterward, when they couldn't decide how the tragedy had happened, they brought us all in for a whipping; perhaps they thought the belt would draw it out of us as cleanly as it drew blood to the skin. The difficulty was that nobody except me knew the truth. Nobody else had been there. They sensed a secret, dark and dreadful, rippling through the dormitories like an electrical charge, but I was the only girl who knew and I wasn't about to share it. So I kept my lips shut and I let the lashes come for me and for the others, and time passed and term ended and school finished not long after that.

I blink, and take my gloves off.

"Where are the children?" I ask. "I should like to introduce myself."

Tom gives me a strange look. "The captain asked us to settle you in first, miss. The twins can get overexcited. They like to play games."

"Well, they're children, aren't they?"

He pauses, as if my query might have some other answer.

"What happened to their previous governess? The woman before me?"

"She left," Tom replies, too quickly and smoothly for it to be the truth. "One morning, suddenly. We had no warning, miss, honestly. She sent word days later — a family emergency. She was mighty sad about it, hated letting the captain down. We all of us hate to let the captain down. It'd be horrible if he was let down again, wouldn't it, miss? After the effort he's gone to, to bring you down here. There's only so much a man can take. The captain said there was no way round it, and the world exists outside Winterbourne whether we like it or not. Because you do feel that way, miss, here, after a while. Like Winterbourne is all there is, just the house and sea. You find you don't need anything else." His expression is unfathomable, doggedly loyal.

"Do the children miss her terribly?" I am not sure if I am talking about the governess or the children's mother: this pair of doomed women, for a moment, seem bound in a fundamental, terrifying way, but the thought flits free before I can catch it.

"Of course they do," Tom says. "But they'll warm to you even better."

I'm about to ask my predecessor's name — it seems important to know it — when there is a noise on the staircase: a shuffle of footsteps, a slow, lilting gait, punctuated by the unmistakable point of a cane. When my employer comes into view, I take a step back. I have never seen anyone in my life who looks like this.

"The new governess," he says bluntly, twisting his cane into the stair.

For a moment I forget my name.

"Alice Miller," I say at last.

The man steps forward, into a pit of shadow so that I can no longer see his face. *Captain Jonathan de Grey.* The name that has followed me from London, from that interview that seems like years ago in spite of it being days — from before then, even, if that were possible. "I trust you had a good journey," he says, in a peculiar, remote voice. "We're very pleased that you're here. Very pleased indeed."

CHAPTER 3

NEW YORK, PRESENT DAY

Rachel Wright stepped on to the podium to address her guests. Pride filled her as she took in the gallery launch, the people mingling, the inspiring artworks and the sheer transformation of the space she had purchased six months ago from rundown warehouse to edgy exhibition. Immediately, she felt his eyes on her.

"Ladies and gentlemen," Paul, her assistant, announced as he tapped the microphone. "May I introduce the woman responsible for tonight: Founder and Director of the Square Peg Gallery — Rachel Wright!" Paul smiled as he led the applause. He wanted to please her. Everyone did. Rachel commanded respect. Little was known about her private life and the care with which she protected it was a point of staunch admiration. Paul and the others knew about the big thing, of course. But nobody mentioned it.

"Thank you all for being here tonight," Rachel began. "And thanks especially to our sponsors, without whom none of this would be possible — in particular White Label Inc. and G&V Assets." She deliberately named his firm second; it was a stupid power thing. More applause, for them or for her, it didn't matter. She needed their funds and they needed her association. She'd said as much in her pitch. Where was their commitment to community culture? Were their rivals delivering on social responsibility? She remembered launching her petition in his boardroom, the way his black eyes had trained into her as they trained into her now, challenging her. How did he always manage it? Rachel could present to sponsors from here to Milan, could sit opposite the greatest creatives in the world, but with him, well, he made her feel the spotlight. It was the excitement of their arrangement, she supposed.

"If this gallery hasn't stopped to breathe, then neither have I," Rachel told her audience, thinking of the three hours' sleep she had grown accustomed to snatching; of the caffeine she lived off and the cigarettes she was trying to give up but that sometimes pushed her that extra hour into the night, of the determination — "my mother had another word for it," she joked — that took an idea out of one's head and made it a reality; of the team she'd had behind her; of her Upper West Side apartment that she never spent any time in and that had become overtaken by work. Talking about the gallery was like talking about herself, for she had given everything to it over the past eighteen months. Art was her passion and her purpose. She had always found sanctuary in it, in its possibility and lack of boundary, in its subjectivity and beauty, in its strength to innovate and energize, to change minds and start dialogues. Since she could remember, she'd been happiest staring into a painting or admiring a sculpture, imagining the stories that went into it and, in doing so, she was able to forget her own.

As always when Rachel spoke in front of big crowds, she wound up feeling they were waiting for more. Perhaps they were. They knew, after all, what had happened to her back in 2012. It had been in the papers, talked about over breakfast tables. Did they expect her to reference it? She wondered, sometimes, if she should. That maybe if she mentioned it once, that would be enough. That would sate their curiosity about whether it was an event she acknowledged and accepted, an event she had dealt with.

Perhaps she didn't ever bring it up because she hadn't dealt with it.

Her speech closed to the sound of rapturous appreciation. Rachel dared herself to find his face. It wasn't difficult. She could just imagine the scent of his aftershave, which she caught when they embraced, just inside the angle of his shirt collar.

Of course he followed her back from the launch. Mutually they had decided not to be seen together in public. On the surface neither wanted their position to be compromised — his investment muddied the waters somewhat — but deep down it was their shared reluctance to commit. A no-strings arrangement suited both fine. Secret liaisons at her apartment or his heightened the thrill. Being linked officially made it too serious, too much of a fact. Rachel wasn't ready for that. She liked the emotional distance.

She was stepping into the shower when she heard the buzzer go.

"Aaron." She answered the door in her gown. "It's two a.m. Can't you sleep?"

He grinned. "Not without you." He leaned in and she turned her face away, just a fraction, to tease him, even though she knew she would let herself be kissed.

"You were sensational tonight," he said, his arms looping round her waist.

"Thank you."

"I mean it. I was impressed."

She could never tell how sincere he was being. Aaron Grewal was arrogant and proud (as she suspected were many multi-millionaires), and she had a reasonable inkling he slept with other women. But she didn't care. This wasn't about heart and soul; it was about danger and distraction. Aaron was different to what she was used to . . . to what was missing. He was like her late nights, her coffee, her deadlines, a quick fix to get through, nothing permanent or serious, nothing it would hurt to lose.

Afterward, they lay in each other's arms. It was nice to be held, to hear the warm beat of another person's heart. When she'd won the pitch from Aaron's firm, they'd told her she was one of the strongest candidates they'd seen. The word had stayed with her, become part of why she'd been drawn into romance with Aaron in the first place. He saw her strength and recognized it. Strength was the reason she was still here. It was how she'd got ahead, being decisive, being convinced: it was how she'd survived.

In the glow of the streetlight, Rachel made out the room around her: a student's room, a rented room, a room lived in for hours at a time. Interspersed with her plans for the gallery, drawings, reports and journals filled with sketches and emails and wish lists, was a litter of empty cups, perfumes, piled-up books, pictures that never made it on to the walls, propped up against wash racks, clothes strewn across the floor, handbags and pill packets and phone chargers . . .

There were no photographs. Aaron had commented on it when he'd first come over. No framed family, no memories, nothing personal. It hadn't been intentional, just how things were. She couldn't help it. The past was a stranger.

"Goodnight, Success Story," Aaron murmured, kissing the top of her head.

She smiled into his chest, feeling the urge to cry. Exhaustion, that was all. And an expression of tenderness she had long learned to live without, so that when she received it, it hurt a little. Rachel had cried a lot at the start of her life, and she had cried a lot in 2012, but she hadn't cried since. As a rule she didn't cry. Instead she surrounded herself with noise and lights, with anything but quiet and dark.

It took ages to fall asleep. She would manage a couple of hours and that was what she preferred: a brief sliver of quiet before the day drew her into its comforting, busy embrace. And yet the shorter the sleep, the deeper her dreams . . . Always they came in bursts, the same one on a cycle for weeks at a time. This one had lasted longer than most. Rachel felt herself floating in a familiar space, inexplicable, tantalizing, as known to her as her skin yet as alien as the stars: a dimly lit passage in a huge, impersonal house, a moon-bathed window, coarse floorboards beneath her naked feet. This faraway place called her, whispering, whispering, *This is where you belong.*

CHAPTER 4

He left before she woke the next morning.
Rachel was glad, fixed herself coffee and
opened her emails. Her inbox was filled with
messages of congratulation. They'd made a
mint on some of the more expensive works
last night and several write-ups had already
appeared in the morning's coverage, calling
the Square Peg launch "a triumph" and "an
enthralling odyssey into the city's burning
talent." Paul had written with news that
tickets for next month's exhibition had sold
out, and that a renowned London artist
wished to make an appearance at the weekend. Rachel summoned Paul for brunch and
closed her tablet.

It took minutes to get ready. Despite her
lack of sleep, the bathroom mirror told her
she looked good. With neat brown hair,
warm hazel eyes and a smattering of freckles
across her nose, Rachel was no supermodel,
but she had a fine figure, great skin and she

carried herself well. For a long time she had puzzled over the roots of her appearance. Most people didn't have to — their parents were right in front of them, or they had pictures to go on, blood relatives to join the dots — and she had thought so many times about what a phenomenon that would be. Imagining her mother and father was a bit like imagining her own hypothetical child, as much of a mystery and a miracle. For she had no positioning in the world, no biological foundation: she wasn't the branch or the leaf on a tree, running deep into the earth, permanent and enduring; she was her own shrub, small and lonely, with roots barely clinging to the soil.

Rachel had got along fine with her adoptive parents, Maggie and Greg. They had longed for a baby and been unable to have one of their own, and when they'd welcomed her at a week old, it had been the answer to their prayers. She was lucky, she knew: they'd been loving, supportive, attentive, and truthful with her, explaining her adoption as soon as she was old enough to understand. But, really, one was never old enough to understand something like that, to properly get to grips with and accept deep inside without umbrage or bitterness that you weren't loved enough to be kept in the first place. "We chose you," Maggie used to say over and over, "because you were special. We adored you from the second we laid eyes on you." And Rachel used to take reassurance from this — that she might have been cast aside by one set of parents but at least she'd been picked up by another — until her older, more complicated years, when she had learned about the adoption process and that Maggie and Greg hadn't selected her, she had simply been the first baby to come along. It was hard to get a baby, most childless couples wished for babies and there weren't enough to go round, so no wonder her adoptive parents had felt she was meant to be.

Rachel knew this was ungrateful and unhelpful, so she'd stifled the truth of her emotions and instead focused on the future, always the next thing, getting ahead, refusing to look behind. When she'd referenced her mother in the gallery speech, she'd been remembering how Maggie used to describe her as "bloody-minded." It was meant, for the most part, affectionately, but in her teenage years it had caused toxic fights. Rachel's stubbornness, her iron will, whether it concerned dating a boy or staying out or refusing to finish her studies, came from a place that neither Maggie nor Greg could trace in themselves, a place so remote and unknown that it served only to remind them what was missing. That Rachel had a family out there who were just like her, and it was their blood that was running through her veins, not the Wrights'.

Maggie and Greg had died within a year of each other when she was eighteen, so she hadn't had all that much of them either. At the time she'd mourned, but she never shed as many tears over them as she had over her imagined, other parents. It had seemed thankless and hurtful to pursue her heritage while Maggie and Greg were alive, but after they went there was nothing stopping her. Rachel knew she'd been born in England to English parents, and had ideas about traveling there, to some charming retreat or else a townhouse in London, and being welcomed by a woman smelling of vanilla sponge, a friendly wirehaired dog trailing at her feet. However, her ideas came to nothing and her search was short-lived: Rachel discovered inside a week that her birth mother was dead and she had no father listed. That was when she'd decided to close the door on the past. She spoke to no one about it. Nobody knew she was adopted and she preferred it that way. Keeping a lid on her feelings was a trick she'd learned early on, and it had certainly protected her since.

The sound of the mail hitting the mat pulled her from her thoughts. She grabbed her jacket and bent to scoop up the letters to look at later, but a single white envelope drew her up short. It was one of those envelopes that made you look twice. There was nothing menacing about it, nothing especially unusual but for the UK postal address and a red stamp reading STRICTLY CONFIDENTIAL.

She picked it up and turned it over. *Private documents enclosed.* There was a return address, a Quakers Oatley & Sons Solicitors in Mayfair, London.

She ran her nail along the seal and opened it.

CHAPTER 5

CORNWALL, 1947

Only when the captain moves to shake my hand does his face return to the light. It is a fine, distinguished face: the product of centuries of ancestral perfection. His eyes are blue and clear, startlingly bright in comparison with the rest of him. His hair is black and has grown out of its cut, longer and more disheveled than is the fashion for gentlemen, and there is a faint shadow of, or prelude to, a beard, although that could be the gloom hitting him from beneath. The chin is striking, square and sharp, and his mouth is wide, the lips parted slightly, with a curl that could be mistaken for a sneer. It isn't a kind mouth.

I notice all this before I notice the most obvious thing: his scars. I was warned about the captain's war wounds, but I hadn't known about his burns. His left cheek is pitted like fruit peel, the skin pulled tight toward the angle where his jaw meets his earlobe, where it melts into spilled candle wax.

His clear, blue eyes, as they meet mine, dare me to comment. For a shameful moment I am glad of his disfiguration, for if he were flawless I might not know how to speak. There is a scent about him, of tobacco and scorched wood.

"Thank you, Tom," he says, "but I will show Miss Miller to her room."

"Very well, Captain."

The mouth lifts then, but it isn't quite a smile. Nonetheless I return it and follow him up to the landing. We make slow, awkward progress, and I see how much discomfort his leg causes him but also the pride that prevents him from admitting it.

"Tell me," he starts, "what are your first impressions of Winterbourne?"

"Well, I've only just arrived." We pass a glass case filled with stuffed birds: a hawk alights on a branch, wings wide, beak screaming. "But I should say what strikes me is that it's very beautiful."

"Beautiful." The captain repeats the word, as if it's foreign. "Winterbourne has been described as many things, but beautiful isn't one of them."

"No? I'm surprised."

"It was built by a band of lunatics. Hardly

the way to speak of one's ancestors, but there's the long and short of it. Too much money and too little discrimination. They thought they were recreating Notre-Dame, I'm sure. That families should be expected to live here, generations of us, hardly came into it. No — I've heard *daunting, intimidating, bleak, desolate . . .* but I've never heard *beautiful.*"

"You don't like your home, Captain?"

He gives a short, hollow laugh. "It isn't a question of me not liking it. Rather the other way round."

I frown, but before I can speak he stops at a door and draws a chain of keys from his pocket. It is necessary for him to lean against the wall to do this, wheezing slightly, and my instinct is to help him but I don't. We are at the end of a passage. Looking back, the way we've come appears impossibly long, distortedly so, a carpeted corridor flickering in the glow of feeble bulbs. Ahead is a narrow staircase, presumably the servants' access.

"This is your room," he says, and the door creaks open.

The first thing I notice is the smell of age, a musty scent that seems to rise from the floorboards and seep from the walls. The atmosphere is deep, as weighty as the green velvet drapes that hang from the high window. There is a wooden four-poster bed, carved ornately in the Jacobean style, its quilts piled extravagantly. Chenille rugs adorn the boards beneath my feet, and behind me, on the wall we have stepped through, is an elaborate scenic mural depicting some dark, tangled foliage. Its pattern is dizzyingly complicated, impossible to follow one twisted vine without getting lost in the knots of the others.

"Will this be adequate for you?" says Jonathan de Grey. I nod. Of course it will be. It is, presumably, where his previous governess slept. She flits into my mind then vanishes just as quickly. I wonder about her sleeping here, watching the forest mural from her bed, trying to follow those creepers then unable to find her way out.

"It's lovely," I say. It isn't true, just as perhaps *beautiful* wasn't quite true for Winterbourne. Just something people say to make things well. "I shall be very comfortable here." I go to the window, pull the curtains and flood the room with light. Already, it looks better. There is a little writing desk, a handsome wardrobe and an adjacent washing and dressing room. I think of my miserable lodgings in London and am once again amazed at the fortune that brought me here. All *will* be well.

"I'll leave you now," says the captain, stepping back. For a moment the daylight catches his features, the taut, pockmarked side of his face, and he shies from it like a creature of the night. "Mrs. Yarrow will collect you shortly."

The door closes and I am alone. Gradually the captain's footsteps cease, and against the silence my ears tune into quieter sounds: sounds sewn into the building. I hear a soft tapping, most likely the flick of a branch at the window, but when I look out the wild trees are distant. I travel from one surface to another, the foot of the bed, the top of the wardrobe; I smile, as if the tapping is playing with me, a silly parlor game. It sounds louder at the desk so I open the drawer. Abruptly, the tapping stops — it was a draft behind the wall, or a mouse scratching at wood. Inside is a clock, small and round, 1920s, silver. The time reads twenty-five minutes to three, but the second hand isn't working. There is an engraving on the back:

L. Until the end of time.

I remove the clock and put it on the table. I'll see later if it can't be fixed.

From the window, the view is tremendous. I must be on the westernmost gable because the sea appears huge and immediate, with no cliffs to separate us, as if it is washing right up to Winterbourne's walls; or we could be on the Polcreath tower light, rising straight up out of the ocean, its root chalky with salt and seaweed. The water is dark, perfectly still closer to shore but in the distance little white crests jump and retreat on its surface. The sky is frozen white and copper, like a Turner painting, dashed with smears of dirty raincloud. I met a former lighthouse keeper, once, during the war. His house had been blown to dust in a bad Blitz. As I held his hand and waited for the ambulance to arrive, he told me of his time, years before, on a remote Atlantic outpost, and that he could never be afraid of the sea, no matter how it churned or roared. "The sea's my friend," he assured me, his face blackened with ash. "If I fell into it, it would toss me back up. The sea would never take me." He missed the water like a lost love, he said; even through the noise and fury of war it called to him, calling him back to its lonely perfection. "It's all right," he'd kept saying, as I told him he would find safety and a way to rebuild his life, "this wasn't my life anyway. My life is out on the water," and he'd wept for a loss he could not express.

I consider if this sea will become my friend, looking at it every day, and it looking at me. So different from the rush and noise of London, which, once peace was declared, people told me would be a welcome diversion. Everyone was grieving, everyone was spent; everyone had known terrible things and faced terrible truths. But the city pumped on like an unstoppable heart, whisking us up with it, forcing us to go on even if some days we felt like lying down in the middle of the street and closing our eyes and never waking again. *Carry on, carry on,* that was the message throughout the war. What about after it ended? Carry on, they said, carry on. It was hard for me to carry on. There are some things from which you cannot carry on. Some things hurt too much. Things we did. Things we let happen. I close my eyes, unwilling to remember. A grasping hand, swirling hair, and her eyes, her eyes . . .

I am about to go and find Mrs. Yarrow, whom I assume to be the cook, when something catches my eye that I didn't notice before.

It is a painting, hanging in the shadow of the dark green curtain and no bigger than a place mat on a dining table. The frame, too, is large, so that the print inside is really quite small and delicate, and I have to lean in to see what it portrays.

It's a little farm scene, a barn surrounded by hay bales and a gray band of sea just visible in the distance. A cow chews on a tuft of grass. Milking pails lie abandoned. A cluster of dark firs borders a simple cottage, its chimney smoking and a full moon hovering over its roof. The landscape is curiously recognizable as that around Winterbourne: we are here, in this place, at some distant, irretrievable point in the past. The moors are unmistakable, their wild desolation, the color of the earth.

Perhaps it's instinctive to look for a human face in these things, because I do, but even though I am looking it still comes as a surprise to me when I see her. She is merely a detail, an impression, not really a person; it's more the feeling of her, looking out at the window, looking right back at me. Her head must be the size of a farthing, if that, with a wisp of dark hair and two green eyes. The artist has made a point of her eyes, the brightest color in the picture. I think of the girl peering out at me, just as, a moment before, I was peering out at the sea from my own window. I think of us peering at each other, and for an instant the effect is unsettling, because it really appears that she is seeing me, and I her. *Not really a person. Not really.*

"Miss Miller?" There is a knock at the door.

I tie the curtain back, obscuring the print, and go to answer it.

I don't realize I am hungry until Mrs. Yarrow puts soup and a sandwich in front of me, a doorstop of cheese and ham. I remember sharing my butter ration with Mrs. Wilson at Quakers Oatley after her husband died, and what another world London seems.

Mrs. Yarrow fusses about me like a mother, fetching milk, then a pudding of lemon meringue pie with gingerbread biscuits. I haven't eaten so much in months.

"Well, I've had practice," she says, when I compliment her on her cooking. "I've worked here for the captain for twenty years, and practice makes perfect, as they say." She has a West Country burr, is plump and pink-cheeked, and her frizzy brown hair escapes in soft tendrils from her cap. She sits opposite me, her hands in her lap.

"Are we pleased to have you joining us, miss," she says, with such visible relief that it seems almost inappropriate.

"I'm pleased to be here."

"I don't know how much longer the captain could have coped. Things have been . . . testing."

"Since my predecessor left?"

Mrs. Yarrow nods. "I've been in charge of the children. As you can imagine, I have my hands full enough with the daily running of things. It was really too much. But none of us wants to let the captain down."

"Of course not."

"It will be good for the children to have proper care." Mrs. Yarrow shifts in her seat; she has the manner of somebody loose-tongued trying not to tell a secret. "All this up and down, here and gone, no consistency, miss, that's the problem."

"It must have been confusing for them." I sip my tea.

"Yes. Confusing. That's it."

"And to have lost their poor mother, as well."

"Oh, yes, miss. That were quite a thing."

I want to ask again after Mrs. de Grey; I want her to tell me. But Mrs. Yarrow has reddened and her eyes have fallen to her lap. She looks afraid.

"I must say I feel fond of the twins already," I say instead. "To be so young and to go through so much."

"Ah, but the young are strong," says Mrs. Yarrow. "Stronger than I, in any case. You'll see what I mean when you meet them."

She sees me gazing up at the kitchen shelves, at the soup tureens and jelly molds coated in dust, at the giant mixing bowls and tarnished ladles, at the china plates and casseroles and long-unused tea sets with their chipped edges and mismatched saucers. The space is cavernous, great wooden worktops and a central island around which we sit, but it's drafty now in the early evening and its size only summons the buzz and activity that's missing. Once, this would have been the hub of the house. Today, it's a graveyard: a ghost of times gone by. I wonder if Mrs. de Grey cooked here, her hands dusted with flour and her babies crawling round her skirts. Or perhaps she cut a remote figure, closeted away with her thoughts, wringing her fingers, which I picture as studded with jewels. I know how treacherous thoughts can be. That if you are left alone with them for too long, they can turn against you.

"It was strange how the war brought Winterbourne back to us," says Mrs. Yarrow, brightening. "When we had the children here — the evacuees — it was like old times.

Voices everywhere, running feet, excitement. You wouldn't have recognized this place." She gestures about her. "We had littl-uns piled all round this table, sticking their fingers into cake mix, playing hide-and-seek in the tower, getting up to mischief with the bell box. Bells were ringing all through the house, miss, and we soon found out why! That was just after the twins came along. Madam used to complain that she couldn't get any sleep because of the noise. She'd go upstairs to lie down in the day, while I took the babes, and she couldn't rest for all the shrieking. But, now they've gone, it does seem quiet, doesn't it?" Mrs. Yarrow shakes her head, as if at a fond memory. "I still think I hear them sometimes, isn't that a funny thing? It's a trick of Winterbourne, lots of creaks and knocks where the wind gets in. And the twins, of course, they can cause a racket — they can make enough noise for twenty children. You'll have your hands full with them, miss."

"By all accounts they're well behaved."

"Oh, absolutely," agrees Mrs. Yarrow, wholeheartedly, as if in swift correction of having spoken out of turn. She slips a finger beneath the elastic of her cap and scratches her head. "I mean only that they're tiring for a woman my age. Do you have children, miss?" The question is so abrupt and unexpected that I glance away.

"No."

"I'm sorry. I don't mean to pry. I didn't suppose you would, in accepting this station."

"You're right. One day, perhaps." I force a smile. It takes an enormous effort of will, but I must manage it because she returns it easily, our awkwardness forgotten.

"Well," I say, changing the subject, "I expect you'll be a veritable mine of information and knowledge for me over the coming days."

Mrs. Yarrow nods. "Of course, I'd be delighted. Although," she lowers her voice, "between you and me, I confess I'm thinking about moving on."

"You are?"

"It's early days. But I'm getting too long in the tooth for this, miss. Since the last girl left . . ." She swallows, an audible, dry contraction. Is it my imagination, or has the cook turned pale, her skin appearing waxen in the fading light, her brow heavy and her eyes deep with some unfathomable terror? "It hasn't been easy. Looking after the children hasn't been easy. It's better if I have a fresh start, somewhere new. The captain won't like it, but he'll have you. You'll be the woman of this house next, miss. And you'll like it. Winterbourne is a special place, a very special place."

At once, there is clamor from the staircase, a storm of battering, hurrying footsteps like the ack-ack gunfire of home, and Mrs. Yarrow forgets her worried turn, straightens and smiles, smoothing her apron as if about to curtsy to the king.

"Speak of the devils," she says, "here they come now. Would you like to come and meet them, miss? Edmund and Constance de Grey. They've been so looking forward to this."

CHAPTER 6

The twins run straight into me, their arms around my waist. It almost knocks me over. I laugh, as if being greeted by dogs, friendly, tails wagging, craving attention.

"Miss Miller, Miss Miller, what a delight!" The girl looks up at me, impossibly pretty, her grin wide to expose a row of little teeth, as neat as a bracelet. A velvet clip holds her blond ringlets back and her blue eyes are shining. She has the face of a doll, precise and sweet, with a dimple in her chin that you struggle not to press with your thumb. She is the loveliest thing I have ever seen.

"Oh, call me Alice!" I say.

"May we play with her, Father?" the boy says, and only then do I realize that the captain is present, his cane in hand. It must be an effort for him to stand because he lowers himself into a chair by the fire. "May we *please*?"

"Be gentle, Edmund," he answers.

Looking at Edmund, it is impossible to imagine the boy being anything but. For all their twinship, the children do not look alike. Edmund has been blessed with copper curls, a crop of them that shine like burnished gold. Across his nose is a light dusting of freckles, and his skin is porcelain-pale and smooth as cream.

They are a pair of angels. Constance tugs my hand and I crouch so I can look up at them both. I have never seen two such innocent faces, shining with happiness and every good thing. "I have something for you," Constance whispers. Edmund nudges her: "Give it to her, silly!" Constance fishes in the pocket of her dress.

It's a chain, woven out of grass. The thought is so pure and touching that for a moment I don't know what to say. Nobody told me how enchanting these children were, not my contact in London, not Tom, not Mrs. Yarrow, not even Jonathan de Grey. But enchanting they are, smiling down at me, awaiting my response.

"How clever of you," I say, admiring the grass. "And how kind."

"Put it on, put it on!" Constance helps me.

In a flash I am reminded of another time, another bracelet, somebody else helping me to fasten the clasp. That bracelet was gold, and if I concentrate hard I can feel his thumbs on that part of my wrist, over my pulse, his skin warm against mine . . .

"There!" cries Constance triumphantly.

"Well," I say, "doesn't that look splendid."

"Capital!" agrees Edmund.

"Miss Miller is going to be tired," says their father. I glance at him, and for an odd, unaccountable moment the four of us seem absolutely right, together in this dim hall, with Mrs. Yarrow hanging dutifully back, as if *we* are the family, and I am the wife, and I am the mother . . . The impression vanishes as soon as it appears.

"She says we can call her Alice!" says Constance, tugging at my hand once more, her fingers looped through mine. It's infectious, I'll admit, and I laugh. It sounds unfamiliar in my throat, girlish, as if it's a younger me making the sound.

"Very well," says the captain. "Alice," he pauses, tasting my name: I see him taste it, "will be tired. You're to let her rest this evening. Tomorrow is another day."

"But we can't sleep," objects Edmund. "We want to play with her — *please,* Father? Please may we play with her, please?"

The captain stands, his cane striking the floor in a deafening blow. Mrs. Yarrow gasps.

I get to my feet. The children drop my hands.

"Do I need to repeat myself?" the captain says.

Edmund shakes his head.

"Did you hear me the first time, boy?"

The child nods.

"Then I neither expect nor welcome your protest. You are to follow my instructions to the letter, do you understand? And, from tonight, you are to follow Miss Miller's." He turns to me. "Miss Miller, if you would . . . ?" I try not to feel afraid, for the growl of his voice and the thunder of his cane casts a shadow across the house.

"Up to bed, children," I say softly. "Cook will bring you some cocoa."

The children retreat, sloping upstairs like kittens in the rain. It troubles me to see the spirit pinched out of them. It troubles me how fast the captain's temper caught light. Now he bids us goodnight and slips away to another part of the house.

"The captain prefers the children to be seen and not heard," says Mrs. Yarrow.

"Yes," I say. "I rather got that impression."

Morning arrives with a burst of sunshine. I wake in my four-poster bed, shrugging off a deep, dreamless sleep, the likes of which I haven't had since before the war, and go straight to the window to welcome the day. Despite the thick drapes, sunlight razes through the cracks like an outline of fire. I pull them open and let it in. The sea is green today, light, sparkling green, and the sky above a hazy blue. I prise open the window, a hook on a rusted latch, and a draft of fresh, salty air hits my nostrils. I feel like a girl on Christmas morning. I cannot wait to see the twins once more.

When I tie back the curtains, I spy that painting again — the little girl looking out of the cottage. She has one hand flat against the panes, a detail I hadn't noticed yesterday. The hand is raised as if in greeting or acknowledgment. Or warning.

A bell sounds downstairs. It makes me jump. I feel as I did at Burstead, late for breakfast, the house matrons stalking the corridors with their starched bosoms and shrill whistles. *"Come on, Miller! Get dressed, Miller! What are you doing, girl?"*

In minutes I'm downstairs — but the bell wasn't for me, of course, it was for the children. Mrs. Yarrow has bowls of porridge steaming on the table, decorated with honey and walnuts. "Did you sleep well, miss?" she asks me.

"Very well, thank you."

65

"You didn't hear the dogs?"

"What dogs?"

"We've got a wandering madcap," she rattles cutlery out of a drawer, "Marlin, they call him. Well, he's got these giant hounds and walks them on the cliffs at night." She lays the spoons on the table. "God knows why, miss. And they make the most terrible noise, howling and yowling and yelping at the moon. It used to keep Madam awake something rotten. The children, too, when they were babes. Luckily he doesn't come as close to Winterbourne as he used to, since the captain and he had words. But do you know what this man Marlin said to the captain? He said: *It's your house that makes my dogs afraid. It's your house that's the trouble.* So the captain says not to bother walking them round here again, if that's the way he feels. But still he does."

"Is he a local man?"

"Lived here for years. Not the most sociable person you'll meet."

"I do like dogs. What breed are they?"

The cook goes to the bell a second time, rings it. "You won't like these ones, miss. These aren't right. They're great snarling things with huge teeth, and paws that could fell a man in a stroke. To think of them being scared by a big old house is a nonsense.

The captain chooses not to let it vex him, but I hate to hear them at night."

"I didn't hear them."

She turns her back. "You must have slept soundly."

We are interrupted by the children's arrival, a tornado of gold and copper and neatly pressed shirts and shorts, a frill of dress, twinkling eyes and gracious smiles. "Miss Miller! Alice! See, I said we didn't dream her!" In the glow of the kitchen, Constance and Edmund appear even more adorable than they did last evening.

Constance takes my hand, her small, perfect fingers looping through mine.

"Father said we're not to touch her," says Edmund. "Remember?"

"Alice doesn't mind," says Constance, "do you, Alice?"

"I won't break."

"Constance breaks *all* her toys," says Edmund. "That's why I won't let her play with any of mine. Especially my locomotives."

"I do not!" objects the girl.

"Chop-chop, children," says Mrs. Yarrow, encouraging them to sit. "Miss Miller will want to get on with your lessons this morning. Eat your breakfast first."

"I can eat one-handed," says Constance. "I'm not letting go."

I ought to deter her, follow the captain's rules. But there is such charm about her, about them both, that I am happy to be held.

I'm not letting go.

I was told that before, in another life, when I was another girl. It's not an easy thing to hear, neither is it easy to resist. And I was let go, wasn't I? Our hands parted, and I fell.

Thus far the children have been educated in an upstairs bedroom, one of the many chambers at Winterbourne that otherwise go unused. On seeing the forlorn space, a dark turret with the oppressive atmosphere of a sanatorium, I immediately decide to relocate. "Oh, I never liked it," agrees Mrs. Yarrow, as she helps Tom and me carry the desks to the drawing room. As the stand-in between governesses, she'd been employed short-term in the twins' tutelage. "Too dingy, and the children kept complaining of coughs and chills. Besides, I could feel *her* watching me all the time."

"Her?"

"The woman who was here before you," Mrs. Yarrow says quickly, under Tom's dissatisfied glare. "She had her ways of doing things. That's all."

"What sort of ways?"

"Oh, nothing, nothing important . . ."

"Is this very well for you, miss?" Tom squares the desks so they're facing the window. "Will you need anything else?"

"Thank you, Tom, that will be all. Children should be educated in a good light, don't you agree, Mrs. Yarrow? I want Edmund and Constance to feel inspired by our lessons, and where better place to start than with a fine view of nature."

"Right you are."

And I must admit, an hour later, I am feeling positive about our progress. The de Grey twins continue to amaze me in their enthusiasm, their confidence, and their understanding that whatever they know is a mere grain when set against what still remains to be found. They are unfailingly polite, amenable characters with a zest for learning, making my job no less than a pleasure. I had worried, slightly, for the educative aspect. I had been honest about my lack of teaching experience but feared it would prove a challenge. Now I see why my honesty didn't count against me: these pupils are just about the easiest, loveliest, most rewarding novices a teacher could hope to influence. Whatever methods my predecessor had, they must have worked.

After lunch, the three of us venture into parkland. The lawns at Winterbourne would once have been impeccably tended, but now, as I observed in the Rolls when we first approached, they are hopelessly over-grown. Creepers straggle across the paths; chipped stone planters are covered in moss, and two lion heads at the top of a run of steps have ears and eyes missing, stolen by the elements. The topiary is melted out of shape and the whole impression is one of a garden underwater, liquid and strange. Behind us, Winterbourne rises in giant, eerie magnificence. I hear the sea, an incessant, rhythmic breath as it washes into shore.

"This afternoon," I tell them as we take the path to the wood, "we're going to draw a picture." I'm invigorated by the day: the sun, the sky and the birdsong.

"Like a flower?" says Constance.

"Like a fox," says Edmund.

"A flower would be easier to draw than a fox," I say, "because we need to be able to really look at it. We're going to look at it in incredible detail, and keep looking at it as we draw, so that we can reproduce as ac-curate a likeness as possible."

"It has to be still, then," says Edmund.

"That's absolutely right. One can draw a moving thing, of course one can, but one isn't able to study it with as much care." We pick our way over a twisted tree branch. The children are used to coming this way for they step over it easily, while I am obliged to stop and adjust my skirt. "Tom found a dead fox," says Edmund. He collects a stick and pokes the ground with it. "He's always finding dead foxes."

"Edmund!" Constance covers her ears.

"It's all right, Constance." I smile. "Nature is red in tooth and claw."

"I don't like it."

"Could I draw a dead fox?" says Edmund.

"You could if you wanted. But it's rather morbid, don't you think?"

"But I could study it, in detail, then, as you say. It wouldn't be able to get away from me. It wouldn't be able to run away."

"True. But when you looked at your picture afterward, you wouldn't think of the fox as living, would you? You wouldn't remember how clever you were to reproduce its detail as it rushed through the wood. You'd remember it as a body."

"And you'd hate to look at it," says Constance. "It would make you sad."

"I suppose," says Edmund. A neat frown puckers his childish brow. "But Father has his case of birds — those stuffed crows on the landing. They used to scare us, didn't

71

they, Connie? We'd run past them with our eyes shut in case they jumped out and pecked us! People like to look at those, and that's the same thing, isn't it?"

I spy a place for us to sketch, a soft clearing, surrounded by flora.

"It depends on the person," I say. "Everybody likes different things. Hence the multiplicity of art."

"What does multiplicity mean?"

"A big collection, full of variety."

"*I'm* going to draw a flower," says Constance.

"That's boring," says the boy.

"In your opinion," I tell him. "And that's what we're talking about. Art is preference. Art is personal. Constance prefers the flower, while you prefer the fox. Neither is right or wrong. It's about what you wish to see in the thing you're looking at. Do you wish to observe a living soul, or do you wish to capture it?"

Edmund thinks about it for a moment. Then he smiles cunningly and says, "May we draw you, miss?"

"That isn't really the object of the exercise."

"Alice is a pretty name," interjects Constance.

"Thank you."

"I wish I were called Alice."

"Constance is lovely. It means forever."

"That's what Mummy used to say."

The mention of their mother catches me off guard. Another detail, another candle held up to the frozen mist I hold in my mind. What did Mrs. de Grey look like? Was she fair, like me, or dark like her husband? She must have been very beautiful, I think, to have such beautiful children and to have attracted a man like the captain.

It is a relief to reach the clearing, and to incite the children to sit and open their sketchbooks. Perhaps it is the ghost of Mrs. de Grey still clinging to our collective mood, or perhaps it is the sheer sweetness of their faces as they gaze hopefully up at me, but before I know it I have agreed to Edmund's request and am sitting opposite on a blanket, preparing to be drawn. "Wait — !" calls Constance, and she jumps up and brings a daisy to me, which she threads through my hair.

"There," she says, kissing my cheek. "Now it's perfect."

"Be kind to me, won't you?" I say.

"We're always kind," says Edmund.

CHAPTER 7

NEW YORK, PRESENT DAY

Quakers Oatley Solicitors
St. James House
Richmond Square
Mayfair
London W1 —

Ms. Rachel Wright
Apt 243E
West 72nd Street, NY —

9 September 2016

Dear Ms. Wright

Re: Winterbourne Hall, Polcreath, Cornwall

It is with regret that I write to inform you of the death of your aunt Constance de Grey, who passed away at her ancestral home in the early hours of Sunday morning.

I am conscious that this might come as something of a surprise, as I believe you were unaware of your connection with the Winterbourne Estate. Nonetheless, as the de Grey family solicitor, it is my duty to inform you that, being Miss de Grey's next of kin, the park and all its land and contents now fall directly into your possession.

I would appreciate a swift response indicating how you would like to proceed. Under these circumstances, I normally advise a visit to our offices in London, where we can make the necessary inroads before granting you access to your inheritance.

Yours faithfully
Stephen Oatley, Esq.

CHAPTER 8

Rachel read the letter, then read it again. Her first thought was that it was a joke. She even looked about her, expecting a camera to be on her, or a crowd to appear, ready to laugh along. But her apartment was unchanged. Outside, the traffic droned on.

Her hands were shaking. Quickly she replaced the letter in its envelope, sitting down because her knees had turned to jelly. The envelope, that anodyne thing, seemed to pulse on the kitchen table. She folded it back out, looked again. *Impossible.* It was totally impossible. She searched for a clue to its falsehood; her mind tripped over a dozen hoaxes but none fitted with such an outrageous set of claims as this. And yet a voice whispered, *It's plausible, it might be,* louder and more insistent each time.

Her phone rang. It was Paul. "Hey," he said, "guess what? The *City* wants to interview you, tomorrow at ten; I've booked you a spot at Jacob's. Sound good?"

She was slow to reply, unlike her. "I don't know, I . . ."

He was surprised at her reticence. "I can put them back, if you like?"

"Listen, Paul," she said, making a decision, "I think you'll have to. In fact, you can clear my schedule for the rest of the week. Next week, too."

There was a pause. "Is everything OK?"

"Everything's fine." Rachel fingered the edges of the letter, half expecting it to vanish beneath her touch. "Something's come up. Something important. At least, I think it is." She thought quickly. "I might have to go abroad for a while," she said, "I don't know how long. You'll look after things here, won't you?"

"Of course. But . . ."

"Thank you. I knew I could count on you. I'll call you later, OK?"

She hung up. Her apartment seemed changed, submerged, a place she wasn't quite part of and could no longer stand to be in. As if it were a stage set, with cardboard walls and doors that led nowhere, and plastic pieces of fruit gathering dust in a bowl. She went to the park and walked and walked, and watched the people sailing past in their safe, happy worlds, with families and homes they had always known and loved, a hurrying, babbling stream while she remained a solitary rock, confounded by the noise and rush. All the while the letter glowed with promise in her pocket. She sat on a bench, waiting for her coffee to grow cold.

"Are you sure it's a good idea?" said Aaron, when she told him that night.

She'd known he'd question her — he, who had two loving parents and an elder sister who called him "Rookie" and sixteen cousins with who knew how many kids.

"How will I know if I don't give it a chance?"

He read the letter again. "It looks real," he said, with a shrug, turning the page over, as if the word FORGERY might be stamped on its back.

Oh, Rachel knew it was real. She'd spoken to Quakers Oatley Solicitors and the story stacked up. The firm had sounded relieved to hear from her, as if the de Grey estate were one it was seeking to move on from. She had conducted herself as if she were in a business meeting, arrangements, dates, agendas, plans; yes, she would travel to England; yes, she would visit the house called Winterbourne. But she didn't tell them what she was hoping to find there — some clue to her past, some inkling, however faint, about where she had come from and the people who had made her. It was too much to hope for, wasn't it? But there *was* hope, now, at least.

"What about the gallery?" Aaron asked. They were in his penthouse, a rooftop tower overlooking Central Park. The vodka in Rachel's hand was mercifully robust. It had been a sober realization that really, other than her colleagues, she had no one else here to inform of her intention, just him. "Seems like you're just getting started," he said.

She was conscious at moments like these that Aaron wasn't merely her lover: he was her investor. "I am," she replied. "A week or two away won't change that. I'll be online if I'm needed; in the meantime Paul takes charge, he's more than capable."

"You think a week or two is all it'll be?"

"Honestly, I don't know." She put down her glass. "It depends what I find. A rickety old house, most probably, and a bunch of junk that needs sorting."

Privately, the thought of that junk containing just one photograph of a man and woman who might have been her parents, or her grandparents, or her aunt and uncle or cousins or anyone, really, made her flush with adrenaline.

"Will you be OK in such a big place on your own?" Aaron came to her and rested his forehead against hers, winding her fingers through his. They kissed; he smiled mischievously. "It looks kind of . . . foreboding. Like a haunted house."

She laughed. "You believe in that stuff?" she asked.

"You might."

"I certainly don't. Make-believe isn't my thing."

"You don't think we're a bit make-believe?"

She frowned, amused. "How do you mean?"

"We're playing pretend, aren't we? Pretending we're together, but we're not really, not properly. All I'm saying is that make-believe has its perks."

"I'm sure it does." Rachel reached for her drink, encouraging him to take a step back. "But I'm more interested in the facts at Winterbourne. This may be my only shot at finding them. How many adopted kids get a chance like this?"

"I'm only suggesting you might want a little company while you're out there."

"I'll be fine," she said. "Creaks and bumps

80

don't scare me."

He folded his arms, watching her affectionately. "What does, Rachel Wright?"

She finished the vodka, emboldened by it. "What kind of question is that?"

"What does scare you? Because I'm wondering if Winterbourne represents a chance for you," he said, "to run away from what's happened here, from real life." In that barefaced way of his, he struck her right where it hurt, forging on, heedless of her dismay. "Because you haven't been happy, even I can see that, and by my own admission I don't know you that well. Working all hours, pouring everything you've got into the gallery, barely pausing to breathe — it's impressive, sure, and I was impressed by you the moment you walked into my office with a torch in your eyes that told me you'd stop at nothing to achieve it. But managing all that has meant you've been able to close other, more personal, doors, hasn't it?"

Seeing her expression, he added, "I don't want to speak out of turn —"

"You have spoken out of turn," she said, coldly. "I'm not running away, Aaron. I'm running toward something. Something I've been trying for years to find."

"I know."

"You don't know. You've never been able

to get this. I need to see that place. I need to find out about where I came from, the people I came from, my mother, my father, I have no clue who they were. I'll probably never know, now this last link is gone. But I have to go there, be there, touch it and feel it. I've thought of nothing else since I read that letter — and it goes back to way before then. I've thought about this, or some version of it, ever since I found out I was adopted. Finally I've got the chance at resolution. And once I find that resolution, I can come home."

Aaron ran a hand through his hair. "You've been through a lot, Rachel."

"I know what I've been through."

"I don't want to see you go through any more."

"You won't. I'm going on my own. You won't have to see anything."

Perhaps she should have kept the whole thing to herself. She supposed that she had wanted to share it with someone. She had wanted to talk about it with someone because it was too big to take in on her own.

It was hard to think about the person she really wished to discuss it with. His wisdom, his good sense, his kindness, how he would have taken her in his arms . . . He had always been her first port of call, and Rachel liked that expression because it was true: he'd been the harbor for her little ship that had been bouncing alone on the tides for too many years. He had taken her in, given her shelter, and she'd put too much on him, of course she had, mistaking him for the whole family she lacked, so that when he left it wasn't just a husband, someone she had hoped to have kids with. It was everyone. It was the past as well as the future. She missed him. Oh, she did.

"I have to do this, Aaron," she said. "And frankly I don't care what you think."

He nodded. She waited. But the day Aaron Grewal apologized would be the day the sky fell in. "Let's have tonight together, OK?" he said instead.

She kissed him, an answer he seemed to accept. The future vibrated with nothing and everything, an empty, fearsome space, yet its promise was the closest she had held to her heart in as long as she could remember. Winterbourne would relinquish its secrets. And if it fought her, if it dared make her wait longer than she already had, she would force its mysteries to the surface through sheer dark grit. She was good at that.

CHAPTER 9

CORNWALL, PRESENT DAY

Rachel didn't like to delay once her mind was set. Twenty-four hours later she was boarding a train at Paddington, the key to Winterbourne safe in her pocket. She kept touching it, running her fingers over its ancient contours. It looked like a key that could open another world, the key to a trapdoor in the ground, beyond which strange creatures roamed and slept, and the sun rose at dusk and the moon rose at dawn.

A woman sat opposite her with a young girl. The girl was applying nail stickers, her focus entire. The woman flipped out a magazine, its cover detailing minor celebrities on vacation, with the headline SKINNY AND MISERABLE!

The train eased from its platform and a voice announced: *"Welcome to this South West Trains service to Penzance, calling at . . ."* Rachel reached for her tablet and checked her mail, but it was no good, she couldn't focus. Instead she looked through the window. It took a while to chug out of London, past the terraces under their drab gray sky, and the motion of the train made her tired. She hadn't slept on the plane, had barely rested or stopped since she'd opened the letter, and she put her head back now and tried to relax. Each time she closed her eyes, she saw the faces of the two solicitors at Quakers Oatley, sitting opposite her, their expressions by turns fascinated and grave. She had been Alice in Wonderland, tumbling down the rabbit hole, and they were as captivated by her as she was by them. These gatekeepers were about to change her life, everything she had ever thought about herself, every presumption overturned. Her instinct about their being keen to move the case on had been right. Rachel had the impression that Winterbourne was an albatross for them and they welcomed the chance to get rid of its legacy. "We weren't sure we'd be able to find you," the woman had said, adjusting her papers in the prim, efficient manner of one pleased at their own good luck, "or, if we did, what your reaction would be."

The man had run through what they knew. Rachel craved more, each answer insufficient, each explanation scattered with holes. She yearned for the names of her mother and father but was left wanting. Her grandfather was identified as a Captain Jonathan de Grey, making Constance, as the letter made clear, Rachel's aunt. But there was no grandmother. "What about the captain's wife?" she'd asked, scouring the scant family tree as the solicitors looked apologetically on. "That was her, right?" But the man shook his head. "Your mother," he said gently, "had different parentage . . ."

It was his way of saying that Captain de Grey had gone elsewhere, and that Rachel's mother had been born a bastard as a result of his affair. But who had she been? Who was the poor woman who had given birth to Rachel in a London hospital, looked into her baby's eyes and decided to give her up? Allegedly Constance had been the only person who knew about Rachel, and about this American orphan's connection to her family. Why hadn't Constance sought to find her? Why hadn't she spoken out? Rachel tried not to feel bruised, but it was hard. All her life she had felt fundamentally rejected, and even at the threshold of this incredible discovery that same rejection snapped at her heels. Her aunt had known of her and done nothing, content to let Rachel unearth whatever truths were left behind after she'd died. It didn't make sense. More questions, more uncertainties: it seemed the more Rachel learned, the more clueless she grew.

When she asked about Constance, the glance the solicitors exchanged implied that she hadn't been an easy woman. Rachel told herself that, for all the romance and surprise of Winterbourne just falling into her life like a first drift of January snow, she couldn't for a moment imagine a fairy-tale ending. All her life she had invented pictures that made sense to her — that her birth mother had been unable to cope, or that Rachel had been taken against her will, or that someone had forced her mother to give her up — and there was safety in those knowable limits. Now, every version she'd held dear exploded. It all came to this: this house, this family, and these doubts she might never be able to assuage. Quakers Oatley had dealt with the de Greys for years, but they didn't know how Rachel fitted in — only that Constance, on her deathbed, had made an assertion that turned out to be true.

It seemed alarmingly easy to inherit one of the country's grandest estates. Rachel signed documents, provided identification and settled a fee.

In return: a key.

"The only one," said the woman, before letting it go, and Rachel felt the sheer weight of it in her hand and wondered how many had held it in years gone by. It occurred to her that the key was the only thing she had ever touched that her mother, too, might also have touched — apart from herself, of course: her own skin.

She must have dozed because the next thing she knew they were rolling through unbroken countryside and the sun was setting over the hills. The woman opposite and her daughter had gone. Rachel's carriage was empty.

"Excuse me," she asked a steward on his way past, "where are we?"

"Next stop Polcreath," he told her.

She sat back and watched the blackening landscape.

Dusk was nearly complete by the time they pulled into the station. The platform was empty apart from a man on a bench, his head tucked into the collar of his coat, and a couple of passengers who had disembarked with her. A sign read TAXI and Rachel followed it out to the road, where a car was parked with its headlights on. She went to the window and named her destination. The driver seemed surprised.

"You sure?" he said. "I thought it was derelict. No one's lived there in years."

"My aunt lived there." It felt wonderful to say it. *My.*

"Climb in, then."

She was hoping he wouldn't talk. But: "You American?" he asked.

"Yes."

"Where from?"

"New York."

"So what brings you here? Winterbourne Hall's not much of a tourist destination."

"Like I said, I have family here. Had. My aunt died recently."

"I'm sorry to hear that."

Rachel sat back, handling the key once more in her pocket. It felt warm, as if radiant, shimmering in anticipation of reaching home.

"I expect you've got lots to sort out, then," said the driver, folding a stick of gum into his mouth. He looked at her in the rearview mirror.

"What do you mean?"

"Well, family affairs and the like. After someone dies. You know."

"Yes. Yes, I have."

"You'll be staying a while?"

"As long as it takes."

"There're people round here that can

89

show you around, if you like."

"I'll be fine. But thank you."

"Always friendly faces in Polcreath, you'll see. And if you're *really* short on company, I'm in the Landogger Inn most nights."

"I'll bear that in mind." But he'd said it with a twist of humor, which she returned. "The Landogger — that's an unusual name."

"Named after the cliffs," he said, "right by Winterbourne. They'll surround you. Lethal they are, too: a sudden drop. The house is right on the Landogger Bluff."

"You seem to know a lot about Winterbourne."

"Not much. Just that for those of us who've been in Polcreath all our lives, it's the stuff of legends. Always there, you know, there on the hill, but no one ever goes."

"You must remember my family." It was a difficult thought, the idea that this man, friendly though he was, had been closer to her ancestors than she would ever be — that he might have seen them, heard their voices, and maybe even met them. She didn't know how to feel as the cab drew closer to Winterbourne. A ripple of frustrated anger obscured any sense of homecoming. She wanted to know why she'd been dismissed and forgotten about: why her whole family, it seemed, had cast her aside.

"I never met them," the driver said. "They were, and I don't mean no offense by this, curious. Liked to keep themselves to themselves. I'm going way back now, to the sixties, when I was a boy." Rachel could tell by his voice that he liked the memory. "The de Grey children . . . Well, isn't that a posh name? They weren't children any more by the sixties, of course, but they stayed on at Winterbourne, a lad and a woman, coming up for thirty, they were. People said there was something funny about the lad, that he was gone in the head. I always thought it was odd, even then, that they should have remained at the house, unmarried, with no families of their own. It was as if they were married to each other. But listen to me, just an idle gossip, talking about your people like I knew them myself."

He met her gaze in the mirror and she was thankful night was falling. She didn't want him to see the naked truth: that these were mysteries she could not yet answer. That he, an "idle gossip," knew more about her family than she did.

"Are we close?" Rachel said.

"Not far now," he replied. "Not far at all."

It was, in fact, another half an hour, and by

91

the time they reached the Winterbourne gates the night outside was pitch-black. They'd left the last settlement many miles ago, and the house was so alone and remote that not one light of civilization could be seen anywhere across the black, boundless moors. The only glow was the glow of the moon, which hung above them like a marble, throwing the sea into glittering gray.

As Rachel stepped out of the cab, glad of its reassuring interior bulbs and the familiar hum of its engine, she looked above at the sky. The stars were immense. Stars like this didn't exist above New York. Exotic words surfaced in her mind — *Cassiopeia, Betelgeuse, Europa.* She must have learned them long ago and forgotten, or else had little reason to remember, but here, beneath the vast beauty of space, the stars appeared to her as jewels, unfathomably rare and precious.

"You sure you'll be all right?" The driver leaned over as she got out. "There's a warm bed at the Landogger, I'll bet. I can always take you back there."

Rachel shook her head. "I'll be fine." Winterbourne was hers, after all. Staying here alone might be a foreboding prospect, but she felt as if the house and its ghosts had thrown her a challenge. She had been held back for too many years, against her will, ignorant of its existence, robbed of her choice, letting the years drain out like bath water. She had a choice now, and she'd never find answers if she ran away.

She paid the driver and watched his taillights disappear into the night. She turned to the mansion, her eyes traveling up its enormous façade, whose shape, in the darkness, she could barely decipher. It loomed, shadow-like, amorphous and huge, a lake of black except where the moonlight caught it and a detail could be glimpsed, like the snap of glass in a window or the gnarled arm of a tree. She regretted her decision — although it hadn't been conscious, just the way things had worked out — to arrive so late. *It'll be better in the morning,* she told herself, bracing herself against the long night ahead. *Wait for the daylight.* She could hear the roar of the sea against the Landogger cliffs, the foam and spit of it as it churned against rocks.

She took the key from her pocket and let herself in.

CHAPTER 10
CORNWALL, 1947

My first week passes in a contented haze. Being around the children is a constant tonic, their smiles and laughter warming me utterly and their sweet inquiries occupying my mind in a way it hasn't known in years. I realize that I was merely treading water back in London: working at the solicitors' office was a way to earn money but it was also a way to let time pass, to allow my life to wash past me in a flat tide. Here, at Winterbourne, with Constance hanging off my arm and Edmund running ahead, I feel hopeful and alive. There is nothing to be afraid of any longer.

Why my predecessor absconded I shall never understand. If a matter should arise of such urgency that I should be called away, that would be very well, but to disappear completely from my charges' lives? I cannot imagine turning my back on the twins, accepting that I would never see them again. Already, and these are early days, Constance and Edmund have become part of me. Simply, I adore them. Each morning I wait for the sound of running footsteps on the landing above, the excitement of their squeals and their smiles lit up across the breakfast table. I was deeply touched on the afternoon they sketched me in the clearing; I should have known by their furtive whispers that they were planning a surprise, but when I saw the finished portraits I couldn't help but gasp. They had drawn me all in white, in a sumptuous wedding dress with a full skirt and pretty sleeves, just as I had always dreamed of for myself, and just as I might have had, had I not lost the only man I ever loved. *My love, my dearest love . . .* For a fleeting moment the sun disappeared and I had simply stared, wondering how intuitive these angels could be to sense what had happened to me — the happiness that now remained forever beyond my reach — and the heady mix of irony and sweet enticement their drawings provoked . . . before their laughter drew me from my reverie and reminded me it was children's folly, nothing more. "You'd make a beautiful bride," Constance said, kissing my cheek. That the previous nurse could have left such heavenly companions in her wake astonishes me.

I spoke to Mrs. Yarrow on Friday:

"Isn't it odd that the last governess sent no word of her whereabouts?"

"It was a family matter," Mrs. Yarrow replied.

"Yes, Tom explained. But, knowing the children as I do, I find it strange to say the least. The captain hasn't heard from her since?"

"No one has."

"Did she have friends here? In the village?"

"I wouldn't know the first thing about her private life, miss."

"Of course not. Forgive me."

Since our exchange, I have tried not to think too deeply about it. Just because I have found an intense connection with Edmund and Constance does not mean every woman would. I can only praise the governess, whoever she was, for the work she completed before her departure. Her students are courteous, inspired, loving and tender. I dote on them as I would my own. But I am training myself away from such fancies, for the children are my wards and there it ends.

Captain de Grey seems pleased with the arrangement, as far as it is possible to tell. I have only encountered my employer twice since that first day, and one of those encounters constituted barely a passing nod on his part. The second was while selecting books in the library for our afternoon study, when I caught him watching me from the door. "Are you finding everything you need?" he asked, but I knew when I turned that he had been standing there longer than was necessary, and longer than an ordinary man would were he hoping to ask such a pedestrian question as that. I replied that I was, thank you, and he retreated to whatever preoccupation holds him in thrall from day to day in his study. Still, even after he'd gone, I felt his eyes on my back and I wondered for how long he had waited, unseen, behind me, before he spoke. It ought to have unnerved me but instead I found it a thrill. I find him a thrill. The surprise of him, appearing as if from nowhere, dangerously quiet and dangerously handsome . . .

Alice Miller — for heaven's sake, wake up!

Mrs. Wilson's admonition at Quakers Oatley: I am dreaming again. I am imagining. Always prone to such things, or so I am told.

It is a fine September day, unusually warm for the onset of autumn. This afternoon, the children and I head across the parkland to a promised lake. Part of my concern is to ensure the twins' physical exercise, and their favorite pastime is swimming. It seemed to me we would be spoiled for water, with the sea surrounding us, but Mrs. Yarrow was quick to extinguish that notion. "Oh no," she said quickly. "Absolutely not, miss. The captain would never allow it. The sea is off limits."

"We wouldn't go far. Mere paddling."

"No, miss. Captain de Grey forbids it. No child of his will ever set foot in that water. You mustn't think of it. Swear to me you won't."

Of course, I had no option but to swear, and the children accommodated my embargo with their usual charm and gentleness, directing me instead to a pool in a sheltered glade. It is an almost precise circle, bordered by reeds and the fat, happy heads of bulrushes. A dragonfly hovers over the still, blue surface.

"Geronimo!" Edmund leaps in in his shirt and shorts, splashing like a dog.

"Edmund," Constance cries, "you're not in your bathing suit!"

"I know! Isn't it splendid?"

I ought to chide the boy but the sheer ebullience of his performance brings a smile to my face, after which my scolding would be pointless. "Just for today," I tell him, sitting with my hands looped round my knees, enjoying the warm breeze as it teases my skirt. Constance obediently changes into her swimming suit and lowers herself gingerly into the water. Edmund promptly splashes her.

"No! I don't like to get my hair wet!"

"Don't be such a girl."

"I *am* a girl."

I watch them frolic with childish abandon, the water spraying over their arms and heads in bursts of silver. I find their courage and resilience admirable — the courage and resilience of all children, I suppose. They scarcely knew their mother before she died; they will hardly have a mind picture of her. And yet they carry no bitterness, no sullenness, simply a love of life. I think back to my own childhood and try to pinpoint a moment at which things seemed straightforward, but it's difficult. When I think of bathing, I think of the dank green bathroom at my parents' house in Surrey, of the crust of mold around the bathroom taps and the cracked soap in a tray on the sink. I think of the water, cooling around my ten-year-old body, the wrinkled skin on my toes and fingertips but I still didn't want to climb out. I could hear my parents arguing downstairs, a slammed door then the angry stomp of footsteps on the stairs. My father's fist would pound on the door. *"Are you still in there, girl?"*

Or I think of the baths at Burstead, those harsh iron troughs, a naked bulb swinging above my head and the shrieks and yelps of girls in the yard outside. When I first arrived at boarding school, I cried in the bath. I cried because I was lonely, and I hadn't any friends, and I wanted my parents even though I hated them and I wanted my home even though I hated it, and everything was confusing. A girl called Ginny Pettifer had found me crying, and brought her friends to look in at me and laugh. I close my eyes, pushing down the dreadful memories. Of that miserable bath, yes, and of Ginny's gleeful face at the door — but then of years later, and more water, much more, blooming the most perfect shade of red like a lover's rose, and a tangle of hair and two panicked, swollen eyes, a hand reaching for mine and grasping air . . .

My parents had imagined that Burstead was the answer to their problems. I spent seven years at that school and the first five were miserable. Then, all of a sudden, Burstead stopped answering their problems, and started answering mine.

"Alice, Alice, look!" Constance's cry brings me back to the present. She is on the rim of the pond, ready to jump. "I'm going to jump! Look, look!"

"I'm looking!"

With a splash, she's back in the water. Edmund complains at the impact, splashing her back. For a moment I let myself become part of the joyful scene, really part of it, as if I were one of the children here, a long time ago. No mistakes made, no loss, no suffering. *Stop daydreaming, Alice.* Daydreaming is for fools.

When the time comes for them to get out, I reach in and offer my arm. Constance takes it first, warm and definite, full of trust, then the boy.

The twins giggle as they dry off in the sun. *See?* I think. *I did the right thing. This time, I did.*

Later that day, while the children are taking their supper, I hear a motor car approach the house and then the sound of a slamming door.

"Are we expecting anyone, Mrs. Yarrow?"

"Only the captain's doctor."

I go to greet him. The man on the doorstep is a little older than me, with a mop of brown hair and a neat mustache. He carries a doctor's bag and there is a wire-haired pointer at his heels. "You must be Alice Miller," he says, amiably.

"How do you do."

The man nods his cap, removes it. "Henry Marsh, the captain's physician."

"So I understand. Won't you come in."

In the hall, Henry Marsh takes off his coat. The dog trails after him, a splash of white on the tip of his tail. He makes a comment about the animal being his trusted assistant, and how Captain de Grey has no objections to his attendance. I smile and stroke the dog, fussing round his ears and his gruff, wizened face. The doctor watches me kindly, inquisitively.

"How are you settling in?"

"Very well, thank you."

"Is the man of the house up and about today?"

"I haven't seen him — but that doesn't mean he's not."

Henry smiles back. "It's a big place, Winterbourne, isn't it?"

"Certainly."

"It takes some getting used to?"

"I'm used to it already. The children have helped me with that."

Henry's smile doesn't move or change, but his eyes no longer concur. "I'm sure," he says. "If you'll excuse me, I must see to my patient."

"Of course."

An hour later, the doctor is back in the hall, the dog keeping close to his heels.

"Is everything well, Doctor?" I ask.

He appears somewhat troubled; I offer him a drink. "No, thank you," he says. "I'd best be on my way. I've another appointment in Polcreath."

I see him move to go, then, on impulse, I place a hand on the door.

"Doctor," I begin, checking swiftly behind me that we are alone, "forgive my impertinence, but I wonder if the captain is quite well. You will of course be the person to ask about this — and of course you will tell me if it is not my concern. But his leg appears to be causing him great pain and I worry that he refuses to admit it."

The doctor steps back. In the same moment, without warning, the wire-haired pointer makes a sudden dash for the bowels of the house, scooting off in a flash of fur to the lower stairs. "Hell and damnation!" Henry cries. "Tipper, get back here!"

"I'm sorry," he turns to me, "he occasionally does this. Normally I can get him out before he does. It must be rats down there; he's picking up a scent."

103

"Let's follow," I say, thinking it rather good luck. We walk. He talks.

"Jonathan is that breed of man who doesn't readily admit weakness," the doctor says carefully, his instinct toward friendliness wishing to answer my question but his professionalism keeping him within reasonable bounds. It interests me that he refers to the captain by his name — it makes my employer seem less remote, more like an ordinary person, no one to be afraid of. "He comes from that sort of family," Henry says, "old English, stiff upper lip, that sort of thing. When he went off to war, there was no question of his surviving. The de Greys were — are — an institution in Polcreath; the idea of one of them falling victim to as trifling a matter as war was unthinkable. The captain wasn't just to live: he was to triumph."

We embark down the stairs. "Tipper!" he calls. "Damn dog. Sorry for my language. He's old; I shouldn't bring him on my rounds any more."

"Are the captain's injuries very bad?"

The doctor considers his reply. "They are as they appear," he says at length, as he helps me down the steps. It's cold and dank, this lower part of Winterbourne shut off from the rest of the house so that it feels as if we are trespassing. "When his Hawker Tempest went down over France, it was a miracle he was dragged out alive. Some might say a few burns and a dicky knee were a small price to pay."

"Is there potential for improvement?"

"With the knee, certainly, but with injuries like this, a big part of the patient's recovery is caught up in his outlook. Frustration doesn't come close to describing it, particularly for a man in Jonathan's position. He sees his war wounds as failings, where others might see them as strengths, badges of honor, however you like to describe it. Jonathan is a brave man, no doubt about it. But he isn't the most open to accepting a doctor's help. If he didn't have to see me at all, I'm sure he'd be glad."

We emerge into a fusty corridor, sooty with dust and cobwebs.

"This must be the old servants' quarters," I say out loud, and Henry nods, remembering I don't yet know the house. From the way he stalks ahead, peering behind doors after his dog, it's clear he's been down here several times, probably for the same reason. I look up and see the bell box Mrs. Yarrow was talking about, the one the evacuees used to play havoc with. It's a handsome thing, its gold edges tarnished but the dozens of names beneath the chimes are visible: DIN-ING ROOM, STUDY, LIBRARY, MAS-TER BEDROOM . . . . I imagine the servants rushing along this corridor in another decade, bright with bustle. Now, it's as quiet as a graveyard.

"Tipper!" Henry is shouting. "Get back here, you useless mutt!"

The doctor encourages me to turn back; he'll be up with the dog soon enough. But I'm looking at that bell box, picturing the maids rushing up to the captain's bedside. I'm picturing the woman in bed beside him.

"Did his wife die while he was away?" The darkness makes me bold. Here we cannot be heard, cannot be seen. Here, I can say what I like.

Henry shakes his head. "The captain's crash happened in '41. He was no good to the effort after that and came straight back to Winterbourne. She'd struggled while he was absent, of course, coping with two babies on her own. But it wasn't until the following year that she died." There, he stops. He knows we have stumbled off limits.

"I don't mean to speak out of turn," I say, hoping to assure him of my loyalty. "It's just I feel such affiliation with Edmund and Constance, and in turn with Winterbourne, and in turn with the captain. I care for them all."

"I understand. But the death of Laura de Grey isn't a matter for discussion, here or anywhere in Polcreath. I should never have entertained it."

Her name coats me like heat. It's the first time I have heard it. *Laura.*

I have an almost overwhelming desire to say it aloud, but I don't. Her husband would have left to fight right after their twins were born, leaving her to deal with their infancy by herself. I recall Mrs. Yarrow talking about the evacuees and the bell box, about those howling hounds belonging to the man called Marlin, and how Laura was kept awake at night, exhausted and alone, prey to two screaming nurslings, growing to hate Winterbourne and its severe outlook, its arched windows and gloom-laden passages, the thrashing sea outside mirroring the thrashing in her mind, wishing fervently for her husband's return . . . And when the captain did come back, had he been the same? Physically he was compromised, yes, but was he the man she'd married, in spirit, in soul, in temperament? Did he look at her in the same way; did he talk to her as he had? *Laura.* The mother. The wife. The powerful. *Laura.*

"I shouldn't have raised it," I say. "I'm sorry."

We are interrupted by a frantic bark. "At last!" the doctor mutters, and I follow him down the hall and toward another set of descending steps. Just how deep does Winterbourne go? "I should have known he'd be here," says Henry, as the barking becomes a higher pitched yap, a moan, nearly, as if Tipper has hurt himself. "The cellar — again!" We arrive in a small, damp room: the full stop of the house. It can't be longer than a few meters, and the walls are exposed stone, mottled black. There are a few empty crates on their sides on the dusty ground.

"Is he all right?"

Henry grabs the dog's collar and attempts to soothe him, but the animal is wild. I take a step back: Tipper's eyes are mad, his mouth pulled over his gums, his teeth bared. Saliva darts from his tongue with each expulsion. His fur stands on end, his spine arched, his tail set. He yelps then cowers, yelps then cowers.

"Come now, boy," says the doctor gently, "it's just a silly old door."

I see the door he means, though I didn't at first. It is set in the corner, lost in shadow but not quite. It is unfeasibly old-looking, and small, so small as to be uncertain if it

108

was intended for a person to walk or crawl through. Its wood is cracked and splintered with age. In the style of the house, it wears a Gothic arch, with a heavy rounded handle partway down. I try the handle but it doesn't give.

"Why is he afraid?" I ask.

"He's an old dog full of bad habits," says the doctor lightly, although I can see he's as keen to get back upstairs as I am.

"Where does it lead?"

Henry doesn't know. "I should think there's a lot of old rubbish behind there," he says. "Tipper can smell it." He's struggling to restrain the dog. "Let's go."

We head back the way we've come, Tipper dipping his head, his tail bowed, staying tight to his master's heel. "That's the last time I bring you with me, do you hear?" he says gently to the hound. Before we ascend the final staircase, I look behind, wondering at this cold, abandoned netherworld, seeing that strange door, beyond which Tipper knew about something we did not.

I hear her name again.

Laura.

CHAPTER 11

I sleep well that night. When I wake at the usual time, I imagine for a moment that it is still the small hours, for my room is drenched in a sooty, dim light.

Climbing out of bed, I pull the curtains and see why. The mists have rolled in. I can scarcely see a foot from the window, the air obscured with dense, swirling fog. The sea has vanished, the sky invisible. I glimpse the position of Winterbourne in my mind's eye, high on the Landogger Bluff, closeted in vapor; cold mists press against the walls and turrets, drifting beneath the arches, smothering the roof of the chapel . . .

All is quiet. All is still.

As ever when I go to tie back the drapes, I am faced with that eerie painting. Each day, I like it less. Something prevents me from taking it down, some sense that it has been here longer than I. Today, I try not to examine it, focusing instead on the silk knots that draw the curtains into place. And yet I cannot resist. The girl at the window lures me, as determinedly and insidiously as the fogs that roll in off the sea, creeping overnight, slowly, stealthily; it is as if she is whispering to me: *Look, look . . .* Is it my fancy, or has her gaze changed? Her regard has moved to one side, toward me, toward the ancient, indecipherable sea. I could swear that yesterday it was not so.

Don't be ridiculous, Alice, I tell myself. The print is honestly so small, and the girl within it even smaller, that to pick out such an unlikely discrepancy is absurd.

At Burstead, my lover and I once spent a night together in the music school. I remember those handsome, silent pianos, dozens of them, and the way they shone in the moonlight, like war heroes at a gathering, mute but magnificent. I kept thinking, then, that I heard noises in the dark, people who had found us as we lay in Practice Room 3, or some noise beyond, a flit of wings, a whisper, some flight of my nervous disposition. *"There's nothing,"* he said to me, as he turned to kiss me in the purple light. *"There's no one here except you and me . . ."* I try to hear him now, but his voice grows fainter with every passing year. *There's no one here. Just me.*

I obscure the painting as far as is possible with the material and go to my dressing room, slipping off my nightdress and laying it on the bed. It's only when I'm buttoning my skirt that I notice the smudge on the inside of my elbow, where the skin creases and softens in the bend of my arm. Thinking it must be soot from the fire, I try to wipe it away and when it doesn't come, I lick my thumb and try again. Pressing harder this time, it smarts. It's a bruise, clearly: bluish-brown and shaped like an almond. It seems an odd place to have it, not the sort of bump one might acquire from walking into a bedframe or knocking one's arm on the newel post.

Surely I struck it in a game with the children. I've been so occupied with those happy souls since arriving at Winterbourne that I can't promise I'd even have noticed. Filled with pleasure at the thought of seeing them at breakfast, I finish dressing and go downstairs to greet my wards.

"Be careful, miss," says Tom as he helps us into our coats and boots. "The captain doesn't like the children to go out when the mists are in. It's awful cold and damp."

"We'll be fine, Tom. Fresh air is good for the children — and, besides, we've already sought the captain's permission." This is only true in part. I would have sooner received consent directly, but when I tapped on de Grey's study door an hour previously, asking if we might venture out for a walk, I was met only by silence.

Instead it fell to the boy Edmund to reassure me that his father had given approval. "It's quite all right, Alice," Edmund told me with confidence. "I met Father in the drawing room and he agreed we could go. He trusts you, Alice," he said, his eyes sparkling, "he knows you'll take care of us." I flushed at the unexpected compliment. Could the captain have formed a positive opinion of me so fast, and in such an obvious way that it would be clear to the children?

"Take this," says Tom, producing an old dog whistle and looping it round my neck. "Like I said, you'll fast lose your bearings."

"We're not going far."

"I'm excited!" Constance is pulling on her mittens. Next to her, Edmund yanks his cap down over his ears. "We're going on an adventure," he says.

I smile at Tom in a way I hope reassures him that we are doing no such thing. But Tom doesn't look reassured.

"Take the whistle," he says, "and watch

your step."

Minutes later, the door closes behind us. I cannot wait to get out on the moors. The world seems changed, magical and deeply peaceful, as if we might slip into it unheeded, like woods on a snowy morning awaiting a first footprint.

"Can you hear the sea?" Constance cries. "I can hear it — but I can't see it!"

She's right. It's an odd impression because we are so close to the cliff drop and yet we cannot detect a thing. The sea crashes in with a deep, mellow roar, which takes on a new personality in this muffled, sunken world. Without bearings to situate us — a few steps from the house and it disappears completely — our senses are primed elsewhere. The tide bellows louder; the cold snap in the air smells startlingly clean.

"Hold my hands, children."

"Look at our boots!" Edmund exclaims as we walk, emerging in pockets of better vision that enable me to reclaim our situation, before we are engulfed once more. Our boots do indeed look strange, uncannily real as they plod ahead, three pairs in a line, two small, one big, and bizarrely separate from the rest of us. It is as if we are walking on clouds, and for a moment the ground beneath us feels precarious, as if we could fall through it at any moment.

I stop. The fog is closing in, too close. I cannot breathe.

"What's the matter, Alice?" Constance asks.

"Nothing, I —" My lungs strain. "Nothing."

"Listen for the lighthouse," says Edmund, in a voice that sounds much older than his own. "That's how you can tell where you are."

"Do you often come out in the mists?" I ask, with a nervous laugh. Edmund doesn't reply. I listen for the Polcreath tower, and its sharp fog blasts tell me we are over the westernmost brow and close to the sea. But in the next instant, I wonder that I don't hear it to my other side, or above, or behind. The blasts grow louder and more aggressive. My knees weaken. I'm back in London, on a cold March night during the Blitz, and the air-raid sirens are wailing, louder and louder, louder and louder . . .

"Bombs away!"

Edmund releases my hand and runs into the wall of fog. I turn, turn, turn, gripping Constance tightly, but I cannot see a thing. I cannot see him.

"Edmund!"

I think I hear him whooping in the distance, then it is only the ravens' caws I can hear, and if I can't see a meter in front of me then how can he? How can he see the cliff edge, the churning swell of the sea, the dagger-sharp rocks below?

"Edmund! *Come back here now!*"

But how will he know where we are? How will he see me?

"EDMUND!"

"Don't worry, Alice," says Constance, her little-girl voice light and singsong. "He'll be all right. He knows Winterbourne better than you, remember."

All at once the very sound of Constance, my sweet, sweet Constance, turns on me. I cannot see the child's face, only the pale grip of her small hand in mine, and our joined palms appear ghostly, dismembered, horrifying. All at once I remember that other hand, *her* hand, years ago, in the water, reaching for mine, and for a shocking instant it *could* be hers, her clammy grip, rigid with fear, threatening to drag me in!

"We both know Winterbourne better than you."

Why does she talk to me in that tone?

"EDMUND!"

"Don't be silly, Alice. You are being silly now."

I release her hand, drawing mine sharply

116

away as if something black and slippery has crawled over it. Constance starts crying.

"Oh, my Constance!" I kneel to her, find her face with my hands and embrace her. Suddenly she is my Constance again, the strangeness dissolved. She is but a child! "I'm sorry, my darling. I'm worried for your brother — that is all. We must find him. Do you know where he is? Do you know where he might have run to?"

The girl sniffs. She wipes her eyes. Her features soften and morph in the eerie half-light, and for a second she looks canny, before her innocence resumes.

"What are you looking at, child?" For Constance's gaze is trained over my shoulder. I turn but see nothing. "What are you looking at?"

And then I see her. The mist spools patiently across the cliffs and in one glimmer of clarity I see her. There is a woman. She is facing the sea. She wears all black, head to toe, like a widow. I squint, trying to draw her more sharply into focus, but the more I look, the more she escapes my definition. She flickers and fades, in moments as real as day and in the next a mere black shape, impossibly still and impossibly menacing. What is she doing there? She is right on the bluff; she must be mere inches from its edge. Who is she? "Hello?" I call. "Is somebody there?"

Constance has my hand again, and her thumb tickles mine for an instant, as if she is stroking it, as if she is the one replying, *Yes, somebody is.* The vision itself does not reply. The woman does not move. I have the blinding, improbable notion that she has taken Edmund, stolen him and flung him over the edge into the roiling swell . . .

She's come back for you, Alice.

You always knew she would.

I cannot bear for Constance to witness her. Whirling back on the girl, I capture her in my cloak, shutting out our dark companion.

"Alice, Alice, I can't see a thing!"

I crouch to her, my eyes wild. "I don't want you to see, my darling."

"Why?" She snivels, wipes her nose, at once a little girl again, my harmless child. "I'm scared, Alice — you're scaring me!"

I turn my head to the cliff edge but the woman has disappeared.

"She's gone," I say, searching left and right. "Where did she go?"

"Who?" Constance is crying again now, gripping my cloak with one hand but seeming to pull away at the same time, as if she can't be sure where the danger lies. But I

118

know where it lies. It lies with that specter, which, now vanished, seems all the more looming for its absence. There is nowhere the woman can have gone. The mist churns silently across the landscape, exposing the hill as it goes. If she had moved off, I would have caught her by now. She is nowhere. Not unless . . .

Beneath us, out of sight, the tide rolls on, a thunderous crash of waves.

"Didn't you see her?" I shiver, pulling the girl close. "She was right there!"

"I didn't see anyone."

I crouch to her again and search her face. I want to tell Constance that I *saw* her looking, I *saw* her, before I turned to the phantom myself — but the words dry on my tongue. Constance's lip is trembling, her eyes wet with tears. Am I mistaken?

"It doesn't matter," I manage, and pull her toward me. I must get a hold on myself. This sweet girl is my charge. Her arms wrap round me and her hair is fragrant gold: once again she is my angel, and we neither of us saw the devil on the cliff.

As we pull apart, her hands cross over my elbow. I feel pressure on the bruise inside my arm, as if her tiny fingers have pressed it.

I stand and call his name. Nothing. The

whistle blows, short and shrill.

Tom is with us quickly. "I'm sorry," I stammer, "he ran off. Edmund ran off. Didn't he, Constance, darling? He just let go. I don't know where he is. Oh, help us, Tom!"

The houseman looks to Constance, who neither supports nor denies my claims. "It's all right," he puts a hand on my shoulder, "we'll find him." He steers me over the hill and then I see the house emerge from the fog — it must be clearing now, daylight beginning to break through — far closer than I had expected.

"Go back indoors," he says, "and wait for us there."

We obey. My fingers and toes are numb with cold, or fear. Mrs. Yarrow meets us and gives us mugs of warmed milk, but I can't drink mine while I'm thinking of Edmund out in the wild, frozen and alone. I feel disgraced by my idiotic confidence, stalking out into the savage mist as if it posed no threat whatsoever. I feel dismayed by my failure to speak to the captain in person about our endeavor, and the vanity that had coaxed me into it, enjoying the captain's trust in me and wanting to see that trust rewarded. "Mrs. Yarrow," I splutter, once Constance is safely by the fire and out of earshot. "Were you out there just now? Were you out in the fog?"

"Certainly not, miss!"

"I saw a woman. She was standing on the cliff."

"Are you sure?"

"Perfectly. She was . . . Oh, she was horrible!"

"The fog plays tricks on us, miss," says the cook. "There'd be nobody foolish enough to go walking alone on a morning like this."

"I swear I saw her. Constance did, too, but she won't admit it."

Mrs. Yarrow washes out the milk pan. "Constance saw her?"

"Yes. I might not have noticed this fiend were it not for her."

The cook puts the pan on the draining board to dry. "This was after Edmund ran away from you?"

"Yes!"

"Children like to play games."

"What are you suggesting?"

"Especially with a new prospect such as yourself, miss."

"Please be frank, Mrs. Yarrow."

The cook appears undecided as to whether to speak further. She peers past me to check the hallway is clear, before: "Ever since I

121

can recall," she says, "those twins have had a mischief to them. Goodness knows I struggled to cope with them on my own, before you arrived. Always playing pranks on me, they were. Hiding my belongings. Tricking me into believing I'd said words I hadn't. Knocking on my door late at night and then running away, so that I became convinced of some ghoul! Once, the boy even put a nasty big spider in my bed, and when I pulled back the covers I screamed the house down — and I knew it was him, I knew!"

"I cannot accept it, Mrs. Yarrow. The children are impeccable."

"So impeccable as to tease you into disobeying their father?"

"I beg your pardon?"

"Knowing the captain as I do, miss, there is slim chance he would have given blessing to your expedition. I'll wager it was one of the children, was it not?"

I swallow. Edmund is a boy, full of the boldness of youth. What child hasn't told a white lie in defiance of a parent? That I will pay the price of that lie is unfortunate. I struggle to answer Mrs. Yarrow, but my silence is answer enough.

The cook sits. "All I'm suggesting, miss, is that being without their mother might have . . . addled their natures somewhat. Is it possible that your woman on the cliff was in fact the boy himself? That the twins persuaded you into the outing as a way to pursue their game? These children know Winterbourne and its surrounds better than anyone. It's their home. They've no fear of tumbling into the sea or tripping on a stray log — they know every inch. It's their playground."

We're interrupted by the sound of a closing door.

"Edmund!" I jump up.

The boy is huddled next to Tom, the houseman's coat wrapped around his small shoulders. He is pale and cold, his teeth chattering, and his copper hair is plastered to his forehead with precipitation or clammy fright.

"Found him in the copse," says Tom, "and a good job, too."

Mrs. Yarrow steers him into the kitchen. "Let's get you warmed up, lovey."

"Edmund, darling," I step forward, "are you all right?"

As the boy's meek form travels past me, I feel the urge to apologize — though for what, I do not know. He was the one who ran from me. I cannot bear to think of the accusations that passed the cook's lips just moments before. Seeing Edmund's frail body, shivering and innocent, I cannot entertain it for a heartbeat. I think of him shaking and alone on the moors and want to scoop him into my arms.

But it seems I am required elsewhere. Captain de Grey appears in the hall.

"Miss Miller, I must see you immediately."

Amid the brutal shadow of his face, his blue eyes glint like diamonds. They frighten and excite me, both at once.

I turn to Edmund but the boy is being led away. For an instant, he glances behind him and sharply meets my eye.

"Just what in hell do you think you were doing?"

"I'm sorry, Captain. It was foolish to leave Winterbourne. Accept my apology."

"Did you not deem it necessary to ask me first?"

"I'm very sorry," I say, for I cannot think of anything else. Edmund is a child, and I could always have overridden his claim.

The captain pours himself a drink — brandy, strong, in a cut-glass tumbler — and knocks it back. "Do you want one?" He pours another.

"No, thank you." He drinks more. He wipes the back of his hand across his mouth and I notice the coarse black hairs on the outside of his wrist.

"Sit down," he tells me. I do.

"Do you have any idea," he says, "what those children mean to me?"

"Yes, Captain."

"Do you have children?"

"I do not."

"Then you lie." He sits at his desk. It is scattered with paper, an ashtray bearing the stubs of several cigars, and a framed photograph whose picture I cannot see from this angle. "You cannot possibly grasp what it might be to lose a child," he says. "I could have lost Edmund today. Do you hear me? Do you understand?"

I swallow dryly. I have no idea what it is to lose . . .

Oh, but I do, Jonathan, I want to say. *Oh, but I do.* And I think that if I were Laura de Grey, with this husband and these children, I would have wanted to live forever and a day. I would have risked losing nothing. I would have held them all to my heart so tightly that none of them could get away.

"I accept full responsibility for what happened," I manage. Any protest that Edmund orchestrated his own fate would sound petty on my part. If the price is the captain's anger then so be it. "It was reckless to leave

125

Winterbourne."

I wonder where the captain was this morning, when I came knocking. Possibly he was sleeping, or possibly he'd been drinking. But for a tired man, for a drunk, his eyes are piercingly clear. The burned side of his face is in shadow (does he always sit so as to ensure this?) and his dark hair is unkempt. He trails a long finger around the rim of his brandy glass, watching me.

"I agree," he says. "Reckless. And it won't happen again."

"You have my absolute assurance of that."

Abruptly, the captain stands. "Are you engaged to be married?" he asks, walking to the window.

The question surprises me. "No."

"Then what is your position?"

"I beg your pardon?"

"Your position, Miss Miller," he says. "A woman of your . . ." He waves a hand around in lieu of a word. "You must have a sweetheart at home."

I meet his eye. "I lost my sweetheart during the war."

The captain lifts his chin a notch. "I see. Did he see action?"

"If your question is whether he died in action, the answer is yes."

"I'm sorry."

"The war was cruel."

"Was yours a long affair?"

I laugh, uncomfortably. "Forgive me, Captain, but I cannot see what this has to do with what happened in the mist."

"It has everything to do with what happened in the mist. I am trying to ascertain what attachments you might have in your personal life, Miss Miller — attachments which enable you to look after my children to a satisfactory degree. Now, for a woman to have never been obligated, at least not in any serious way, and to have no children of her own, well, that was the problem with our last governess. I cannot entertain a possibility of that repeating. To care for my family, to understand how high a stake they represent to me, you must first appreciate high stakes in your own life. I am invested in my children. What are you invested in, Miss Miller?"

I glance to the floor. I think of my father in the house in Surrey, demanding my intentions, just as the captain is now. *"You're a silly, stupid girl. I'm ashamed to call you my daughter. Do you know how ashamed I am?"*

Captain de Grey's study is like the chapel at Burstead, dark wood paneling and oriel windows, high-backed chairs (or pews in the chapel's case) where we would all stand

127

in neat rows to say our prayers. *Forgive us our trespasses* . . . Winterbourne bears down on me, seems to *watch* me with hidden eyes, curiously looking, curiously poking the soft parts of my flesh, testing to see what makes me wince.

My trespass cannot be forgiven. What I did — or didn't do. The choice I made.

Those are my stakes. Higher than them all.

"I was engaged to be married," I say. "We had plans for after the war." I don't disclose those plans to the captain — it is too painful, too raw, even after years have passed. "Captain," I meet his blue eyes, "I know what it is to love. I know what it is to have that love taken away. I would not wish the heartache I have suffered on my worst enemy. I will protect your children as if they were mine. You can be assured of that."

He surveys me for a moment, so intensely that I have to look away.

"As if they are yours?" he repeats.

"As if they are mine."

He nods. "I'm assured," he says, softly. "You may go."

CHAPTER 12

CORNWALL, PRESENT DAY

Rachel stepped inside. She fumbled for a light switch, then, finding none, used her phone to illuminate the way. On the fireplace were a collection of altar candles and a box of matches, which she knelt to and lit. From there she could spot the basket of firewood and bucket of kindling, which she assembled in the hearth. She took a newspaper from her bag and packed balls of it under the tinder, so that when she held a flame to the arrangement it swiftly licked orange and the wood cracked and sparked.

It was amazing how little glow was needed to irradiate a dark space. Rachel stood and looked about her. Her surroundings were vast. High above in the entrance hall, a roof lantern let the moon peer in, as curious an eye as hers, and after a few moments she could start to make out every shape and contour as if she were seeing them twelve hours from now. No doubt about it, the place was creepy. She thought of her aunt shuffling around here in her final days, ancient and alone, and a sudden snap made her turn her head — but it was only the firewood as it splintered and burned.

"Get a grip!" she scolded herself. Her voice sounded funny in the dark: she half expected it to fly back at her or for some sound to answer it.

All the same, it was a relief to spy the solitary switch at the foot of the stairs. To Rachel's amazement, when she pressed it, the chandelier spluttered to life. She sneezed, as all of a sudden the dark romance of the hall was eclipsed by its stark, neglected reality. Cobwebs hung in swathes between the rafters; the fireplace was coated in silver: everything from the framed pictures on the walls to the banister on the staircase to the shabby, frayed rugs on the flagstone floor was devoured by age.

It couldn't have been updated in decades, and why should it have? Rachel imagined her ancestors here, the "curious" de Greys, whose conversations had rippled through this space, whose calls had wound down the stairs, whose laughter had gathered round the fire. Now, the house was silent. Empty. But despite its dereliction, of all the works of art Rachel had seen, of all the visionary imaginings she had helped promote and display, of all the galleries she had spent hours in getting lost in a beautiful fantasy, those contained at Winterbourne — the very bones of Winterbourne, from its architecture to its fittings — were by far the most beautiful fantasy of them all. Whoever had designed and built this had been inspired to the point of madness.

Rachel thought of her apartment in Manhattan with the blare of traffic outside, the reassuring glow of the streetlights holding her until she fell asleep . . . Here, she was on her own. There was no phone ringing off the hook, no late-night coffee shops, no Aaron Grewal messaging her with an invitation for that evening. She could hear her own breath. Her heartbeat. There was nobody for miles around, just her, the house, and the wide, sprawling sea. But she wasn't afraid. It simply didn't occur to her to be afraid. It didn't occur to her to consider the long trek back to civilization and warm lodgings, or to regret not taking the cab driver up on his offer of returning her to town. Winterbourne had already cast her under a fascinated spell. She had entered a priceless masterpiece, was standing in it, breathing its antique air.

It was late. She decided to head to bed,

resolving to see to the house in the morning. She found the first chamber she could and collapsed in sleep.

Birdsong woke her. It took a moment to remember where she was but the cold soon brought her to her senses. Rachel was still wearing last night's coat, her knees tucked in tight — she must have crashed out as soon as her head hit the pillow, not even bothering to slip beneath the covers. Turning over, she decided that it might have been for the best: the four-poster was as dust-caked as everything else, the brocade bedding stiff with disuse. She coughed, getting up to open the window and let in the fresh air. It took several attempts to release the latch but when she did, it was as if the house inhaled, its aged scent dispelled by the crisp Cornish breeze. The empty seascape was beautiful, the water blue and twinkling in the cool September sunshine and the sky adrift with clouds. She detected a fishing boat in the distance, the only sign of life.

All she could think about was having a shower. Such a thing seemed doubtful at Winterbourne, and as she ventured to explore the labyrinth of rooms her instinct was confirmed. The bathroom on this floor was straight out of the 1900s. There was an iron tub and the loo looked archaic. It was also freezing. She searched the walls and found an old-fashioned convection heater, shaped like a zeppelin, and was gratified when she pulled its cord and heard a reassuring groan before the element glowed to life. The taps on the bath were rusted so hard that she almost gave up, before one of them surrendered and a brown choke of water splurged on to her hands. In minutes the corrosion passed through and the water began to clear, but there was nothing warm about it. She resolved to figure that part out later.

Remarkably, she found a couple of clean towels in the cupboard. She dried and dressed quickly, in part because of the bitter cold (despite the heater, which was now emitting a burned, charred smell: she switched it off) and in part because her stomach was growling. She had bought a few basics before leaving London — bread, milk, eggs, coffee — and realized she hadn't eaten a decent meal in days.

It seemed simplest to keep the room she'd slept in, so she unpacked, dusted off the dresser and set out her belongings. She thought how in need of decoration the whole place was: a new ream of wallpaper, for a start, to go over the botched job someone had done in covering up the mural opposite her bed. She only half glanced at it now, and wondered what beautiful design had once detailed its surface.

Only before she left did she notice the painting. It was discreet, tucked behind the drapes, and depicted a tiny cottage, golden hay bales, a cow waiting to be milked . . . Rachel smiled, liking it immediately. It was just the sort of thing she'd love to take back to New York and share with the gallery.

She searched the painting for a sign of human life, some face to greet hers, but there was none. Only an open upstairs window, a small square of empty black, flung open to the night as if someone, or something, had escaped.

After breakfast, she set about cleaning. Unsurprisingly there wasn't much to use, just an old mop and a dustpan and brush. She unearthed a bucket under the kitchen sink and filled it with soapy water, then dragged the whole lot into the hall. She focused on her own room, the bathroom and the kitchen. The rest would have to wait.

The rest, she swiftly learned, was considerable. Rachel was incredulous at the spaces that continued to open at Winterbourne, on and on they went, one maze of rooms that led to another. On the ground floor alone was a grand study, steeped in the scent of old books and leather, a library addled with damp (what room wasn't?), a drawing room with two small desks pressed up against the window, a scullery, a chapel, a ballroom, and downstairs were the old servants' quarters, which Rachel closed the door on. Upstairs, along from her bedroom, were half a dozen more, some with single beds, some with four-posters, some with no sleeping arrangements at all. Two other stories climbed above, which she explored with amazement, marveling at the sheer grandiosity of the place. Doubtless, it was eccentric. The mansion was homage to all things Gothic, its turrets and spires like elaborate peaks of icing; its grave, studded furniture soaked in rich history; its candle holders and wall tapestries as sumptuous as they came. It was like a museum. She half expected red rope to be looped across doorways with a polite sign reading: *Please do not touch.*

Only, it was hers to touch. All of it. Every piece.

Never in her wildest dreams could Rachel have connected herself with this lavishness. It was preposterous. All those years wondering about where she had come from, all those tears she had shed thinking she would never know, all that anguish over discovering her birth mother was dead, all those teenage fall-outs with Maggie and Greg (imagine if they were alive to see Winterbourne), it all came to this: this splendid, impossible palace in the middle of nowhere on the Cornish coast. She felt like an impostor, a pretender to the throne. It wasn't *hers*. She had no right to it.

But she did. Her grandfather had been Jonathan de Grey.

Still, she thought of her elusive grandmother. Who had she been? The woman was an essential shadow, the key to Rachel's parentage. She wasn't Laura, the captain's wife. Who, then? Someone with whom de Grey had strayed — and there was a passion and romance she clung to in this because without those elements it sounded sordid, to have gone behind the back of a wife and mother. And through that passion her grandparents had created Rachel's mother. *My mother . . .* To think that mysterious woman had begun her life here, in this house, on the floorboards Rachel now walked on, was crazy. Which room had she slept in? What toys had she played with?

At once, a door banged shut behind her. Rachel flew round, before chiding herself for being easily spooked. She pushed the door, expecting it to open as easily as it had closed, but it didn't give. She leaned her body against it but it wouldn't budge. Strange. She rattled the handle — it was stuck.

A distant voice inquired: "Hello?"

Rachel's heart pounded. She waited, her breath hard, wondering if jet lag was getting the better of her. The voice came again:

"Hello?"

It was coming from downstairs. Rachel grabbed the mop and held the stick firmly. She left the locked room and headed down two flights, the mop held aloft like some cocked baseball bat. She saw the top of a man's head before she saw anything else, as she peered down through the banister. It was pleasing, for a moment, to be unobserved and yet observing, and a relief (if bizarrely anticlimactic) to recognize her impostor as real, unconnected with the sealed room upstairs, nothing to do with Winterbourne's slamming doors or chill drafts.

"Can I help you?" Rachel asked sharply, stepping into the hall, resenting the stranger for catching her at a vulnerable moment and making her lose her head.

"Hi," said the man, turning. He carried a crate of produce — fruit, bread, meat and a bottle of wine — and wore an easy, steady smile. "I'm Jack. Jack Wyatt. Thought I'd bring you up some stuff. Sorry to let myself in. I tried ringing, but the bell's broken."

Rachel leaned the mop against the wall and ran an arm across her brow. The man called Jack was a little older than her, and very tall. He had brown hair that was slightly graying round the ears. His complexion was tanned, as if he spent a lot of time outdoors. His grin was wide and slightly lopsided, which made it interesting.

"Thank you," she said. "That's thoughtful."

"Can I put it down?"

"Yes, anywhere." She motioned to the kitchen, which held the first acceptably clean surface. "I have coffee, but no tea. Would you like a cup?"

Jack set down the crate and removed a box of teabags. "Americans don't go in for tea, do they? I should have known."

"But you do, I expect."

"I'm a farmer. I don't just drink tea: I *need* tea."

There was no kettle, but she had worked out from her morning coffee that a saucepan over the stove worked just as well, if not quite so efficiently. Jack had his hands in his pockets — big hands; they had struck her as big when he was holding the crate — and he was looking up and around. "I've never been inside before," he said.

"It doesn't sound as if many people have."

"Have you?"

"This is my first time."

"Pete said you're a de Grey."

Ah, the cab driver. Rachel could just imagine him returning to the pub after he'd dropped her and relaying his ride: the American who'd arrived at Winterbourne.

"Not strictly." She stirred his tea. "Well, I mean, I am. After the fact. Sort of." She looked at him: he was frowning. "I'm not explaining myself. It's complicated."

He sat. "None of my business anyway."

"I hope you don't take sugar," she said, putting the mug before him.

"Not today, it appears. So how are you finding it?"

"Large."

For some reason, Jack found this amusing and laughed. He blew on his tea and then drank a huge gulp of it, even though it would still have been hot.

"Do you know much about the house?" Rachel asked.

"Its history, you mean?"

"More like how to get the immersion on."

He laughed again. "I can take a look. They

139

said I might have to."

"They?"

Jack ran one of his big hands across the back of his big neck. His knuckles were work-roughened, with the nails cut short and square. "Down at the Landogger," he said. "We all thought you'd be in for a bit of a rough ride, cut off at Winterbourne in the middle of a cold spell. It's not the most hospitable of places, is it?"

"So you collectively estimated I'd need help?"

Rachel bristled. No, more than bristled: it was downright annoying. She resented the thought that a bunch of men had been sitting round a table with their pints discussing a damsel in distress. She was perfectly able to look after herself.

"Don't you?"

Rachel sat straight. "Actually, I don't. I'll sort it out myself."

"No need to be like that."

"And you were elected my knight in shining armor?"

"Yeah, I always get the short straw."

She couldn't tell if he was joking or not. He watched her over his mug of tea and she decided that he was. But she couldn't be sure.

"Well, I appreciate your concern but it

isn't necessary." Rachel knew she sounded stuffy and uptight. The fact was that she was out of her comfort zone. Her zone was in New York, working with artists and organizers, ruling her world to the finest detail, juggling twenty things at once. In the course of her career she had sat opposite some of the most powerful players in the world. Sitting opposite Jack Wyatt, now, felt implausibly uncomfortable. "I won't be here for long, in any case."

He raised an eyebrow. "Not thinking of Polcreath as your next home?"

It was her turn to laugh. "I haven't been into Polcreath yet."

"I'll have to show you around."

Rachel looked away. "I was wondering about getting out, actually. I need to get hooked up."

He folded his arms, smirked a little. She decided he was rude.

"What the hell does that mean?" he asked.

"To the internet. I need to get online."

The smirk turned into a guffaw. "Ridiculous," he said.

"Excuse me?"

"*I need to get online.* Who *needs* to get online? You *need* water and a roof over your head and someone to hold at night. You don't *need* the bloody internet."

"You needed tea a moment ago," she countered. "You said farmers need tea."

"Yeah, they do. Add that to the list. Tea."

"My job *requires* me to get online — is that more acceptable?"

"A little. What is it you do?"

"I own a gallery. In New York. We just launched."

"I don't go to galleries."

"Something told me you didn't."

"Going well, is it?"

"Like I said, we just launched."

"And you've come out here to deepest, darkest Cornwall and there's no internet." He laughed a little more. She didn't like him. "Shouldn't think there'll be a phone signal either. You'll have to use the box down in the village." He seemed to be finding this very amusing. She imagined he lived on his farm with his chickens and sheep and probably didn't even own a television.

"I guess I'm asking the wrong person then," she said stiffly.

"Sorry, sorry, I'm being unhelpful. Have you got wheels?"

"Excuse me?"

"Did you hire a car?"

"No. I hadn't realized how remote the house was."

"OK," he spread his hands on the table,

"here's the thing. I drive past the south gate every morning at eight. If you want a lift into town any day, just be waiting there when I come past. There'll be places you can 'hook up' there. That's your best bet. I wouldn't want to think of you here, dying of internet deprivation."

"That's very funny."

He laughed again, as if they were sharing the joke.

"Well, I'd better get off. Thanks for the tea."

She felt she should thank him too, for bringing the food, for offering the rides, but for some reason she couldn't produce the words.

"Do you want me to take a look at that immersion before I go?"

"It's fine." She stood. "I'll manage myself."

She did manage — after an hour-long hunt to find the thing. She ran the usable taps through for several minutes to clear the rust, and even achieved a shallow, lukewarm bath later that afternoon. It had been a tiring day but her progress was pleasing. Tomorrow she would hitch a lift into Polcreath with Jack (a prospect she didn't relish) and catch up on emails. It would be good to reconnect with the world.

Seven p.m. with nothing to do. The light outside had faded, the sea a glittering mauve. Rachel cooked scrambled eggs and ate them from a cracked plate, gazing out of the window at the distant tower light. She wondered what Aaron was doing, if he missed her. Did she miss him? She didn't know. Maybe. Somehow she couldn't picture him here: Cornwall was another world, removed from the buzz of the city.

Another night's sleep, she thought, her eyes threatening to close. She couldn't remember sleeping as well, or for so long, as she had last night. It was as if those lost hours were catching up with her at last, demanding to be taken.

There had been no nightmares. She had not dreamed of that day, that phone call, the morning the world crashed down . . . Rachel didn't need a therapist to tell her that she avoided sleep for fear of returning to the trauma. The trauma was a constant friend at her back, nudging her in vulnerable places, whispering souvenirs in the dark.

Before heading to her room, on a whim she climbed the two flights to the door that had slammed on her earlier. She wanted to see if the wood had relaxed, if perhaps she could persuade it with a shove this time. As she passed along the corridor it occurred to her that this was the sort of house people might pay to spend the night in, as part of those team-building haunted weekends away. The sort of house nobody without a vested interest would elect to pass the time in alone.

Rachel didn't believe in things like that. There were the facts in front of you, the things you could see and touch, or there was nothing at all.

She was considering this as she met the surprise, and it was so perfectly timed that she almost spluttered a laugh. For there, where she expected to meet the stuck door, there was instead an open space. The door had unbolted again. She stopped.

It was an invitation; it had been waiting for her. *Don't be absurd.* But the impression was strong. As if Rachel hadn't just stepped up to the house, but that the house had stepped up to her. *Come and see,* it seemed to say. *I'll show you.*

Inside, it was bitterly cold. Ah, so that was it. The window was lifted a fraction and a sharp current of air blew through: the door had likely been closing and opening itself all afternoon. There were two single beds, close together, and the one nearest the door was set up for an old woman. This was where Constance de Grey had spent her final days, she realized. There was a walker, a plastic cup and straw, a hardback book and a crocheted blanket. On the wall was a naïve painting of a jar of lilies. Rachel went to the bed and brushed her fingers across the blanket. She picked up the book, which was a mighty tome entitled *The Wonderful Story of the Sea.*

Who had taken the other bed? It seemed strange that Constance should have preferred to stay in a small single when there were so many larger rooms available. She recalled what the taxi driver had said about Constance and her brother living here their whole lives, "as if they were married to each other." Had this been their childhood room? Had they stayed in it, clinging to each other, as the decades passed?

Rachel snapped the window shut. She left the room and closed the door tightly behind her. It would stay shut now. She went down the lonely corridor, her footsteps quiet on the steps, and descended the stairs. Outside, an owl hooted, a soft, low call.

Down in her own bedroom, she lit a small fire in the grate. Crooked shadows circled.

Rachel had noticed the remnants of the

mural this morning but hadn't paid it attention. Now she peered closer, running her fingertips across the wall opposite her bed and wondering: Whose room was this once? Who sat where Rachel sat now, warming their bones by the fire? Originally the hand-painted mural would have covered the length and breadth of the wall, a design she guessed, from the scraps left, boasted a lavish pattern of dark, tangled foliage. She could see the ghosts of its swirls and loops creeping above the skirting and emerging in ragged, weirdly sumptuous blotches. But what she saw now, contrary to what she'd first thought, was that the picture hadn't in fact been covered up: instead, *the wall itself* had been clawed at to the point of its very material coming away. It looked as if the task had been done with violence, the surface of the plaster ripped in wide, frenzied ribbons, and the lasting effect was like badly scratched skin. It looked in pain. A ghastly image dawned on Rachel, of the previous occupant, or some occupant long ago, tearing at the wall, tearing and tearing until their nails chipped and bled. She pictured a woman, but the woman frightened her so much that she switched off the thought as cleanly as a light. She had trained herself to do this. The mind could be a dangerous thing.

Rachel set about undressing. It was a trick of her tiredness that she felt exposed in doing so, as if someone was watching. Her naked skin prickled, the fine hairs on her arms and neck standing on end. She turned away from the window, away from that little painting of the lonely cottage, and climbed into bed.

CHAPTER 13
CORNWALL, 1947

Poor Edmund is laid low with a chill. There is a veil of accusation over the house that I am the person responsible for this, so I tend to him as best I can with warm soup and bedtime stories, and must admit I enjoy the nursing role. In the evenings, Edmund nestles into the crook of one arm and Constance in the other, and we turn the pages of an adventure about an orphan at Moonacre Manor, or hear the roll of the waves in *The Wonderful Story of the Sea*. "Alice, I love it when you read to us," says sweet Constance, while Edmund wipes sleepy eyes and snuggles down in his soft pajamas. Mrs. Yarrow ought to see them like this, I think, where no person on earth could imagine a rotten bone in their bodies. The cook does not care for them as I do. I am special to them.

On one such evening, we visit a story about a boy who runs away from home.

"Did you run away, Edmund?" I ask gently. It's the first time we have referenced that morning in the mist. He looks up at me with solemn, rheumy eyes and I instantly regret raising it. Yet it bothers me. I cannot move past it. I need to know why.

"No," he says, his copper hair gleaming in the candlelight. "You let me go."

I pull back. He's sleepy; possibly he's delirious. "What do you mean?"

"You let me go," he says again. "You told me to."

"I never did."

"You said I must go back to the house. That it was dangerous out there. There was someone with us, a stranger. She was looking at us. You said I had to go."

I touch the boy's forehead: he is burning up.

"Go to sleep, darling," I force out, standing to tuck him in.

"Who was she, Alice?" Edmund looks at me sharply then, as if no longer the boy in the grip of a fever but a man, fascinated, watching for my reaction.

"You're dreaming, darling." I smooth his blankets with undue attention. "It was just the three of us. The mist plays tricks, it had us all tricked that day."

"I'm sorry if I worried you. Poor Alice.

150

Dear Alice."

Constance slips into her adjacent bed and pulls the covers to her chin. "I don't feel very well," she whimpers.

I go to her. Her temperature is normal and her eyes are bright. I kiss her cheek.

"Both of you need your sleep," I say softly, and pinch the candle out. "All will be well when the sun comes up. Goodnight, Constance. Goodnight, Edmund."

"Goodnight, Alice," they chime. When I close the door, I think I hear the soft titter of laughter, but when I press my ear against the wood there is nothing.

Of course, the twins do everything together, which includes being ill. The following morning Constance is ailing with coughs and shivers alongside her brother, and Mrs. Yarrow and I take breakfast to their beds, refresh their hot water bottles and make sure they're comfortable. "We want coloring books," says Edmund, "and a game of snakes and ladders. And marshmallows toasted on the fire."

"If you're well enough for snakes and ladders and marshmallows, you're well enough for school," says Mrs. Yarrow.

"Please, Alice, can we?"

"Later on, perhaps."

Edmund flops back on his pillows. "We'll have to make our own fun, Connie."

"What you need is rest," I put in. "I'll be back to see you at lunchtime. No games now, do you hear?"

The cook and I leave. Mrs. Yarrow turns to me in the hallway.

"They don't look poorly to me," she says.

"Edmund had a fever last night," I reply, unwilling to engage in any more talk against the children: my loyalties lie with them and with Captain de Grey. "They're best off up here. Will you watch them this morning? I'd like to take some air."

"Certainly."

I decide to head down to the beach, that narrow strip of sand and rocks beneath the Landogger Bluff. I haven't ventured to the shoreline before and to get down off the hill will feel a welcome change — to be on a level with the sea, able to meet it and touch it, instead of hearing its groans and roars at some higher altitude, hopelessly blind to its movements. I pull on my coat and hat and step out of the house. As usual there is no sign of life, just the sober, quiet parkland and the clenched fists of ancient trees that appear like watercolor paintings, implausibly still and lifeless.

I pass through overgrown topiary and into

152

what would once have been the formal gardens. Box hedges sprawl around a dead rose garden, a nest of vines as thick as wrists. The air is flaccid and gray. Against the wall sits a summerhouse, but its roof has slipped and its windows are empty, blank holes where a finger might once have tapped: *Can I come in?* There is a little veranda at the front and I picture Laura de Grey sitting on it in a deckchair, admiring her roses.

Two ravens swoop out of the sky, their caws severing the quiet. One lands on the summerhouse and flaps its wings, a heavy, audible motion. Its black eye is watchful, and seems to rest on me for a moment. Its feathers are dark, liquid-looking.

It feels ominous to turn my back on the bird, so I wait for it to fly off before continuing to the perimeter. It's strange how the land seems to end so abruptly, a run of green then beyond it the drop. Tom told me that the way down is via a number of steps, and I find them between two firs. I glance back at Winterbourne, keen to see it from this angle, keen to see it from every new angle because it appears different and enthralling each time. From here the battlements dominate, those medieval-looking crenellations like the molars of a gnashing beast. Spitting gargoyles jut from its sides, from this distance no more than fishhooks, ready to snag at passing prey. The house is a monstrosity in many ways, outrageous and grotesque in its flamboyant architecture yet brazen enough to carry it with style, and no small degree of beauty.

The steps to the beach are precarious, steep and muddy, and I clutch tufts of grass to steady my descent. It's a significant plunge and the sand appears horribly far away, until at last the steps become gritty with silt and my traction improves, and finally my feet touch solid ground. The sea is black-iron beneath a brooding sky and the shore is treacherous with boulders and rocks. It isn't a pleasure beach. The water is high and seething, and where it meets land it swirls and crashes around prehistoric stones. Caves like black slits are carved into the rock; slick, dark weed tangles and knots in shallow pools. Tom warned me that the tide rushes in here fast, so I am not to venture too far from the steps. Looking down the beach I see that it runs for miles, right out of sight. I pick up a pebble and throw it into the surf. The wind rushes back at me, filling my nostrils with a sharp blast of salty air.

The sound of a dog barking startles me.

At first I assume it to be Henry Marsh and Tipper, but then I am seeing a much older man in a sou'wester, and there are three dogs at his heels, not one. The man passes me with a look of curious distrust, his face scarcely visible. The dogs are low-backed, long-tailed creatures, sniffing the ground with whiskery snouts, their large paws molesting the sand. They are part Irish wolfhound and part something else.

"Good day," I say.

"Not much o' one," he growls back. I had expected the man to pass without comment, such was his bearing, so I am satisfied that he stops. "Rain's comin' in," he says in a broad West Country accent, "you're best off indoors. This in't no place for a lady. You're the one up at Winterbourne, are you? I might've guessed. You've got the look."

"My name's Alice Miller. You must be Marlin."

"They already told you about me, did they? That meddling housekeeper reckons she hears the dogs at night. She'll be lucky. We don't go near that place any more. It's evil. Got a bad spirit in it — or so they say. My dogs know better."

"Mrs. Yarrow mentioned you walk the dogs on the cliffs."

"No fear I do," he says. The drizzle is

coming down steadily now, an integral sort of wetness that seems to come from inside the air rather than falling from it. "We used to take our walks u' there when Mrs. de Grey was alive. Then it went bad. There's a funny thing about that house, make no mistake."

"What do you mean, a funny thing?"

"The dogs won't have it. They can smell it, whatever it is. I trust my dogs. They're just about the only things I do trust. They know when something's wrong." The dogs are paddling round his boots, staying close to their master. I think of Tipper at the cellar door, barking and frothing at the mouth, his ears flat, his eyes wild.

"That housekeeper don't hear a thing these days," he goes on. "We stay down here where we know what's what. Tide can catch you fast, be sure, unless you're friendly with the sea. But still the capt'n tells us to go. I said to him, do you own the sea as well? I told him he's got a bad thing at Winterbourne. We don't want to be there no more than it wants us to be there. But he don't own the whole o' Cornwall."

"You said things went bad after Mrs. de Grey died?"

I hear the sound of the rain spitting against his sou'wester, and the contrasting quiet as it hits mine: I'll be soaked. But I am absorbed by Marlin. Part of me estimates he's senseless, while another is compelled.

"Things were bad before she died," he says. "That's why she died. The bad thing didn't want her there. It don't want anyone there."

"How did she die?"

His lips part, revealing a line of brownish, chipped teeth. His grin is grisly, horribly knowing. "You want to ask your master about that," he says.

The dogs start to yowl, a thin, reedy chorus, and the rain spits down harder.

"Come along, you lot," says Marlin, moving off, "time to get home." He turns to me. "You take care, lady. You take care inside that house. And you can tell your old keeper there that she's hearing things. Likely it's the sounds inside 'er own head — for that's what Winterbourne does. She's no fear of us coming close, be sure o' that."

"Where do you live?" I ask.

"On a boat called *Old Lymer,* down at Polcreath Hollow."

He goes back the way he's come, and I picture the shoreline winding round the crags, an endless, rugged shoreline, all around the country, and if I were to follow it for hundreds of days I would eventually come back here, to this point where I am standing now. Marlin is mad. Mrs. Yarrow told me as much. He is trying to make me fearful but I will not be afraid. The captain is the victim — of the war, of his wife's death, of his injuries. He is a man trying to do the best for his family, which includes protecting them from local dissenters. Marlin has invented a falsehood because he is angry at being told to stay away from the park. And yet I remember Tipper at that cellar door, the way the doctor could scarcely restrain him, his bloodcurdling howls . . .

Wrapping my coat tight against the rain, I mount the steps away from the beach. To the east I see the faint figures of Marlin and his dogs moving further along the tide. It is only when I round a bend in the ascent that I turn to the west.

What I see surprises me. I had imagined the beach to be deserted. I cannot imagine how anyone could have climbed down, as Tom assured me this was the only access for miles. But there it is. A dark shape, a hundred yards or so from where I stand; it is fleeting, there and then not, and then there again, most definitely there, flickering like a black candle in the distance. The space between us, and the now driving rain, makes it hard to decipher exactly. Squinting, I detect a lurching gait to its walk. I want to believe that it is Captain de Grey — for who else could it be, limping and lilting along the shoreline with a beastly determination? — and yet I don't think it can be. It doesn't appear to have a walking cane (although I could be mistaken: the shape shudders and shivers in the poor weather and gets further away from me still), and the thought of him stumbling down the harsh rocks is nigh on impossible.

"Hello?" I call out, but the rain swallows the word. "Hello there!"

Still the figure plows on. In an instant it seems to melt against the sea, seeming to lower itself to the ground, seeming to *crawl;* in the next it is walking with that horrible pitching gait, a dark blemish. I blink, desperate to catch it, desperate to be clear. For a startling moment I believe it is expanding in my view, it is coming *closer . . .* and I rush up the steps, grappling the mud, before realizing my mistake.

My mistake is this. My mistake is not noticing. For, right above the figure on the beach is the spot where I saw her. The woman on the cliff. My dark companion.

CHAPTER 14

I rush back to Winterbourne and close the door behind me. My breath is strained from running, and I go to the window and watch the approach, biting my nails, convinced I am about to see her black shape advancing toward us through the trees.

"My goodness, you're soaked!"

Mrs. Yarrow makes me startle.

"Get out of that coat, come along now."

"I'd like to lie down, Mrs. Yarrow," I say. "I'm feeling unwell."

"I'm not surprised, miss, catching cold like that. You'll soon have what the children have, I don't doubt." She helps me out of my coat and makes me dry off by the fire while she fetches a pot of tea. "Take this up with you," she says, "and get some rest. I'll keep an eye on the twins. I haven't had a peep out of them so far."

I do as instructed, unable to help checking on Constance and Edmund beforehand, due to a nameless fear that they might have been harmed. All is well, of course. I think I hear a scuffle as I approach their door, but when I peer round the children are slumbering soundly in their beds, a picture of pure innocence.

In my own room, I fall asleep quickly. When I wake in an hour's time I feel clearer and less afraid. Suddenly the figure on the shore loses its menace: Tom would have made a mistake about the steps being the only access to the beach; it was nothing but a walker caught in the rain. The coincidence with the cliff edge was nothing more than that — an accident. There was no way I could be sure, in any case, of the direct correlation between the two, the distance was too far and the weather too bleary. I imagined the crooked gait. And yet that is the detail that haunts and harrows me, the memory of that distorted limp . . .

My stomach is empty. Downstairs, Mrs. Yarrow has left soup on the stove, which I eat with crusts of bread while scorning myself for my folly. The man Marlin has set me on edge. All his talk of the bad thing at Winterbourne, every word of it nonsense, made me believe in what wasn't there. *Stop daydreaming, Alice.*

Afterward, learning that the children are

161

playing cards in their dressing gowns in the drawing room, I help Mrs. Yarrow with that evening's supper.

"Go out to the kitchen garden, would you, miss?" she asks. "We need a sprig of parsley."

I haven't been through this way before, and am surprised to find a side door in the pantry that leads through to the glasshouses. Like so much else at Winterbourne, they are in a state of decline. It's akin to being inside an algae-coated fish bowl; the glass mottled and stained, the light coming through as an eerie bluish-green. Planters and vines push through in a show of resilience particular to organic life: a crop of tomatoes in the last breath of summer, a burst of red peppers in a terracotta pot.

I wonder if Laura de Grey tended her garden. Once upon a time, somebody cared for these glasshouses with deep affection. A pair of Wellington boots sits by the door, one knocked on its side. There is a watering can with a spider's web strewn across it, and a ball of twine which, when I reach to collect it, clings momentarily to its wooden surface, sticky with age. A seedling tray, half filled with graying soil, is discarded next to a pair of rusted pruning shears. I feel as if I have stumbled into a shipwreck. Everything is masked in this sunken, pinched-out light, and I have the sense that it has been undisturbed for some time, allowed to flourish untended, the plants taking over and starting to strangle the building. At points the creepers escape between panes of glass, reappearing on the outside and peering back in. I think of Laura in her summerhouse, Laura in her rose garden, Laura in her deck chair, Laura here, her fine, pale fingers planting the saplings and pressing the soil, her smile as she watches them grow. I think she may have done all of these things, or none at all.

Through the other side and out into the courtyard, a trough of soil relinquishes Mrs. Yarrow's herbs. It takes no time to find the parsley. I decide to head back round the front of the house to avoid returning the way I've come.

Before I reach the north front, I catch sight of the captain. He is across the yard, at the old stables, leaning on his cane.

"Captain," I go to him, "good afternoon." It strikes me as awkward that I'm still holding the parsley, as if I am presenting a bouquet. I tuck it into my apron.

"Good afternoon." He turns to show me the unmarked side of his face, and I note how he winces with discomfort at the movement. "How are the children?"

"They'll be right as rain tomorrow."

There follows a scuffle behind the stable door, a warm stamp of hooves, and when a horse puts its head up to greet us I can't help but gasp with pleasure.

"I had no idea!"

"She belonged to my wife."

I smooth the animal's nose, its hot, soft muzzle and silken ears. Her eyes are blue-black and full of soul and kindness in the way that horses' are, and her coat is the most exquisite shade of silvery ash, lightening to white on her flanks where her age is catching up with her. "She's absolutely beautiful," I say. "What's her name?"

"Storm."

"Nobody told me."

"Nobody really thinks of her any more, apart from me. I like to tend to her myself, for obvious reasons."

"Of course."

"My wife loved her."

"I can imagine. Did she ride a lot?"

"Every day." The captain's mouth lifts in a half-smile, and he is lost for a moment. "Storm hasn't been out riding in years," he says.

"The twins aren't enamored by her? I would have been, at their age!"

"Constance took a fall when she was young. She funked it after that. And Edmund, well, he doesn't like animals."

I make a mental note to rectify this through our studies, getting the children out to experience wildlife as well as read their way to enlightenment. No boy of mine — or rather, no boy under my charge — will grow up so gravely mistaken.

The captain runs a hand through Storm's silver mane, his forehead so close to the horse that they are nearly touching. I notice the holes in the elbows of the captain's jacket, and his crumpled shirt. His hair needs a cut. For a wild moment I imagine my hands on him as his are on Storm: a potent creature, barely restrained, burning with passion yet quiet with dignity and grace. I have to look away.

"You met my doctor the other day," he says.

"I did indeed. I found him very amenable."

"He found you very amenable, too."

I meet his eye. "I beg your pardon, Captain?"

"I've known Henry for a long time. He's a bachelor, as I expect you gathered."

"I hadn't considered it," I reply.

"He visited again this morning and was

hoping to see you."

"I was out for a walk."

"Indeed," says the captain, his eyes still fixed on the horse. "Nevertheless I would like to remind you that a . . . dalliance of any kind would be wholly inappropriate while you are occupying this post. The children require your full attention and I would not permit any distractions from your devotion to their case."

"It hadn't crossed my mind — and certainly won't now."

The captain drops his touch from the animal and leans on his cane. I see him fighting the pain, unwilling to disclose it.

"Is there anything I can do for you?" I ask, and as I ask it I realize the request is for me as much as for him. I fight a strong desire to reach out and touch him. I want to make him better. I want to care for him, as I am caring for his children.

"I'm fine." He steadies himself. Storm nuzzles his shoulder. It is a relief when he begins to talk about Laura again because my inappropriate thoughts lurch to a halt. "It's more than the leg, isn't it," he says grimly. "It's more than the burns and it's more than the leg. It's the state of things. It's this house. It's the house that Laura died in."

"I'm so very sorry about your wife."

"You can't be sorry; you didn't know her." But then he appears to remember my confidence on the last occasion we spoke and his voice softens. "Would you believe me if I told you that things were very different before? When we were first married, before the war; before Constance and Edmund, we were happy?"

"I believe it," I say.

"But then things changed. The house got into her." His brow drops, his eyes veiled by dark confusion. "The house was always against her. It bided its time; it let us embrace our happiness and then it ripped it away. All these years I've tried to unravel it, Miss Miller; I've tried to remember what happened, but I get so far and the rest is blank. Henry Marsh calls it shellshock, great swathes of time unaccounted for, holes and cracks where the picture should be entire. I dream about my hands — my hands, Miss Miller, held in front of me in a corridor, shaking and reaching out." He looks to me but I cannot speak. "Only, I do not know what for. And sometimes I do not recognize these hands as my own, for they are softer and younger, like Laura's hands only different. And I believe in the blackest, truest part of my heart that these hands have been here all along, claiming people and claiming lives and there is nothing I can do to stop it. My parents before me and their parents too, right back to when Winterbourne was built! They each fell prey to tragedy, their lives stolen, like Laura's, too young. I look about me now and I see it taking us all, one by one, every part of what we were until nothing will be left, nothing at all . . ."

I am dismayed by his trouble and shocked at his words. "You mustn't think that," I whisper. "Winterbourne is magnificent. The children adore it."

The captain shakes his head in disgust. "The house is falling down around us, a brick at a time. It's a weight around my neck, a damned money pit. I feel it mocking me, now that I can't leap to repairs as I used to, waiting for me to fail, laughing at my failure. I wish I could leave. I wish it had never been mine in the first place."

"Why don't you, then? Why don't you leave?"

"And let it win?" he answers. "Let my ancestors laugh down the ages at me, at my failure, at my incompetence, at my surrender?"

"But if you're worried for your safety and the children's . . . ?"

It pains me to pose it, to consent to his

madness, for his thoughts are raving and illogical with grief and cannot have any
foundation in fact. Yet he appears so desperate, this strong, brilliant man brave enough
to show me his weakness.

"The house will get us either way," he
says. "It doesn't matter where we go. It's
caught me like a moth on a pin, afraid to let
my children out for fear of an accident
befalling them; equally I'm afraid to keep
them here. We're despised."

"You can't mean that, Captain."

"Can't I? Winterbourne has dismantled
my life, piece by piece. It's made me . . . do
things."

"Do what?"

"Things I can't remember. Things I don't
want to remember."

"Captain, if I might be so bold, but Winterbourne is bricks and mortar. Might there
be truth to Henry's conclusions of
shellshock? I can only imagine —"

He slams his fist on the stable door, making the horse startle.

"Bricks and mortar!" he mimics, showing
me his full face now, the misshapen, melted
side that contorts in imitation of my gross
naivety. "You'll say that now," he rasps, "but
you'll soon understand. Do you suppose
that Winterbourne likes you? You might

believe it does, and it might let you think that for a while, because that's what it does, don't you see? Look at what happened to Laura. Look at what's happened to me. It's bitter. It *wants* you to suffer. It will show you joy for the sole pleasure of robbing you of it —" He trails off, blinks and moves back, as if awoken from a dreadful possession. He reassembles himself. "Forgive me, Miss Miller. Forgive my outburst. I — it's a bad day for me. I'm struggling with the bank — and now, seeing Storm, I . . ."

"There's no need to explain." But it's hard to hide the fact that I'm shaking, by turns afraid of and enthralled by his fervor. The way his blue eyes flashed danger.

"Please, go," he says, and I realize he cannot make a swift departure himself and how horribly ensnaring this must be. "I wish to be alone."

"Of course."

"And, Alice," he stops me before I do, "I'm sorry. I'm very sorry."

"It's all right."

I touch his arm, just fleetingly, but it is enough to set my own on fire.

The cook is looking anxiously out of the scullery window when I return. "I was starting to think you'd got lost!" she says, as I

170

hand over the herb.

But I am not lost. I am thinking perfectly clearly. Jonathan de Grey needs my help and so do the children. Without me, this house will fall apart! It is plain to me now. The previous governess hadn't the strength to protect this family — but I do.

"I met Storm," I say.

"Ah, yes." Mrs. Yarrow chops the parsley. "She's a beautiful beast, isn't she? Apple of the captain's eye."

"And Laura's, apparently."

Mrs. Yarrow glances sharply at me, as if surprised that I would utter her name.

"Indeed," she says. "Could you pass me that bowl, please?"

I reach for it. Then I ask forthrightly: "The governess who was here before me — she didn't abscond on a family matter, did she?"

The cook doesn't look up. "I don't know what you're talking about, miss."

"Come now." My hunch is growing by the second, fed by the cook's every evasion. I pass her the bowl, which she gingerly accepts. "That woman didn't leave Winterbourne abruptly. There was no home emergency, was there?"

Mrs. Yarrow stirs for a moment then rests the spoon. She looks about her to check we are alone, before leaning in to whisper: "I've been forbid to tell you, miss. All of us have. You mustn't breathe a word, please, promise me."

"I promise."

"She killed 'erself, miss. It was the most terrible business. Everything seemed fine, she never let on she was troubled and then one day . . . Such a shock, it was!"

I remember being asked at my interview if I was of sound mind. *Could you reassure us that you have no history of mental disturbances?* So that was why. The governess before me had lost her mind. I remember the man's expression as he asked me, intent on sniffing out my secrets. Only I hid them well.

"What did she do?" I say.

"She threw herself off those cliffs there." Mrs. Yarrow closes her eyes, remembering it yet hating to remember. When her eyes open, they are moist with fear. "Oh, it were dreadful, miss. Right there on the Landogger Bluff."

My mouth goes dry. "Who found her?"

"The captain did, miss. And the worst part was that she didn't die straight away, oh no. She broke every bone in her body. By the time he got to her, she was a sack of skin. But still —" Mrs. Yarrow swallows hard, her face ashen. "Still she was trying to

172

crawl toward the sea. I don't know why. There was nothing left of her, but she was dragging herself into that water. She died before she reached it."

Images creep into my mind. The figure I saw on the beach, limping and crawling, that slithering shape . . . "We heard her screams," says Mrs. Yarrow. "It were a horrible sound. Have you ever heard foxes scrapping at night? It was like that, like moaning from hell. And that's why the captain won't have the children anywhere near the sea, miss. That's why the sea's off limits. He thinks she's still there, waiting to drag them in." Mrs. Yarrow shudders. "You mustn't tell a soul, miss. I should never have said. The captain keeps it quiet, there's been enough suffering already."

I consider my question; I almost don't ask. "Were she and the captain close?"

"What do you mean, miss?"

"Did they have a close relationship? I'm wondering, after Laura . . ."

"Oh, you must never suggest such a thing! Oh, my dear girl, you must never suggest it to me again! The captain could never betray his wife's memory. He is a good man, a kind and a decent man. I wish you had not thought it!"

"I'm sorry."

"If anything," the cook checks about her, "he did not hold that woman in high regard. I used to hear him shouting at her. It could be awful frightening."

"What had she done?"

"I couldn't tell you, miss. I wouldn't know."

"And there was nothing unusual about her behavior before it happened?"

Mrs. Yarrow scratches the strip of hair escaping her cap. "Only that she stayed in her room more in those last few days. Said she was ailing. And when they took in her body . . . well, it were covered in marks. Lots of red marks, strange they were too — scratches and scabs, bruises and the like." She looks at me. "She had your room, miss, the one you sleep in. I suppose you'd rather I didn't tell you that. I was going to say it on the day you arrived but the captain put you there and who was I to object?"

"Yes. He did put me there, didn't he."

"I wouldn't think on it, miss. It was — is — the old nurse's room, is all."

We jump at the sound of the great door opening. Tom enters with a bundle of firewood and we resume preparing the meal as if nothing has been said.

That night, as I undress for bed, I notice

that the color of the bruise on my arm has deepened, not eased — and surrounding it is a pattern of tiny scratches, as if made by a small, sharp, determined nail. I cover the marks with the sleeve of my gown and lie awake in the dark for a long time, my eyes wide open and watchful, waiting for sleep.

CHAPTER 15

CORNWALL, PRESENT DAY

Rachel hadn't seen the exterior in daylight before. Now, in the bright morning, the house appeared kinder than it had when she arrived, and grander than any showpiece she had ever seen. Its dramatic arches reminded her of Parisian cathedrals, and the high turrets with their tremendous gargoyles brought to mind fortresses buried deep in the Romanian hills. Gleaming stained glass adorned the chapel windows, and crowning the spire was a decorative finial that shone and glittered in the optimistic sun.

It was with some reluctance that she crossed the overgrown parkland to get down to the south gate. She didn't relish the thought of seeing Jack Wyatt again, much less accepting a favor from him, but she had little choice: the gallery would be wondering what edge of the world she had slipped over, and she'd promised Paul she would stay in touch. Here, she was completely cut off. She hadn't even checked the news since her arrival in London — a meteorite could have wiped out the whole of the west coast for all she knew. Her boots swished through the long grass and she could hear the gentle tumble of the sea as it washed into shore. Turning back to Winterbourne, she shielded her eyes and watched as a swoop of large black birds descended on its roof. *That's my house,* she thought, incredulously. *It's mine.*

Then she was down over the next dip and Winterbourne was out of sight. Rachel had underestimated the walk to the perimeter — the estate was huge — and when she arrived at the gate it was quarter past, and she thought she'd missed him.

But there was the Land Rover, with Jack inside it.

"I saw you coming down the hill," he said, releasing the passenger door so she could climb inside. "I thought Americans were sticklers for punctuality."

She ignored him. "It's good of you to give me a ride."

"I was a little surprised, to be honest," he released the clutch and they moved off, bouncing down a narrow dirt track away from the estate, "you taking me up on my offer on day one. Couldn't you wait to see me again?"

She changed the subject. "You have dogs?"

Jack grinned his slightly off-center grin. It transformed his face, Rachel thought, into something quite warm and compelling. But then he spoke. "You really are Sherlock Holmes." However, it didn't take much detective work to attribute the carpet of hairs on the back seat and the array of blankets gathered there to a band of hounds. There was also an earnest, wheaty fragrance that brought to mind cozy November nights and dogs resting by the hearth, not unpleasant, in fact rather cheering.

The inside of the Land Rover was suggestive of more haphazard living. Several bits of material — rags covered in engine oil; chamois leather — were stuffed beneath the handbrake. A stash of old cassette tapes was jammed in her door pocket. A notepad lay discarded in the footwell, a list of some sort, untidily scrawled.

"I thought I'd spare you the circus," he told her. "The dogs are a bit too friendly for some people. Especially women."

"That's sexist."

"Not really, just an observation."

"Based on . . . ?"

"Most of the women I've been out with." Jack turned on to the main road. "Given the choice they'd rather not be mauled by muddy paws, or have bad breath in their face, or stub their toe on a knackered chew trying to get to the sofa."

"And what didn't they like about the dogs?"

"Ha." But he thought it was funny because his grin reappeared, wider this time, and she noticed the crease in his cheek. "They used to hate having the dogs in the house, thought I should tie them up outside in the barn, even in winter when the ground was frozen. I always think if a person is kind to a dog then they're all right."

"I've never had a dog."

"Well, you've missed out."

Rachel wondered if the de Greys had kept animals. What else had she missed out on in her childhood? What else could her upbringing have contained if she had stayed with her birth mother and been raised at Winterbourne? It was a parallel universe, an impossible one, and yet one that had been at her fingertips from the very start, her fate decided by a woman she had never met. It was difficult to picture herself in that grand castle, running through the corridors as her mother would have, as Constance and her brother would have, playing with the dolls' houses and rocking horse, clamoring on the piano and climbing the shelves in the library.

Instead, she'd had Maggie and Greg — decent, honest, good-hearted people — in their suburban mainstream home. She hated to sound spoiled, and it wasn't that, really. It was just hard to consider how that altered background might have changed things at the most innate level: the way Rachel connected with life, the people she met, the chances she had. She might never have met Seth, the man who threw light on her small planet, and she might never have lost him. Sliding doors. Pointless fiction.

Seth . . .

Rachel focused on the here and now, on what she could see and feel, as she had trained herself to since the accident: Jack's hands on the steering wheel, his paint-splashed trousers, the road rushing past. Except it hadn't been an accident, had it?

There were only so many words that would do. *Event. Incident. Tragedy.* And the worst of them: *atrocity.* Sometimes she could abide only the vaguest of references, simply *what happened,* or *that day,* or *the phone call.* That last one seemed the easiest to use, the most anodyne, as if Paul had been ringing to discuss the next day's schedule. Still, it had the power to wind her. *It's over. You're here. He's gone.*

"Are you OK?" Jack asked. "Is my driving making you sick?"

"I'm fine," she managed, though his driving was haywire. They undertook a truck and then ducked on to a slip road, which looped back toward the sea.

"Here we are," said Jack. "Welcome to civilization."

The word for Rachel conjured her Manhattan skyline, sushi bars and late-night bistros, subways that ran all night. Polcreath was a fishing town, pretty and compact, with a pub, high street, a church, a waterfront restaurant and a modest settlement that constituted the population. She discovered this as Jack's car wound down through the center and emerged all too quickly at the harbor, prompting her to ask: "Was that it?"

He laughed. "What were you expecting?"

They parked illegally (Jack didn't seem bothered about road signs) and walked up to the high street. "That's your best bet," said Jack, pointing out a café. "I'll see you back at the car at eleven." She wanted to say she'd need longer than that, but before she could he was stalking away in the opposite direction.

Rachel crossed to the café and opened the door. Neat floral-print tablecloths were laid

181

with vintage tea sets, and there was pretty bunting strung up over the counter. "Hello, excuse me," she approached the girl, "do you have Wi-Fi?"

The girl slid the code across and took her order for a flat white. Moments later she was online. Her email account was bursting and she fielded as many as she could, cutting and pasting an outline as to her whereabouts and how the gallery was operating without her. It seemed to be operating very well. Paul had been in touch with a report and had run interviews for her, explaining that she'd been called abroad on business and that that was the price to pay for swift and sudden success. She replied, explaining her lack of connection at the house and promising to be available once a day. *"I owe you,"* she wrote, *"for having my back. Thank you."*

A young man came into the café. He and Rachel exchanged a smile before the man took an adjacent table. He flipped a magazine out of his bag and Rachel had to do a double take, as she saw on its cover a shot of Aaron Grewal, impeccably suited, arms folded, above the banner BUSINESS HAS NEVER LOOKED SO GOOD.

It was weird seeing Aaron, this polished, renowned entrepreneur who was a galaxy away from a tiny teashop at the foot of the UK, where all you could hear was the gentle tap of a spoon on a saucer or the steady slow wash of the sea. She wondered what he was doing, if he was with someone else (they had never agreed on exclusivity) and whether that mattered. Rachel found her heart intact. It always had been, since Seth: losing him had been enough to make her lock it away for good.

Several of her emails were from him. A glance at her phone revealed more attempts at contact. She was surprised by the attention. They'd always kept it casual, and while she'd expected Aaron to be in touch to check she'd arrived, and that the inheritance had gone as planned, she didn't expect the devotions of, well, a boyfriend.

The most recent email, sent late last night, his time, surprised her. It read:

Hey again, elusive R. It hasn't been long but I'm going crazy here without you. I get that things could take a while your end, so why don't I come to you? I'm worried about you, dealing with this. I hate to imagine you on your own. I know you said I didn't get it, but I do. I've been thinking a lot about us, Rachel, and I want to be part of it. I can help, even if it's just taking you for dinner or bringing you coffee in the morning. I can get away this weekend; I'll fly over and we can spend it together. Let me know.

Can't wait.

Aaron x

Rachel absorbed the message with mounting apprehension. She should have found it sweet, kind, romantic, and it was all of those things — but instead alarm bells sounded. *Worry* wasn't a word she had thought to associate with Aaron Grewal. He was composed and unflappable, and he definitely didn't spend his time "thinking about us": that was what couples did, couples who bore secrets and resentments, couples at crossroads. Not them. She didn't want him coming over. It was impossible to picture him at Winterbourne. He'd never occupied a less than five-star dwelling in his life and she could imagine his dismay at the state of the property. Already it felt precious and private to her, something she must keep close to her heart.

It was odd watching the man at the next table read all about her lover while Rachel was mere feet away in a pair of muddy Wellington boots, her hair dragged into a scruffy ponytail, trying to think up how best to reply to him.

She composed a message and quickly pressed Send:

Dear Aaron, Sorry for my radio silence. Turns out Winterbourne's well and truly off grid — who'd have guessed? Anyway, no need to come; I'll be leaving in a few days and will look you up when I'm back.

Hope all's well with you. Rachel x

Feeling better at having touched the outside world, she logged off, drained her coffee and set off to explore her ancestors' town.

Jack found her at a bike stall. "You're late," he said.

"I'm not. I've got five minutes."

"Exactly. It's at least seven to the car."

"Not if I'm on one of these."

Jack put his hands in his pockets, watching the bicycle stall with disdain. "Waste of money," he declared. "I've got an old thing in the garage you can use if you want a bike, give it a bit of grease, she'll be good as new."

The storekeeper came out. "Ten percent discount if you buy before midday," he said, passing Rachel a leaflet. Jack snorted. He was unbelievably rude.

Perhaps it was Jack's rudeness that she felt she had to compensate for, or perhaps it was the sheer fact of his disapproval, but Rachel bought the shiny red bike she'd been looking at with a ten percent discount and felt mightily pleased with herself as she wheeled it away over the cobbles. No, it wasn't strictly necessary for the sake of a few days — but she couldn't bear to ask Jack for another favor (she couldn't bear to see him again at all, as it went), and if she was going to keep her promise to Paul then she had to have her own way of getting in. Besides, being stranded up at the house with no means of escape wasn't a feeling she enjoyed. The bike was better than nothing, and doubly satisfying for the look on Jack's face.

"Actually, I think I'll cycle back," she said when they reached the Land Rover, and Jack opened the tailgate to load it in.

"Really? It looks like rain."

"I don't mind."

"Clearly you haven't been out in a Polcreath wind."

Rachel disliked that he imagined her to be an uninitiated city girl who would wither at the first spot of drizzle. She remembered how he'd been sent by the others at the Landogger Inn to rescue her, and turned her back and mounted the bike.

"Do you want my number?" he said as he was opening the driver's door.

She raised an eyebrow.

"Very funny," he said, and it wasn't clear — nor was it clear to her when she thought about it later that night — what the joke was. "I mean if you need anything at Winterbourne. Right now you've got your boyfriend in America and that's about it."

"Excuse me? You don't know the first thing about my private life."

"Well, he won't be much good over there, will he?"

"I don't have a signal, remember?"

"You will where I picked you up — maybe even before. It's the house that's the black hole." He scribbled on a piece of paper and passed it to her; she tucked it in her pocket. Then he climbed in and gunned the engine, escaping in a cloud of gravel.

All the way back to Winterbourne, Rachel considered Jack's description of the house as a "black hole." He meant of connectivity, of course, but the words seemed laden with another, more serious, meaning. Winterbourne was its own rock, cut off from civilization as much as it was from time. It could be a house in any era, belonging to any family, which in a way was how Rachel had arrived at it.

She'd been wrong about the rain. It started steadily and then settled into a lashing, determined stride, slicing at her from the sea and blasting her cheeks with freezing cold. As she chugged up the hill toward Winterbourne, lungs burning and calves straining, she cursed herself for turning down Jack's ride for nothing more than pride, and now she was soaked from head to toe and everywhere in between. At points she had to close her eyes because the downpour was blinding, catching the road beneath her in staccato frames that made progress slow and unstable. Her knuckles whitened on the handlebars, the clouds above her looming and dark, and when she saw the south gate come into view she almost cried with relief.

Twenty minutes later, she was drying off by the fire. Never had the heat and light of a few burning logs been the source of such bliss, and Rachel wrapped herself in a sweater, poured a big mug of coffee, pulled a chair up to the flames and warmed her hands. She could hear the ongoing lash of the rain against the windows, amplified by Winterbourne's lofty vaults and giant panes of stained glass.

Next she knew she was awake, the rain had stopped and the sky outside was darkening. The fire had reduced to blushing embers, which she stoked until they sparked encouragement, then she threw on more wood, which quickly caught. Rachel wasn't the sort to sleep during the day, as a rule she didn't just "nod off," so it was surprising to discover that several hours had passed since she'd returned.

She switched on a few lights — enough to make a home of the small region of Winterbourne she preferred to reside in — and cooked herself a light supper. Afterward, she headed to the study to try and find a landline: yesterday she'd poked her head round the door and seen a pile of boxes, which she hoped contained a point of contact with the outside world. It was all very well Jack Wyatt giving her his number, but she'd rather not have to venture half a mile away in order to use it. Not that she would be using it — but anyway.

There was a cluster of candles on the windowsill, which she met with a match. The room shivered to half-life, half awake and part of the world she knew, half asleep and belonging to some other, distant state beyond her reach.

It took the best part of an hour to find it, an antiquated contraption with an old-fashioned number dial and heavy receiver. When Rachel at last located the wall socket, she didn't for a moment expect it to work, but after a few uncertain pips she detected the reassuring monotone of a connection. She fished Jack's number out of her pocket and put it next to the phone. For some reason, she felt better with it there.

Night was encroaching on the windows, capturing her in its cloak. Shadows lengthened and deepened. Rachel wondered, when the time came to part with Winterbourne, what the new buyers would make of it. Doubtless they would waste no time in modernizing, gutting the bedrooms for lush en suites and demolishing walls for open-plan living. The thought made her sad but she pushed sentimentality away. There was no option but to sell. She couldn't stay here forever, closeted away like Rapunzel in the tower with only Jack and his crowd at the Landogger Inn for company. She had to return to America and real life, her career, her home.

Even so, the thought of letting Winterbourne go filled her with grief. The house was in her blood, yes, but it was more than that. Already it had cast her under a rich and heady spell, as if it had been waiting for her, as if it had been calling to her, whispering at night of secrets yet to be found, caressing her skin as she slept, tapping on the glass to be let in, and the more time she spent here the deeper she fell . . .

As a habit Rachel didn't like to become attached. It was all the more reason to move as quickly as she could, and her email exchange with Aaron had been the prompt she needed. Tomorrow she would set the ball rolling. Get someone out to value Winterbourne and its contents, and then pass it into their safekeeping until a sale was agreed. It would be good to return to New York. Rachel thought of her gleaming desk at home and the view of Manhattan from her window. Soon she would be back, and for the first time she would know her roots, the place she came from, the people who were her family. Finally, she had done it: she had found the missing piece. And if all Winterbourne could give her was what it had already given — its dusty shelves, its creaky beds, its ancient floorboards — then that was enough. She could fill in the rest, in the years to come. She could imagine it.

As Rachel was closing the last box, something caught her eye. Perhaps it was the single loop of red string around the letter

— it was romantic, like an ancient scroll sealed with candle wax. She lifted it out and unfurled it. The letter was written in a ragged hand, so ragged, in fact, it was alarming, a bloodcurdling scrawl blotched with ink, the paper spiked where the pen had driven through it, and was addressed to Captain Jonathan de Grey of Winterbourne Hall, Polcreath. It was signed by a name she hadn't heard before: Alice Miller. Rachel read it, her unease rising.

How could you send me away? the letter read. *You know the truth about me. You know the secret I carry. How could you, Jonathan — how could you?*

CHAPTER 16

CORNWALL, 1947

Sunday morning and we are getting ready for church. The children are recovered, at least the boy is, and he is compensating for the past days' torpor with a show of riotousness. All throughout breakfast he was kicking the underside of the table, despite my admonishments, and refused to touch his porridge.

My patience runs thin today because of the previous night's lack of sleep. At a little before three I woke to the sound of footsteps outside my door, which strangely enough I first imagined to be furniture being dragged across the landing. It wasn't until I greeted the sight in the passage that my addled brain caught up.

Constance was sleepwalking — a habitual pursuit, I've since learned — and had somehow managed to pass down the stairs from her floor to mine without accident. The girl's slippers were scraping the boards as she advanced to a point in the hallway and then, curiously, she stopped to look up at the ceiling. There was something undeniably sinister about our wordless encounter, and Constance made quite a sight, her nightdress bathed in moonlight and her ringlets curled on the nape of her neck. I gently held her shoulders, steering her round: I had heard that one should never rouse a sleepwalker, and though I had never questioned why, I wasn't about to start then. We returned upstairs to the bed she'd left empty next to Edmund. The boy was alert when we appeared, but unconcerned. "Connie's always done it," he told me, with the childish satisfaction of knowing better than an adult. "She's done it since our mother died. I'm tired of going to fetch her." I tucked the girl back in and kissed her brow.

"Will she sleep peacefully now?"

"It depends," said Edmund.

"On what?"

"On whether she's called," he said. "If she's called, she'll go."

"Called?" I was perplexed. "By whom?"

But he had rolled over and pulled his sheets tight. I decided the boy must have been half asleep. Even so, by the time I returned to my own chamber I could not shake a feeling of discomfiture, which continued throughout a restless night.

One thought bothered me, and continues to bother me now. I checked my watch when I first heard Constance outside my room. The time read twenty-five minutes to three, the same time as Laura's stopped clock — *L. Until the end of time.* Nothing but a coincidence, I'm sure, but I cannot forget the oddity of the detail.

Tom is waiting outside with the car. I stifle my yawn, helping the twins with their coats and then putting on my own. We follow Mrs. Yarrow through the door.

"Is the captain joining us?" I ask, trying to keep the hope from my voice.

"Oh, no," murmurs Mrs. Yarrow, "the captain doesn't go to church."

I trust my disappointment doesn't show. "Did he once?"

"Indeed, before the war. He hasn't been since Laura."

As the car advances down the rutted drive, I remember what the captain said to me at the stables. He certainly sounded, then, like a man who had lost his faith.

"Children, behave!" I chide, as Edmund and Constance squirm and giggle next to me. They are pinching each other's knees, little nails twisting, half laughing and half complaining at the sting. They exchange an impish glance then collect their hands in their laps, gazing out of the window in what appears a mockery of good conduct. I think again of the marks on my elbow and cover my arm.

Polcreath Church is a sweet building, positioned on a mount overlooking the sea and surrounded by a protective shelter of cedars. Unlike at Winterbourne, the cliff position seems peaceful and undisturbed, hopeful as it perches against the horizon.

"I hate coming here," says Edmund, as we exit the car.

"Edmund!"

"I do. Why should I lie? God says not to lie — so there."

Constance snickers. I frown at her and she stops.

"You must be Miss Miller." The reverend steps out to greet us before I can complete my rebuke. "It's a pleasure to welcome you to Polcreath."

"Thank you."

"Quite different from London, I should think?"

"I must confess this is my first trip in. I've been occupied at Winterbourne."

"Of course you have." The reverend takes

my hands; his are soft and warm, like rising bread dough. "It's big enough to be its own town, up there."

"Indeed it is."

"But if you need anything, Miss Miller, the church is here for you." He holds my hand a little longer, as if there is more he wishes to say, but then releases it.

Inside, we file into pews at the front. I ensure the children are positioned between Mrs. Yarrow and me because I will not abide them showing me up. The sea of captivated faces suggests the entire Polcreath population knows about the new governess arriving from the city, and no doubt rumors and gossip abound about my experience and appointment. I wonder if the town knows about my predecessor. Is that why they watch me with fascination? Do they know about that poor woman's death? Do they know that her mind was sick and her spirit in distress? Do they know that she threw herself on to the Landogger rocks because she saw no other escape?

Since Mrs. Yarrow's confidence, I have tried to come to terms with the tragedy — but perhaps there are no terms to be found. That woman was senseless, driven mad by a creeping rot in her system, and who knew what her private circumstances were? I confess that I, too, have visited the brink of that strange landscape, a land of brittle trees and arid soil, a world turned on its head and turned inside out and is it any wonder, with the hurts of my past? But there is no point in thinking about it now. The difference between us is that I pulled myself back. How awful that she could not.

"It's a blessing to see so many of you here," the reverend begins, "fortifying our community, pulling together as one, as is needed in these fragile, fractured years. We open our arms to old friends and likewise embrace our new. Let us pray."

The congregation bows its head. I follow suit but the prayer skims off me like water, its words hollow and meaningless. Is this how Captain de Grey felt, before he turned his back on God? I am not sure if I have turned my back, or if I was facing the right way to begin with. It strikes me that we learn not to turn away from points of danger but to always keep them in sight. Is this what faith has become to the captain? Is this what it has become to me? And yet I can trace it right back to the start, attending church with my parents in an ironed frock. I would see the altar, the body of Christ, and feel not as I ought, not as the dozens of worshippers around me felt, in awe and reverence, blindly following. I felt detached. An outsider.

We are strangers, He and I. We always have been. Seeing the children next to me, their misbehavior elapsed in the presence of the Lord, I wonder that I was never like them. Their angelic bearing puts me to shame. The weight of their loss humiliates me, for my own, when set against theirs, is trifling. After all, I engineered my own fate. I brought despair to my own door. Not like them, the innocents.

I wish to clasp the children to me, to cherish and protect them. In the same moment I fear for their corruption, that I might tarnish them in some way and the bad thing I did will find its way beneath their flawless skin and ruin them forever.

Meanwhile they, in return, remind me of everything that is guilt- and grief-stricken in my own life, their purity gleaming against my sin.

My parents sent me to Burstead for religious education as well as academic. That their daughter should have wound up transgressing in the most despicable way was a bitter pill they could not swallow. And even then they did not see the full picture: the true, atrocious, unsalvageable depths of my crime. How were they to know that if the devil is in the child already, no degree of edification can wring it out?

I am relieved when the service concludes and we are released into fresh air. Mrs. Yarrow takes the children back to the car while I linger in the graveyard to greet Henry Marsh, the captain's physician, whose face I noticed as we filed out.

"I was hoping to see you today," says Henry, with his friendly smile. "How's Jonathan?"

The use of the captain's first name arrests me as much as last time. It seems a violation to use it, but, I confess, a thrilling one. I turn away from the church. "The captain remains the captain." I am not bold enough to use it myself, but Henry appears to find my response pleasing, and droll, because he laughs.

"And Tipper?" I ask, returning his smile. "Has he recovered from his visit?"

Henry shakes his head. "I am sorry about that. It was a mistake to bring him, in hindsight. He's too old. I suppose I'm yearning for the days when he was a pup."

"There's no need to apologize. I enjoyed meeting you both."

Henry straightens a little, as if emboldened by that. "Miss Miller, this might seem terribly forthright, but would you like to have supper with me one night?"

It is surprise more than anything that compels me to answer, "I'd be delighted." His smile widens and he takes off his cap, then puts it on again.

"How about tomorrow evening?" he says. "I can collect you when I finish my rounds, at, say, eight o'clock?"

"I'll see you at eight." The children will be in bed by then, and my evenings are my own, so how I choose to spend them is a private matter. "One thing, Doctor," I say regardless, "but I would prefer it if the captain weren't to know."

"I quite agree."

"While I'm in his employment —"

"As am I —"

"It would seem appropriate "

"Miss Miller," he touches my arm, "I quite agree."

"Good day, Doctor."

"Good day, Miss Miller."

I walk down the path toward Tom and the car, holding my hat against the flipping breeze. The wind picks up, blowing clouds across the sky. The sea churns gray, frothing at its surface. We had better get back and light the fires.

■ ■ ■ ■

The following afternoon, the children and I
are studying in the drawing room. I have
asked them to complete a writing assign-
ment and am trying, as I mark last week's
papers, to ignore the incessant tapping of
Edmund's pencil on his notebook.

"Is there a problem?" I ask him.

The boy watches me. The pencil keeps
tapping.

"Have you managed any work at all?"

Next to him, Constance lifts her head and
shoots her brother a glance.

"You're distracting Constance," I say,
though as the girl returns to her learning,
this patently isn't true. "May I see what
you've done?"

Edmund lifts his paper and predictably it
is blank. "I haven't any ideas," he says. His
copper hair is smoothed around his pale
complexion, and his eyes are wide and
imploring. "I can't think of anything to say."

"I've asked you to write about your happiest memory at Winterbourne."

"I haven't any."

"Nonsense."

But clearly the boy has had the same
problem fulfilling his prep. As I turn over

his submission, expecting to find the essay I asked for, instead I discover an empty page, save for the scribbled words: *Hello, Alice . . .*

Then, a little further down:

It's me, Alice.

Are you there?

Do you remember?

For a moment I am unsettled, before I see it for the silliness it is, the pointless rebellion. I can only surmise Edmund's insolence to be a legacy of his illness. Perhaps he has not quite recovered. I bite my tongue, reassemble my patience and go to him.

"You mustn't neglect your schoolwork, Edmund," I say.

"This isn't school."

"It very well is."

"There's a school in town, but Father won't allow us there. Isn't that right, Connie?" The sister looks up, then away. "He wants to keep us at Winterbourne so we never get out. Whoever heard of a school for two? Father's a coward, that's all."

"Your father is anything but."

Edmund regards me again with that look of satisfaction, older than his years, making fun of me. "We *told* him he should make friends with it. It's nice to you, if you make friends with it. If you don't . . . Well, I wouldn't know, because it likes me."

I swallow. "Your father has nothing but love for you," I say, dismissing his words as procrastination. "He wishes to shelter you, that is all."

Edmund's eyes narrow. "Not you as well," he says shortly.

"I beg your pardon?"

"The last one grew soupy over Father, too."

Constance's voice is meek. "That's enough, Edmund. Don't talk about that."

"And now we're stuck here, with only you stupid women for company."

I seize his shoulder and lift him out of his chair.

"I will not tolerate such talk in my classroom," I say, opening the door and releasing him. "You will stand there against that wall until I tell you to come back in — and until I do, you will reflect on what you have just said. Do I make myself clear?"

Edmund lowers his head, snivels, and for a moment I think he is crying. Oh, but he is just a boy! A poor, lost, frightened boy! And the frustration of his captivity must be too much to bear, and I ought to understand; I am, after all, his carer, and often it feels I am more than that, so strong is my instinct toward these children. I rush to him, my arms outstretched, but then he looks up and into my eyes, and I see that he is not weeping at all but laughing. It is a dry, thin sort of laugh. I straighten, my hands trembling, and re-enter the drawing room, shutting the door behind me.

"He won't stay there," says Constance. "He never does."

Constance works diligently for the rest of the afternoon. If only I could say the same for myself because my thoughts grow as tangled as the forest wallpaper in my bedroom, twisting and looping until I can make sense of neither head nor tail. Edmund is damaged, that much is clear, and it is my duty to help him — to help them all, to bring this family back together and breathe the heart back into Winterbourne! I long to take Constance's face in my hands and kiss it over and over, to kiss his too, these precious children, these children in need, for surely that is all it is; surely Edmund's behavior is a simple consequence of the trauma he has suffered? No child should ever lose his mother. I must be patient. I must find a solution. I must save him!

And the girl is not without my concern. Constance's disturbance might be less evident than her brother's, but still it is glaringly real. I read about somnambulism and learned that it invariably has a psychological cause. The fact she has experienced repeated episodes proves her upset. Dear, unfortunate child! I realize that I have been brought to Winterbourne not just to tend to these children's daily needs, but also to address a greater one beyond. Perhaps the captain is aware of it, perhaps he is not, but I will not rest until I have made progress. Mrs. Yarrow's allegations make sense. The twins *have* likely stepped out of line — on occasion they might have leaped right over it. But I see the root of their problems. I understand that they are not at fault. It is another force at work inside this house, the legacy of their doomed mother and the ordeal they suffered when she died — not to mention what happened to the poor woman before me! The children are not to blame.

Neither is the captain. With each hour that passes, he continues to fascinate and distract me. How I wish I could help him, as much for his benefit as for my own. In Jonathan de Grey I see a man I can mend, with affection, with devotion, with loyalty, and in mending him I can make right the wrongs of both our pasts.

"My darling," I go to her desk, "I wish to speak with you."

"About Edmund? About the woman we had before you?"

"No, darling, not that."

"Because he didn't mean to . . . I'm sure he didn't mean to."

I shake my head. "Didn't mean to do what, sweetheart?"

Constance's blue eyes are imploring, her words coming fast. "She didn't like it, Alice; she didn't like what he did — and it wasn't kind, really it wasn't. But neither of us meant to. We were told to do it. Told to say it. Then she went and killed herself, out there on those rocks. And Father found her, and we never said anything because we didn't want to get into trouble. But we thought it would make her pleased with us!"

I take my child in my arms, my dear, sweet child, and stroke her silken hair.

"Hush now," I say, "there's nothing to be frightened of. I'm here."

"And so is *she*!"

"Constance," I draw back, "it's just you and me."

"Then who is that?"

I startle, pull away, look about me. "Who?"

"She was right there, behind you, right at your shoulder. Her!"

"Stop it, Constance," I demand, my voice trembling. "That's enough. You're seeing things. You're tired, and of course you are, you spent half the night walking about Winterbourne. That's what I wanted to talk to you about, not this nonsense, not Edmund. Now pull yourself together, both of you. What would your father say?"

Constance watches me. "She's going to get me," she says. "She's going to get us all. Then you'll know. Then you'll know why."

At half past seven, I change my clothes for my appointment with Henry Marsh. Already I can picture the interior of the Landogger Inn, its reassuring fire and the comforting chatter of locals as they gather round it. Normality. Ease. Winterbourne has seemed a fiend to me today, and while I try to put the twins' behavior to the back of my mind it is difficult. At the same time I am aware of my own inclination toward getting carried away; everything I have been privy to at the house has a reasonable explanation, and that explanation is the deaths of two women. I must keep a level head. I must see to the plain truth. An evening with the doctor is precisely what I need: kind, logical Henry with his medical good sense.

Before I pull my bedroom curtains shut, I check that the front of the house is quiet. No captain. No Mrs. Yarrow. No Tom. They will have retired to their respective diversions for the evening. I have agreed to meet Henry on the drive, out of sight.

I see my reflection in the darkening glass, the blush of lipstick the likes of which I haven't worn since the war. I close my eyes. I remember how I used to get ready to see my love, the excitement and anticipation of his lips meeting mine, his arms round my waist, and for a moment I can conjure his smile so exactly that it takes my breath away and I must open my eyes again to make it stop. It is too painful.

I haven't gone out with many men since. Thinking about it, I have been a one-man girl since I was seventeen. A tear escapes. I wipe it away. Those days are gone. I rest my hand on my stomach, warm, tender, and torment myself with another ending, one where he hadn't died, one where we had all been together. *Stop daydreaming, Alice.* It is pointless wishing for what cannot be. Pointless and painful. What is, is.

And I deserve it — don't I?

I pull the curtains shut. As I do, I see the little farmyard painting on the wall. Peering in, it seems to me now as if the girl at the cottage window has turned her back to me, and she is smaller still, making her way further into the house. I cannot swear it; I cannot swear I saw her face the times before. Did I? It's hard to be sure. A chill trails down my spine and I tell myself I am fine, I am well, there is nothing to fear. I step back and turn away myself. I take my purse and prepare to sneak downstairs.

CHAPTER 17

ALICE, LONDON, DECEMBER 1940

Betty woke me in the small hours. The night outside was absolute, the dark around me so close that it seemed to fill my mouth and ears. In the distance, or perhaps it was my surfacing perception that created the distance, erupted the shaking blast of a falling bomb, closely followed by the spit of ack-ack gunfire. For a moment I forgot. And then I remembered. A dull cramp had started in my belly. Maybe it had even been part of my dream: I dreamed I was being carried across the desert on a stretcher, wounded in some way to my abdomen, the sun flashing and superb above me in the sky, and I didn't know if I was being carried toward him or away from him.

"What's the time?" I whispered to Betty.

"Half past two," she whispered back. It seemed a violation, at that hour, to do anything other than whisper. Perhaps we were fearful of the Germans hearing us. We

211

dressed in the dark. I laced my boots and tied my coat and tried not to dwell on the ache in my stomach, receding at points like a forgiving tide and in others butting forward, fast becoming pain. I winced, but turned away to do it. Betty didn't know. Nobody here knew. My shame bore me down and wore me out.

"Are you all right?" she asked me. "You look pale."

"Just tired."

Everyone was tired: it was an acceptable response. In the canteen, we lit the stove and made the tea, pouring it into large urns ready to serve when we arrived at our destination. The depot told us it was a trench shelter in Green Park. The bombs were still falling. Houses there had been blown to smithereens. People were afraid.

The pies turned my stomach as I put them into the gas oven. I clenched my jaw to bite away the sickness. Weeks ago, when I'd first found out, it had been a terrible sickness, a constant heaving sea — and that was how I'd first known, really, because my bleeding had often been erratic and it wasn't unusual for me to be late. But now the sickness caught me off guard, suddenly strangling before melting away. It was akin to my dread, in fact, because in some hours the whole predicament seemed manageable, even desirable: this was the very last piece I had of him and I loved it, I loved it fiercely, and no matter what I had to do we would come through this together. But in other hours my panic overwhelmed me. I knew I was completely alone. I had no idea what I would do or where I would go, or who would have me.

At three-thirty a.m. Betty and I hitched the canteen on to the car. It was a considerable effort, especially as we were aided only by torchlight, and one of us had to hold the torch so there were only three hands between us. Over the wall of the depot I could see pockets of sky illuminated, bruised pink and flashing orange, and the low grumble of enemy aircraft. The air smelled of soot and burning, an acrid, chemical stench that mixed with the hot sweetness of the pies and made me want to retch. The cramping in my stomach was getting worse. I climbed behind the wheel.

Betty guided me out of the depot. It was difficult to see by the thin light of the torch but presently we were away. I knew the streets like the back of my hand and appreciated the focus of the drive, away from my own problems and into a bigger picture. It was amazing how bright the moonshine seemed when there were no other lights to be seen. London was a blackened city in more ways than one, and the shapes of its landmarks — the spires of Parliament, the dome of St. Paul's — crept out of the deep night like black cats on a high wall.

Minutes later we arrived at the park, reporting to the ARP warden at his post.

"It's been a bad night," he said. "We're thankful for the WVS."

Betty and I attached our steel helmets and set about preparing the canteen. For a moment I lost my troubles in the plain occupation of the job. Londoners emerged from their night-long shelter with hands outstretched, cold fingers longing for a warm mug of tea, bellies grumbling for sustenance. It felt satisfying to pour the tea and hand out the pies and buns, which were for the most part enjoyed in silence. In a quiet moment Betty stepped outside the canteen and lit a cigarette; I could see the flare of the match as it lit up the inside of her hands, then the glow of the tip of her smoke.

As night began to break to morning and the all-clear sounded, we could start to make out the devastation around us. Buildings had collapsed; heaps of rubble stood in their place, and where they had fallen, swathes of sky appeared that shouldn't have been there, the surprising blowouts between buildings like missing teeth.

We loaded our trays with food and drink to take down to the shelter. Not everybody was able to come up to the canteen, those who were old or infirm, or plain scared. In the trench we were met by relieved faces — relief at the raid being over, relief at seeing us — and we passed the refreshments into grateful hands. An elderly couple had brought a table and chairs from home and I wondered how long they had been there. The woman looked at me with crinkly eyes that seemed to linger on me a moment too long, as if she could tell, as if she knew, and her silent sympathy made me weep. When I passed her her tea, she held my fingers in her soft ones and whispered, "Thank you." Betty called for me to come back up.

It was frightfully cold. Outside the canteen, I bent to the ground to wash the tea mugs in a bowl of water and the water stung my hands. I could see my breath in the wintry air, and on a nearby bench the first light of day illuminated a white sheen of frost. Men had arrived to clear the debris from this raid, having spent the night in the same employment elsewhere, and were glad of the hot tea and the chance to smoke. It was as I was leaning over Betty to collect a pack of cigarettes that the cramp in my belly intensified, and buckled me over. Betty caught me.

"Alice — what's the matter?"

"I need to sit down," I said.

"Here." She guided me gently to the stool at the back, sitting me down and touching my shoulder. She thrust a warm mug into my hands. "Drink this."

"I don't feel well. I think something's wrong."

"What's wrong?"

But I couldn't say. My mouth was dry with fear and sickness, and a terrible, stretching, opening sadness, and the sadness seemed to come from nowhere and was the worst thing of all. "Alice," Betty pressed, "what's happened?"

"Something I ate," I forced out. "I'll be all right."

Betty didn't look convinced, but she returned to her post and did the job for two of us. When we were done at Green Park, Betty washed the mugs and I helped her stack them on to the trays, despite her objections.

"I don't want to sit around," I said. "I don't want to do nothing."

But Betty insisted on driving to our next stop. As we leaped and bumped over the ruts in the road, my stomach tightened and loosened. I rested my head against the window. I felt weak. It was without thinking that I touched my belly and thought about the tiny person inside, and yearned for them yet was afraid of that yearning, and loved them deeply yet was afraid of that love, and wanted them but didn't want them.

"Alice," Betty asked, turning to me. "Are you in trouble?"

I hadn't needed to reply because she had already stopped the canteen, in a side street off Holborn. She touched my arm. "Oh, Alice," she said.

I shook my head. "I'm losing it anyway," I said, and a hot choke escaped. "It doesn't feel right. Not today. It's leaving me. I can feel it."

"Is he married?" she asked. "Is he a soldier?"

I squeezed my eyes and the tears wrung out like water from a twisted knot. "No," I whispered, "not married. But he was a soldier. He died."

"And did he know . . . ?"

"No."

Betty passed me a napkin to wipe my eyes. I kept my hands pressed over my face. "Alice, it happened to me too," she said. "It happens to girls all over. The war doesn't change things, doesn't make it go away. Mine was married; I had to see a doctor — well, he called himself a doctor — to stop it. If you are losing it, maybe it's for the best. Maybe it's not the right time to have a baby. You're barely twenty."

"I'm twenty-one."

"You've got your life ahead of you."

"My life was supposed to be with him. Oh, Betty, I'm scared!"

"Does your family know?"

I turned away. I remembered the glass falling from my mother's hand, the arc of spilled liquid; I remembered my father's inhuman expression, gray and closed and utterly unfeeling. "I'm on my own," I said, and never had it felt so true — because whatever was inside me, whatever had been inside me up to that point, holding me as tightly as I held it, had gone. I knew it as clearly as the day of the week. The cramps, the waning nausea, the growing sensation of dampness between my legs . . .

"This," I touched my stomach, "was all I had left."

"But, Alice, a woman can't do this on her own — especially now. What will you do? Where will you go? Would you give it away?"

"I couldn't."

"You might have to, if you can't look after it."

"He asked me to marry him before he left. He promised me we'd be together. I wish I could have told him about the baby, I wish I'd known before he left. I expect him to send me word from abroad, there's been a mistake and he's still alive . . ."

Betty's eyes were full of sympathy, as only a woman's can be.

"War is a time for pragmatism," she said. "You have to be strong — whatever cards you're dealt. All this is is a bad hand. You'll be dealt a better one, in time." Seeing my expression, she added softly: "Alice, you don't know that you've lost it."

I turned to her. "Look away," I said, and she did.

It was difficult to maneuver in the tight space, but at that point I barely cared who saw. I unbelted my coat, lifted my bottom from the car seat and raised my skirt. I pulled my stockings down my thighs and bent so I could see inside my knickers.

"I need to visit the bathroom," I said to Betty, in a small, strange voice. I didn't want to see her expression so I didn't turn to meet it. All I could think was, *This was always going to happen. You've lost everything, and it's exactly what you deserve.*

She started the engine and we drove on, through burned-out streets and burned-out houses, traversing the graveyard of London, where somewhere, although it was nowhere that I could see, life clung on for all it was worth.

Chapter 18

CORNWALL, PRESENT DAY

The letter she found was just the beginning. Over the next two days Rachel unearthed a trove of missives, all roped up inside those study boxes and all in the same vein — this woman, Alice Miller, was imploring Jonathan de Grey to bring her home.

Home, Alice wrote in one letter. *I have come to call Winterbourne my home. Did you know, Jonathan, that I have never named another place such? Winterbourne is where I belong, with you, with Constance and Edmund. With the secret I now carry.*

It was hard to be sure from where Alice Miller was writing. Each letter was stamped in the top corner with a red badge, CERTIFIED, but there was no return address. Only late at night, when she was sifting the dirt off another bundle, did she uncover the record. It was a typed sheet, stained sepia, brittle to touch.

On it was a form, with most of the requirements filled in. *Name: Alice Elizabeth Miller. Born: August 3, 1919. Place of birth: Epsom, Surrey. Occupation: Governess.*

Rachel skimmed the sheet. At the foot she found what she was looking for.

Reasons for confinement: Hysteria, Melancholy, Delusion.

Methods of treatment: Psychotherapy, Sedative, Electroconvulsive.

She struggled to make sense of it. Questions abounded. Had Alice worked for Jonathan de Grey? Had she been his children's governess? Why had she been taken to this asylum against her will, and kept despite her protests? The "secret" she was carrying, could it have been a child? And, if it were, had it been his?

An idea occurred to Rachel as she sat surrounded by upturned crates in the dwindling firelight. Supposing Alice Miller was the grandmother she'd been searching for. Supposing Alice had had an affair with her employer and become pregnant with his child — with Rachel's birth mother. Supposing she had been sent away to have the baby . . . It had been common in those days, women left alone to deal with the consequences of a mutual act, and the derision and pain they endured.

Why hadn't Jonathan responded? Whatever Alice had been to him, to ignore such desperate correspondence showed a hard-hearted man. It seemed that the captain had read these letters then forgotten them, parceling them up out of sight.

Rachel held the record to her chest, as if by keeping it close she could connect with this woman in another time, who had been in this very house; this woman who had known suffering in whatever place she was kept, her pleas falling on deaf ears . . . She imagined the infamy de Grey's affair would have brought on him, his children finding out and the rampant town gossip. He had already lost his wife during the war. Would he have realized his mistake and forced Alice out of Winterbourne?

Rachel checked herself. Her every invention could be just that: wholly untrue. And yet try as she might, she could not shake the vision of Alice Miller and Jonathan de Grey, and that somehow they were the key to her story. And that the "secret" Alice spoke of wasn't just her own: it belonged to Rachel, too.

The adrenaline she felt over those forty-eight hours could only be likened to the energy she'd run on in New York. Sleep was a necessity, not an indulgence; food was required instead of enjoyed. Anything that got in the way of her discoveries was a nuisance, and Rachel would wake after a burst of sleep desperate to resume her task. She dreamed fevered dreams of the woman called Alice and the man called Jonathan; she imagined in her half-awake state that she heard children's cries in the hall vaults, snapping floorboards, the sound of smothered laughter and the patter of running feet. And all the while a ghostly hand seemed to hover at her back, guiding her forward, showing her the way, *willing* her to unearth the truth. Rachel wondered at the baby Alice had been carrying, if indeed it was a baby, and she reached for that possibility tentatively, hesitantly, as if frightened it would evaporate the moment they touched. Since discovering her link to Winterbourne she had assumed her birth mother would have been raised here, but now Rachel considered that perhaps she hadn't. Perhaps her mother had never so much as seen the house, perhaps she had been born far away, and been denied her heritage just as Rachel had been denied hers. Each time she shed light on one mystery, a dozen more appeared. Possibilities grew before her eyes.

Only when she had emptied the last of the boxes and read everything they contained

— from the beseeching letters to the notes of aching love; from the fury Alice Miller felt against her employer to the longing she harbored to be with him; from the manic rants against Winterbourne to the odes of affection toward it; from the hateful messages about the "devil-sent" twins to the remorseful retractions thereof; from the fear she felt at her pregnancy to the joy that they shared this bond — Rachel was exhausted. She bathed in a shallow bath and lit fires in the kitchen, where she curled her fingers round a mug of cocoa and worked out her next move.

There was no way she could relinquish Winterbourne now and return to America. She would have to stay and see this discovery through, for it might be her only shot. For a long time, when she was a girl, Rachel had envisaged families as being tied together by an invisible cord. Her own, drooping from her navel, was untethered at its other end, and she would watch everybody else tied up and it was only she who floated alone. Alice and Jonathan were her moorings: she was sure of it.

There was just one missing piece, the piece that joined them.

My mother.

She was startled by a sound from downstairs. It was a sharp bump, like something heavy falling from a shelf. Rachel stood and went through the hall to the little staircase beyond, opening the door. She had never crossed into the servants' quarters, that subterranean labyrinth beneath her feet, and as the cool, dark pit glared back at her she admitted it was far from enticing. What was down there apart from a ton of cobwebs and yet more neglected rooms? Nothing to be afraid of.

The sharp gust of cool air that wafted up to greet her brought to mind a bygone, foreign world, a world of ringing bells and rushing servants, of supper trays and hurrying footsteps, smelling as it did of leather and damp, of cold stone and rot. She shone her flashlight on the steps, which were slippery beneath a drip in the ceiling, and her descent made a peculiar, muffled sound, as if there were a delay between the instant her foot met the surface and the instant Rachel heard it.

At the bottom of the steps was a long passage. She shone her light on it, rendering it harshly bright up close and then dissolving into murk. High on the wall was a tarnished bell box, its glass case so stippled that it was scarcely possible to see the labels beneath. *Drip, drip* . . . The leaks continued, fissures in the stone that wept to the floor. The passage was lined with doors and she peered behind some: empty rooms, long since cleared, and there was a gloomy pantry still cluttered with stained tins and cans.

Rachel was deciding that she had imagined the thumping noise, for what could possibly have made it down here, when she noticed, at the end of the passage, another flight of steps. This one was shorter, just a few, and she had to duck under the low ceiling to get down. The space she emerged into could only be the cellar: it still carried a very faint tang of wine, and a pile of crates was stacked up on a bottle rack.

The thing her eye was drawn to, however, was a small access in the mold-covered stone, set beneath a Gothic peak. It was bizarrely small, as if intended for someone to crawl instead of walk through. Rachel's torch exposed its cracked veneer and the circular handle that wouldn't budge, though she gave it her best shove. Frowning, she shoved it again. That was strange, for the sound her effort made echoed exactly the sound she had detected from upstairs. How could that be?

She settled on there being some draft pipe on the other side of the door — though it occurred to her, even as she rested on the conclusion, that what she had heard (to hear it two floors up and on the wrong side of the house) must have been caused by an awfully big draft. Rachel tried the handle again and to her surprise it rotated smoothly this time. She pushed the door but nothing happened. And then, as quickly as it had given, the handle locked again, partway round, which was absurd because she had just released it — and more absurd still because the loop didn't feel as if it had snagged on a mechanism, rather it felt as if somebody, *somebody on the other side,* had it in their grip. As she continued to try the handle, and as whatever had caught it continued their objection, it felt as if they were in a stalemate. Rachel had the sensation of being connected to a living thing, her will against theirs, both stooped with effort, invisible to the other and with only this strange little door between them. For a moment the sensation was so strong that she dropped the handle, burned.

"Suit yourself," she muttered, and the sound of her voice was reassuring in the dark — normal and ordinary. The dark was so close down here, close enough to be a physical thing, all around her, filling her ears and mouth. All at once a feeling of hopelessness overtook her. Loneliness assaulted her from nowhere — and not just physical loneliness at being in this vast house on her own, but a basic, inescapable, emotional loneliness, the loneliness she had lived with since Seth. Defeated, she slumped down, her back against the door. She missed him so much that it went beyond tears, became calm, became numb, that familiar emptiness. Was she always going to feel this lonely? Would she ever find a place in the world that welcomed her, that showed her belonging and wanted her close? Rachel flicked off the flashlight and the dark rushed in at her, thick as mud. Doggedly she remained in it, remained here in the dark, alone, in the silence, because this was her fear, the solitude she avoided at all costs because it brought up her memories: recollections of the day she lost Seth.

She flicked the light on again, breaking through the surface. And then off — pitch-black, covering her face and eyes like a shroud. In the dark she could draw the memories out as real as day, all the facts she ran from in her daily life, busying herself because she was running from this, this very thing, this darkness, this stillness, this was it. She could see his face, the last time she had kissed it before he left for work. She could hear the phone bleating, could hear the voice as she picked it up, a voice she would never forget. *Rachel, it's not good news. But you know already, right?*

On the light went. She filled her lungs. Then she dove back down, absolute black, and this time it was his voice she heard, on her birthday, at the picnic he had organized for her, just the two of them. He had kissed her. *I'll never leave you, Rachel. You've been left before, I know, but this is where it ends. With me . . . Us.*

Us.

She clicked the torch once more, unable to bear it any longer — and it was hard to tell what happened first because the light was on and then she saw it, or she saw it as the light came on, or maybe before, maybe she felt it before she saw it, but then there it was — *it* — only it was impossible, she was dreaming; she was tired, sleep-deprived, it couldn't be there. *A woman.*

A dreadful woman, a dreadful shape, no, it couldn't be, it was impossible. Rachel gasped, staggered to her feet, the flashlight falling from her hands; it struck the floor and spun, coating the walls in light she was horrified to meet, and she stooped to grab it and then she ran. She ran up the little steps and along the servants' corridor, every part of her shaking, hearing scurrying

230

footsteps behind her but terrified to turn back, terrified, and she ran up, up, up to the main floor and then suddenly the bells were ringing, from nowhere, louder and louder and louder, chimes clamoring from the bell box on the wall, operated by some terrible, invisible hand, bells clattering this way and that like shrieking children caught in a fire. On and on they rang their ceaseless, deafening chime, ringing all around, above, below, just as the darkness had surrounded her, a terrible uproar, and still she heard that scampering at her heels like the paws of a ravenous animal —

She reached the hall and banged the door shut behind her. She had no key for it and so dragged the heavy chest across to meet it, jamming it against the wood. The hall appeared dreadful, she was losing herself, losing herself to the memories that crawled and crept and pulled her down — only she had gone down, just then, willingly, hadn't she, inviting herself to the dark! She should have known; she should never have gone. She stopped, breathed, and there were no bells. No rushing footsteps.

Nothing. Silence.

I'm tired. Rachel repeated it like a mantra. *That's all. I'm tired. I'm tired.*

It was late, she had to sleep, and she went

there and lay on the sheets, shivering with cold and fear, waiting for that awful din to start up again, thinking she could still hear it, that the bells had been as real as the nightmare downstairs, and it might have been hours before sleep claimed her or it might have been minutes.

CHAPTER 19

It didn't take long, come the morning, for Rachel to dismiss the previous night's events as fantastical. With the clear band of daylight that streamed into her bedroom and the steady wash of the sea, so her lucidity returned. It was obvious, now, that her preoccupation with Alice Miller's correspondence had put her on edge and had made her hear, and see, things that weren't there. Her imaginings had got the better of her.

There was no doubt that Winterbourne was kinder in the day. As Rachel pulled on jeans and a shirt, she reflected that the very architecture of the place, especially by night, was enough to play with the most level of heads. At times it felt so isolated that it was possible to believe she was the last person left on earth — that there was nobody else alive, no other people anywhere, just her.

So it was with a concentrated sort of

dispassion that Rachel perceived the black stains on her way downstairs. They affected the large arched window on the west front and were so defined, and so at odds with the clear panes adorning every other aperture, that she stopped. She went to touch the glass but the stains were on the outside; and on closer inspection appeared to have some kind of organic matter contained inside them, as if someone had thrown a sack at the window filled with paint, and what appeared to be, though surely couldn't be, small clumps of fur.

She stepped outside. The day was bracing, encouraging, and she walked round to the west gable, expecting to have to wrench a ladder from the stables in order to decipher the problem — but it transpired to be simpler than that. Rachel saw the dark heap immediately, a queer, localized massacre, and bent to examine it.

Bats. Dozens of them, their bodies crumpled, and when she looked up at the window from this new vantage she could only think that they had flown straight into it. Puzzled, she lifted one of the bats' wings — it was amazingly light and translucent, and completely without life — and let it drop. It was beyond peculiar. Rachel had been aware of bats at Winterbourne, swooping at dusk and nesting among the gargoyles, but why they should have annihilated themselves in this way was extraordinary.

"You're still alive, then."

She had been so absorbed that she hadn't heard Jack arrive, and now turned to see his car parked out front. He was leaning against the wall, all six-feet-whatever of him, his big hands in his pockets. "I haven't seen you since Polcreath," he said. "Wondered if you'd ridden your bike into a ditch."

"How thoughtful."

He peered past her to the bats. "That's a mess," he said.

"No kidding."

"What happened?"

"I have no idea. I just found them."

Jack crouched to the pile. She saw the patch of lightly graying hair at the tops of his ears and thought it might be attractive, were it not for the rest of him.

"Poor things must've got spooked," he said.

"Does that happen?"

He squinted up at her. "I can imagine it happens at Winterbourne." Then, with a note of humor, "No need to look so worried. Animals are unpredictable. All it takes is one of them to go batty," he was pleased at his own joke, "and it sets the whole lot of them off. Pack instinct. Or, in this case, colony."

"Hmm."

"You want help clearing it up?"

She couldn't say no, and was grateful for the help with the ladder and buckets as they wiped clean the window and heaped the unfortunate bodies on to a shovel. Jack talked the entire time, about his dogs, about his farm, about his sister and her kids who were coming to visit this weekend and how he was preparing himself for a full-scale assault because his nephews never left him alone.

"Have you got little ones in your family?" he asked.

Rachel shook her head. "I don't really have any family."

"No?" He gestured to the building. "What about this lot?"

She leaned on the shovel, and the truth seemed suddenly easy to speak.

"I never knew them," she admitted. "I was adopted from England when I was a baby and taken to the States. My adoptive parents are dead now, and I never had any brothers or sisters. Last week I found out about Winterbourne and, well, here I am. I've got a chance now to find out about the parents I never met, and their parents, and all of the de Greys. It's a part of myself I never knew. I still don't know it. I'm just finding out." She stopped. Jack was listening, looking at her deeply, and she felt that she had to say more so she added, "It's nice to hear about busy, bustling families like yours. I always kind of wanted that. Lots of people, lots of love."

He was still watching her. "Yeah," he said. "But I'm sorry, you know, about your adoption."

"It was a happy adoption. They were good people."

"But I didn't realize. I'm sorry."

"How could you have?" She smiled. "It's fine. Really."

He was quieter after that, and they finished the job swiftly. Jack seemed keen to stick around — was there anything else she needed help with? He had the morning free — so she invited him in for a well-earned mug of tea.

"What's that doing there?" he asked inside the hall. Rachel clocked the Elizabethan chest pushed up against the door to the downstairs, and laughed.

"I got a little freaked in the night," she confessed. "It was nothing."

"It doesn't look like nothing. How did you move that thing on your own?"

"I don't know." She conceded it looked impossibly hefty now. "But I did."

"What's down there?"

"The old servants' rooms. They're as much of a wreck as you can imagine. I thought I heard something so I followed it down there, but I was mistaken. I hadn't slept and . . ." She trailed off. "Anyway, it seemed like the right thing to do at the time."

"What did you hear?"

"Those bats against the window, probably." Rachel tried to make light of it but Jack regarded her seriously. "And then I was down in the cellar, and . . ." She shook her head. "It was crazy, but I could swear someone was with me."

"Someone?"

She wouldn't have told him, were it not for the way his eyes appeared suddenly kinder and more understanding than they had to her before.

"A woman," she said, recalling the brief flash that her torch had illuminated, the horrible sight that had made her run. If she concentrated, she could pick the image out as clear as day. "She was facing the wall. I only saw the back of her, and only for a second . . . . But like I say, it was a trick of the dark. My own shadow, I expect."

"Why would she have been facing the wall?"

"Exactly. It's insane. There was nobody there. I dreamed it."

Jack helped her move the chest. "You're sure you wouldn't feel safer keeping it there?" he teased, and she wanted to say something clever but didn't. She'd thought he would tease her much more than this and he hadn't, for which she was grateful.

"I'm intrigued now," he said. "Think I should go in and find her?"

"OK, OK, I'm an idiot."

"I'm not saying that. I wouldn't want to sleep at Winterbourne on my own."

"Really?" She made a face. "You don't seem the type."

"What type?"

"To be afraid of the dark."

"I'm not afraid of the dark," he said. "I might be afraid of what's *in* the dark."

A thought struck Rachel.

"Actually," she said, "there is something you can help me with."

The farce of last night's panic settled ever more firmly on Rachel as they made their way down the servants' corridor. To think she had skittered up here in fright twelve hours before seemed ridiculous. Who was that girl? Not her. Today the deserted quarters seemed sad rather than spooky, the antique bell box a bruised relic that clearly hadn't sounded in decades. There was nothing intimidating about it, just dank, leaking walls and the stink of neglect. Another dip and they came to the cellar.

"There it is," said Rachel. Jack went to the stunted door and pushed it.

"Weird little thing, isn't it?" he said.

"Can you open it?"

"Sure, if you don't mind it getting wrecked in the process."

She nodded. The door would have to be sacrificed. It pained her to demolish part of Winterbourne, however minor it was, but she needed to see behind it. She needed it brought to the sensible light of day just as the rest of the house had been.

Jack's bulk made light work of it, and several shoves later the door broke through. He tore the remaining shards of wood from inside the frame and stood back.

"Be my guest," he said.

Rachel crept inside with the torch. "Don't you dare shut me in," she called back, as much to hear the comfort of his reply as for any other reason.

"And what would I do that with?"

She looked about her. The chamber was

240

as compact as the door had implied, an unevenly shaped room with a low ceiling. She couldn't think what it had been used for, with space for maybe five or six huddled together. It was incredibly cold.

"There's nothing in here."

"Great, we can leave."

"Oh my god!"

Rachel's own reflection had almost given her a heart attack — for her torch had crossed a large, oval standing mirror on the opposite wall. Because of the proportions of the room, her image, with its startled expression, had seemed obscenely close.

"What is it?"

"Nothing. A damn mirror — sorry."

"What's a mirror doing in there?"

"I have no idea. Help me lift it out?"

Jack climbed in and together they tilted the mirror from the wall. It was extremely heavy and an awkward shape to persuade through the access. Nonetheless Rachel felt sure that she didn't want to leave it there: it was unnerving, the thought of a glass reflecting nothing but the dark, endlessly.

"Let's get it upstairs," she said. Jack took it from her and went ahead, and when they emerged into the hall he shut the door and spent a few moments mucking about with the catch.

"There," he said, "little trick I learned. It's locked. Feel better?"

"I felt fine before." But she did feel better, a bit.

They examined the mirror, resting glass-out by the fireplace. It resembled a washed-up sea creature, something with many tentacles spewed up on a beach. Rachel had never seen anything so aggressively ornate in her life, and the eccentric shows and private viewings she'd attended made that a bold claim.

"It's monstrous," said Jack, but Rachel disagreed. There was a theatric beauty about the mirror that fitted utterly with Winterbourne. Its Gothic frame was elaborate, bringing to mind a nest of snakes or else a tangle of foliage, parts of which appeared sharp enough to cause injury. The glass was blemished by age and the whole thing as tall and wide as she was. Like so much else at Winterbourne, she wished she could take it back to her gallery, imagined it as the centerpiece for a new exhibition.

"It looks like it belongs to a wicked queen," she said.

Jack nudged her. "It does now."

"I don't like myself in it. Don't you think we look strange?"

"This is just what we look like."

But she thought they did look strange. It was curious to consider that the glass had lain hidden and unused all this time — who knew for how long? — and now it had finally opened its observant eye, here, in this hall, and was witnessing them as keenly as they witnessed it. "Do you think it belonged to Constance?" said Rachel.

"I doubt it belonged to her father. The brother was a bit alternative, though."

Rachel turned to him. "Do you ever take anything seriously?"

"Of course I do." He smiled at her. "The serious stuff."

"I ought to hang it," she said. "I don't know where."

"It'd look good on the fire. Nice bit of kindling, that frame."

She folded her arms. "You're suggesting I *burn* a mirror. How many years of bad luck would that be?"

"This one looks like it'd curse you for eternity."

She laughed, then went to the mirror and ran her fingers over the loops and spikes that made up its surround. "I just feel it *wants* to be hung, don't you?"

"I feel I want that cup of tea."

They went to the kitchen to make it. Jack sat at the table.

"Thanks for coming up," said Rachel. "I'm glad you did."

"I've no doubt." He drank his tea fast again, even though it had just been poured. "Bats and cellars and mirrors — it's quite *The Castle of Otranto* up here."

"Since when have you read *The Castle of Otranto*?" She grinned, then realized how she came across. "I'm sorry, that sounded patronizing."

"Because it was patronizing," said Jack. "Just because I don't go in for art galleries."

"You could go in for both."

"I'd go in for yours."

She blushed.

"Anyway," he said, "I came up because I figured you probably wouldn't be here for much longer. In fact, I thought you might already have gone."

"Not that I'd ridden my bike into a ditch?"

"Or that."

"As it goes, I've decided to stick around." She decided to be straight with him. "The reason I was exhausted last night was because I found some letters in de Grey's study. Letters my grandparents wrote, secret letters that no one else was supposed to read, and now I can't get them out of my mind. I'm trying to piece stuff together, my history, and this is just the beginning. I need to know what happened here and where my mother wound up. I need to know if she was OK."

"What about your job? What about your boyfriend?"

"My job will survive. I have a good team."

"And your boyfriend?"

"Shut up, Jack." But she smiled.

They were pulled from the moment by a polite knocking at the door. Rachel went to answer it, as Jack pulled on his coat and said, "I'd better get going."

When she opened it, with Jack behind her, for a moment the person waiting there made no sense at all. It was a woman in a skirt suit with a satchel over one shoulder. Her hair was coiffed and her lips were pink and she looked hopelessly out of place and hopelessly optimistic. She must have come to the wrong place.

As if Winterbourne could be mistaken for the wrong place.

"I'm Wanda Pearlman," the woman said, extending her manicured hand with a quiver of excitement. "I'm a director with Brightside Estates in Polcreath, and may I take this opportunity to say what a thrill and a privilege it is to be selling your home."

Chapter 20

CORNWALL, 1947

The morning after my supper with Henry Marsh, I am surprised to find a crude bouquet of wild flowers outside my bedroom door. My first illogical thought is that Henry himself has left them there, before I see the note accompanying them.

> I'm sorry for being bad. I won't do it again.
> I love you very much.
>
> Edmund.

I smile, a little mystified, and tuck the note into the pocket of my skirt. Downstairs, over breakfast, I murmur to him, "Did Mrs. Yarrow put you up to this?"

The boy shakes his head and appears to me as he did when I first met him, utterly sweet and benign. "I picked the flowers myself," Edmund explains. "Well, Connie helped me." Across the table, Constance nods her assent. "I was a brat yesterday," he says, "a silly, spoiled brat, as Father would say. Will you forgive me?"

I squeeze his hand. "You're already for-given."

Privately, though, I deem there nothing to forgive. My evening with Henry put it all in perspective. Over our meal, I couldn't help but confide in the doctor about the chil-dren's mischief, sharing with him Mrs. Yar-row's claim that they had tormented her before I arrived, Edmund's vanishing that day in the mist, his conduct in class and then Constance's attempt to put the frights up me with talk of spooks and ghouls.

"What are you afraid of?" Henry had asked me in the candlelight.

"That it could be true."

"What could be true?"

He made me say it — and in saying it I heard how ludicrous it sounded. "That the poor woman before me," I faltered, "might still be at Winterbourne."

"As a ghost?"

"Oh, I know, it's madness."

Henry had dabbed his mustache with a napkin. "It was a terrible shock when she died," he said. "Such a violent way to do it . . . But she was troubled, Alice, you must understand. Deeply troubled." He'd reached across for my hand, squeezing it before let-ting it go. "Did you know she was hurting herself? When she was brought in, she was covered in cuts and scratches, head to toe. Now, we doctors claim to be experts about the human body, but the mind is a new landscape entirely. And it would stand to reason that an event like that would affect small children. How could it not?"

"I quite agree," I'd said, "and to lose their mother, as well. They must expect me to disappear at any moment. All their other carers seem to."

Henry had placed his cutlery together; I could tell by his body language that he wasn't comfortable talking about Laura. "Do you believe in ghosts?" he asked.

"Do you?"

"I'm a man of science. Of course I don't."

I couldn't answer the question myself. All I knew was that I had to be privy to every part of the de Greys, to see what they saw, to know what they knew, to be inseparable from them in that way families are, all of us together, facing whichever adversity came our way. I wanted to be integral to them, for them to depend on me, to need me, to never doubt me nor I them. The children had appealed to me, and so had Jonathan. They had shown me how important I was and the significance of the role I filled. Right from the start when the twins had sketched me in a wedding dress — *"You'd make a beautiful bride"* — they had been communicating a yearning they were too young to understand. But I understood. It was my duty to return their devotion.

Edmund taps my arm, drawing me back to the present.

"May we get down from the table, Alice?"

"Of course you may," I say. "Now go and get ready for class. Nine a.m. sharp."

I wonder, as I watch the children obediently leave the kitchen, whether Henry has ever lost anyone close to him — and whether, when the stakes are high, it's as easy to be a person of science. But I must admit that the doctor's good sense has settled my mind. He agreed that the twins' playing up was a consequence of their situation. Between him and me, Winterbourne was an extreme sort of place, Captain de Grey was an extreme sort of man, and with the upheaval of the past few years it was a small miracle they hadn't taken leave of their senses altogether.

"The best you can be is a constant," Henry had advised, "and be sure to stand your ground. That's the way with children: they'll try to get the better of you but they don't really want to manage it. They're testing you, Alice, that's all."

■ ■ ■ ■

For the rest of the morning they don't test me at all. Edmund and Constance are exemplary students: keen, interested, sweetly engaged. I return the girl's project to her on her happiest memory at Winterbourne, with my comments at the foot: *Thank you for sharing this with me, Constance. It's a wonderful memory.* To Edmund, following his outburst, I have only reassurance that he might complete the same task for next time. "What did you write about, Connie?" he asks, a touch sheepishly.

"Mummy," she replies. "Mummy in the mirror."

He nods, as if this needs no elaboration. To be frank, I am not convinced that Constance's memory is altogether accurate — after all, she was three when she last saw her mother alive. But the way her little paragraph conjured the image of Laura de Grey brushing her hair in the mirror bewitched me utterly, not least because it gave me those physical details about Laura that I craved. Constance wrote about her "lashings of black hair" and her "pale, lovely face" and the skin that was "like powder to touch." She wrote about Laura's red lips and green eyes. The mirror, I assume, had been hanging in the de Greys' bedroom, and it is so easy to picture the wife at her dressing table, with Constance looking admiringly on from behind, that it is almost as if I am remembering a scene of myself from a long time ago.

Stop daydreaming, Alice.

"It was an excellent piece," I say, smiling at the girl, "and well written."

"Connie wants to be a writer when she's grown up," says Edmund.

"She'd make a very good one."

"She likes to make things up. Don't you, Connie?"

Constance nods. The children watch me serenely. And then I am struck by an idea. "Come outside," I tell them, "come on! Coats on, wrap up warm, here we go." The children are surprised and pleased to get out of the drawing room. I clap my hands to hurry them along, as if afraid that to pause will change my mind.

Minutes later we are at the stables. Storm is chewing lazily on a clump of grass and the solid, languid sound of her hooves as she approaches the door is enough to make Constance squeal with excitement. It's a cold October day and we can see our breath in the air, bite-sized clouds. The sky is gray

251

and the sea is gray and there is barely a line in between. Warm steam rises from the hay in the stable.

"Father never lets us come!" says Constance. "Can I stroke her? Can I?"

Storm puts her patient head over the door and Constance reaches to touch it.

"Hello, Storm," she whispers, as the horse grunts through its nostrils, a hot, whickery expulsion. "Do you remember us?"

"I think she does," I say, pleased to see them together. If Laura loved this horse, and she loved the children, then surely it is right that this happens.

Behind, Edmund scuffs his feet on the ground. I recall what his father told me about his dislike of animals, but I wonder how much he was ever encouraged.

"Edmund," I say, "would you like to stroke Storm?" He shakes his head. "What's the matter?" I ask. "Don't you like horses? There's no need to be afraid. See how gentle she is! She won't hurt you. Look, come here, that's it —"

"Will you ride her, Alice?" Constance interrupts.

"Goodness, no! I wouldn't dream of it."

"But she wants to be ridden. I can tell. She hasn't been ridden in years."

"I hardly think I'm the person to take her out."

"Who else will do it?" Constance turns to me, and smiles the smile that only I see: one that speaks of the deep affection she has for me. "Please, Alice, will you? Mummy would have liked you to. Mummy would ask you, if only she could. It would make us so happy, as well, to see Storm out on the moors again, just like old times."

"Miss Miller."

I start at the deep voice. It rings deep in the cool, vibrating air. Captain de Grey stands before us; he must have been watching from a high window, or perhaps he followed us. Sometimes I feel him following me, if not his body then his gaze; I feel his eyes on my back when he thinks I don't realize.

"Good morning, Captain."

The children shrink, afraid. Indeed, in the quiet, still courtyard with Winterbourne soaring behind, the captain cuts a menacing figure. He is dressed darkly, as ever, and his hair is growing wildly past the collar of his long coat. It strikes me how tall he is, far taller than me. His eyes appear shockingly blue.

"May I have a word," he says.

"Certainly. Children, run along. Resume

253

with Tennyson, I'll be in shortly."

Once we are alone, he says, "I would rather the children did not come here."

"Why not?"

I have spoken out of turn. His expression confirms it.

"Forgive me, Captain, I should never have —"

"Because this was their mother's place," he says coldly. "Laura loved to come to the stables. The twins don't understand. It's painful for them."

I bow my head. It takes might not to dispute my employer. I want to shake him and remind him what wonderful children he has and how his children are a gift, a gift not everybody has the fortune to experience, and if he only spent a little more time with them, loving them, cuddling them, they wouldn't be frightened of him.

"I could help them to understand," I venture. "If you think it would benefit."

"All the children need benefit from is your tutelage."

I nod. "Of course."

"And they would also benefit from having a governess who is committed to their care and not concerned with her own affairs."

"I beg your pardon, Captain?"

"I think you heard."

254

I'm stunned. "Sir, to doubt my commitment to your children is —"

"I understand you met with Henry Marsh last night."

Unable to deny it, I lift my chin. There is no need to ask how he knows: I can imagine it already, my naivety in thinking I could go unnoticed through the back pass when all along the captain was watching me, trailing me, why does he observe me so?

"You admit it," he says.

"I do. The children were in bed. My evening was my own."

"I had specifically requested that you avoid Henry Marsh."

"I'm sorry. I hadn't realized it was an instruction." Although I must have, because why else would I have engaged in secrecy? I acknowledge the thrill it gave me to disobey the captain and to conceal my disobedience from him. I acknowledge that throughout my evening with the doctor, I had the captain in my mind, not the doctor at all but the captain, picturing him in his study, smoking, writing, his dark silhouette brooding against the candlelight. I enjoyed the fact that Henry was his physician and that I was coming between them; I enjoyed the clandestine quiver of my defiance and the promise, however faint, of my punishment.

I realize that I wanted the captain to find out. I needed him to. I am becoming as addicted to him as I have only been addicted to one other before in my life. I never thought I would feel this way again, as if love might save me. It frightens me how quickly I am falling.

"I'm not in the habit of being misread, Miss Miller."

"I quite understand."

"I don't think you do. The children showed me the drawing they did of you in the glade, dressed as a bride. They brought it to my desk and I must say I was quite alarmed. I would appreciate it if you would refrain from imposing your fantasies on their impressionable minds, especially on Constance, for whom, as a girl, such ideas hold special allure. Whatever your reasons, it isn't correct conduct for a governess."

I laugh. "But that was the twins' suggestion, Captain, I hardly think —"

"No, it doesn't appear that you do."

I remember the twins' sweet enthusiasm and the innocence of their task. They would have been excited to show the captain, and likely received a rebuke for their effort. But another, more appealing, thought surfaces. That the children wished their father to see me as I might one day appear to him, as his beloved and betrothed. That an unconscious desire propelled them to draw me like that in the first place, a desire to have me as their mother, and as his wife, and for Winterbourne to belong to us all . . .

"Hopefully you will think on this," the captain says, interrupting my contemplation. "Aside from the impropriety of your outing when you are employed at Winterbourne under my authority, you must take my advice when it comes to Henry Marsh. He is a fine doctor — but the man is not to be trusted."

I frown. It is hard to think of a more trustworthy man than the doctor.

"Captain, you need not concern yourself —"

"Oh, but I must," he says, and for an instant the burns on his face tighten. "I have known the doctor for many years. He was my wife's physician as well as mine. I am better informed to pass judgment on his character than you are."

"Then why are you trusting him with your injuries?" It is a brave challenge, the first time his wounds have been recognized, but he meets it unswervingly.

"It is not his capability as a medic that I doubt," he says. "It is his dishonesty."

"Excuse me?"

But the captain has said too much. He leans more heavily on his cane. "I am merely confirming my point to you, Miss Miller. My reasons for warning you away from Henry Marsh are not simply in Winterbourne's interests, although I do feel that your direction should be solely placed here — they are to ensure your own safety and well-being." He speaks this last part with an endearing self-consciousness that is at odds with his command. "In any case," he finishes, as if done with the matter, "do as you wish. You are aware of my preference. Think of it what you will."

The captain turns and makes his way back to the house, his collar turned up against the cold. A chill wind blows in from the sea, flipping his coat like the dark wings of a bird. Behind me, Storm retreats into her stable and I wonder if I am standing now where Laura once stood, watching her husband, knowing he is hers, and marveling that Winterbourne and all it contains is mine, all mine, all mine.

The rest of the day passes without a glimpse of Captain de Grey. I confess I am looking for him, hoping to see him, for his company both terrifies and excites me. With Henry Marsh I am Alice Miller, ordinary, unexceptional, familiar; with the captain I am somebody else. I don't know whom. I don't know if I trust her.

I have always craved to be that other woman. How could I not? Ever since school, since the crime I committed when I was seventeen years old, I have yearned to step into new shoes. I detest what I did. I wake at night sweating and sick with it. What frightens me almost as much as being discovered is the cold hard stone that became of my heart; that I was able to walk from the scene, calmly and coolly, and return to my dormitory, brush my teeth and comb my hair and wait patiently for lights-out, wishing Matron a polite goodnight, all the while knowing what I had left and what would be revealed in the morning. What sort of a person can do that? Me. I could. I did. And I got away with it, too. Who would have suspected meek, mild Alice Miller, who wouldn't say boo to a goose? Nobody saw me there. It was a tragic accident, that was what they said, poor girl, such a shame, such a loss, so young and full of promise. Assemblies in memoriam, a collection for her parents, a project room named in her honor . . . I nodded along, pretending to wipe my eyes.

Now the nightmares come and come,

louder and brighter each time.

At Winterbourne, with the captain, I could put my crime behind me. I could start again. I could stop longing for a life that didn't work out and begin an untainted one. Jonathan de Grey is a new species, one I have never encountered before. I yearn to strike him and to be struck by him; I yearn to be kissed by him until my lips bleed.

Later that night, when I am alone, I try to talk myself out of my preoccupation. Jonathan sees nothing in me; I am his children's instructor. He is still in love with his wife. As if to torment myself with this, I lift the silver clock from where I set it on the table when I first arrived, thinking it might be fixed. *L. Until the end of time . . .*

The engraving stares back at me, devastatingly real and heartfelt. The hands read twenty-five minutes to three. In this stilled hour, Laura herself has been stilled. The captain's love for her has been stilled. Their marriage has been preserved in a moment, perfect and eternal, untouchable to mortals like me.

"The captain stopped it when she died," Mrs. Yarrow explained to me, when I inquired about it. I didn't need to ask the significance of the hour — it was the same hour that Constance had been sleepwalking

outside my room, and the same hour on which, I'd noticed, the other clocks in the house had been stopped, the ormolu in the captain's study, the carriage clocks in the dining room, the grandfather in the hall.

"Time ground to a halt for the poor man after she went," said Mrs. Yarrow. *"I thought it would pass, that we could start the blessed things up again, but when I went to wind the carriage, all hell broke loose. I vowed I'd never go near them again."*

I touch Laura's clock now. The cook told me that the children had insisted it be put in my room before I'd even arrived, a pretty token for their new governess, and now I find myself consumed by its power, taunted by it, tempted by it. How can I compete? Laura, with her lashings of hair and glimmering eyes; Laura, the mother of his children; Laura, with the romance of death . . . I cannot. And yet I am unable to deny my jealousy.

I wish her husband to be mine. I wish her children to be mine, and her home to be mine, and her horse to be mine; every part of her life I wish to swap for my own. I wish to wear her clothes and be draped in her jewels; I wish to dance on a moonlit night with a wild-haired captain; I wish to know his secrets as she must have, to kiss him tenderly and make love with him fiercely; I wish to be his confidante, his friend, his mistress. But Laura is a woman against whom I stand no chance. She towers over me, mighty, powerful, a goddess, and I am nobody. I am not she.

My desire for the captain exhausts me. I admit it. It will not be denied.

I undress slowly; the curtains are open so that the black shiver of the sea can be glimpsed in the burgeoning dark. I want the captain to be watching.

I want him to see me, like this. For him.

I glance down at my nakedness and the pattern of red marks that run up my arm. The spots have spread since I arrived, some of them mellowed to bruises and some of them fresh, recently made. I touch the skin to see if they hurt, but they don't. I must be sensitive to something in this house, some fabric or else a contagion in the air. And yet I don't mind them. With each day that passes, with each day my passion thrives, so my blood appears to rise to my skin in coin-sized petals, no bigger than a thumbprint, attesting my devotion. I wish him to kiss them away, to kiss me all over.

Finally I draw the drapes closed, the material soft against my body.

Did my predecessor stand where I am?

Did she long for him as I do?

I slip into my nightdress and crawl between the sheets, where I lie awake for some time, gazing into the dark and struggling to capture the details of his face.

Chapter 21

The week passes in a state of high tension. Winterbourne feels like a storm about to break, the air charged with unknowable forces. I see the captain only once, standing alone on the Landogger Bluff, during my afternoon walk with the children.

"Isn't that Father?" Constance asks me. "What is he doing?" I wish I knew. But the more intense and isolated Captain de Grey becomes, the more he enthralls me.

"Come along," I say hurriedly, "your father will be in presently."

It is an effort to hide my craving from the children, and from Mrs. Yarrow. Each time the captain arises in conversation I must turn away, for surely my racing heart will give me away. They seem not to notice, for which I am grateful.

On Wednesday, after breakfast, we have a fright. The last I saw of the children was my dismissal of them and instruction to go and dress; but thirty minutes later I am still waiting in the classroom. I go to Mrs. Yarrow. "Have you seen them?" I ask.

"No, miss. I thought they were with you."

Together, we ascend to the twins' bedroom and their beds are neatly made; the clothes I laid out for them last night are not in evidence.

"Well, at least the mites are dressed," says Mrs. Yarrow, in that mistrustful tone I have become used to, seeming to suggest that the children are engaged in some unsavory activity, with us as the butts of their joke. I do not address her disloyalty for now is not the time. Instead I say, "Perhaps they're with Tom."

We find Tom outside, up a ladder, clearing the rain gutter of leaves. He climbs down when he sees us, but confesses he's had no sight of them either.

"Oh, Lordy!" Mrs. Yarrow wrings her hands.

"Keep your head, Mrs. Yarrow," I say, "there will be a perfectly reasonable explanation." I am just praying that explanation arrives before Captain de Grey does, for I feel his eyes on me again, watching me all the time, everywhere, always.

"They wouldn't 'a' gone downstairs, would they?" says Tom.

"Downstairs?"

He nods. "To the cellar."

"Why on earth would they do that?"

"The girl was talking about a mirror," Tom says. "She wanted to show you, miss." He pauses, averts his gaze, and his next words are an effort. "It were a mirror of Madam's," he manages. "All her things were moved down there after she left."

"It's true," says Mrs. Yarrow. "The captain wanted them out of sight, all of Madam's possessions. We don't use those rooms any more, in any case."

The three of us hurry inside and head for the bowels of the house. I haven't ventured this way since Tipper led Henry and me on a mission, the first time the doctor visited, and it smells as dank and disused as it did then. Down the servants' corridor and getting closer to that weird room with the diminutive entrance, we hear the tinkle of children's laughter. "There they are!" I cry. "I hear them!"

I am surprised to find the strange, small door open, and it strikes me as odd that the children should be giggling if what Tom said was true and they are sitting surrounded by their dead mother's belongings. Was that what Tipper was barking at, just a trove of old effects? Why was he so afraid? I long to

266

creep inside and touch the fabrics this woman wore, to glimpse the life she led, but then the laughter stops and the children appear at the hatch. The light is so faded that it is hard to make out their shapes, but I would know my children anywhere.

"Help us," urges Edmund, "Tom!"

Now I see why. They are attempting to carry a considerable weight and as its outline appears through the alcove I see it is the mirror. Laura de Grey's mirror.

I rush to help and between us we wrench the glass through. Mrs. Yarrow falls back, disapproving, and I ought to share her disapproval but cannot, for the intrigue is too great for me to contest. Tom stands the mirror and for a moment we all gaze at it, as if a new person has joined us. It is oval in shape, the glass plain enough but the frame is beguiling. It is twisted and black like a froth of serpents, or the head of Medusa, and one has the sensation of reaching to touch it and one of its tentacles coming alive in one's hands. It reminds me of the mural in my room — that writhing greenery — where I cannot trace a stem of it without becoming lost.

My vision of Laura at her dressing table was wrong. She was not sitting but standing. The beauty of her head alone was not enough.

Constance snivels. She was not laughing in there, but crying!

I kneel to her. "What is it, darling?"

"This was my mummy's," she says.

"I know it was. But you hoped to find it? Tom said you did."

Constance nods. "Edmund promised he'd help me. I wanted to see it again. May we bring it upstairs, Alice, please? I don't like it being down here. It isn't happy down here." I look up at the others, at Mrs. Yarrow and Tom, and they are doubtful.

"The captain won't like it," says Tom.

I stand, smoothing my skirt. The captain's rage flies toward me on wings made of gold. "I am sure he'll understand once I explain it to him."

The private reprimand I am hoping for doesn't arrive; instead, we are all of us present when the captain sees the excavated mirror, and all of us are subject to his anger.

Anger, though, is not nearly the right word. Instead the captain receives our find as if absorbing a blow to the stomach: quiet, controlled and steady.

"Constance wishes to keep it here, in the hall," I say. "Could we?"

The captain eyes each of us in turn. I can

hear Mrs. Yarrow's protests without her needing to speak: *"It weren't me, Captain, I didn't want anything to do with it, it's a horrible thing anyway; forgive me, Captain, it were the children's doing, the children and her!"* He watches the mirror carefully, as if it is an old adversary.

"Is that right, Constance?"

The children no longer hold my hands; they have stepped away from me. Edmund's glance flits over me: a shiver of conspiracy passes through the hallway then disappears. "Mummy used to brush her hair in it," says Constance faintly.

The captain's shoulders drop, surrendering to a great exhale.

"Very well," he says, "you may keep it above stairs. But not here." He doesn't have to say: *Not here where I can see it. Not here where I must be reminded of her.*

"In Alice's room," says Constance, as if this has been the plan all along.

Startled, I turn to her.

"Alice will take the mirror," she goes on, and there is that quiver of collusion again; I cannot put my finger on it. "Then we can see it any time we like. Alice will look perfect in it. Don't you think, Father? It's a waste for it to be hidden away."

"Come now, children," I object, "I

269

wouldn't assume —"

"If she wishes it," says the captain, meeting my eye with his cold blue glare.

I cannot speak. The mirror observes me. The children are pleased.

Tom lifts the glass with some effort. Leaving behind our companions, we take it to my room. "Is here all right?" he asks, settling it by the window.

"That's fine. Thank you, Tom."

Before he leaves, he asks, "You're sure about this, miss?"

"It is the children's wish," I answer; "I am happy to entertain it."

"Mrs. de Grey used to love that mirror." He hesitates. "She'd be in front of it every day — obsessed, she was — brushing her hair or admiring the new clothes the captain bought for her. But she hated it by the end. She weren't at all keen on it by then. Said it gave her a fright."

"Well, I'm not about to let a rusted antique do such a thing to me."

"Of course not, miss."

I am relieved when he goes and I am alone, looking at myself in the glass and liking how it makes a grander person of me. I find myself smiling, despite the strain of the morning, and a warm beam of sunshine pools on the floor around my ankles.

Oh, but that is a most peculiar thing.

The painting on the wall has changed. I move closer, to make sure, and when I see what has happened I gasp, blood rising in my chest. The last time I saw the girl in the picture, she was most definitely *inside the farmhouse.* Now, she is outside.

It cannot be.

Alarmed, I take a step back. Something horrible is caught in my throat. I must be seeing things — or else this is a different picture, swapped without my knowledge, without my being here, but then by whom? I cannot move, dread pinning me to the spot, and it is not so much my dread at the image itself coming alive as it is at the possibility that *I am the one moving:* that my mind has moved her, somehow. That I am not as well as I think I have been. That my mind is failing me again.

You're perfectly fine, Alice, I tell myself. *Stop daydreaming.*

Gently I touch the girl's portrait with my finger, expecting what I do not know — warmth, breath, for the tip of my finger to penetrate its surface? It is cool, the oils decades old and rippled with age, and when I peer in I see that she is not looking to me at all, but instead to the mirror at my back, as if stepping near to see herself in it.

■ ■ ■ ■

It is with difficulty that we pass the morning in study, for I cannot prevent my mind from wandering away from the drawing room, upstairs to the mirror and the impossible painting, or else down to the cellar and toward Laura's belongings. The cellar seems to call to me, pulsing with promise, seducing me with secrets it has yet to reveal. Laura is the key. If I could just find out what happened to her . . .

At lunchtime, with the twins playing outside, Mrs. Yarrow is pale, her eyes rimmed. "Oh, miss," she says wearily, "the time has come. I cannot bear it any more."

"You cannot bear what?"

"Here. Winterbourne. The children. Danger is coming."

I turn to her. "Mrs. Yarrow?"

The cook folds a heap of towels in order to avoid looking at me. "When I said before about moving on, miss, I meant it. My sister works for a house up in Norfolk. There's an opening there in the kitchen, the pay is good and the family fair —"

"Winterbourne needs you," I object. "You can't leave."

"That's what I thought," she says, "to

begin with. But Winterbourne has never been right, miss; it wasn't right with Madam, and I daresay it wasn't right before."

I scoff. "Mrs. Yarrow, this is lunacy."

"No," she cuts me off, "I'll tell you what is lunacy. That boy and that girl. They're lunacy. Haven't you seen the way they look at you?"

I push my plate away. "I have no idea what you mean."

"They're laughing at you. Don't you see? They used to laugh at me, but now they have you to play with. You can think what you like, miss, about why they are the way they are, you can think of the excuses you want. But I know the truth."

"Then speak it!"

"They're wrong, those children. They've put a spell on this place — or else it's put a spell on them. I've pretended long enough that I can stand it. But Winterbourne is slipping away, miss: the old Winterbourne, the Winterbourne I knew. It belongs to the twins now, and there's nothing you or I or anyone can do about it."

"It's their home, Mrs. Yarrow," I say tightly.

"Indeed. But I used to have a home here too. I used to run this house, but now the twins run everything: their father, Tom, you. All that business with Edmund running away in the mist, their feigning illness, their disobedience, then today the mirror! Oh, miss, surely you see, with the mirror —"

"Mrs. Yarrow, I will not hear it." I stand and turn to leave, unable to hear her poisonous words. "If you believe such lies then perhaps it is best if you go."

"It was better, before they were born," blathers the cook, her fingers shaking so that she buries them in her apron, but still her voice quavers. "They made their mother sick — sick in the head! Madam told me she could not stand to touch them!"

"Mrs. Yarrow!"

"Madam died and then the other woman died. I will not let it happen to me —"

I strike my fist on the table. How dare Mrs. Yarrow cast such aspersions on the cherubs who play on the lawn? Through the window I see the twins frolicking on the grass, Edmund's copper curls like a harp of gold and Constance's skirts bouncing as she leaps. I will not give the cook audience. She has already tempted me toward doubting the children once and I will not let her again. I know better now. It is a pity she does not. "Enough," I say evenly. "I ought to report your words to the captain."

"All that business with Madam's mirror, don't you see their trick?"

"They miss their mother. They should be comforted, not chastised."

"That were Madam's mirror but it turned against her in the end. She did not like herself in it by the time she died."

"Was she sick? Her appearance changed?"

Mrs. Yarrow says no, not quite, perhaps, in a way.

"The children sense it," she says. "They can't have known it, they were young, but they *sense it*. I saw how they dragged that thing out from its den. Didn't you hear their laughter, miss, down in the cellar? They want you to have the mirror. Or else something in this house told them to give it to you."

"I will not listen!"

"Ask yourself why, miss. Why did they give it to you?"

"Because they love me, Mrs. Yarrow!"

That succeeds in quieting her, though I wish I hadn't said it. It is a private wish, close to a belief, and I am not ready to share it.

"You are a fool, if that is what you suppose."

"Why shouldn't I suppose it? You speak gibberish; that mirror is a piece of glass and

275

nothing more: a gift, and a striking one, from them to me. Don't you see that I am the closest thing they have to a mother now? I dote on them, never doubt it, and never doubt that I will defend those children with my life if the occasion arises."

Mrs. Yarrow turns from me, her hands braced on the rim of the sink.

"You are not their mother," she says warningly. "You are not the mistress of Winterbourne. You must never imagine yourself to be such. This house will not have it. That was the mistake the woman before you made."

"She can't have made it," I say tightly. "Or she would never have left them."

The cook remains where she is. So do I.

"Good afternoon, Mrs. Yarrow," I say, and head out to find the children.

We finish lessons early. I see the strain the day's activities have taken on Edmund and Constance, and find myself longing to get out of the house. That's the way with Winterbourne: its atmosphere changes as fast as the breeze on the Landogger Bluff.

"To your room, darlings; you can finish your work there."

The children do as they're told and I seize my coat from the hall.

"Are you heading out, miss?" asks Tom, as we pass each other in the porch. "There's heavy rain coming in, be warned."

"Thank you, Tom."

But I pay no heed to a spot of rain, and instead walk out over the parkland, through the tall grasses and toward the cliffs. I position myself in the windswept spot where I saw the dark-dressed woman and let my gaze fall to the beach, half hoping I will find her there, a staggering black shape, crawling, crawling toward the sea . . .

But the sand is empty. Gloomy clouds heap on the horizon. I wonder how close their last governess stood before she stepped over the brink. Did she put one toe over first? Did she brace herself like a diver, or tumble like a rag doll? Was she afraid?

It makes me envious to imagine her with the children, with the captain, playing at the role I now hold dear. Mrs. Yarrow knows not of what she speaks. I am different. Winterbourne knows I am different. This house is my salvation.

I have been too focused on the dead and not focused enough on the living. Inside Winterbourne is a living, breathing man — it makes me shudder to think of him — and two children who need my love. Henry Marsh asked if I believed in ghosts. No, I do not. I cannot. I would already have been hunted to my grave.

I turn from the sea to head back to the house, but then I spy the low line of the stables and am drawn in that direction instead. The rain has started to spit, stinging my cheeks. I gather my coat. Above, thunder rolls across the darkening sky.

Storm is sheltering in the warm enclosure. I stroke her ears and mane and a light in her eyes catches mine. Before I can think better of it — because given another minute, surely I would — I unbolt the door and locate the reins, long unused, suspended in a tangle from a rafter. There is no saddle but I prefer it that way.

"She wants to be ridden. She hasn't been ridden in years . . ."

I loop the reins around Storm's neck and she accepts them gratefully, dancing her hooves with anticipation. My heart beats wildly; my throat is dry.

"Mummy would have liked you to. Mummy would ask you, if only she could . . ."

"Come along, girl," I say. "Come along, Storm."

I lead her out and she follows on unsteady legs, head flicking against the rain. The white in her mane reminds me she is old but seeing her out of the stable, against the

278

roll of the Cornish moors, she strikes me as a new animal. The muscles in her legs and flanks are ready to work, eager to run. Out of sight of the house, I mount her. Her coat is quickly soaked. The rain falls torrentially now, huge drops that hang from my eyelashes and nose. My coat is drenched and my hat seeping so I throw it on to the grass. With my thighs I grip the horse's sides, clasping the leather straps in my hand.

"Yah!" I shout, kicking back my heels. The beast springs from under me. I have never flown but I imagine that this is how it feels to fly. Storm seems to know the terrain, as well she might, and together we soar across the heath, the rain whirling and spinning from the sky. I kick harder, keeping her speed, and we move so fast it seems entirely plausible that we are ready to step up into the heavens . . . It is too fast, I know, and to come across a ditch or rut would throw me clean over the edge, but I don't care. I am free. I am flying. I am wetted through and it makes me alive. I am not sure if I have ever felt alive, not like this. I can leave it all behind, my childhood, my crime, my doomed romance and the future I lost. Those were the things that brought me here, to Winterbourne. This house has shown me I can have it yet: I too can be happy. I too

can know love. I too can claim my chance. Nothing can catch me now, not riding Storm in the driving rain, the rhythm of our bodies working against the other, the horse's hooves churning the ground and our hearts racing in tandem.

I could be her, I think. *Laura de Grey of Winterbourne.*

And, for a moment, I am.

I am Laura.

The thought sends such a primitive thrill through me that I have to tug the reins to bring Storm to a slower pace. The horse wheezes and chuffs but she is as exhilarated as I, her chest pumping and her muscles straining for more.

We turn back to the house, now an outline in the distance. I recall Mrs. Yarrow's words to me when I first arrived at Winterbourne, when she first told me of her intended departure:

"You'll be the woman of this house next, miss. And you'll like it."

I tilt my face to the sky and allow the rain to take me. I open my mouth and let it come inside. For an instant the arc above me illuminates in a flash of lightning, white and shocking, then there is the answering call of thunder.

I twitch the reins and we move off, galloping back toward the house.

Storm is returned to the stables and I am walking, dripping, to Winterbourne when I stop. I see a silhouette in the chapel's arched window. It is the captain.

"Miss Miller." He steps out. The pouring rain slices across my vision, blurring his edges, smoothing his features, so his burns are scarcely visible. He looks at me with those cool blue eyes, his black hair soaked in moments. "Come."

I am reminded of a story I read as a child. He is the wolf. I am the flesh he wishes to bite. Inside, the rebuke I am expecting both thrills and dismays me.

"I saw you," he says quietly, "out with Storm." The rolling sky echoes his displeasure. "Have you taken leave of your senses?"

"Captain, I . . ." But there is no justification for what I did. I wanted to be caught. I wanted this. I wanted him, and me, and to feel the force of his rage.

"I granted you acquittal over the mirror," he says, "but this? Taking my dead wife's horse, when you are aware of how much she means to me?" It isn't clear whether he means Laura or the animal. I suppose it makes no difference.

"I'm sorry. I saw Storm and I wanted her

to run —"

"You had *no right!*" The captain turns to the chapel altar and for a wild second I believe he is going to drop to his knees, before he whirls back round to face me. His features are contorted, his eyes savage. I have never been so attracted to a man before in my life. "Nothing you say can make this better. There are no excuses."

Your daughter told me to. I could say it. Just as I could say that Edmund lured me out that day in the mist. Just as I could say that they depicted me as Jonathan's bride, so he would see me that way and imagine us together. Just as they wanted me to have their mother's mirror, so I could be more like her, so I could assume my place as mistress of Winterbourne. That the children are, it would seem, moving us together like a pawn and a king in a game of chess. *They want it.* They have plotted it since the moment I entered the house. It is they I can thank for these intimate encounters, they who have stoked the fire of their father's passion and placed me in front to feel its warmth. They wish for him to capture me, and now I am but one square away.

Behind the captain, the crucifixion bears down. Even in dark daylight, the stained glass of the chapel windows glows with punishment. I shiver, the rain coursing now off my chin and the ends of my hair, snaking down my neck.

"Do you know the worst part?" It is almost a groan, heavy with regret and an attempt to restrain some other feeling, harder for me to pinpoint. "You looked just like her." The captain steps toward me; instinctively, I step back. I say nothing. "Out there on the moors," he says, "it was like seeing Laura again. As if you were her ghost."

My skin is freezing. Goose bumps prickle my back. Yet there is heat within me too, and heat seems to come off the captain, and still I am unable to speak.

There are no words to defend my actions and besides I do not wish to defend them. I wish to be Laura, just as he described me. The chapel flashes with lightning.

"You devilish creature," he rasps — and then he comes toward me and takes my chin in his hands; and I go to speak his name but before I can, he kisses me.

CHAPTER 22

CORNWALL, PRESENT DAY

Rachel rode her bike into town. Jack had offered her a ride but she refused. She'd been short with him — in her anger at the estate agent's visit, the brief ceasefire they'd shared had been called off. He was back to his condescending self.

"Rachel," he'd said before she turned him out, "who cares about that woman? So what if she wants to sell Winterbourne, it's your house. What you say goes."

So what? She should have expected his lackadaisical response. Then he had dared to tell her to calm down; he would drive her to Polcreath because she was in no fit state to go on her own. What Jack didn't realize was that Rachel had always gone on her own, all through her life; it was how she did things and she did them well. She would have slapped him had she not had more pressing issues on her mind.

In Polcreath, the day was bright and clear.

Seagulls flapped on the low seawall and gossamer clouds drifted across the sky. Rachel headed straight for the café and resumed her usual table. In moments her suspicions were confirmed. An email from Aaron told her in noble terms that he had found a representative for Winterbourne: Rachel would be absolved of the "pressure" of selling in no time, realizing the fortune that was hers to inherit, and that "Winterfield" would soon be a thing of the past. She wasn't sure what was the worst part — that Aaron imagined all she cared about was money or that he had no clue what the place meant to her, despite the things she had told him. She realized that he didn't understand her at all. How could he have imagined he had the right to take such action without consulting her first? Clearly he figured he was doing her a favor, but the fact remained it was none of his business.

She composed her message:

Aaron, you shouldn't have done this. It was a breach of my trust, and something only I, given the circumstances, should have arranged. I would have arranged it when I was ready.

Rachel sat back and chewed her thumb.

She thought of the nights they had spent together, the kisses and the comfort he had given her. She thought of his smile, the ambition she'd been attracted to. It had been nice to have someone on her side.

I'd have preferred not to do this by email but I feel you've left me no choice. It's over, Aaron. It was never meant to be serious between us so I hope you will accept this easily.

Take care and good luck. Rachel x

Tucking her tablet into her bag, she downed her coffee and left the shop.

In time she would sell Winterbourne and its land — but not yet. Not until she had revealed its story. She owed it to her mother and her grandmother. Rachel felt the women waiting for her, watching her, their eyes in the walls and their breath on the windows, willing her to uncover the truth that had buried them.

Winterbourne was transformed in the sunshine. Its walls blazed peach in the afternoon and its turrets and towers appeared classically romantic against the sky. The glass in the hothouses bounced light instead of swallowing it, and the crumbling stone frame of the orangery resembled an Italianate villa, nestled in the Tuscan hills. Rachel decided that, should she have been here in Winterbourne's prime, the orangery would have been her favorite place. Yes, it had fallen to rack and ruin like the rest of the estate, yet it retained a timeless elegance and sense of peace that was lacking in other parts of the house. She took a walk down to the cliffs, and when she turned back to the building it seemed to regard her in a new way, gratefully, as if relieved at having been kept hold of.

We belong to each other, she thought.

Wanda Pearlman hadn't been pleased. The Realtor thought she'd had the sale of a lifetime on her hands. No doubt tales of Rachel's passionate protest would find their way out of Brightside Lettings and into Polcreath proper, and everyone's suspicions about the eccentric family member up at Winterbourne would be confirmed. The thought made Rachel smile. In their eyes she was a de Grey, part of that messy, strange, isolated clan who could behave as single-mindedly as they liked.

The sea was glittering blue. It was incredible how profoundly it could change. In New York, weather came and went and occasionally Rachel would glimpse a postage-stamp-sized window of it between the highrises. There, the sky was a mosaic; here, it was entire, a canopy that when reflected in the wide water gave a strange effect of seamless continuity. She could imagine Winterbourne caught in the sphere, like a design trapped in a paperweight, and she even smaller, the only sign of life.

Only, here was another. Rachel heard a car. Turning to the hill, she was in time to spot Jack's Land Rover approaching the house.

"Back again so soon?" she said when she reached him.

He got out and closed the door. "Thought I'd see how you are."

"Well, you'll be relieved to know I made it into Polcreath without falling into an hysterical collapse."

He grinned. "Sometimes I feel I can't put a foot right with you."

His candor stumped her.

"Anyway," he said, "and this is a bit of a curveball, but my sister's in town and we're having some drinks at my house tonight. Do you want to come?"

"I really shouldn't," she said automatically, "I've got things to do here."

"Things that can't wait? Come on," he

urged, "those letters will still be here when you get back. It's nothing formal, just some friends, food, booze . . ." Seeing her doubtful expression, he added, "My sister'll kill me if I don't bring you. She doesn't like to think of you up here on your own. I'm under strict instruction. Help me out."

Rachel had to admit that the idea of a party was appealing: company, warm bodies mingling, a glass or several of wine and a chance to take her mind off Aaron. She'd been up at Winterbourne on her own for days. Maybe she could do with this.

"OK," she said, before she could change her mind. "What time?"

"Sevenish? I'm at the farmhouse across the field from the Landogger. I'll come collect you if you like."

"It's fine, I'll make my own way."

"Why doesn't that surprise me?"

She smiled back and raised a hand. "Bye, Jack." She was still smiling when she went inside.

Getting ready for a party in Polcreath was different to getting ready for a party in New York. Out there, she'd either finish up a frantic day and head straight to the venue in her work wear, or else she'd glam up for the night in a limited-edition gown donated to her by a sponsor. Here, she had none of those robes with her, and even if she had, she'd feel a fool turning up to Jack's farmhouse wearing one of them.

She decided on a shirt and skinny jeans, with lots of jewelry. She left her hair loose and applied lipstick, feeling stylish but not overdone. In mounting her bike as the sun went down and the last shot of warmth went out of the day, she conceded that she might have been better off accepting Jack's offer of a pickup. It was a habit she had, Maggie always told her so, of cutting her nose to spite her face. At least it wasn't raining, and the track down to the Landogger was straightforward.

Less could be said for the field she needed to cross in order to reach Jack's house. Rachel stopped outside the Landogger Inn and surveyed her options. The road that looped round gave way to a main carriageway, which was no good on two wheels. In the interests of avoiding comment from the pint-swilling locals gathered outside the pub, she chained her bike to the gate and then passed through the gate on foot. Luckily she had rejected heels in favor of Converse, and the field wasn't muddy.

As she came closer to the farmhouse, she saw how beautiful it was. She had pictured

290

a ramshackle affair with crumpling roofs and bashed-in cowsheds, but in fact the house itself was very well kept. It was large, even quite grand, with a low thatched roof and plenty of windows, through which emanated a warm amber glow. She caught the sharp agricultural tang coming from the barns, not unpleasant, and when she turned to the view Jack must see every day from his porch, Polcreath was lit up in a flurry of tiny lights, gently climbing the hillside. On top of that hill, high, higher, almost touching the clouds, it seemed, was the dark shape of Winterbourne.

"Rachel!" The door opened and with it a gust of welcoming heat, and the aroma of wine. "At least I'm guessing it's you," said the woman in the doorway, beaming from ear to ear, "Jack told me you were glamorous. I'm Kirsty, by the way."

"Jack's sister?"

"For my sins." They shook hands. "Come in, come in."

Kirsty looked a lot like her brother: she had the same-shaped face and slate-gray eyes. "Can I get you a glass of wine? My kids went to bed an hour ago and I'm afraid I might have already finished all the decent stuff." She grinned. "Sure there's some red around here though . . . ." Rachel followed her into the living room, deciding she liked Jack's sister, a straightaway, uncomplicated sort of liking. The space was filled with chatting friends and easy laughter, and she felt just as comfortable and inconspicuous as she would have had she stepped into a friendly downtown bar. They stood beneath low ceilings, crisscrossed with beams, and a fire roared in the hearth. There were books everywhere, in piles, on tables and filling the shelves. Several squidgy sofas were drawn close to the heat, draped in various throws and blankets; a sheepdog snoozed on one, his paws twitching in the middle of a dream.

"Here." Kirsty handed her a glass. "So how are you settling into Polcreath?"

She was still thinking about how Jack had described her as glamorous, and the very many times he had seen her in muddy Wellingtons with scragged-back hair.

"Oh, I'm not looking to settle in," said Rachel. "Winterbourne's just a stop."

And why had he been describing her to his sister at all?

"Jack and I grew up here," said Kirsty. "As children we were fascinated by the house. Did you used to come a lot, to spend time with your family?"

But he hadn't shared Rachel's confidence

about her adoption.

"No," she said, sipping her wine. "Actually, this is the first time I've been. I didn't realize I was related to the de Greys until recently."

Kirsty's eyes widened. "Gosh," she said, "I'm sorry."

"What for?"

"I don't know. Putting my foot in it? It runs in our family."

"That's been the odd thing for me," said Rachel, "not knowing *what* runs in mine." She smiled. "And anyway, your brother's been very kind to me."

"Even though he's the most annoying man in the world."

Rachel laughed. "Are you close?"

"Very. Always have been. Maybe that's why I find him annoying." Kirsty returned her laugh. "No, seriously, I'd have been lost without him. When my marriage broke down, Jack was there. He helped me out of a bad situation, helped with the children; he's a fantastic uncle, they love him. He let me stay here and put myself back together. So I guess I have no right to tell him to do the washing up properly or take off his filthy boots before he tramples mud all through the house."

"You don't live locally any more?"

"London. Jack lived there too, for a while, but it didn't work out."

Rachel was surprised. Not that it hadn't worked out, but that he'd been there in the first place. The idea of Jack in the city seemed wrong; he was as sewn into Cornwall as the sea and the sky. "Did he work there?" she asked.

"No, it was a girl. Totally wrong for him, I thought, and turns out I was right. Anyway, when he came back here it was like we could all breathe a sigh of relief. And we love visiting — the boys, especially. It's a magical place."

Jack joined them. "I see you found each other," he said, with his usual smug grin. "I thought you might." He was wearing a green-checkered shirt that looked worn and soft to touch, and there was another sheepdog trailing at his heels.

"Kirsty's been telling me about your life in London," said Rachel.

Jack rolled his eyes. "The less said about that the better." But he sent his sister a pointed look and she shrugged, as if to say, *What was I meant to do? She asked.*

Kirsty left them to refill her glass. "She's on a mission tonight," said Rachel.

"Believe me, once you meet those boys you'll know why." Then, as if he'd perhaps said something too forward, Jack asked, "Do you like the house?"

"Are you auditioning for Wanda Pearlman?"

Jack smirked. "What kind of a name is that anyway?"

Rachel looked about at the sweetness of the living room, its inherent ease and allure, and found that the answer was simple. "Yes, I do, very much. It's . . ."

"Charming? Quaint? Olde-worlde? I don't know what expression your arty friends would use."

"That's an uninitiated thing to say."

"Then initiate me." He drank from his glass. She did the same, unsure how to reply. Then Jack said: "Are they missing you?"

Rachel thought of the call she'd put through to Paul earlier today. "They're fine. You know, coming here has made me realize that it's not all on me. Other people do things quite well, too."

"But not as well as you."

"It's hard, when you've nurtured and cared for something, to let it go."

"I feel the same about my pigs."

She laughed. "We really are from different worlds, Jack Wyatt."

He looked away, then back, and smiled

with her. "We are."

After midnight, people began to leave. Rachel said goodbye to Kirsty and was surprised when the sister hugged her. They were both a little drunk and the world seemed drunk with them. "Come again, Rachel," she said warmly. "Come again soon."

She had thought Jack had melted off to the pub with the others, but instead he was outside smoking. When she opened the door he moved to stub out the cigarette, then saw who it was and relaxed. "Sorry," he said, "thought you were Kirsty."

"Just me," she pulled on her coat, "and I'll steal one of those, thanks."

He lit one for her and passed it over. They smoked in silence for a moment.

"Thanks for inviting me," she said. "I had a really good time."

"You're welcome."

"Your sister's nice."

"Yeah, she's OK. Most of the time."

"You sound about fifteen."

She felt him smile rather than saw it: the night was black, with only the pale moon to shine on it. Abundant stars decorated the canopy above.

"What were you doing at fifteen, Rachel Wright?" he asked.

"Arguing with my mother, most likely."

"About what?"

"Oh, I don't know. Makeup. Pot. Staying out with a boy."

"Didn't you get on with her?"

"Yes, on the whole . . . Parents and teenagers don't mix, though, do they?"

"I certainly didn't with mine."

Rachel blew out a satisfying plume of smoke. She turned to him, feeling bold.

"So what about the girl in London?" She smiled. "Was she the one who didn't like dogs?"

He waved a hand. "Kirsty always has the habit of saying precisely what I don't want her to say. It was nothing. Just a weird time in my life."

"We've all had those. I'm still having them."

"Trying to figure out what I wanted," he said. "Trying to separate what I *thought* I wanted from what I actually did. She worked in finance, a perfectly nice girl but not for me. Manicures and gym member-ship, that kind of thing."

"I can't see you with that."

"Nobody could. But I had a try. Your soul always catches you in the end." He turned to her in the night. "What about you? How's your boyfriend?"

She could be honest with him now. "It's over."

"It is?"

She nodded. "A long story, and you don't want to hear it."

"Try me."

Now she laughed. Jack would have a field day with the idea of Aaron Grewal. To think of the two men together was comical. They couldn't be more different.

"Can I try you with something else?" she said.

The tip of his cigarette crackled as he drew on it. "Sure."

"I was married," she said, "a few years ago. I got married when I was twenty-five, so quite young by some people's standards." She focused on the dark shapes in the night: the hulk of hedges and the distant twinkle of the Landogger Inn across the field. "My husband, Seth, saved me — at least I thought that at the time. I'd never belonged anywhere but I felt I belonged with him. I had this idea of settling down quickly and making a family from nothing, the family I'd never had. I'd be at the center of it."

Jack waited. After a moment, he said, "You're divorced?"

"No," she said, "he died."

Jack said nothing, even when she was

298

quiet for some time.

"He died on a Monday morning in 2012, less than six months after we were married. A terror attack on the office he was working in. He was there one day and gone the next." Rachel closed her eyes. She had never said this to anyone, not to Paul, not to Aaron, not to anyone. "I saw it on the news and I just thought, it's impossible. He'll call me. He'll say he went out for coffee, or he was late getting the train and we'll cook dinner tonight and feel lucky, so much luckier than those other poor people. But he didn't call me. Instead, his brother did. The first thing he said to me was, 'Rachel, it's Seth. But you know already, right?' And I did. I knew. I looked around our kitchen and his cup was still on the side where he'd drunk from it before he'd left. The paper he'd been reading was open on the same page, page seventeen, on some article about drug busts in Philly. It all seemed so normal. The world kept turning. Grass kept growing. Planes kept flying. News items about the bombing wound up after ten minutes and moved on to another matter. Ten minutes, was that all we got?

"It took me months to stop playing over the last time I saw him. It was so insignificant, that quick kiss goodbye; I think I reminded him about something banal like picking up milk. And then the what-ifs . . . What if there'd been a delay on the subway that day, or he'd been too sick to go in, or there'd been a freak snowfall like the one we had the winter before and we couldn't even get to the end of our street? But all that counts is what happened. There's only one version of what happened, and what is, is, and what isn't, isn't. That was what happened to me. To us."

She was expecting to weep, perhaps she was already weeping. But no, her face was dry. She had come through it.

"Did they catch the people who did it?" Jack asked.

"Two of them," she said. "Suicide bombers. Just walked right in there, plain as anything. But it goes deeper than that. It's an ongoing war. Capturing them was no comfort, at least not to me. It's still happening. People are still dying, for no reason."

"I think I read about your Monday," he said softly, remembering. "It was in the papers over here."

"It would have been. It was everywhere. The city felt broken but we didn't let them win. We couldn't be afraid to go into work, to the shops, we had to survive."

"Rachel, I'm sorry. I'm sad and I'm sorry."

"It isn't your fault."

"No, but it isn't yours either. It shouldn't have happened to you."

"But it did give me something." She faced him. It was strange: Jack's details were impossible to pick out in the darkness, but the shape of him exuded compassion and kindness and those qualities seemed almost as real as an eye or mouth. "It made me strong," she said. "It made me rely on myself. It made me succeed. It made me driven. I consider those to be gifts given to me by Seth. It's why the gallery matters to me so much. I know you think it pretentious, but it isn't to me."

"I never said it was pretentious. And god, Rachel, I never would now."

"But finding Winterbourne, it's like a second chance, you know? That chance, again, of belonging. That solicitor's letter arriving, telling me about the de Greys; I was at home at the time and it just felt like the universe was calling me up, like it was saying, *Hey, Rachel, we've got something else for you, it isn't over yet.*"

"Because it's not, is it?" Jack reached for her hand.

She let him hold it. They stood like that for a minute, maybe more, before he let her go. "I'm sorry," she said. "I'm drunk. It's easy to talk."

"I'm glad you did. I'm glad you told me."

"So am I."

"I know you'll find what you're looking for, here."

"What am I looking for?"

"You said it. Belonging. But it's more than just the walls of the house, isn't it? You're looking to understand your past and the people who brought you into the world. It's important. I'll help you. I'd like to."

Rachel opened her mouth to reply but the door opened and Kirsty stepped out. The spell was broken. "Whoops!" she said. "Didn't realize there was anyone out here."

"I was just going," said Rachel.

"How are you getting back?" asked Jack.

"I left my bike at the Landogger."

"Nonsense," he said, "I'll call a cab." He ducked inside to the phone.

Kirsty folded her arms against the cold. "You'll be careful with him, won't you?" she said. At Rachel's puzzlement, she added, "Jack. You'll be careful with him."

In the cab, riding back to Winterbourne, Rachel thought about what Kirsty had said. She was amazed that she had told Jack her secret, and amazed, more, that he had seemed to understand the cost at which it came. *I'll help you. I'd like to.*

For the first time, like a bud opening to the flush of spring, Rachel considered it — letting another person close, letting herself be trusted and to trust in return . . .

She was alive. That was another thing Seth had given her, the gift of her life, ever more valuable for its comparison with the loss of his. She was on the brink of a discovery that would change her world, the discovery at the heart of Winterbourne.

But, as the taxi hurtled toward the daunting house on the hill, she could never have anticipated how great the discovery would be.

CHAPTER 23

CORNWALL, 1947

Every part of Winterbourne is improved this morning. The sky is a deeper blue. The sea is a softer sigh. The birds chirp more sweetly in the trees. How could the world not be changed? *Jonathan!* I wish to cry his name a thousand times, each refrain louder than the last. I cried his name in the chapel last night; I cried it over and over again as our love at last came to fruition, the inevitable collision of our physical bodies when our spirits had been joined for so long. I am shocked at the ease with which I surrendered myself to him, and yet not surprised at all. I dismissed decorum; I did away with finesse. Our union had been inescapable since I first arrived at Winterbourne, and now, though I never believed it would happen again, I am happy.

Before the captain kissed me, I was convinced I was about to be discharged. Riding Storm was the final disgrace and I could no longer be responsible for his children or his home. But no, Jonathan had other ideas. He wished to keep me, and to keep me more certainly than I dreamed! Passion does not come close to conveying the night we passed. I am reborn. I am awake. I ought to blush at the fleshly extremes of our affections but I cannot. I am too content. After the war, I never thought I would know feelings like it again. I thought I had lost the only man I would ever adore — but no, here, like an angel, is another! Jonathan is my savior, my future, my light.

Over a formal breakfast, I wonder that my feelings are not clear for all to see. I try to catch the captain's eye at the head of the table but he avoids meeting me. Who can blame him? It seems absurd, to say the least, that we can be present, together, at this prim arrangement of butter dishes and silver cutlery and china plates, when mere hours ago we were tangled in desire, two bodies made one, his hair between my fingers and his tongue in my mouth.

It is unpardonable! A delicious offense! Last night is a dreamscape of strange and brilliant things, so distant and impossible-seeming today that I would think I had imagined it all, were it not for the scent of him still lingering on my skin.

"Alice, could you pass the jam, please?" Constance asks.

"Of course, my dear." My eyes flit over the captain again, his dark brow focused on the morning paper. They call him a cripple, but they cannot know what they describe. No man capable of the love he showed me could be painted as such.

Then again, my love has eased his pain. With my kisses I soothed his burns; with my lips I caressed his legs, and every other part of him. Already I am foreseeing a later point in the day, when I can approach him in a private moment and we can be together. Jonathan (what a thrill it is to use his name!) will turn to me with a ravenous expression and say: "Oh, Alice, my sweet Alice, I have been dreaming of you all day," and it will be all we can manage not to devour each other completely.

But we will need to advance with care, for the sake of the children. The twins are exceptional and will easily pick out the truth if given so much as a whisper.

I must be patient. I know what is at stake, for them as well as for me. They have lost a mother and will not — should not — accept another so easily in her place. But for me, well, there can be no other outcome. I have coveted this since I set foot here. No, that is a lie. I coveted it before I even caught a *sense* of Winterbourne, before my interview in London, before I took the job at Quakers Oatley & Sons, before the war . . . even before the man I lost, the baby I lost? I have always yearned to be part of tenderness like this, a loving, secure family. To think I could fill such a pivotal role for them as wife and mother, for once an Alice Miller to be respected and looked up to, who had achieved, who had realized something concrete, is alluring. I yearn to start again, with no past, no guilt, no demons at my back . . .

Jonathan will have a plan. As I steal glances at him from the other end of the table (an impossible distance — but to think that I could do away with the breakfast dishes and climb on to its surface, and take his face in my hands and kiss him; I could do that, were it not for my judgment!), I see how hard he is contemplating our next move. He will have spent the hours since our union contemplating it, and he will not share it with me until it is completed in his mind. Only then will he disclose our love to the children and the staff, and only then can it be absorbed into the house. For Winterbourne is part of our family, too. Winterbourne is my new home.

"Alice, aren't you hungry?" Edmund is gazing inquiringly at me.

I look down at my untouched bowl. I ought to be famished for the energy I've expended, but the mere proximity of Jonathan is enough to sate my appetite.

"I'm quite all right, darling," I say, holding my hands in my lap because I am afraid their tremble will give me away. "Would you like to be excused?"

It is as if I am addressing their father, because at once Jonathan stands from the table, lets his newspaper drop to his chair and abruptly leaves the room. The children scramble to follow, to get ready for the classroom, though I have no idea how I will gather my thoughts for the morning. I finish my coffee and hope for the best.

At lunchtime, Henry Marsh arrives at the house. I meet him coming away from his appointment with Jonathan, his doctor's bag in hand.

"Alice!" He greets me in the hall, his smile wide. "I was hoping to see you."

"Yes. I'm sorry I haven't been in touch."

"Would you have time for a walk?"

I nod. It must be done, and sooner rather than later.

We step outside. The day is fresh, its

autumn colors fading. Leaves are beginning to fall and the high branches of trees shiver naked against the sky. The grass is damp with frozen dew. Ravens caw amid the topiary.

"How is the captain today?" I ask as we head down the slopes toward the lake. Henry walks close enough to me that the material of his jacket grazes my elbow. I wonder if Jonathan is watching us. Part of me wishes him to.

"Not quite himself," Henry replies, with a frown. "His mind seemed occupied. I don't suppose you'd know by what? Are the children in good spirits?"

"They're very well."

Henry shakes his head; I think what a kind face he has, open and willing. Just the kind of man my parents would have urged me toward, a sensible medical man.

"I oughtn't to discuss this with you, Alice, but . . ." We stop by the reeds, the little copse behind us; the doctor has ensured we are out of sight of the house. "But since our outing last week, I have confidence to. I fear that Jonathan is against me."

"Against you?" I am surprised. "How?"

"He does not trust me. I used to have his trust, but I don't any more."

Elation washes through me. *I know why,* I

think. *He doesn't trust you because he's resentful of our friendship. He cannot stand another man taking what he desires!*

"We had a good relationship when I first started treating him," says Henry, "when he first came back from the war. But something changed before Laura died. He withdrew from me; it's difficult to explain, and I suppose I ought to be able, making my business from explanations. Jonathan no longer opened up to me. What promised to grow into friendship shrank to mere professionalism. Well, I oughtn't to mind, I know, after all I am here to tend his injuries, but I wish I knew the grounds of it."

I consider, then, that it can't be about me. Not if it started before Laura died.

"Never mind," he says hurriedly, "I shouldn't have bothered you with it."

"I wish I could help," I say. "But I wouldn't know what to advise."

"Of course not."

"I could speak with him, if you think that would benefit?"

Henry looks perplexed. "You have that closeness?"

"Why wouldn't we?"

He checks behind him, as if fearful someone has joined us. "I assumed a governess might not approach her employer on a personal matter."

"And I take it you would rather I did not on this one."

Henry still wears a look of confusion, but then he smiles and it dissolves.

"Alice, I'm glad to see you today." He takes my hands. "I wondered when I would again. My dear, I've thought of little but you. Tell me you have felt the same."

I take my hands away.

"It's all right," he urges, "there is nobody here."

"I know there isn't," I say, hating to hurt this good man but knowing that I must. "But Henry, it's only fair that I tell you the truth. I admire you as a doctor and respect you as a friend but it can be nothing more. I hope you understand."

A moment passes. Hurt crosses his features, before he straightens.

"Of course I understand, Miss Miller."

"It's a personal . . . complication," I say, not wanting him to think it is any shortcoming of his. "My circumstances have changed."

"Is it him?"

"I'm sorry?"

"The captain, has he forbid you from meeting me?" Henry seems ignited by this idea, and turns back to the house.

"No!" I stop him. "No, it's not. Nothing like that."

If only I could tell him. I am bursting to tell someone, a friend like Betty, whom I volunteered with in the war, a girl I can relive it with, who will clamor for all the details and I would be only too happy to divulge them. But I can't.

"But you don't wish to see me again," he says.

"It isn't possible. I'm very sorry, Henry."

After a moment he nods, assembling himself, and proceeds to act with dignity. He takes my hands again but this time it is definite, firmer, as if readying an ally to advance into the fray. "You be careful, Miss Miller," he says. His next words falter. "You're an exceptional woman. I don't know if you have been told that before, but you are. Jonathan and his children are lucky to have you at Winterbourne."

"Thank you."

He lingers, as if unsure whether to say more. But there is clearly nothing more to say, for he drops my hands and turns back up the hill, to return to his car.

I wait until the rumble of Henry's car has faded completely before I move. It is growing cold; the gusts of wind that blow in off the sea are sharp with winter's bite.

I delay my return to the house while I reflect on what I have done. In abandoning the doctor I have abandoned any reason to hold back: nothing, now, stands in Jonathan's and my way. Despite the chill I am filled with heat.

It is with some uncertainty that, as I approach the drive, I see the ancient Rolls-Royce parked out front. Tom has the bonnet up. "Are we going somewhere?" I ask.

Tom wipes his hands on an oilcloth and slams the bonnet shut.

"You'll need to ask the cook about that."

When I step inside, I understand what is happening. Mrs. Yarrow had meant what she said when we spoke. The cook is surrounded by a collection of her bags. When she sees me she kneels to the children, kissing both of them goodbye.

Jonathan is on the stairs. I feel him before I see him. He leans on his cane, and I long to run to him and ease his suffering but he does not glance my way.

"Mrs. Yarrow . . . ?" I start.

The cook faces me. We have not spoken since our dispute and it saddens me that her expression is closed, as if she is meeting me for the first time, hello and goodbye, as if none of our confidences have passed and

313

none of our hours been shared. "The Norfolk house came good, miss," she says detachedly. "My sister will be waiting for me there. It's been a pleasure knowing you, miss."

Her words are flat. I look to the children for emotion but they show little: it is impossible to know if they are upset by the cook's departure or not. Another woman gone, another carer leaving, is it any wonder they greet it with fortitude? I am furious with Mrs. Yarrow. *I will never abandon them,* I vow. *They will have to drag me out of here in a wooden box before that happens.*

"I wish you the best, Mrs. Yarrow," I say. "Winterbourne will miss you."

The cook lifts her chin, silently defiant. I expect she is waiting for an apology but I cannot give it. I stand by my refusal to entertain her treacherous imaginings and, in any case, it would be reckless to rake over our fight in front of the de Greys.

"Why are you going?" Constance asks the cook. She comes to take my hand, and I, only too pleased to be her anchor, draw her close.

"I've been here a long time, lovey," says Mrs. Yarrow. "It's time for a change."

"But why?"

"I'm getting old. My family lives far away

and I'd rather be close to them."

"Aren't you sad to say goodbye?"

"I am, dear, but it's the right decision. Your father understands."

Again, I try to engage with Jonathan but he merely nods his assent. The cook opens the door, lingering on the handle. She looks behind her one last time, seeming to inhale the many years she's spent in Winterbourne's service.

Outside, once Tom has packed the bags into the car, he suggests we take a group photograph. "Everybody against the house — what do you think, Captain?"

"Very well."

As a couple we stand together, the children in front, our hands resting on their shoulders. All is right in the world, all is just. Mrs. Yarrow does not wish to take part — "I'm not one for photographs," she says tightly — so we are about to disband for surely her presence is the point, before Tom offers to arrange for the image to be dispatched to Mrs. Yarrow at her new post, as a memento. The camera clicks and the four of us, the de Grey family, he and I and our beautiful children, are caught in a moment. With Winterbourne gazing approvingly on, my happiness is enough for us all.

Mrs. Yarrow climbs into the car. She does

not look at us.

The Rolls moves off.

"Back to class, children," I say, briskly clapping my hands. Edmund takes his sister's arm and together they return inside the house. I want to speak with Jonathan, and imagine that this is our chance, but before I can he has followed them.

Early evening, I prepare the children's supper. The kitchen seems strange without Mrs. Yarrow. I keep stumbling across her ghosts: the chipped postbox-red mug she insisted on using for tea; the neatly folded napkins in the scullery drawer, organized by color; the jar of sweets she kept in the pantry for when the twins were sickly.

"I don't like it," says Edmund, prodding his potatoes with his fork.

"Come along, darling," I encourage, "it's your favorite."

"No, it's not. I only like it how Cook does it."

"Well, Cook isn't here any more," I say, "so you'll learn to like this instead."

Constance starts crying. "Did Father send her away?" she asks.

"Of course not!"

"We didn't have to get rid of her; she didn't mean Winterbourne any harm."

"Of course she didn't," I say, thinking it an odd thing to say.

"Then why did she go?"

I put my arms round both their shoulders. "You heard what Mrs. Yarrow said," I soothe. "She wanted to see her sister and be close to where she grew up. When you're grown up, won't you want to stay close to Winterbourne?"

"I won't," says Edmund.

"Whyever not?"

He lifts his shoulders. I remember what he said in the classroom that day about Jonathan not allowing them to attend school. *Father's afraid.* "I'll be tired," he says.

"Of what?"

"Of doing what I'm told."

I laugh. "You'll be an adult, then, Edmund. You'll be surprised at what you can do independently from your father."

"I'm not talking about him," he says.

"Then who?"

The boy looks at Constance. And she, swiftly changing the subject, asks:

"What's that? Have you hurt yourself?"

Instantly I put a hand to my neck. The marks on my skin have spread, more ferociously since my encounter with the captain; now they have crept up my chest, over my shoulders, climbing my throat. Constance has noticed the crimson scratch above my collar. I thought I had covered it up, but evidently not sufficiently.

"It's nothing, sweetheart; I snagged myself on a necklace."

When I saw in Laura's mirror how the marks had multiplied, though, I fretted at the captain's reaction. Had he observed them, and been appalled? But there had not been this many last evening, I am sure. They have reproduced tenfold today. And when I consulted the girl in the painting, she was waiting for me with a smile. I have grown used to her subtle changes; I have come to expect them. It seems that with every leap I take at Winterbourne — owning the mirror, owning the children, owning, now, the man of the house — she grows and morphs before my eyes. My dark companion.

"It must have been sore," says Edmund, and both children watch me indulgently, and I cannot decipher if I am reading sympathy or derision.

"It was at the time," I answer, "but not any more."

In the end, I clear the meat and potatoes away and offer them pudding instead. Afterward we read by the fire, and all I have in my mind is to be their comfort. I stroke their foreheads as we read, and with their bodies snuggled up against mine I feel utterly at peace. The best part of the evening is surely yet to come.

With the twins safely tucked up in bed, I prepare Jonathan's meal and take it to him. A sliver of light escapes his study door, promising the heat within; will we make love on his desk of papers, will he fling his photographs of Laura to the wall?

Laura. Did she carry her husband's supper on a tray, like I do? Did she wait here, outside this room, shivering in anticipation of his embrace?

"Come in," he says when I knock.

"I've brought you some food," I say, setting down the tray. His back is to me; he faces the fire. For what seems like a long time, I wait, before at last he turns. His hands are steepled beneath his chin. His blue eyes shine in the flickering light. I feel stripped, of my clothes, my defenses, of everything I had planned to say. *Jonathan . . .*

"Sit down, Miss Miller," he says. I do.

"If this is about Mrs. Yarrow leaving," I say, "you needn't worry. I can handle her role as well as my own. I know it could be an adjustment for us all but when I accepted

319

this position I was aware there might be additional responsibilities —"

"It isn't about Mrs. Yarrow," says Jonathan. "Although, on that note, I will be hiring a housekeeper: I believe it to be the best course of action on every front."

"Really, Jonathan, that isn't necessary."

His eyebrow lifts, unkindly.

"You will address me as Captain, Miss Miller," he says. "Is that quite clear?"

"Forgive me." I look to my lap, humiliation burning. I wonder if this is his idea of a game, an added spice to our dalliance. I should continue to observe his authority and address him correctly as such. I raise my head. "Forgive me," I say again.

"Hiring a housekeeper is perfectly necessary," he says, returning to point. "These responsibilities are too much to manage on your own."

"But I wish to manage them."

He narrows his eyes. "And I wish to hire." Promptly, he stands. "I fear you are forgetting your place here, Miss Miller. I do not abide my employees challenging my will, nor do I accept their speaking to me as if we are equals. You are my subordinate: you care for my children and that is where it ends. You are a governess, and you remain at Winterbourne only at my discretion." He clears his throat, gruffly. "Given what happened between us last night," he says, "I ought to dismiss you immediately. But my children are fond of you. I have enjoyed watching them respond to your teaching and I believe you have their best interests at heart."

"I do! But, Captain —"

"So I will extend you this courtesy and allow you to stay. But the condition is this. We will, neither of us, speak of the madness that overcame us in the chapel yesterday evening. I am sure you are as regretful of it as I. I must certainly have taken leave of my senses and I apologize for the situation I put you in."

"There is no need to be sorry." My mouth is numb. My heart is numb. Jonathan goes to the window, where freezing rain slices against the panes.

"A reckless illusion," he says, in a gentler voice, "that is all it was. Miss Miller, I mistook you for another woman. I mistook you for my wife. Truly, I am sorry."

I long to object. *You didn't mistake me for her, you didn't! Not the whole time! Not when you were looking into my eyes, you saw me, you did!* But I stay where I am, fingers clasped, and all I can think about is his supper growing cold.

He said a new housekeeper would be the best action "on every front." Does that include, then, implementing distance between us? Disgrace floods through me, imagining like a foolish child that he felt as I did when all along he was seeking out ways to avoid us being together. It would seem a horror to him to be at Winterbourne with just his children and me, where, to me, it would seem a heaven.

Stupid Alice, stop daydreaming! You silly, stupid girl!

"Do you hear me, Miss Miller?" he says softly, and turns to face me.

I only meet his eyes for a heartbeat before it becomes too painful. I can still feel his touch on my skin, and it is scarcely possible that this time twenty-four hours ago we were entwined, when now we are strangers. "Yes," I answer. "I hear you."

CHAPTER 24

ALICE, SURREY, NOVEMBER 1940

Tick tock, tick tock, tick tock . . .

The dining room was stifling hot. Fire roared in the hearth and my dress stuck to my back. I had never liked that clock, with its shagreen, lizardy casing and its way of spitting out seconds like someone trying to clear their mouth of orange pith.

It was torturous. Waiting. Waiting. Beef fritter congealing on my plate, and it was the plate with the flaked rim that we had used to give to Grandma because she said it had "character." I wished for character, then. I wished for bravery.

"What's the matter, girl?" said my father. The three of us were sitting for lunch. It was Sunday, after church, and he held fort at the helm of the table, masticating bread pudding. I loathed the way he ate. "Food not good enough for you?"

"I'm not hungry," I said, withering beneath my father's glare. *Tick tock, tick tock, tick tock* . . . Every second tormented me. *Do it. Say it now.*

"I need a drink," said my mother, pushing back her chair and rising unsteadily to her feet. My father muttered something. I didn't need to hear what.

Could I blame her for her depression? No, I could not. Trapped in this house with him, his demands and his put-downs, his subtle tyranny. And it was subtle. There was no shouting, no beating or bruising. Other women had it worse; she'd even said that to me once. It was difficult to know which had come first, his cruelty or her drinking. Each fed the other. For days my mother would take to her bed (they no longer shared a room) and the house would "fall to rack and ruin." He wanted a diligent wife, one who took as much pride in her homestead as she did in her appearance. As I watched my mother shuffle from the dining room, hair unbrushed and a stoop to her shoulders, I wondered if he took other women. It was likely. And it would make his imminent demonstration of morality an even bitterer pill to swallow.

I could have benefited from alcohol as well, but of course I didn't admit it. My father sliced his fritter, slopped out meaty gravy; I watched its brown gloop clinging to the neck of the gravy boat, before he caught it with a finger and licked it clean. The heat from the fire made everything fatter and more sickening, too close, too much.

I'll do it when she comes back, I thought.

But she did come back, gin in shaking hand, and I stayed silent. So many times I had rehearsed the words, the order of them: some magical, elusive sequence that would mitigate my transgression, make it sound milder. It seemed impossible to embark on the confession, as unlikely as stepping off a tall building into thin air.

The girls at Burstead had mostly done away with their parents. At the start of term they had been dropped at the gates by an employee of their family, the girl's own mother and father either too busy or else preoccupied abroad. There had been a collective sense right from the start, as we lay in our dormitories staring into the night, of necessary amputation. For me, aged ten, it had been a precise rejection — my parents didn't want me, I doubted that they had ever wanted me — and if I was to survive then I would need to learn to fend for myself. For others it was less clear-cut; they might have been lavished with love and promised that Burstead was in their best interests, but the seed of resentment remained and grew. We had been let go. Our childhood was over. Our parents were breathing a sigh of relief.

"I don't care a bit for my lot," Ginny Pettifer had used to say, somewhat proudly, as she shirked lacrosse in favor of painting her toenails in the daygirls' study room. *"And they don't care for me."* Her family was like a group of people introduced at a party, she'd claimed, quickly realizing they didn't like each other but knowing they were stuck. Ginny was an only child, too. Plenty of Burstead girls were.

I could barely think of Ginny. Each hour she crawled and crept on the periphery of my imaginings, an incessant knuckle on a locked door. I saw her in dreams; I met her in nightmares. Our year's leaving assembly had been a hushed affair, an echo of the funeral that some of us would make and some of us wouldn't. I didn't go. How could I have? Instead I spent the day in bed, claiming a headache.

"What is the problem with you women?" my father said as he completed his meal and pushed his plate away. "This country's at war and you let good food go to waste?" He wiped his mouth with a napkin; I noticed the graying hairs on the backs of his hands, and the skin beneath, papery and thin. My father had always seemed old, even when he was young. "How about pudding, Maud?" He trained his eye on his wife, that same hawk eye that had pursued me all my life, ever watchful, ever judgmental: nothing was good enough for that hawk eye; nothing was sufficient.

I heard my mother move from her chair. Opposite me, the empty side of the table was charged with absence. What might it have been like to have a sibling? Where would the power have lain, then? For that was the word I associated with him. *Power.* He had the power to crush me, not physically but with words, with criticism.

Often I questioned why they had gone ahead with a child at all. Once or twice my mother had admitted I'd been a mistake, only to retract it at a later point. As if such a thing could be retracted. When my grandmother died, they came into money. My father, in his arrogance, spent it quickly, and one of his indulgences was my Burstead education. *At last we can get rid of her,* I imagined him saying. Perhaps he hadn't said that, but I could hear it as immediately as if he were speaking it now.

Outside, in the garden, a robin hopped across the barren lawn. It paused and dipped its tail, seeming to look in at me. I wished to be that bird. I longed to fly away. *But then there would be no Robert,* I reminded myself, and my heart lifted in hope.

I will fly away, I thought. *We will fly away together.* That was the reason I was here. Robert was the reason for everything. And if we had a chance of a future together, I would have to be strong. My parents had to be told.

"It's burned."

My mother came back in with a pear crumble.

Tick tock, tick tock, tick tock . . .

"I'm pregnant," I said.

My mother dropped her glass. I dropped with it. I had jumped. Thin air beneath me, the ground hurtling up.

"We're engaged to be married," I said, the ground rushing closer. "We love each other. I'm moving to London. We're going to start our lives together."

I met my mother's gaze, insipid with shock and gin and dismay.

Then my father started laughing. I had braced myself for wrath, for thunder, and to hear his snicker was sinister and shocking. It was a reedy, cruel laugh, a laugh so pitiful and mean that the justifications and defenses I'd prepared evaporated.

"Presumably you're getting rid of it."

328

I shook my head.

My father's fist struck the table, with such impact that the china shuddered.

"I am going to ask you that question again, Alice, so think very carefully."

"We love each other," I repeated. It was all I could say, all that meant anything. I kept thinking: *As long as we love each other, nothing else matters.*

"If you suppose for one moment that I will stand for my name to be dragged through the gutter by some local delinquent —"

"He isn't local." But I couldn't say who he was. Robert had forbid it. I agreed, if for nothing else than to avoid making worse an already scandalous confession.

"Then who is he?"

"Nobody you know."

"Tell me now, girl," my father roared.

"I cannot."

"Wrong. What you cannot do is pursue this situation."

"I am keeping our baby, whether it suits you or not."

My father's quietness was the most horrifying thing of all. I searched the garden to find my robin but she had gone; only the murky yellow lawn stared back at me, mulched with autumn's leaves. I sensed his panicked mind working, piecing it together, the disgrace, the illicit affair, until he arrived at the most reprehensible act of all — the impossible pregnancy, its inescapable fact and inevitable conclusion, a conclusion that would affect not just me (for what did he care for me?) but his own repute. The shame of a daughter who would commit such a felony! My mother whimpered, sitting in front of her burned pear crumble. I looked to her, hoping for support, for in what other aspect of life should a mother be closer to her daughter? But I saw only fear. Her fear of her husband was greater than her love for her child.

I knew then that I should never have come back. It had been futile to imagine they could offer me anything. I had held fast to a blind hope, close to desperation, that they might have opened their arms and told me they would help me and that everything would be all right. Robert would return from the war. He would survive. We would be married. Our baby would arrive safely and there was nothing to dread.

It turned out I was the fool my father always told me I was. A desperate fool, because this was the end of my ideas, this hurtful house and these hurtful people my last remaining options. In London, I had told no one. Bombs were falling. The city was frightening. I had a life inside me, tentative and precious, but I was terrified. I felt utterly alone. If they did not help me, I didn't know what I would do.

"If you think this man will stay with you, Alice, you are wrong." My father stood from the table. There was no bang, no explosion, just a silent uprising. "He'll swear to you that he will. He'll promise you marriage. He might even remain at your side until the child arrives. But after that . . ." His eyes met my mother, her head bowed, silent tears flowing. "We all know what having a child does to a woman."

I tried not to let his words touch me. But they did. I didn't want to be like my mother, to sit here defeated, yet the insinuation that her unhappy state was my fault, was a result of my very existence, was hard to bear. It wasn't true. It was my father's cruelty. But I also knew that that same cruelty was responsible for my own so-called affliction: my "nervous disposition"; my urge to hide in daydreams, to invent worlds that I could inhabit, worlds where I mattered and I was loved. I had none of that here.

Robert didn't know about the pregnancy. He had left to fight before I knew for certain. But I wasn't going to tell my parents that. I wasn't going to hear my father crow about how Robert would abandon me as soon as he discovered it. I knew that Robert wouldn't. A voice whispered inside me: *Do you? Do you really?* Because if Robert knew about Ginny — if anyone knew about Ginny — it would all be over.

My father tried a different tack. He leaned in close, conspiratorially. "You have every reason to put an end to this," he said. "I know a man who can do it."

"I can't," I said.

"He's a vet. It isn't so different. You'll be in and out in a day."

"I don't want to."

"You have no choice."

I looked at him. "Yes, I do," I said firmly. And even if that choice sent me rushing into the abyss, which I surely knew it would, for no girl in my position could possibly make it work, not here, not now, not unmarried at the turn of a new decade with no money or means of support, at least it was a choice I had taken away from him. I knew the reasons why I should not proceed, too many to count, and maybe if I had loved my parents and been afraid of losing them it might have made a difference. But I believed in Robert more. I believed in us. I believed in my reveries about our future together.

Content. Secure. I believed that everything would work out.

And I had paid a price for this. I had protected our affair at the highest cost.

My pregnancy was one life in exchange for another. It was my retribution, my chance to forge something good from the turmoil I had created.

My father picked up his plate and hurled it against the window, where it smashed and left a brown smear across the panes. "I always knew you were impressionable, Alice, but this . . ." He shook his head. "You idiot child — this man of yours doesn't love you. You're nothing but a silly toy he picked up. After what happened to that girl in your year, you'd think you might have more sense, learn to behave, look after yourself. But no, not you." His voice grew quiet. "At first we thought there was something the matter with you. If you'd been a boy, you'd have had more sense. Less time to waste getting caught up in your nerves, you'd have been doing, building, fixing." He delivered this with such hostility that I watched the empty side of the table again, wondering. "But no," he said, "it was just you. And now you're doing it again. Residing inside these pointless fictions that will get you nowhere. Imagining you can survive this. You won't survive this."

"It isn't fiction. It's real."

"I'll tell you what's real," he said savagely. "The war on our doorstep is real. Wake up, little girl. These are difficult times. Have you thought about the outcome of your choice? When your precious lover deserts you — because he will, make no mistake about that — what are your plans, then? Have you thought that far ahead?"

"We'll find a way to stay together. We'll always be together."

"You're a damned fool!" He struck the table.

"Please, Charles — !" begged my mother.

But I didn't need her. I had the shiver of a shadow of something wonderful inside me, deep inside where he couldn't touch it. I pushed back my chair with a scrape and met my father head-on. I hadn't realized until that moment that I was taller than him, not much, but a fraction. He appeared pathetic, small, tragic.

"How would you know what I am? You don't know anything about me."

"I know you're a silly, stupid girl and I'm ashamed to call you my daughter. Do you know how ashamed I am?"

"Your shame can drive you to the grave, for all I care."

My mother started crying.

"I'm sorry, Mother," I said, pulling open the door and refusing to look behind, "but I fear I will not see you again. Please understand my decision."

"Charles, stop her!"

But my father could not stop me. He did not want to stop me. He wanted me as far away from this house as possible; he wanted to pretend I had never been here, to never speak of me again, his disgrace of a daughter, his rotten flesh and blood.

CHAPTER 25

CORNWALL, PRESENT DAY

The morning after Jack's party, Rachel climbed the two flights of stairs to reach Constance de Grey's bedroom. She hadn't ventured here since she had first arrived. Now, it seemed the obvious place to look. Constance had been the last person to leave Winterbourne. Could she have been protecting the key to its history?

The climb was an effort due to her hangover. She hoped to find a distraction — and did, right away, for the bedroom door was unexpectedly open. Rachel stopped, smiled, and it seemed funny for an instant, as if someone was messing with her. She was *certain* she had closed this door on the first day with some force, hadn't she? Seeing it now, she couldn't have. Ignoring her anxiety, she stepped through.

Inside, Constance's room was stuffy considering it was unlived in, as if it had recently held living, breathing bodies. The

336

two single beds were as she remembered, the old woman's walking frame and drinking apparatus a reminder of her latterly decrepit state. There was a faint odor of lavender, which Rachel supposed came from her aunt's clothes; certainly, after Seth died, his belongings retained a scent for far too long. Too long because with every inhalation, every time she held one of his shirts to her face and breathed him in, her agony was refreshed. Months on from the event, she begged his trace to leave her. In time, she found courage to give his clothes away. She kept just one sweater, and on those vulnerable occasions where she needed to hold it, it smelled a little old, a little musty, but nothing more.

Had she been wrong to tell Jack about Seth? She had never shared the truth with anyone — it was too personal, too painful, and exposed the fragile points she preferred to keep hidden. Yet the moment had been right. Cornwall was loosening her defenses, opening her up to the realization that she didn't have to be alone. Had she left the old Rachel behind in New York, struggling at a desk or chained to a phone, or had the real her been here all along, at Winterbourne, waiting to be found?

She went to the old woman's closet, a

lumbering beast made of dark wood, and switched the little key in the door. Inside, the lavender aroma was strong. She ran her fingers over an array of fabrics that seemed to be from every stage of her aunt's life: pretty summer dresses, light as lace, perfect for a sixteen-year-old Constance; a weighty fur she might have worn in her middle age; a lavish fox stole, the animal's head and tail still attached and its glassy eyes shot; a collection of pastel silk blouses that were like water to touch; and several heavy ruched skirts that made Rachel think of stuffy librarians checking overdue fines. There were a few pairs of shoes at the foot of the wardrobe but no sign of what she was searching for.

It didn't take long to scour the rest of the space because it was so sparsely furnished. A chest of drawers revealed little except handkerchiefs and smelling salts, and a box that appeared promising held only pearls. She dropped to her knees to inspect the room from a different angle — and, immediately, spotted it.

The trunk was strapped shut with leather buckles, the kind that belonged on Victorian train platforms next to unaccompanied young boys wearing shorts and knee socks. Rachel expected it to be heavy, maybe unbearably so, but it was surprisingly light and it took only a few attempts to drag it out from underneath Constance's bed. She sneezed from the dust; yet within the powder was the unmistakable pattern of fingerprints, making her think that someone had accessed the trunk relatively recently. To her amazement, the straps unbuckled and the lid swung open without fuss. Inside the top it was handsomely printed: DE GREY, WINTERBOURNE, CORNWALL. A four-word address, no further details needed.

At first she thought it held schoolbooks, dozens of them, some thick with good-quality covers, others notepads that were falling apart at their spines. On some Constance had scribbled her name in a juvenile hand; others were blank. Some were ink-blotched and age-stained; others appeared new, as if they had been bought last week in the newsagent's in Polcreath. Rachel flicked through one, then the next. All contained the same thing: the elaborate handwritten scrawl of Constance de Grey.

It was difficult to work out the chronology. Constance hadn't dated any of her diaries, nor were the books conventionally laid out in weeks and months. Instead they showed a near-continuous soliloquy running across lined pages that might just as easily have been used for shopping lists. The only clue Rachel had was the progression of the writing itself, and that wasn't always reliable. Frequently she would find herself in the middle of a journal, having decided she was reading a teenage Constance, when suddenly a note would bring her up short: a reference to some anachronism like a TV, or else Edmund's thirtieth birthday, which of course would also have been her own.

For hours, she didn't move from that spot in the twins' bedroom. She forgot about her hangover, about Jack, about the chill prickling through the thick yarn of her sweater — even, for the very first time, she forgot about Seth — and the day started to fade, the morning's sun smothered in cloud by lunchtime and drizzling gray by three. Still, she kept reading. It was hard to know how consistently the diaries had been kept. Swathes of time were missing, and Rachel found herself jumping from one childish book to another, more mature one, with seemingly no stepping-stone in between. Some of the entries detailed the conventional musings of a growing girl — observations about Winterbourne, frustrations against her schoolwork, in her teenage years a boy in Polcreath she had dared to hold

hands with — while others were more
bizarre. Constance referred a lot, throughout her life, to an unnamed female:
  She's horrible to me.
  *She's doing it again. Pinching me at night.
Telling me things.*
  *She should never have told us to do it. Now
look what's happened!*
Her first thought was that this had been a
woman employed at Winterbourne, some
cruel professor their father had hired — but
then Rachel would come across a troubling
entry such as, *"Why did she make us play
such a trick? Now it's our fault they're dead,
every one of them, dead!"* scratched in a
manic hand, and wonder that Constance
could be talking about a living being at all
and not some figment of her (evidently)
rather wild imagination. But who had died?
Who had been killed?
  The anonymous pronouns were troublesome. Rachel pondered if the lack of names
was less to do with Constance's familiarity
with whomever she was talking about and
more to do with protecting the identity of
those involved. It was tantalizing to be so
near to her aunt's secrets, yet frustrating to
be deprived of so many contexts. Constance
never needed to qualify her statements. She
had no need to explain for the benefit of a

reader because she was writing for herself, no one else. But then she would say, *"I wonder if my diaries will ever be found. What would they make of our wickedness? If you're there, reader, hello! And goodbye. It is all of it made up."*

A disturbing thought needled at Rachel: that one of the people at the butt of the children's "tricks" was Rachel's own grandmother, Alice Miller. That the asylum hadn't been the worst of it for Alice. Death had come after. *Every one of them, dead!*

Rachel snapped shut the journal she was reading. She forced herself to stop getting carried away. She hadn't even the facts to suggest that Alice Miller *was* her grandmother — it was nothing but a hunch.

Outside, afternoon crept toward evening. Rachel had spent hours immersed in the journals and her stomach moaned with hunger. Folding the book under one arm, she headed downstairs. Had Constance meant for her diaries to be found? In telling the London solicitors about Rachel's existence, had she hoped it would be Rachel's hand that unearthed them? Constance might not have thought about the text being read at the time she wrote it, but an old woman at the end of her life, bathed in secrets, afraid of death . . . The diaries were

342

a confession: Constance's chance at atonement.

In the hall, Rachel passed the mirror that she and Jack had excavated from the cellar. It really was a beastly-looking thing. Who had it belonged to? Its ornate frame resembled a drowning girl's hair, animated in the firelight. Rachel paused in front of it. She looked odd in the glass, not quite herself. Its edges were dappled and a yellow stain crept across the image. Rachel had the impression that she was separate from the person she was looking at, as if they had been peeled apart, as if the woman in front of her could quite easily make a gesture that Rachel, in the real world, had not.

The thought was ghastly. With some effort, she forced the mirror round so it was facing the wood panels, the reverse of it sticky with cobwebs and a whisker-thin spider that picked its way across threads. As she did, she noticed two initials and a surname carved into the back. They were tiny and could easily have been missed, but Rachel was used to deciphering details on old pieces. The letters read: *M. C. Sinnett.*

She frowned. For some reason, a distant chime rang in her mind. She recognized that name, she'd seen it before, but she couldn't say where.

343

As Rachel walked to the kitchen, she felt as if she had left a stranger standing alone, turned to the wall, waiting for her return. She had the sense that her likeness might still be caught inside the mirror. That if she were to return and swing it back round she would see her image as she had left it moments before.

Rachel fixed a sandwich and ate it without appetite, the diary at her side. The Constance writing this diary was elderly: Rachel knew by the spindly script that spun across the pages, and the book itself couldn't have been more than a year or two old. Some of the entries were virtually illegible, others appearing to make no sense at all, and sewn into every line was the writer's aggravation at her depleted state. In clearer moments there were memories of the house, her father, of someone called Tom who lived with the family, and one jotting about "him" (her brother?) that reminded Rachel of the exchange she'd had with the cab driver when she first arrived in Polcreath: something about Edmund being . . . what words had he used? "Gone in the head."

She got him in the end, Constance wrote. *She sent him mad. She shook him so hard he lost his brains. She whispered to him too many times, horrible things, haunting things, poisonous things that addled his mind and made him wish to follow her. He wished to follow her to whatever dark sphere she had come from and he said the only way he could do that was to do what Mother did . . . I have spent most of my grown life trying to stop him. And it's how she got me too, you see, because I had to stay behind to look after him. I could never have found a husband, or had a family of my own at Winterbourne, not with a brother like that. She never wanted me to. She doesn't want ANYONE to be happy here. Winterbourne is HERS and it always will be.*

And then, several pages on, there was this:

We are cursed, all of us. I always knew the curse. I knew the curse from when I was a girl. I felt it. I saw it in shadows. At first I thought it was a friend, someone else to play with. But the games it wanted to play were evil. Mother died. Then Christine died. Then Alice died.

Women. It hates the women.

Rachel read those lines over and over again. They made her afraid.

But she hadn't time to think, because Alice Miller's name appeared on the line after, and the line after that, pulling her deeper down the rabbit hole . . .

Only poor Alice didn't die as quickly as the others. Winterbourne enjoyed its game with her. It made her believe in happiness and then it made her suffer. It made her and her baby suffer. Father didn't know at first that I found out about the baby. He didn't know that I kept Alice's letters from him. She sent so many from where they locked her up but I didn't want him to see, so I waited for the post to arrive each day and I took what I needed. It was for his benefit. He already had us. He would never have wanted a baby. I never even told Edmund that. It was mine.

CHAPTER 26

Rachel woke in a chair by the fire, now dwindled to smoking ash. Disoriented, she consulted her watch and saw it was just past ten. She couldn't recall what time she had fallen asleep. Her hands and feet were numb; one of the diaries was splayed open on her lap. Slowly, glimpses of the previous night's discoveries drifted into her mind.

With a stiff neck she leaned in to encourage the fire, stoking the last ember, blowing on it to bring it back to life. At the first flicker she rested another log and listened to it crackle and burn. *Alice Miller. My grandmother . . .* For Alice had to be — and the baby she had birthed in incarceration was Rachel's mother.

It was a lot to take in. Alice must have suffered such fear and rejection, or seeming rejection, for Jonathan de Grey had apparently never known about the pregnancy thanks to Constance's wiles. And her baby,

Rachel's mother: had she been loved, cared for, had she been looked after? It seemed vital that she had; Rachel couldn't bear it otherwise. But the picture she'd carried all these years of her mother as a functioning, well-adjusted woman who simply hadn't wanted her, a perfectly adequate mother who was able to care for a child (perhaps she'd gone on to have other children?) but just hadn't wanted this one, was broken. Rachel's mother had been born into turmoil. She would never grasp the truth of whatever institution Alice had been locked up in. Why had Alice been locked up? What had she done wrong?

Conclusions pooled in terrifying forms. How Rachel longed for the ghosts of Winterbourne to come alive. How she longed for answers: answers that Constance de Grey's memories were too afraid to give — or that Rachel was too afraid to read.

An itch had nagged at the back of her mind since the previous afternoon. She stood and headed up to her bedroom, where she went straight to the little painting on the wall. She stood before it, her arms wrapped round herself because suddenly it felt cold, and she watched that eerie open window in the upstairs of the cottage, half expecting a figure to appear at it, or a hand to have crept insidiously over the sill.

But the window, as before, was empty: a dark square against a dark night. Rachel's eyes traveled down to the frame and then there it was, tucked into the corner: the name she'd suspected since she'd turned the mirror around in the hall.

M. C. Sinnett.

It was signed in a ragged, virtually illegible hand.

M. C. Sinnett: owner of the mirror and painter of the cottage. Had this woman lived at the house once? Was she connected to a de Grey? Perhaps she was simply an artist whom the family had admired, and they had sought to purchase her work?

Rachel frowned and ran a finger across the name. She looked once more at that empty window, the curtain inside it blowing against a murmuring wind, and was so immersed in the impression of solitude and, somehow, deep sadness, that when a battering descended on the door downstairs, she stepped back and gasped in fear.

Her first thought was that it was Jack, and as she hurried down through the hall to open it she didn't care to analyze why she hastily twisted the mirror back round to inspect her reflection. What she saw wasn't good. Her hair was a nest; her smudged eyes were rimmed and her clothes were the same slouchy ones as yesterday, only now they carried a smoky, musty scent that wasn't just to do with the fire but with the house itself. Oh, she thought, who cared? It was just Jack. But all the same she was pleased to see him, she realized, and would be glad of his company after an unsettling twenty-four hours. She tied her hair back and pinched the skin on her cheeks.

Rachel opened the door, not realizing how much she had lifted at the prospect of seeing Jack until it wasn't him. It was someone else — someone so incongruous with Winterbourne that he might as well have landed from outer space.

Aaron Grewal.

"Aaron," she stammered. "What are you doing here?"

"Hello, stranger," he answered, the bouquet of flowers in his arms so huge that it obscured his head. When he was able to get a clear view of her, he struggled to conceal his surprise. Rachel imagined how she must look, in scuffed jeans, a shapeless sweater and no makeup. It was a far cry from her image in New York.

"You look great," he said, compelled toward the lie because the truth was too flagrant. "Are you surprised to see me? Here, these are for you. Obviously."

She took the flowers and stood back to let him in. He embraced her, kissed her cheek but not her lips, and gazed up in wonder at the enormity of Winterbourne's hall.

"Wow," he said. "This is something else."

Rachel marveled, too, at the arrival of this gleaming man. Aaron appeared artificial, like a 1930s actor superimposed on a beach scene. He wore a crisp shirt tucked into pressed jeans, and his brogues shone like fall conkers. When she went to close the door, she saw a glistening Porsche parked on the drive, and couldn't help but think of Jack's beaten-up old Land Rover that was filled with dog blankets and chewed-up cassette tapes. She took in Aaron's perfectly shaved jaw and thick, coiffed hair. What had people made of him in Polcreath? Had he been recognized? Then she realized that of course he wouldn't have come that way. He'd have flown by private jet straight into London, then picked up the Porsche and driven down from there.

"Aaron, I . . ." She shook her head. "What are you doing here?" she said again.

Aaron turned to her. "Is that all the welcome I get?" And he slipped his arms round her waist. She eased out of his embrace. His touch felt wrong.

"Didn't you get my email?" she asked.

"Of course I did," he said, as if it were obvious, "and that's why I'm here. Rachel, I can't let you go. Not over a misunderstanding like that. I've missed you. I wanted to see you. And I wanted to see Winterbourne. I mean, check out this place!"

It surprised Rachel that he should react in such a way, he who was used to the grandest properties the world had to offer, he who spared no expense in any aspect of his life. Despite the circumstances she felt proud of her ancestry, of her belonging at Winterbourne, as proud as if she were welcoming someone into her own home, which, in a sense, she was. But it didn't change the fact that her mind was made up.

"It wasn't a misunderstanding," she said. "You tried to sell Winterbourne behind my back, organizing for that woman to come round, telling her I wanted rid of my inheritance without asking me first. You should never have done it."

He held up his hands, prepared for her rebuke. "I know, I know," he said. "That's what I came here to tell you. It was a bad move."

"What were you thinking?"

"That I was helping. I kept imagining you

352

here, alone, and I know you're independent — maybe you were afraid to ask for support." He sighed, ran a hand through his hair. "I don't know, Rachel, I care about you — is that OK, can I say that? I figured you were getting on with the emotional stuff, so if I could step in and take the onerous business of selling off your hands, maybe it would lighten the load?"

She thought about it from his point of view. Maybe she'd been unfair.

"And you traveled thousands of miles just to tell me that?" she said.

"Some women might call it romantic."

"Contacting that Realtor wasn't a decision you had authority to make."

"Rachel, I know. I understand. I was worried, that's all, about you coping."

"I've been coping just fine."

"I can see that." She thought he said it straight up, but there was a note of pomposity there that implied her current appearance — and, indeed, the state of the hall, littered as it was with scattered diaries, not to mention the heaped-up piles of plates and coffee cups just visible in the kitchen — suggested otherwise.

"I meant well," Aaron said quietly. "Can you forgive me?"

Rachel felt tired. "Of course I forgive you."

Aaron stepped across the diaries to reach her, barely seeming to notice them under his polished shoes. "Rachel," he said, "please reconsider what you said about us. That's all I ask, just think about it. I don't want to say more because I don't want to frighten you off, but there is more, the way I feel about you, and I mean it. Being without you has made me reflect on things and, well, I know what I want."

His words disturbed her. Things had always been easy between them; it was how she'd liked it, and she wasn't sure if she wanted this new intensity. Had Aaron been concealing his feelings all along? She wasn't ready for a relationship; she didn't want to settle down. Was he saying he loved her? No one had loved her since Seth.

"You can stay until tomorrow," she said, "but I'm not promising anything." She knew she sounded cold, like the closed, brittle self she had left behind in America — not the girl smoking against Jack's farmhouse wall, letting secrets fall like rain.

"OK," he said. "But you'll at least let me take you for dinner, won't you?"

The afternoon was a struggle. Aaron had expected to be welcomed as a lover and she could offer him no more than a slightly uncomfortable friendship. Politely Rachel asked after his business and the family Thanksgiving he had coming up (to which he rather sorely admitted he'd been planning to invite her), while he, quite justifiably, refrained from returning too many questions. Instead, he focused on Winterbourne.

Rachel was grateful for the distraction of the house, a talking point so vast she dared hope they could avoid personal interaction altogether. Aaron was enamored by it. As they passed through the endless passageways of the majestic building, he stood at every painting, every artifact, every column, every urn, every hanging or tapestry or bookcase or chandelier, fascinated. Rachel found his fervor amusing. Aaron was used to five-star splendor, and was perhaps indulging her a little. She didn't mind. The sheer gothic opulence at Winterbourne would be unlike any glitzy residence he had seen. She was glad of the difference: that this was hers, incomparable, unique.

Then, over a cobbled-together lunch of bread and cheese, Aaron asked if Wanda Pearlman had valued the property. "Of course not," she said.

He was eating standing up, a habit of his, leaning back against the counter. He could be on a billion-dollar-settlement conference call, she thought, were it not for the dust-caked soup tureens above his head, the enormous Belfast sink and cracked jelly molds. Who had worked in this kitchen, she wondered, their sleeves rolled up, apron caked in flour as they beat flour and eggs and pulled cakes out of the oven? Each time she thought of the diaries, another universe opened: a shadow alongside this one. Had Alice cooked? Had Mrs. de Grey? Had the woman called Christine?

"You should find out," commented Aaron, swilling the glass in his hand. "I can't even estimate. Guess I'm not clued up on real estate over here. There's all the land as well, of course. You'd be talking tens of millions, maybe more."

Rachel put her chin on her hand. "I'm planning to sell," she said, "eventually. But I'm not ready yet. There's too much still to find."

"Like what?"

"It's complicated."

"I can do complicated."

Rachel looked into his eyes. She drew a breath.

"Do you remember how you told me, back in New York, that I'd been through a lot?" He nodded. "Well," she said, "you were right. And it started way back at the beginning, before you, before the gallery, before I lost my husband, before I found out I was adopted, before any of that. It started here, at Winterbourne. This house is it. It's my past, and until I fill it with something I can touch, something I can take home, I won't be able to put the things I've been through behind me and move on."

"I get it, Rachel. I do."

"My real mom is only a step away, and who knows what, then, I'll learn about myself? I've never known anything about myself, not even the name I was born with. Can you imagine what it will mean, to know those things for sure? To know how I came into the world? Winterbourne is more than an auction. It's my home."

"But you can't keep it. You can't live here."

"I can until I'm done with it. Or it's done with me, whatever."

"It's a drafty old castle, Rachel. It's not a person."

She couldn't stop, now that she'd started. She had to confide in someone. She had to have someone as levelheaded as Aaron tell her it was nonsense, though she wasn't sure if that would be a relief or a disappointment. She needed perspective.

"I'm afraid that something bad happened

to them, Aaron," she said, "my mother and my grandmother — to both of them. I found these journals belonging to my aunt and they talk about this curse on Winterbourne, on the women who lived here —"

Aaron started laughing, then stopped when he saw her expression.

"I'm sorry, Rachel, but you can't be serious. A *curse*?"

"I know it sounds ridiculous. But it's what my aunt believed."

"And what you believe, by the sounds of it."

At her failure to reply, he went on, "Listen, this is what I was afraid of. It's part of why I came out here, to see if you were holding up. On your own in this place, I knew it could be bad. Then when you emailed telling me we were off, it was like I suddenly realized, yeah, that's what's happened. She isn't thinking straight."

"I'm thinking fine," said Rachel. "I've never been thinking more clearly."

"But you're entertaining the idea of a Winterbourne curse? Come on."

It had been a mistake to tell Aaron anything. She should have told Jack; he knew Polcreath and the house and he wouldn't have judged her. But what hurt most was that maybe Aaron was right. Maybe she *had* spent so much time locked up at Winterbourne with that dank cellar and that creepy mirror and the bats that flew into the windows at night, that she had lost her grip on what was real and what wasn't.

Constance was hardly a reliable narrator. Her diaries could pour forth any kind of fiction and Rachel was a fool to take them at face value. But the alternative, somehow, seemed worse: that there was no truth to any of it, that every word in the diaries was made up, and she was no better off than when she started.

Aaron insisted on driving into Polcreath in the early evening. Rachel would have preferred to walk given the roaring beacon of attention that was the cherry-red Porsche, but he wouldn't be deterred. In New York Aaron preferred to keep a low profile; she suspected that, here, he rather relished the idea of shaking up a sleepy English coastal town. She thought of the mud-caked boots and musty Barbours hanging by the door to the Landogger Inn, the damp dogs dozing by the fire and the locals sucking tops off their pints, and prayed to go anywhere but there.

"There's a nice-looking bistro on the water," she volunteered as they parked in the harbor. "Shall we try that? Great lobster, I've heard." She made that bit up.

"Hmm." Aaron stepped out of the Porsche and breathed in the sea air. Gulls swooped overhead, their wings buffeted on a bracing wind. "I'd rather somewhere authentic. Let's go local. How about that pub over there?"

Rachel's heart sank. The Landogger did indeed look attractive, nestled in the hillside amid a cluster of sparkling lights. "It's not that great," she said. "There's another place, similar, on the other side of town. How about we . . . ?"

"No, let's go there," he said, with the single-mindedness that had drawn her to him in the first place; and, smiling winningly, he took her arm and they walked along the shingly sea path. She hadn't come this way before. The water glittered lilac and there was scarcely anyone in sight. Aaron was dressed in an Armani suit, loosened at the neck, and his usual brand of cologne. The less people saw them, the better.

"Look," said Aaron, as the tree line momentarily parted and Winterbourne's turrets came into view, "there you are, on top of the world." He said it so simply and nicely that Rachel squeezed his arm, a rush of affection warming her heart. It had been sweet of him to come. The Wanda Pearlman thing had been a mix-up. It would be nice to have him here, after all. But the sight of a group of men outside the Landogger quickly extinguished any resurgence of optimism. One was noticeably taller than the others, and shaped horribly like Jack Wyatt. As they came closer, her fears were confirmed. Jack raised his hand to wave at her, and she nodded back.

"Hello," he said as they reached the door, immediately eyeballing Aaron. "How was the hangover yesterday?" His companions drifted inside.

"Uh yeah," she said, "not great. Um, this is Aaron."

"Pleased to meet you," said Jack, although he looked anything but.

"Aaron Grewal," said Aaron. "And you are . . . ?"

"Oh, sorry," said Rachel. "This is Jack. He's been helping me up at the house." She wished instantly that she hadn't said that.

"Has he?" said Aaron, interested.

"We're just coming in for a drink," said Rachel quickly.

"Strange choice of place," said Jack.

"How do you mean?"

"I would have thought Raffini's was a better fit with Armani." He said it in a friendly enough way and fortunately Aaron took it as a compliment.

"Anyway, see you later." She ushered Aaron inside but Jack caught her arm.

"This is the one it's over with?"

"I'm not in the mood, Jack."

"He isn't you," he said. "He definitely isn't you."

"What would you know about what is or isn't me?"

"More than you think."

She turned on him. "Tell me, Jack: how does it feel to be right all the time? Does it ever get boring?"

"Not really."

"It does for other people."

"Him? Seriously? Rachel, that guy looks like he *moisturizes.*"

"You're the one who knows an Armani suit when he sees one."

"What can I say? I'm not all cowsheds and dog whistles."

"Leave me alone."

"Never. You're stuck. I like you."

She shrugged Jack off, wishing they had never come anywhere near the Landogger — and, when she stepped inside, her wish multiplied. Aaron was standing at the bar perusing its menu of jacket potatoes and cottage pie, while the eyes of all the locals were trained on him. Fishermen in rubber boots ogled his *haute couture;* round-bellied darts players nudged each other; dog walkers raised eyebrows.

"Let's sit down," she murmured to him, leading him to a corner table. Luckily the place resumed its chatter and Rachel went to the bar to order. When she returned with wine and poured a hefty slug into her own glass, she felt mildly better. But it didn't help that Jack was occupying a bar stool in her direct line of vision and she was aware of his eyes on her throughout her entire conversation with Aaron. She hated the idea that he was critiquing her life — re-evaluating it, even — based on the signals her companion gave off. When they'd first met, Jack had dismissed her as a soulless city girl. He'd since discovered she wasn't. *Oh, what do I care?* she thought furiously. It didn't matter what Jack thought. He could think any damn thing he liked.

Besides, she felt defensive of Aaron. These people could judge him all they liked, and they could judge her too. They had as much right to be here as anyone else.

When their lasagna arrived, Aaron surprised her by producing a copy of *City* magazine. "Here," he said, passing it to her, "I thought you'd want to see this. Front-page news." He squeezed her fingers as she took it. "I'm proud of you," he said.

Rachel read the article, a generous spread boasting a banner of the gallery exterior with Rachel standing outside it, grinning widely. Paul had run a sensational item, name checking her several times, and the exhibition critique was outstanding.

"Thank you," she said, meaning it. Seeing the gallery moved her. Reading Paul's words moved her. To think that this whole world had been turning far away from Cornwall and she had virtually forgotten about it, her life in New York, her apartment, the team she worked with, it all seemed so distant.

When she finally gazed up at Aaron, he seemed to anticipate this.

"This is who you are, Rachel," he said gently, reaching in to touch her arm. "You belong in New York, with your job, with the career you've built."

She nodded.

"Those guys need you." He lowered his voice. "*I* need you. Come home. Please."

Rachel couldn't stop looking at the picture. She felt a pang for the gallery, the color and activity it generated that was such a far cry from the world she inhabited here. Aaron watched her earnestly. She had never considered herself a runaway: she had always faced things. But was that what she'd been doing in England? Had she deliberately lost herself in Winterbourne as a means of escape, in pursuing a maze that might just as easily spit her out exactly in the place she'd begun? What if the truth wasn't at Winterbourne at all, but back in the real world? She had worked so hard for this success, striving ever since childhood to accomplish something she could be proud of. Well, here it was. And here she was, thousands of miles away.

"I know you're searching," said Aaron, "but this is it." He tapped the cover of the magazine with his finger. "This is you, Rachel, not a heap of old diaries in a spooky house in the middle of nowhere. *This*. Your creation."

She looked up and her eyes flitted across Jack at the bar. He would never know the person she was in New York. He knew her here, and barely, but it wasn't the same. He knew none of her ambition, her brilliance or resilience. Aaron did. The gallery reminded her of it: the same gallery that Jack would make fun of.

Aaron was right. Perhaps it was time to go home. Winterbourne had nothing left to offer her but upset. Did she even want to find out about Alice and her mother? Did she want to face yet more tragedy and sadness, over facts she couldn't change?

She would pack her belongings in the morning and set in motion a sale. Aaron would help her. He had always helped her, always been good to her — and she saw that now, in the fact he'd traveled such a distance to be with her. He cared about her, the real her, and he'd known what was right even when she couldn't.

When Jack left the pub minutes later she tried not to look, and to focus instead on Aaron's plans for their return, the places he'd take her, the shows he wanted her to see and the new apartment he'd bought off Broadway. No pressure, he pledged, they'd take it a day at a time: he only wanted her to be happy.

Rachel watched the door close behind Jack, and pictured him walking back to the old farmhouse across the dark, still fields.

She raised her glass to Aaron's and clinked it.

CHAPTER 27

CORNWALL, 1947

Autumn tips into winter. Gray skies freeze; the sea churns black. Winterbourne stands like a citadel on the hill, indifferent to the icy mists, as lonely as the light at Polcreath tower. I watch the tower, that single beacon out at sea, standing at my bedroom window or on the windswept cliffs. It is more visible on some days than others. I imagine the men working the light and their isolation chimes with my own. Jonathan has cast me out on a hostile sea. When the tower light blinks at night, the last punctuation mark before the wild Atlantic begins, inside my heart bleeds darkness.

I long for him as readily as the fires in the hearth take flame; the slightest kindling and I warm once more, before a sharp gust blows my hope to ash. He avoids me these days. He spends more time than ever locked away in his study, smoking and gazing at pictures of Laura. Accordingly I harden as surely as the garden's frozen lawns, stiff in the morning with sparkling dew, their trees naked and shivering.

The imminence of a new housekeeper lurks over me like a guillotine. For this precious, painful time, I can pretend that we four are a family, my husband distant because of his injuries; and I must play the doting, patient wife while my children run around my skirts and laugh softly in dimly lit corners. But with the new arrival, I will no longer be the woman of this house. I will be plain, misguided Alice Miller, a governess with no home of her own. Jonathan will not be dissuaded. Since our last exchange I dare not speak to him on the most trifling matter, let alone this.

On a night in November — I know not which one — I retire to bed early. I pause a while, as I always do, in front of Laura de Grey's mirror. I enjoy how it makes me look, an altered version. If I wear my hair loose (which I do more now: Constance likes to comb it; she says it reminds her of her mother and I embrace the flattery like a child), and the light is subtle, I can imagine I see somebody else. If I concentrate, I can turn that woman into Laura de Grey, for Laura captured her husband's heart; Laura hadn't been a one-night affair; Laura had been enough to bewitch him . . .

Laura, Laura, Laura . . .

I don't want to be me any more. My life as Alice has ended. I long instead to become this woman in the mirror, with her storm-black eyes and her pale, rising chest. I have taken to wearing long sleeves and a high collar to conceal the marks that have overtaken my body. I know not how they came to be. There are too many and they are too far spreading to be the product of any one impact. I notice the dark patches under my fingernails, as if I am the one who has drawn blood. Perhaps I am ill: they say the worst infections begin with bruises. Yet I have never felt so well, the strength of my obsession bringing color to my cheeks and vigor to my heart.

My bed is cold. I think I will never sleep in this cold but then suddenly I am awake, hours later, my candle gone out and the room swamped in darkness. I hear a steady, soft pattering, like moths against a light, and when I climb from the bed and pull the curtains I see large plumes of snow drifting and spitting against the windowpanes. Snow falls heavily, more heavily than I have seen, the night alive and flickering white. Everything is impossibly quiet, like a held breath.

The little painting appears alive in the

uncertain light. The girl has moved again. I knew she would. Now she is closer, close to stepping out of the frame.

She seems to grow as I inspect her, as if she is coming closer still. I am frightened but I cannot let her see my fright. *Stop daydreaming, Alice; you're imagining things, Alice . . .* Why does she observe me? What do I have that she wants?

"Go back," I whisper to her. But when I peer in at the paint, the girl is as still and lifeless as could be, and I see the dashes of oil that have been used to create her.

A voice calls. Only I cannot make sense of what it says.

It comes from the hallway. Then I hear my own name, sharp and sudden.

Alice.

I light a candle and open the door, knowing what to expect — and sure enough there she is, my child, my love, in the spot in the hall that she always occupies. Constance is sleeping, her hands at her sides, her head raised to the ceiling, the frill of her nightdress brushing her bare toes. How cold she must be! I rush to her — only this time, unlike the other times, her eyes are not glazed but focused.

"It was here," Constance murmurs to me. *"It happened here . . ."*

Twenty-five minutes to three, the dead of night. It is Laura's time.

This is the first occasion she has spoken in such a state. I gather her to me. She looks so lucid, so *present,* that I have the absurd notion of being afraid. "Come along, darling," I tell her, gently guiding her down the passage, up the stairs and back to bed.

In the twins' room, Edmund is soundless beneath his covers, unusually soundless for one in deep sleep. As I tuck the girl back in, I wonder if he is listening to me — the words I croon that are meant for her ears only. It is with relief that I leave their chamber and return to my own. When I climb into bed, facing the open curtains and the dreamlike snow, my back to the forest on the wall that beckons me, curling its finger, *come in, come in,* but by turns needing to face the painting that horrifies me, the little girl watching, I wonder who is awake and who is asleep, and which I am, or what is between, and the thought is so tiring that I lose my grip and then it is morning.

After breakfast, the children are squealing to be let out in the snow. The stuff has settled foot-deep on the parkland and the gardens look enchanted glimpsed through

Winterbourne's frosted windows. Tree boughs hang heavy under ice and the blanket covering the lawns is pristine. "May we, Alice, may we play?" Constance, having no memory of her nighttime excursion, tugs my hand, while Edmund pulls on his boots.

"Wait for me," I tell them. "I must first ask your father."

But I have another motive in speaking with Jonathan. I find him in the library, sitting in a chair by the window. His leg is on a footstool and there is a cigar between his lips. His hair spills over the collar of his coat. It is early for him to be smoking and I wonder that he passed a bad night, as I did. Has he been thinking of me? Was he tempted to venture to my bed? The thought makes me hollow with longing.

"Yes, Miss Miller?" He greets me formally.

After securing his permission to venture outside, I say:

"I wish to talk to you about Constance."

"What about her?"

I close the library door, wait for him to invite me to sit but he doesn't.

"You must be aware of her sleepwalking," I say. "It used to be infrequent but it is happening now several times a week. I am concerned for her well-being."

He draws hard on the cigar. The tip glows orange.

"Constance is perfectly well," he says.

"She cannot be expected to concentrate in lessons if she's barely had any rest."

"Does she appear tired to you this morning?" Out in the hall, we hear the twins exclaiming at the snow, and Constance's enthusiastic laughter.

"No —"

"Nor does she to me. Is that all, Miss Miller?"

I turn to go, then change my mind.

"Constance spoke to me last night, Captain. Normally she is quiet, caught up in her trance. But last night she said, 'It happened here.' What did she mean?"

"She was sleeping, Miss Miller. Her talk is the stuff of dreams. Have you never dreamed a dream that made no sense?"

I dream of you, I yearn to say. *And it makes all the sense in the world.*

"She seemed convinced," I tell him.

"I'm sure she did."

"And she always stops in the same place, in the hallway outside my bedroom, to look up at the beams. Don't you think it odd?"

Jonathan turns his chair to face me. He takes the cigar from his mouth and grinds it out in an ashtray, taking his time, blowing out smoke. How could the burns to his face repel anyone? How could he imagine they did? I cannot picture him without them, his scars as much a part of his handsomeness as his untidy hair and his strong hands and his sharp light eyes, the eyes of a wolf.

"She is disturbing you, then," he says. "This is about you."

"Oh, it's not. Really, Captain, I don't mind."

"I'll have you moved to another room."

"No!" For some reason I cannot bear the thought. The painting and the mural, Laura's clock, her mirror, those things belong to me; they hold me in thrall; I am as addicted to them as I am to the captain! The idea of shutting them away is wrong, like shutting away a living creature in need of light. I am afraid of turning my back, as if in doing so I am turning against myself, the soft tricks of my mind that creep back to claim me and I cannot resist them or they will punish me for it. I could have asked to move when I learned of my predecessor's fate, but I did not; instead the room brought me closer to that unfortunate woman, knowing she had lain where I lay, between my sheets; she had stood at the window as I did and felt desperate for him, as I did. Had she held Laura's clock to her at night and felt its dead heart against her own?

I clarify: "I mean to say, Captain, that I am happy where I am. It is Constance's welfare that concerns me, not my own."

"You need have no concern," the captain says coldly, turning back to the view. Strange words to emerge from a man whose expression could only be described as concerned. He knows about the sleepwalking. He knows about the hallway. He knows why his daughter stops there. What he doesn't know is how to stop me finding out.

When I return to the porch, I am surprised to find the children gone. Their coats and boots are vanished from the usual place. "Constance?" I call. "Edmund?"

I pull my own coat on and step outside. The air is unbelievably still; the day is patient and pure, white within white within white. Even the sea is hushed: I have to strain to hear it. The twins' footprints are a giveaway, the only disturbance to the immaculate snow save for the occasional twitch and jump of a bird.

I follow their steps, two alongside two, until at the frozen lake they diverge. One set follows the lake round; the other heads off to the bluff. At the center of the ice-smothered lake is a hole where someone has thrown in a rock. I picture Edmund, cajoling his sister on, though I cannot detect whose footprints are whose, and I start to feel troubled. I turn, thinking I hear a child's cry, but there is no sign of life. No birds, no movement, no sound. Just Winterbourne, its arched windows blankly watching.

I stare down at my hands, the skin cracked, ravaged with cold.

"Edmund!" I call, louder this time.

I elect to follow the prints to the bluff, the chill air stealing the breath from my lungs. My coat is thin and my boots are poor. I think of Laura, tramping pink-cheeked through these conditions, her boots fur-lined and her shawl made of velvet. I think of blood on snow, red lips on a pale face, and shudder as the sea comes close.

"Constance!" I'm reminded of my first week here, that horrible morning I lost the boy and Tom had to come to our rescue. The weather steals them. The mists come in and the snow comes in, and the weather takes them away.

"Edmund!"

I'm reminded of the woman I saw on the cliff, and the shape I saw on the beach, creeping and crawling away from me, or toward me. I think of that same woman climbing into the mural in my bedroom and she fits exactly, coating herself in the vines that kiss and cradle her form. Is this where she lives? Does she come to the cliff in the day, and creep back to the forest at night?

I stop at the drop. So do the child's footprints. I peer over the edge to the foaming sea and I don't know what I expect to see, but for a reckless moment I can draw in fine detail the broken body of a child. I gasp, drawing back from the edge, shocked at my vision! Then I see more prints. Only it can't be; it surely isn't possible that the child's prints continue alongside another set, a larger one belonging without doubt to an adult . . . I peer closer, presuming the size and grain of Tom's boots but no, these are slighter, the prints of a woman. I put my own next to hers and draw away to compare the impressions. One is a direct copy of the other.

For a frenzied moment I expect to see myself up at the house, entering with Edmund at my side. Who, then, is the person looking on? Who, then, am I?

Unsteadily I walk on, tracking the prints, those larger ones alongside a child's, close enough to be holding hands. And then, up by the topiary, a third set joins them, what can only be the other twin's, and the whole arrangement seems horrific, as if *this is a grown-up the children know,* falling so easily into step alongside her.

Who is she? Who has my children?

"Constance! Edmund!"

The prints lead me to the stables and then they vanish. I turn about, searching the indifferent white but it relinquishes nothing. Storm comes to the door and I put my head over, thinking the twins have perhaps taken shelter — but it is empty. Panic fills my throat. What will I tell the captain? There must be some clue: people don't evaporate into thin air. It occurs to me that a car might have taken them, but I have heard no car. They have to be on the estate, still. I will find them. I must!

But the snow renders my world unfamiliar. The stone steps and ancient trees, the dips and curves and corners of the parkland I have grown accustomed to appear changed, absent, not right. Every familiarity is concealed. I hurry back to the house, opening and closing the door behind me, leaning back against it to close my eyes and catch my breath. How I wish Mrs. Yarrow were here! Or else the doctor, Henry Marsh, any person who could catch me and call me back, for I am falling again. *Silly Alice, stupid Alice!* Tom is nowhere to be seen. I dash between the windows, scanning the bleached landscape but too frightened to become part of it. Whyever did I let them out of my sight? I must never let them out of my sight, ever again! There is somebody here, a trespasser: an intruder who means to harm my darlings. She has tempted them with a devilish offering and they, weak children, have fallen for her charms! She must have sneaked in overnight, masked in her hiding place. She waited. She waited.

I wait now, but no one comes. I pace the floor, I listen for cries; I wring my hands and hold them in prayer. *Please,* I beg, *please bring my children home.* And all the while I am watching his study, terrified that his door will open and the captain will emerge and my sins will be spread for all to see. Jonathan will order me to leave Winterbourne for good. *No!* I think. *It cannot happen!* I cannot contemplate never seeing him again, or the children, or this house, and just as I am opening the door to stride outside there is a battering of tiny fists on the kitchen window. I rush in through the scullery. There, beyond the glass, are Edmund and Constance. They are crying, both the children are crying, and I cry too, sobbing with relief.

"I'm coming!" I splutter. "My darlings,

I'm coming!"

When I return to the door they are there on the other side.

"My darlings!" The twins rush in, shivering, teeth chattering. "Oh, my loves!"

They are freezing. I try to warm their hands in mine but they resist; I try to draw them to me to heat them up but they pull away. The poor mites are in shock.

"Where have you been?" I ask, forgetting my anger, forgetting, even, the woman who took them, for the sheer reassurance that they are well.

"You locked us out!" Edmund cries. His curls are frosted and his lips gray with cold. Constance grips his hand, and I see not relief in her eyes but fear.

"My sweethearts — how could you think such a thing?"

"We couldn't get in!" Constance weeps. "We tried and tried!"

"I've been here," I say; "I was listening for you. It isn't possible."

"You locked the door!" says Edmund. "You locked us out!"

I did lock the door. I was afraid of that woman. But I would have heard them; I would, if they had come knocking! I heard them at the kitchen, didn't I?

"Who were you with?" I demand. But they

are bewildered. Nobody, they tell me, they were with me the whole time. We went out together and we looked at the cliffs and then we went to the stables to visit Storm; on the way back they stopped to throw snow and I returned on my own. I bolted the door behind me, shutting them out. "Who was she?" I ask, wanting to shake them. "Who was that woman?"

"What woman? We were with you. Alice, you're scaring us!"

Somehow I command them to go to their room, and promise to bring up warm towels and cocoa. Alone, I steady myself. My mind is spinning. My heart is thumping. *Nobody*, the twins had said, wide-eyed and sincere. *Just you.*

It cannot be. I am well. I haven't been ill in a long time.

I venture back out to the snow. I will know when I see the prints. I will know and then I'll show them and then I will drag out the truth. But all I see is a zigzag reflection of my hunt, here and there and all around, the trails of a madwoman, back and forth and back and forth, so many prints there is scarcely a space between them.

CHAPTER 28

Mrs. Rackstile arrives at Winterbourne like a witch. That is how she appears to me, having traveled overnight through the slowly thawing snow that might have thwarted one in possession of a less determined disposition. By the neat brim of her hat and the shine on her shoes she could have journeyed door to door by first-class train. She is unmarried, in her fifties, has a narrow, angular face, a sweep of graying hair clipped back at the neck and a pursed, joyless mouth. She presents an instant threat, not least because the children flock ecstatically to her as they did when I first arrived, embracing her, bringing her drawings, treating her to their sweetest smiles. I believe they are punishing me for yesterday. I begged them not to inform their father of what happened and they agreed. Now they would serve me, it seems, a separate penalty.

"Captain de Grey." Mrs. Rackstile shakes

his hand matter-of-factly; and of course she should greet him first, he is her employer, but still I stand overlooked like a girl on the fringes at a party. *This is my house!* I long to cry. *He is my captain!*

"I shall have this place in hand before you know it," she tells him, with a smile. Jonathan returns it and his smile wounds me. I wish I could eradicate every breathing soul at Winterbourne apart from us, alone, alone here forever. I hate her already, without reason. I hate that she is deemed necessary. I hate that she disrupts our family: that she threatens to take the children from me, and Jonathan, and this house. She has no business here. She wants rid of me so she can claim it for herself.

"And this is Alice Miller," says Jonathan, "the children's governess."

I meet Mrs. Rackstile's hand and consider adding that I have been with him; it would be so simple to utter the words, to see what would happen. But of course I do not. Instead Tom shows the housekeeper to her quarters and I resume my demotion, as when Mrs. Yarrow was here. It seems I am always third — third with my parents, third with the twins, third with Jonathan and his beautiful, dead wife. Never can I occupy that elusive first tier. For an instant he and

I are alone and I wish he would give me assurance of my place, my priority, but no: he returns down the corridor without meeting my eye. Why should he, in any case? I am the governess, just as he said. I am nobody else, nobody important. I am nothing. I am invisible.

Mrs. Rackstile's approach to Winterbourne is to make her mark by taking away every one of my own. Every routine I have established, she unpicks. Every preference of mine, swept away. I can tell she deems me frivolous, a silly London girl employed to fill the children's heads with lofty ideas that have no practical use in the real world. She possesses the kind of military conduct that reminds me of my father and of the instructresses at Burstead. After a lifetime serving the gentry, Mrs. Rackstile has her way of doing things and neither hell nor high water will dissuade her from her path.

"Why serve breakfast at eight when the master is up at seven?" she inquires when I share the household timetable. "Bedtime is strict and no stories, it only gives them bad dreams." Gone were runny eggs on Wednesdays, Edmund's favorite. "They will eat whichever meal I serve them and however I choose to serve it." When I tell her about

Constance's sleepwalking, she locks the twins' door. "That will keep her inside. Children need boundaries, Miss Miller; I would have thought you knew that."

The children embrace this new rigidity — they seem to welcome it, even. Privately I know they will tire of it. In asserting their fondness for Mrs. Rackstile, they continue to penalize me. They obey the austerity of their new housekeeper as if she were their father, with the same deference and dread. In loving them and showing that love, I have robbed myself of their respect. They no longer take me seriously. My reprimands fall on deaf ears, as does my praise. They do not care what I think.

On Sunday, Mrs. Rackstile takes the children to church. I plead a headache and remain at Winterbourne, hoping that Jonathan will stay with me, but to my shock and dismay he elects to accompany the group. Has his faith returned? Or is the prospect of meeting a god he does not believe in easier than the prospect of meeting me?

Alone in the house, with only the steady *drip-drip* of the scullery sink that needs to be fixed, I decide what it is I must do. For so long I have been thrown the scraps of Laura de Grey's existence — her elegant looking glass, her beautiful horse, her handsome clock, her lashings of black hair and the powder-softness of her skin — but I am hungry for a feast. With the house empty, I have my opportunity.

Laura possesses me. I am as enamored with this dead woman as I am with her living husband. She is everything that I am not. Even in death she has everything that I crave. When I stand at her mirror, I feel myself transforming. I am not the wisp that Mrs. Rackstile thinks I am; neither am I the distrustful, weakened woman I fear I have become. I can be like Laura. I can spray her scents and wear her clothes. I can show Mrs. Rackstile what the mistress of this house looks like.

Winter has rendered the cellar less habitable than ever. Banks of snow heap against the windows, blocking what scant light still finds a way in. The walls ooze moisture, and where it has frozen is mottled and smooth. I fear the leaks from the low ceiling will snuff my candle, but I make it to the little door with the flame still dancing brightly. The access is open as we left it last and I crouch to get inside.

Hesitant light flickers across the remains of Winterbourne's mistress — those few possessions that the children sat among, the possessions that made the dog Tipper afraid — and it is less than I thought. There are a few framed pictures, one of which presents a simply rendered jar of lilies: its reverse reveals a girlish signature, *Laura Hensley.* So that was her maiden name. *Hensley.* She would have been brought up in a sweet house with a white gate and laurel hedges down the drive. She'd have had a gray, long-haired cat (I had always wanted a cat); her bedroom would have been pink and cream, like meringue, with delicately crocheted quilts and pillows on the window seat. Her parents would have smothered her in kisses. All her life, Laura Hensley was adored. There is a box full of dresses. Jewelry. A bottle of perfume, which I dare to pocket and which is perhaps my most treasured find, for at night I can douse myself in it and smell my body as if it were hers. I consider that Laura's items have been saved, but by whom — by Jonathan? Did he attribute significance to every artifact or was the collection amassed in a rash of grief, grasping what he could of Laura at random, too heartbroken to think straight? I wish I could have helped him; I'd have relished the chance to be here and to comfort him, to take whatever load I could of his suffering.

There is a photograph, which I snatch and hold to the flame to see clearly.

I both love and detest it at once. Jonathan and Laura on their wedding day, the day Miss Hensley became Mrs. de Grey. Of course, beauty is what I expected. The cloud of dark hair, the almond eyes, the heart-shaped face. I trace that face now with my fingertips, and it is her I gaze at for a long time before I even turn to Jonathan. I do not recognize the captain as the man I know now. He is young and unmarked, a less compelling version. Laura is the one who fascinates, Laura in her white dress, Laura smiling widely at the world. I cannot help but compare it with the photograph Tom took of the four of us outside Winterbourne before Mrs. Yarrow left. We had felt like a unit, then, as loving a couple as the one depicted here. Only our version was false. Even Mrs. Yarrow didn't want it. When Tom telephoned to ask after her address so that he could send it on, Mrs. Yarrow said no, she had no desire to receive it.

Seeing Laura on her wedding day reminds me of the drawing the twins made of me when I first arrived. They sketched me in a bridal gown like this one, a delicate veil and flowers in my hair. *Did you want me to be her?* I wonder of them.

For why else would they have encouraged me so? All along, the children have steered me toward a belief that I might one day step into that beautiful woman's shoes, that I might claim the captain as my husband and this house as my own.

They made me believe in my future here, in true love . . .

My weakness to be wanted: my pathetic, throbbing heart.

For a time I remain in the cellar, no longer feeling the cold.

"On a boat called Old Lymer, *down at Polcreath Hollow . . ."*

The single blessing of Mrs. Rackstile's arrival is that, after completing their Sunday prep, the children can take a session with her and the afternoon is my own. What lessons of mine does she seek to unravel? How does she wish to exert her influence on the wards I have shaped as my own? The little girl in the painting was a warning: I see it now. She was trying to warn me that evil was on its way.

"I'm going out," I tell the housekeeper. "I'll be back in time for tea."

"Where are you going?"

"Is it your concern?"

"Everything that happens in this house is

my concern."

I pull up the collar of my coat. "It's just as well that I'm leaving it, then."

Mrs. Rackstile frowns. She looks about to say more, but I go before she can. As I cross to the cliffs and begin the stumble down to the beach, holding my hat to stop it whipping away, I consider it cannot be far: the man Marlin had walked it that day, and probably many days since. The tide is out, the beach empty. Sprawls of seaweed are washed up on the sand, while jagged rocks poke through like molars, rotten and glistening. The weeds are slick and dark, snarled in shallow pits.

I follow the shoreline in Marlin's direction, keeping tight to the cliffs. Their scale dwarfs me, a lone figure hurrying along their base, and the beach seems never-ending. The wind stings my ears. My legs burn. At last, Polcreath Hollow comes into view. It is no more than a shelf of rock with a single boat moored there, a wooden, humble craft. I see its name painted in white down one flank: OLD LYMER.

It is awkward getting off the beach and down on to the ridge of rock. I hear barking and one of the low-backed, long-tailed dogs emerges on deck, growling at me. *I smell of Winterbourne,* I think. *He can smell it on me.*

"Come on, you devil!" Marlin emerges from the boat and takes the dog by the scruff, then, noticing its point of interest, squints at me. When we met before, I didn't see Marlin clearly because of his sou'wester. Now, in the light of day, he appears more ordinary. The sharp, darting eyes I associated with madness regard me evenly.

"I need to speak to you," I say.

Over the past weeks I have become accustomed to cavernous spaces and whistling halls. The simplicity of *Old Lymer,* with its known parameters and gentle movement, is comforting. Marlin orders me to sit by the stove. At his command the dogs lie like sphinxes on their tattered rugs, their paws in front, their heads erect, tongues panting. The galley is a mess with scarcely any visible surfaces, and the camp bed is unmade. "I don't have visitors," says Marlin in his thick West Country accent. "It is what it is."

"I wish to speak with you about Laura," I say.

Marlin sits opposite me. "You don't beat around, do you?"

"When we met," I press, "you said there was something bad at Winterbourne. A bad spirit. That your dogs could sense it and so could you."

Marlin smiles. "And now you know it's true."

"I don't know what to think," I say. "But terrible things have happened." My throat dries. "The children, they're . . ." In a rush I want to echo Mrs. Yarrow's words to me. *They're playing tricks. They're toying with me. Don't you hear their laughter?*

"The children what?"

I shake my head. Close my eyes. Marlin voices what I cannot.

"The children are in bed with it," he says quietly. "Is that what you mean?"

How can I think such a thing? But I do! I do think it!

The footprints in the snow, the woman on the cliff, the marks on my skin, the giggling, the whispering, the scheming, the wide eyes that turn too sharply to glint . . .

Who are they protecting? Who do they love more than me?

"Is it Laura?" I whisper. I watch my hands in the stovelight, cracked and cold, turn them to fists and remember the twins' fists as they battered the kitchen window.

We couldn't get in! We tried and tried!

Marlin shakes his head. The stove crackles. "There was a bad thing at Winterbourne long before Laura," he says. "That's what got her."

"How?" My voice is ragged, desperate. "Tell me, please, how did she die?"

The water laps beneath us. The dogs pant.

"She hanged herself," he says.

I imagine Laura's throat, perfectly white, with the coarse string tight around it. I imagine her stumbling toward her fate, just as Constance stumbles in sleep, her bare feet dragging on the floorboards, her heart leaden with turmoil.

"She hanged herself right there in the passage, choked to death on a rope."

An image enters my mind, a flickering image, of Constance in the hallway, looking up at the ceiling. The girl's pale neck, as pale as her mother's . . .

"They locked her away, so the rumor goes," says Marlin. "That man up there locked 'is own wife away, trapped her in that place day and night seeing no one. He feared she was mad but 'e drove her mad, that's what they say. He put her in a room and buried the key. *Poor old Laura de Grey.* He drove that lady to an early grave."

I shake my head. "There must have been a reason," I say, thinking how Jonathan would have tried to protect her. "Laura lost her mind after the children were born, I've heard of it happening; it happens to healthy women. He was concerned."

"He was concerned, all right," says Marlin, "and you're right, it was after she had those twins. Laura couldn't cope, that's how they tell it. Laura didn't love them. Laura didn't *like* them. They say she did at first, but then whatever fiend's got hold of Winterbourne made sure she lost her mind, and took her own life thereafter. Your captain came out of one war and right into another. He got fright she'd harm them."

"He thought he was helping? He thought by locking her up he could save her?"

Marlin tests me with those eyes of his; tests how far I will go with him, how much I am willing to believe. "You seem awful keen to make a martyr of him," he observes. "But the story goes that your master i'n't quite the innocent, miss. I see it in his eyes: it's guilt, plain as a cloudless day. He thinks those deaths at Winterbourne are his fault, and maybe they are. Who's to say Laura would've died if he hadn't forced her into solitary? Or that other woman, the one before you, they say he scorned her and that's why she did what she did. But make no mistake: whatever's in that house was always going to get them, whether he helped it or not. That's what it does. It wants the women, see, Miss Miller. Every woman who's set foot in that place with hopes of becoming its mistress has come to her end. Laura got further than most, but that's what it likes to do." He grins horribly. "It makes you believe it first."

"I won't accept it! I can't!"

"It uses the children to get what it wants. Children are soft, see, they get molded any way it likes. It tells them what to do, and they do it."

"I reject this; you must not speak any more —"

"Reject it at your peril, for it's the women it wants. Some say it's the spirit of a spurned old witch. She sends the women mad, see, mad with love, with passion, with hate, with what came out of their wombs, mad to their deaths —"

I stand, unable to hear any more. I cannot! I will not. I stagger from the boat, sick with the rocking of the sea, and grab the ladder that will take me back to land, safe land, dry land, with none of these hideous imaginings!

"You know you can't run from it," Marlin calls after me, his words snatched by the bitter wind. "The curse'll catch up wi' you eventually. You came here; you came to me, so I think you know. I think you're frightened it's doing the same to you."

I shakily climb the rotten, weed-coated

ladder, my vision blurred, black water rolling menacingly beneath my feet. I haul myself up on the rocky shelf, but when I look up at the sheer cliff and the wild beach and the destination that waits for me, the clamoring siren of Winterbourne, I wish to plunge into the water and never return.

"Listen," says Marlin, standing on the deck with his three dogs. I am anxious to deem him insane, hear his lunatic words and see his senseless eyes and throw all I have listened to deep into the ocean, but he watches me steadily.

"You get as far from Winterbourne as you can," he warns. "Get far away from him and away from the de Greys. Because if you don't, you'll be next."

CHAPTER 29

CORNWALL, PRESENT DAY

The rest of the week passed decisively for Rachel. She kept the magazine that Aaron had brought on the chest in the hall, a reminder every time she passed it of the life to which she was set to return. She couldn't spend her future trapped in her past.

Aaron contacted a new Realtor about valuing the estate. Despite her initial misgivings, Rachel was grateful for his optimistic companionship. Could she return his feelings, in time? Could she learn to allow him close, even to fall in love with him? On paper Aaron was easy to love — gorgeous, generous, smart, successful — but she'd never considered it before. It hadn't been part of their arrangement, and felt too much like a betrayal of Seth. But as she watched him sort through boxes, as he fixed her meals, as she felt him tenderly rub her shoulders at the end of a tough day, slowly she could start to envisage what their lives might be like together. It would be easy to say yes to him, to be loved and looked after, to share her hopes and fears, to have someone to make breakfast with in the mornings, just as she had when she was married. For this time at Winterbourne, they were that couple. They laughed and talked over late-night suppers; they walked along the bluff after hours cooped up.

Suddenly Aaron didn't seem so at odds with Winterbourne. He appeared less tightly wound, more relaxed, more encouraged somehow. She supposed that, after all, he knew her best. She could talk herself into loving him. She could.

When the Realtor visited, Rachel spent several hours showing him round Winterbourne and its grounds, then discussing her situation and her intention to shift the property from abroad. "Of course, Ms. Wright," said the Realtor, fawningly. "Rest assured we will look after everything, from viewings through offers through auctions — because there will be an auction — right to contracts, and we'll keep you informed every step of the way." Rachel chewed her thumb. She asked about prospective buyers' objectives: could they ask for an indication of how the successful bidder would handle the house? Would they demolish it or extend it; would they put a swimming pool out where the old stables used to be, or a gym in the chapel? She struggled to imagine change and felt protective of the place. "I guess I just want to feel it's going to the right people," she said, and the Realtor smiled his foppish smile and told her that they would do everything they could to manage her wish. When he asked a little pertly if she wouldn't prefer to stay at Winterbourne herself, Aaron stepped up behind and put a hand on Rachel's shoulder: "She wants to sell," he said.

Rachel was grateful to Aaron for maintaining her focus. She dreamed of a young family buying the house, of children's laughter filling the rooms, but knew it was unlikely. More probably it would go to a developer who would raze it to the ground and build a block of apartments. Still, she couldn't afford to be sentimental.

She and Aaron spent their days carefully packing up, sorting and signing paperwork, combing through the details together even when Rachel's eyes were ready to close and Aaron had to all but put the pen in her hand. Much of Winterbourne's contents would be sent to auction, but certain items Rachel wished to take with her: a delicate gold bracelet she decided to believe belonged to her grandmother; an elegant silver clock engraved with the letters *L. Until the end of time,* and, of course, the diaries her aunt had kept, haphazardly arranged inside that boarding-school trunk.

"What about that thing?" Aaron asked one evening, as he passed the mirror by the fireplace. He fingered its ornate Gothic frame, somewhat uneasily, and then laughed at his reflection. "Not all that flattering, is it?"

"I don't like it," said Rachel. "Never have."

"Whose was it?"

"My aunt's, I expect. Though I don't know for sure."

"You're not taking it, then?"

"God, no. The mirror belongs at Winterbourne. I can't picture it anywhere else. I feel as if the house would be furious if I tried to take it away."

Aaron was up early on the day of their flight, loading their travel bags into the Porsche. Rachel stayed a while in her bedroom, watching him out on the drive.

On impulse, she took the painting of the cottage off the wall. The little window was still wide open, a picture of clarity and stillness. Where all else at Winterbourne was flamboyant and looming, the image of the cottage was simple and quiet. It hadn't occurred to her before how at odds it was with the rest of the house, but she liked its difference. Again she scrutinized it for a sign of human life, but naturally there was none: just the brown cow and the milk pails and the gently smoking chimney. She decided to take the painting with her. She would hang it in the gallery in New York, and every time she passed it she would feel a pull in her heart, and look at that name, *M. C. Sinnett,* and wonder to whom it had belonged.

As she was leaving, the corner of wallpaper she'd noticed when she first arrived once again caught her eye — a dark, mossy tangle just above the skirting.

Rachel bent and touched it, and, in doing so, she realized it wasn't wallpaper at all but something painted directly on to the fabric of the house. She'd been wrong in thinking that the wall had been stripped: on the contrary, those violently torn ribbons were instead a spoiled attempt at *covering up* what lay beneath, not removing it. Perhaps several layers of paper had been applied in an effort to conceal it.

She began to pick at the paper. It soon became impulsive, like picking a scab, and the more she picked, the more came away, some in small nubs like the peel of a tightly skinned orange, and some in great sheets like skin after sunburn. She was aware how frantic she would look to anyone who noticed, but Aaron was outside and she was alone and just for now she could afford to be frantic, tearing at the paper without knowing why, just certain she had to see what it was hiding.

Afterward, she stepped back to survey the design. It was blindingly intense.

The corner of moss she had spotted was just the start — a mere shoot in the most sprawling, colossal tree imaginable. Although it wasn't a tree, it was more vaguely amorphous than that, it was *vegetation,* a dense forest of stems and stalks that wound and twisted over and under each other. To follow one tangle was futile, as it disappeared into a nest of its sisters, so intricate and elaborate that it made her eyes swim. The vines were a solid screen of blackest green, the green of seaweed washed up on a pale shore; and as Rachel stood before it, she had the unsettling impression that if she peered hard enough, if she even reached out and parted the branches with her hands, she would glimpse a pair of eyes peering back at her from the other side.

She stepped back, afraid. But the foliage drew her closer, with eyes and voices that flashed and whispered, whispered of something terrible . . .

"Rachel?" Aaron was at the door.

She looked up.

"There's someone here to see you."

CHAPTER 30

Jack was waiting outside. Aaron stood in the doorway behind her, his arms folded.

"Give me a minute, would you?" she asked him.

"We have to leave," he said. "It's a long drive."

"I know. It's OK."

Aaron climbed into the Porsche and told her he'd pass an hour in Polcreath. "Then we really have to get going," he said. "All right?"

"All right."

He slammed the door.

When they were alone, Jack said: "You're leaving Winterbourne?"

"I'm leaving the country," she replied. "I'm going back to the States."

Jack nodded, as if he'd been expecting this. Neither of them spoke for a moment. Rachel tried not to entertain the pleasure she felt at Jack's closeness, the warm solid bulk of him. She tried not to look at his scruffy, work-splashed clothes, so different to Aaron's, or the patches of gray above his ears, one of which was tufting out like a barn owl's. "Can I come in?" he asked. "I've got something for you."

She nodded.

"So you're really serious about this," Jack said inside, looking around at the sealed crates and cartons, the extinguished fire in the grate.

"I am. Aaron made me see sense."

"Which was?"

"Going home. I have a good life in New York."

"Including him?"

Rachel passed Jack his tea. "I haven't figured that out yet."

Jack made a face that suggested he wouldn't press further. She didn't imagine him to be the jealous type — at least not in any obvious way.

"Did you come to say goodbye, then?"

He drank. "I came to give you something. Call it a parting gift." He removed a folder from his bag and handed it to her. As Rachel took it, she ignored the sting in her chest that she would never see this man again. She would never stand in his farmhouse kitchen getting slowly drunk or lean against a wall with him, under the stars. She would never climb into his smelly old Land Rover or stroke his dogs.

"What's this?"

On the front of the folder it read:

PROPERTY OF THE PRIORY OF
ST. JOSEPHINE, WESTWARD,
CORNWALL

CASE FILE 0587

But she knew before Jack spoke. She knew because when she opened the file she saw her grandmother's name: *Alice Elizabeth Miller. Born August 3, 1919.*

"I got talking to this guy in town," said Jack. "His dad used to work at St. Josephine's. The asylum's long gone now — the building's still there, I mean, but it's a school these days. I'm sure you could visit it, if you wanted . . ." He trailed off, then began again: "Some of the patients' records were saved, including Alice's. If you're right about her being your grandmother then it's all here. The missing piece."

Rachel closed the file and slid it across the table.

"Why would I want this?"

He was confused. "I thought you wanted

to know."

"Know what? That my grandmother lost her mind? That they did all sorts of horrible things to her? That my unborn mother never stood a chance?"

"You don't know about your mother. I thought that was the point."

"I know she's dead. I know I'll never meet her. So why bother?" Rachel stood and turned her back to him, wishing he had never come, never brought the folder to her; she wished Aaron would return in the car and they could drive away.

"That's not you talking," said Jack.

"It sure sounds like me."

"No, it doesn't. Look, Rachel, whatever that guy's said about the reasons you should go back — well, what about the reasons you should stay? Don't you think this is important any longer? Don't you believe in the truth? You've wanted the truth your whole life and now here it is, right in front of you, and you're too afraid to look?"

She faced him. "So what if I am afraid," she said. "Wouldn't you be?"

"Yes, I would. But I'd still do it."

"You can't know that."

"I can. It's who I am. Maybe you don't know who you are, and that's the problem."

She shook her head, incredulous. "How

dare you," she said. "You had no right to obtain these records behind my back and you have no right now to come and speak to me like this. I made a decision to leave this behind and I'm sticking to it."

"You don't think you'll regret it?" Jack pushed. "You'll never look back on Winterbourne as the one great question mark of your life — a question you didn't have the guts to answer? Well, I've got the guts. That's why I brought this to you."

"Fine, you're a saint, Jack Wyatt. Is that what you want to hear?"

He came to her and put his hands on her shoulders. They felt big and strong, grounding, and she remembered the first time she had seen those hands, when he'd come to the house all that time ago and told her he'd drawn the short straw.

"I care about you, Rachel," he said. "I want to see you happy."

"Then let me get on with my life."

"This *is* your life. Don't you see? It's the only thing that's going to bring you peace. I honestly feel that if you go back to America now you'll never find peace. You'll never have answers. This is never going to go away. I get that you're scared about what you might find but I'll help you. I'll be there. We'll work through it, whatever it is, together. Think of the people you trust, Rachel, and I don't mean that hopped-up vanity project streaking around town in a Porsche — what would the people you trust say? What about your adoptive parents? What about Seth?"

"Seth isn't here any more."

"But I'm willing to bet I know what he'd tell you to do. He'd tell you to put this house to rest, properly and faithfully, in all the right ways. He wouldn't order you to sell it like your American friend, then kidnap you back across the Atlantic so he can keep you in a cage and tell you to wear a nice dress and get your hair done when I think you're beautiful with mud on your face riding that stupid bike in the rain."

She blinked. She could hear the faulty kitchen tap, *drip drip, drip drip.*

"You should never have brought Seth into this," she said.

"But I have, so deal with it."

His rudeness was appalling, his assumptions, his arrogance. It had been stupid to tell Jack about her husband's death. It could never be retracted, never be forgotten. It could remind her of the things she already knew but that didn't fit with whatever action she'd decided — like the fact that Jack was right: Seth *would* tell her to stay.

409

"I'm sorry, Rachel," he went on, "but this is how I see it. You've been scared for so long you don't even know what you're running from any more. So you'll just keep running, from one thing to the next, without any of it meaning anything. This is your chance to come ashore. This is your chance to stop drifting. You have to let go of the pain you're carrying, instead of pretending it doesn't exist."

She pushed him away, angry. "You have no idea about pain."

"Don't I?"

"How can I pretend it doesn't exist, when it's with me every day?"

"You're doing a fine job of trying. How long is it going to last? How long until you open up again, I mean really open up to someone and allow yourself to be happy? You talk about getting back to your life, Rachel, but all you're talking about is climbing back on a treadmill. You're not really living. You're not really alive. Don't you think you owe it to Seth? Don't you owe it to him to make your life count, if for no other reason than because he can't? Don't you think you can find the courage to meet the facts and accept them, even if you don't like them, the kind of courage your husband found in his last moments? You haven't been living since he died, have you — and that guy out there with the stupid hair doesn't see it but I do."

She slapped him. Her palm stung where she'd done it.

"Get out of my house," she ordered.

Jack accepted it. He even smiled a little, ruefully.

"I want you to feel your heart beating," he said. "I think you have since you've been here. I have, since you've been here — felt mine, I mean." There was a pause. "I came to ask if there was any other reason you might want to stay," he said, "but I guess I have my answer."

She didn't reply. Just kept listening to the tap, her palm burning. After a moment he left, and she heard the rumble of his car as it disappeared down the drive.

She waited a while in the kitchen, too upset to move. Her impulse was to open a bottle of wine, sit tight until Aaron came back and block out the rest. Once she was in America none of it would matter. But something stopped her: the need to prove Jack wrong. She grabbed the folder and stalked through the hall toward Jonathan de Grey's study. Without thinking about it, she opened the file and began to read.

Observation notes: December 16, 1947
Unhappy. Refused medication. Refused food. Obliged to restrain.
Observation notes: December 18, 1947
High spirits. Talk of reconciling with former employer. Alleges he is father of her unborn child.
Observation notes: December 23, 1947
Believes she is living at Winterbourne. Administered ECT/sedatives.
Observation notes: January 19, 1948
Delusional. Maintains she saw footprints in snow outside ward window. Second attempt on life feared possible.
Observation notes: February 12, 1948
In positive mind. Pregnancy beginning to show.

Sitting at de Grey's desk, Rachel read on. As the picture built, so did her sense of injustice. Alice Miller had been incarcerated at St. Josephine's while she was pregnant with the captain's child. How could Jonathan have let this happen? How could he have allowed it while he had all of Winterbourne to offer her? The more she read, the more hateful it seemed. That women had been locked up in these times, and not just in these times but in all the times past and all the world over, with depression, anxiety,

412

stress, with hormones and feelings and emotion; they had been labeled mad with hysteria, mad with their thoughts and impulses, and the longer they were locked up, the more real their frustrations became. The pages blurred as she read and read. She kept thinking she heard Aaron return, but the house stayed quiet.

She followed Alice Miller through her pregnancy, watching her bloom like a lawn in spring. She could picture her grandmother walking through the gardens at St. Josephine's and liked to picture her at peace, her hand laid serenely on her stomach. Had it been like that? She'd never know. Probably it hadn't. The file detailed "breakdowns" and "collapses," labeled Alice as "distracting" to her fellow patients and as "confused" on good days and "maniacal" on others. It catalogued dosages given when Alice was "in a state of tension" or when she displayed "troublesome" or "disruptive" behavior; she frequently reacted badly to medication and the question persisted as to whether she'd have been better off without any interference at all.

Reaching the end of the folder was like anticipating a collision. As the pages began to thin, Rachel knew what was coming. She wasn't surprised when, in July, Alice's baby girl was born. *The child is called Sarah,* the record read.

Sarah. My mother.

She snapped the file shut. She wasn't ready. After all these years, after waiting her whole life, she still wasn't ready. Emotions overtook her: anger, sadness, fear, rejection, and most of all disappointment in herself that she wasn't braver than this. Jack was right. She was still running, and it was here, at Winterbourne, that all roads converged. Tears filled her eyes. She forced herself to say the name aloud — *Sarah* — to make certain it was right, to make sure it fit, because surely she would know when she spoke her mother's name. She wanted time to stop, to stop here where she could imagine Alice holding Sarah and the cocoon of their bond.

But it couldn't stop here. She had to go on and finish what she'd started.

Rachel wiped her eyes. She reopened the case.

The inevitable took only a few lines to come to light. The baby Sarah was taken away. *Mother unfit,* so the records read. *Environment unstable.* Rachel could scarcely imagine the torment this must have caused Alice, that tiny hand prised from hers, that soft head with its sweet smell whisked away

414

down a corridor. *Alternative parenting sought.* And that was what had happened to Rachel, too. *Alternative parenting.* She'd had alternative parents, just like her mother. Suddenly, she shared this vital connection with Sarah. They had both been taken away from the women who birthed them, nursed them, and held them when they cried. *My mother.*

Sarah Miller.

Why not Sarah de Grey? Because Rachel's mother had been denied — that much was clear. What other reason could there be for no further mention of Jonathan? He had either never known about Alice's pregnancy — thanks to Constance keeping the letters quiet — or else he *had* known and chosen to turn his back on it. Rachel looked about her now, at the great man's study, and was filled with a sense of injustice. That he had turned away seemed all too plausible. She could imagine him in his castle, with his splendid children and their impeccable standing, and what a blemish it would be on his widower's reputation to have got a young girl into trouble, let alone one in his employment. And so Sarah Miller, an inconvenience, was vanished into obscurity, away from her mother, never to be seen or heard from again.

Or not, as the case may be — for, as Rachel turned the final page of the file, she saw that there was another document concealed there, an addendum some official had latterly slipped in. She opened the paper and folded it flat, and saw it was a summary of a life. She read it. It only took a minute to read, if that, and there was such pity in this — that a whole life could be compressed into a minute or less — that she put a hand to her mouth and cried. She cried at the sorrow of it, at the waste. She cried at the facts she'd convinced herself of, none of them true. All this time, she hadn't had a clue. She had dismissed her mother as a dropout; someone who had never cared about herself, let alone the daughter she'd given up. How mistaken Rachel had been.

Sarah Thripps, née Miller.
B. July 29, 1948, d. April 3, 1984.

Cause and place of death: traffic accident, Polcreath High Road, Cornwall.

Mr. and Mrs. E. J. Thripps of Ashdown Road, Billericay, Essex, adopted Sarah, daughter of Alice, as an infant. She attended local state school and continued her education at college and university,

416

moving to London aged twenty-three to train as a teacher. Unmarried at thirty-four, she fell pregnant with her daughter (father unknown); the child was born in late 1983 and named Rachel Louise. At the start of 1984 Sarah learned of her adoption, and that her birth mother, Alice, had claimed connection with Winterbourne Hall, Cornwall, owned by the de Grey dynasty. It was on a journey to discover her history at Winterbourne that Sarah was involved in a car accident, her vehicle struck in bad weather by an oncoming lorry. Sarah died on impact but her baby survived the accident and entered the adoption services.

That was it. Ended. It was so cold, so clinical, seeing her mother's life laid out like this. But at its heart was a glowing promise. Sarah hadn't given her up. Sarah had kept her. Sarah had loved her. She and Sarah had been together, and been meant to stay together, and would have stayed together were it not for a freak accident that had left Rachel orphaned, essentially, for there was no word on the identity of her father.

She allowed herself a moment to mourn Sarah Miller, to hold her mother in her heart and then let her go. And in her mourning she found warmth. Warmth in the love Sarah gave her in the first weeks and months of her life; in the fact she had never been rejected, she had been adored; warmth in the knowledge she had been called Rachel from the start, because she hadn't realized until now how much it mattered.

Sarah had been heading to Winterbourne for the very reason Rachel was now here: to seek answers. They had come together, in a way, in the end.

She imagined her mother on the road to Winterbourne, high on the hill in the driving rain. She imagined the headlights of the truck, the blare of its horn, and the steering wheel rushing through Sarah's hands as she lost control and knew she was doomed. What had she thought in her final moments? Had she worried for Rachel? Had she reached out and touched her, told her she'd be OK?

Winterbourne was never the wiser.

Winterbourne never knew Sarah existed.

CHAPTER 31
CORNWALL, 1947

I dream of high towers and high turrets, clouds that pool and dissolve against a midnight sky; I dream of moonlit marshes and figures in white; of torches blazing in a forest, torches descending a hillside, shouting that they will drive me out; I dream of water, dark and clinging, and I dream of diving beneath its surface to a shimmering, glimmering shard on the bed, and when I reach it, it is Laura de Grey's mirror.

I wake, my breath as sharp as glass. I go to the hallway where Constance always stops and force myself to look up at the ceiling — only this time, instead of darkness, I see it: the small, thick black hook driven into the beam. It is a curled finger, a beckoning finger: *Come closer, come close, a little bit closer . . .*

This is where Laura did it. The hook beckoned, and she followed.

Chilled, I creep back to bed.

419

"Winterbourne wants the women . . . Some say it's the spirit of a witch . . ."

I could leave. I could pack my bags and board a train to London, and be rid of this place once and for all. But I cannot abandon him. I cannot abandon my hopes of our future, here, in this house that would, with my help, be happy and peaceful at last, with these children who need me and whom I still adore. Winterbourne is my chance: the only place that has offered me rebirth. Here, I can begin again. So can Jonathan. I still carry this belief and I must carry it carefully, like a candle held in the wind.

By morning, I am cold. I lie watching the foliage on the wall. I follow its stalks but the tangle leads me back on myself, back to where I started, back to front and front to back and there is no sense to it, no reason! It really is most queer.

Time passes. Winter deepens, the frost hardening on the ground and the sky solid gray, as if it is not open air but a leaden, sunken roof. Freezing mists hem us in, and when I look out of the window I see my reflection looking back. Occasionally I hear the fog blast of the tower light, a reminder of those on the sea, cut adrift, and it reminds me of the Sleeping Beauty and how her prince slashed through dense leaves to rouse her, and how I might be roused if I could only slash through mine. But still the foliage gazes back at me, an impossible screen, impenetrable and watching.

Marlin's words haunt my every waking hour. *"Winterbourne wants the women . . ."* My every sleeping hour, too, in toxic, frightful imaginings, terrible imaginings, as the phantasms of these women, invented women, come flying into my dreams on leathery wings. Winterbourne cannot want to destroy me. Winterbourne *likes* me. It has always liked me. It knows me, and wants to give me what I crave.

And then, suddenly, it does.

On Christmas Day, everything changes.

I suppose it should not come as a surprise. These past weeks I have felt a thing latch on to me, draining my energy and blood. Lessons with the twins are a struggle. I drift away while they complete their exercises, or else I visit the lavatory, feeling sick, and sit with my head in my hands, thinking dreadful thoughts. I am thinking back to the war, to Betty and our canteen . . . I am thinking of Betty lighting a cigarette inside her cupped hand, the flare of it, and of my hurting stomach and of lifting up my skirt.

It is an effort to join the celebrations, such as they are. I am tired, very tired. The children squeal over Father Christmas and pillowcases, which they leave at the fireplace with sherry and mince pies. Mrs. Rackstile encourages the decoration of the giant tree, the smartly wrapped presents and red and white paper streamers, pursuits that might formerly have been mine but now she is preferred. The children spoil her with their smiles and love, their kisses and their trust, whereas they regard me warily, as one might a beggar on the street corner, obliged to pass me each day, perhaps even to exchange a word, but secretly wishing I would be cleared away.

I know they are frightened of me. They have not forgotten that morning in the snow, and are convinced of my madness and neglect. The more I grasp for them, the madder I seem. But I force myself to, for if I do not then I will become frightened of them in return. *"It uses the children to get what it wants. It tells them what to do . . ."*

Mrs. Rackstile observes my deterioration with pleasure. She would never crow, for she is too contained. I have never learned to master myself in this way, my feelings too rampant to hold down. Mrs. Rackstile is a study in mastery.

My father would have liked her — something closer to the boy he craved. She reminds me of the matrons at school with their wide cream calves and pleated skirts, looming in the doorway with their hands on their hips. *Come along, Miller, no time to waste; chop-chop, Alice, get on with you, girl!* Those beady eyes are on me now, and I am the fool again. Mrs. Rackstile belittles me in front of the twins: "Let's get on with it, shall we, or we'll be waiting all day for Alice." She makes asides to Jonathan that she thinks I cannot hear: "Are you certain your governess is quite well, Captain? I find her anxious and secretive — and she makes plain her disdain of me." She cannot understand why he keeps me on. *Because he loves me,* I long to say, for then she would see who was the woman of this house.

And he can't get rid of me now, can he? Not now I am carrying his child.

The realization comes at Christmas lunch. Turkey turns in my stomach and the cranberry sauce tastes queer. I have been cramping since Tuesday but there is no blood. My bleed was late last month, so now, surely, here it is. But there is no blood. Before now, alone and dreaming of him, I have let the thought of it cross my mind.

Today I am no longer dreaming. I know.

"You look awfully pale," says Edmund from across the table.

"Manners, young man!" reprimands Mrs. Rackstile. How I wish she did not have to sit with us. I wish Jonathan would banish her to the servants' quarters, for that is where she belongs, and then it would be the four of us — the five! — as a perfect family. So much for Marlin's curse. Winterbourne has granted my wish. It longs not to destroy me but to have me create: to nurture its future and preserve its prosperity.

I fear I am going to be sick, so churning is the lunch in my belly, but instead of vomit, I want to bring up my good news, simply blurt it out to the table.

Dear Jonathan, I think. *Happy Christmas, darling . . .* I wonder what gifts Laura bought her husband over the years. A watch, a leather case — but none so grand as this! This will change everything. This will bring us together.

The feeling passes, and instead I look to Mrs. Rackstile and smile.

"It's quite all right, Mrs. Rackstile," I say, putting my hand to where life grows, in my lap out of sight. Across the room, Jonathan broods long-haired and unshaven, blue eyes searching mine. "It's the excitement of Christmas, that's all."

I must find a way to tell him. I do not sleep

at all Christmas night, thinking of the child inside me, a piece of Jonathan, growing, flourishing. It will be marvelous.

Pregnancy wasn't like this before. Before, I was scared, frightened of war, uncared for and alone. Now, it is different. We are together. Naturally Jonathan will be challenged by our news — it will represent fundamental change at Winterbourne — but his joy will overtake his doubt. This is what he has been waiting for.

I am not afraid of losing it — not this time. This child is meant to be. My child will be born and it will thrive, for it will be a magnificent de Grey.

On Boxing Day, the children are distracted by their presents. Edmund runs up and down the hallways with his fighter airplane, while Constance decorates her dolls' house with wallpaper. Mrs. Rackstile chose the presents. Jonathan praises her for it.

I wonder what the children will make of *my* present — a new sister or brother to play with. They will accept me again, then. They will have to! I will be their stepmother, because Jonathan will have to marry me. He will *want* to marry me. I will become Mrs. Alice de Grey, married by the rector at Polcreath Church.

I try to conjure the image of us as man and wife, but when I see my reflection in Laura's mirror my appearance lets me down. I am lowly. My clothes are drab and plain, my hair limp and my face drawn. What images this mirror has seen! What beauty! With her lashings of hair and embellished gowns, how perfectly suited Laura would have been in preparing for marriage: how seamless a transition from a Hensley to a de Grey. Not so for me. I must work harder. I must be eligible.

Late that night, when the house falls quiet, I descend once more to the cellar. Laura's belongings are as I left them, her robes boxed up, disturbed only where I ran my hand across their tempting surface. I seize the case, my footsteps padding quietly as a cat's. I am a thief. But Laura and I know each other now. Laura will not mind.

I undress in the privacy of my room. My naked skin prickles with cold, the fire in the grate dwindling to ash. I light more candles, which I am glad of because they lend my reflection a romantic, dramatic feel, perfectly in keeping with Laura. The flickering light plays tricks, shifting and moving so that in glimpses my image morphs into hers, overlapping with my own; her spirit is inside me, becoming me. In the little painting by the window, the girl has dropped to the soil outside her cottage; she is on her knees and praying to the sky. A shadow descends the hills beyond, a shadow coming to catch her. She is afraid. I hear their shouts; I see the flames in their hands.

Poor girl.

I am used to her by now. I do not mind her games. I do not mind if I imagine her because it does not matter, not really. All that matters is Jonathan and this family. After that, there will be no need of anyone else. I feel myself falling and I like that feeling. I want to fall and fall and never be caught.

I slip on the costume I prefer best: a high stiff collar and a full red skirt, the kind of costume befitting a lady. In front of the mirror I sway and turn, admiring my reflection. In wearing this creation I can believe that, one day soon, I will be at the helm of this house, swishing through Winterbourne in a fragrant, feminine cloud. I douse Laura's perfume across my neck and wrists. I pin back my hair, as Laura wore hers on her wedding day. In the hesitant candlelight, I am changed — from myself, to Laura, and then on again to another woman, another black-haired woman, maybe two women, maybe three more, swift as blinks, and my gaze, held so cautiously, is not my own but belonging to something far wilder and savage and more ancient than me.

The mirror is powerful. It holds me in thrall. I wonder if the dog Tipper would now bark so dreadfully at the cellar door, or whether it would be my door he feared.

The girl in the painting has gone. They have chased her away.

It is only me, only me who is left, and so immersed am I in the image of the woman in the mirror that I do not see the shadow lurking at my threshold.

CHAPTER 32

Mrs. Rackstile takes my arm and drags me downstairs, handling me like a child. She has made it her business to acquaint herself with every aspect of Winterbourne, and accordingly will have seen pictures of Laura; she will know my purpose. How I detest her! If she weren't here, I could go to Jonathan myself and remind him how it is to gaze upon a woman he loves. Instead, I am released at the door to his office.

"Captain, forgive the interruption," she begins, "but you should be aware . . ."

On Jonathan's desk is a collection of glasses, coated in amber hue. He turns to us, his eyes rheumy and shot with blood. For a moment, he believes I am Laura. He reaches for me, stumbles, then realizes I am not she. His expression is one of such intensity, such loathing and bewilderment and downright desire that I have to grip the edge of the table to stop myself fainting.

He, too, is in the grip of a lethal spell.

"I found her like this," says Mrs. Rackstile. "Dressed up like Mrs. de Grey. Surely, Captain, you see now that she needs help! I will telephone the doctor right away."

Jonathan cannot tear his gaze from mine. I stand transfixed, awaiting my fate; I half fear it, I half fear it will not be delivered. But I do not look away. I am not ashamed. I am beautiful. He comes to me and gently touches my face.

I resist the urge to put his hand on my stomach and tell him, *I am yours.*

"Go downstairs," he tells the housekeeper. "Fetch every item of Laura's that remains in the cellar and bring it here to me. Bring me everything. Now."

Mrs. Rackstile does as she's told. When she has gone, he says:

"Strip."

I assume I have not heard correctly.

"Strip," he says again. "I will not ask you a third time."

There is thrill in my disrobing. Rain spits against the windowpanes like glitter thrown from an endless night. I remove the high collar. I step out of the skirt. I let down my hair. Standing before him in my undergarments I must remind myself that he has seen me naked before. Here, though, it feels like the first time. He surveys my body. I reach to unfasten my brassiere. Jonathan stops me. "Don't do that."

"Why not?"

"Alice . . . Oh, Alice." He covers me with a blanket, wrapping me tight.

"Tell me, Jonathan," I say, his lips close enough to mine now that we could kiss. "Tell me what it is."

He closes his eyes. "You are not safe here. At Winterbourne."

"Yes, I am. I'm safe with you."

"Mrs. Rackstile is right. You should leave. Tomorrow. Tonight."

"I cannot! Captain, you must listen to the truth!"

"Oh, Alice, not you." His eyes open. "I prayed this would not happen to you."

"Nothing has happened to me," I cry. "Nothing has happened to me but *you*! Don't you see? It's you I live for, Jonathan. I have ever since I met you."

His voice breaks. "It's too late," he says. "Look at you."

I glance down at my body. My skin is mottled with thumb-sized bruises, crisscrossed scratches and brittle pinch marks that scatter from my shins to my neck.

"Do they hurt?" he asks.

"No. They'll clear. It's a sensitivity, the

431

sea air, nothing to fret about."

He shakes his head. "It's my fault. I should never have brought you here."

"Yes, you should! You have shown me love, Jonathan, you and the twins, and Winterbourne, all of you. It's all I want. I can be happy here, with you —"

I touch his cheek but in a flare his aggression is back and he strikes me away.

"I am not what you think I am," he says bitterly.

"Then what are you?"

"Not a man you would want in your life."

"I will decide that for myself!"

"There isn't a decision to make." He turns to the window, drink loosening his tongue, his head bowed in confession. "I've never been good for anyone. My mother told me so and she was right. She used to tell me, *Boy, you're a demon; everything you touch rots and dies.* She was a cruel woman, a difficult woman I've since been told, but as I said, she was right. After all, I drove her from Winterbourne; she left in the night without a word and never came back. Then I married the girl I loved and I lost her too. Then the governess before you, Christine: she came to me for help and I turned her away. Now you, Alice, now you . . . It's been proven. My mother was right. I'm no good.

432

I'm dangerous. You should stay away from me, far, far away."

I step toward him and touch his shoulder. "You mustn't believe it," I whisper. "I promise only good things will happen to us."

"It isn't your decision," he rages, "don't you understand? Aren't you listening? It's me, it's this house; it's bigger than you, or us, or any of it! I've tried protecting the people I care for. I stay away from the children. I stay away from Tom, and the doctor, and from Mrs. Yarrow when she was here. God knows I tried to stay away from you, but . . ." His voice breaks. "I ought to let the children away from Winterbourne, send them to board in the city, but I'm fearful of what will become of them. I'm afraid they will meet with some terrible fate, that Winterbourne will wreak vengeance on them for trying to escape! One thing is certain: they will hear dreadful talk about their mother and me, about what I did to her."

"You tried to protect Laura."

"And I failed."

"She would always have died, whatever you did. She wished to die."

"How could she have? We were *happy*. We had two beautiful children. We had a home and a future and we were in love."

It is on the tip of my tongue to say it: Marlin's dreadful vision. Winterbourne plays with its mistresses, lets them believe in joy for the pleasure of stealing it away.

"Jonathan, you must stop blaming yourself." But he is far beyond my reach. There is only one thing left, the quiet miracle that might bring him back to me.

"I have news," I say. I take his hand. "You see —"

Mrs. Rackstile returns, clutching the residue of Laura's possessions, which she holds out to him. The spell of our confidence is broken. Jonathan seizes Laura's clothes and stalks out to the courtyard, through the storm, where he heaps them up in a pile. In the dark, in the wet, they resemble spilled blood, a dark smudge against glistening earth. Rain tears in. The deep howl of a winter gale flips across the cliffs. Jonathan is untiring, limping without his cane, his inky hair plastered across his forehead and his clothes sodden. Box after box he seizes from the housekeeper — the jewels, the fragrances, the photograph of Laura and he on their wedding day.

I am amazed that the furnace catches in the downpour but it does, as if these things have all these years been waiting to burn, the mere switch of a match enough to ignite

434

them. Smoke billows into the night and Jonathan looks on, drenched and dripping to the bone, as the final relics of his lost wife blaze up to meet the stars.

I can still smell smoke on Mrs. Rackstile as she escorts me back to my room. "The captain instructed me to keep you safe," she says. "I am sorry, Alice, but this is for your own good. We cannot have you doing damage to yourself or to others."

"Damage? What kind of damage?"

"You are not well."

"You know nothing about me. You have hated me since you arrived."

The housekeeper is surprised. "I rather think it is you who have hated me, my dear. I have only tried to ease your burden at Winterbourne and to help the captain. It is you who have let your illusions get the better of you. Why, I mean you no harm."

"You mean to take this family away from me."

"It is not your family, Miss Miller. You ought never to cross that line. That is the first rule of housekeeping. We are workers, nothing more."

"I must speak with the captain privately. It is important. Please —"

"You must do no such thing. All you must

do is rest."

"But he has to know, he has to be told!"

Mrs. Rackstile draws me to a stop at the head of the stairs. "Told what?" she asks.

I have the urge to push her back. She is close to the descent — one push and I could end it here. Jonathan and I. Alice and Jonathan. Only us.

"Speak, child," says Mrs. Rackstile. "What is this urgent message of yours?"

I could push her, or I could tell her the truth. Maybe they are both the same.

"I am carrying his baby."

There follows a sliver of a moment in which she believes me — and then her face sags with pity. "My dear girl," she says, and all at once I am back at that Sunday table telling my father and hearing his contempt. "You are even more deluded than I feared. Can you expect me to give such a claim any kind of credence after what I witnessed tonight? Dressing up as his dead wife then purporting to be having his baby?" She shakes her head. "They should have warned you about this when you accepted employment. You are not used to residing in houses such as Winterbourne. You need a stronger constitution. The remoteness and isolation, it has addled your brain. Next you'll be telling me you're in the midst of a love affair with him!"

"He does love me."

Mrs. Rackstile deposits me in my room. I drop to the floor. I feel weak, defeated, inexorably tired. What few possessions I own she scrapes from their ledges and bundles into a sack, before she checks the wardrobe. She is leaving no trace of me here. Just Laura's mirror with me inside it, crouched on the floor, eyes wide and full of fear. The blanket covering me slips from my shoulders.

"What are you doing?" I ask.

"I am keeping you safe from yourself, Miss Miller," she says, taking in my scars. "You cannot be trusted. I will organize a permanent solution in the morning."

"You haven't been listening to me."

"I have, child, and that is why this is necessary. Look at yourself."

"I'm telling the truth."

She looks sorry for me. She, for me!

"It might be your truth," she says softly, "but it is nobody else's."

"I wanted to see how it felt," I cry, "to wear her for a while. That was all, Mrs. Rackstile!" The housekeeper stands in front of the forest mural. I imagine the creepers reaching out and drawing her in until only her outstretched hand is left for me to hold

on to. I will it to do this, its creepers starting to slip and writhe — but then she moves.

"I will check on you after breakfast." She
removes a key from her pocket.

"Do you mean to lock me in?"

"If you are a danger to yourself then you
are a danger to the children."

"The children?" I cry. "You could not possibly think —"

"Couldn't I? Edmund and Constance are
afraid of you. They told me as much. They
said you had lost your mind and were no
longer capable of caring for them. They said
you had become obsessed with the captain
to the detriment of all else."

"They're lying."

"Liars, the twins?" She balks. "I think
not."

"Just as I didn't when I first came here,
but I soon learned."

"And to what a place that learning has
brought you." Mrs. Rackstile surveys my
bruised, shaking limbs. She speaks to me
sympathetically, and there is horror in her
sympathy because it makes me doubt myself, what I think is true. "You are not made
for this life, Alice," she says gently. "You
have ideas above your station and they are
causing you pain. Tell me, what is wrong
with being the help? Is it not good enough

for you?"

"Please," I beg, "please don't leave me here."

"It is all I can do," Mrs. Rackstile says, closing the door. The heavy key switches in the lock and I hear her footsteps march purposefully away.

CHAPTER 33
CORNWALL, PRESENT DAY

Rachel canceled her flight back to America. Aaron was shocked.

"What? Rachel, come on, we've got this —"

"I have to stay," she explained. "I will come back, just not now."

"It's him, isn't it. That Jack guy."

Rachel couldn't think of Jack. She would probably never see him again and that was fine by her. "He gave me something I have to check out," she said.

"What?"

"I can't go into it."

"I'll help you. It'll be quicker."

"No."

Aaron bit down his frustration. She saw him consider his options, before taking her hands and saying calmly, "Why can't we just get rid of the place and you can find all this out afterward? Everything's sorted, Rachel. We're ready to go."

She shook her head. "I'm sorry. Go home. I've appreciated your being here, Aaron, but I didn't ask you to come and I don't ask you to stay. It'll be a few days."

"But I don't understand —"

She lost her patience. "Do you know what?" she said. "I don't understand either. What's any of this to you anyway? Why's it so important?"

He didn't answer. Just watched her, and she had never seen him look so tired and so broken. "I'll see you in New York." He climbed in and gunned the engine.

She read the rest of the diaries that afternoon. Just as she had peeled back the paper covering that forest mural, so the full picture was revealed. Winterbourne's history disclosed itself in a series of giddying revelations. At times Rachel could not accept what she read. Should she accept it? Her aunt's account was all she had, a little girl to an old woman who had lived her life in fear. Yet honesty was sewn into every sentence. Even if it weren't the truth, it was certainly what Constance had believed.

She learned how Christine, the children's first governess, had died.

"Both of us saw how she looked at Father," Constance wrote. *"She blushed from head to*

toe when he spoke to her. She wanted to marry him. When I think back, I wish I had been kinder to Christine. I would make Edmund be kinder. He was never kind. He played games. I told him not to. He said that the house had told him to, and that if he didn't we'd both get into trouble. He said, 'Do you want Christine to take Father away from us, Connie? Because that's what she'll do. She'll marry him and be our mother and then we shall have to call her Mummy. Do you want that, Connie?' "

Rachel thought about the twin beds in her aunt's room. How Edmund had eventually lost his mind and Constance had stayed behind to care for him, putting her own life on hold. Constance wrote on: *"Then Edmund did a terrible thing. He told Christine that Father loved her back. He told her that Father wanted to be her husband and she only had to ask. I'll never forget her face when she heard it, so full of hope. She wanted to trust it and so, against what must have been her wiser judgment, she did. I scolded Edmund. He said he'd had no choice. He was made to do it. A woman had come to our beds and whispered in his ear that he had to do it."*

Rachel pictured Christine gently knocking at the captain's study, waiting for permission to enter. She'd have stammered and stuttered, wrung her hands as she tried to communicate the emotion she felt, waiting for him to put her out of her misery.

But Rachel didn't need to be told what happened next. Jonathan de Grey would have rejected the poor woman straight out, possibly even mocked her, possibly shouted at her, possibly dismissed her with immediate effect. How Christine's hopes were shattered — by sadness, by disappointment, by humiliation.

"When she died, it didn't surprise me. I saw her love and for all my childish ignorance I recognized it as true. The way she did it was horrible, though, leaping from the cliffs and crawling, half dead, to the water. When they found her she was battered and bruised; everyone kept it from us but I overheard Tom describing it to Cook. He said she was 'covered top to toe' in red marks. Some people said Father had done it, and he'd done it to Mummy too. But Edmund and I knew better."

The clock on the mantel ticked solemnly. Part of her didn't want to continue; part of her was compelled. Constance was on a roll now; her scrawl flooded the pages as if whatever was inside her had to get out. Just as Rachel was forced to read on . . .

"I know now, and it's taken fifty years, that whatever lived here with us — whatever still

lives here — took the women from us one by one. It took my mother. It took Christine. It took Alice. It used us to wreak its plans. Before us, it would have used something else, for it has always been here, this thing, at Winterbourne, tempting the women into horrible games then destroying them one by one. I remember a shadow at our door and footsteps on the stairs, murmurs at night, and a hand holding mine . . . Sometimes it would be kind to us, soothe us when we were sick or wipe away our tears. Sometimes it would be angry, if we did not do as it said, and Father's leg would get worse or a chill would strike us down. Sometimes it played with us, giggling in the dark, hide-and-seek or ring-a-roses. But always it was there, as known to us as these walls and gardens, as much a part of this house as we are.

"Who, and why? I know not. All these years I have wondered. As we grew, its spirit became quieter. There were no more women, after Alice. Just me, and it had me where it wanted with Edmund, unable to have a family of my own, no hope of getting married. It's how she got me. Winterbourne is hers. Occasionally I would hear her, mostly at dawn when the sun came up and the morning breeze blew through the trees. I would hear her singing, quiet and sad, of a man she'd

loved and a broken heart . . ."

Rachel shivered. She wished she were not alone. The sky outside was darkening. She could hear the sea thrashing against the cliffs, sucking sand tangled with brown weed. A sliding anxiety gripped her, thinking of Alice, who had died at St. Josephine's asylum for the insane; then of Sarah, her mother, who had died at the car wheel in a storm; then of herself, herself, the third in that line, by blood a de Grey, here, miles from anyone, unearthing secrets and jumping at every snap of the fire . . .

"Stop it," she said out loud. Sarah's accident had been freak. Alice's madness had been born of her love for Jonathan de Grey, as had Christine's. Laura had been in the grip of postnatal depression, misunderstood in those days. It ended there.

"Even now," Constance wrote, *"close to the end, I think about Alice. She is the one I think about most — more than my mother, more than Christine, more than anyone. I think of Alice in the snow when we got lost and she was calling our names. I think of her arms around me when I used to sleepwalk, and sometimes I'd cry and I was afraid. I think of the smell of her nightgown, soft like talcum powder, and her telling me stories until I fell asleep. I think of her laughter. I think of her*

encouragement. She would have made a fine mother. I'm sure she did make a fine mother, eventually, in the short time between her baby being born and the end of her life."

Rachel closed her eyes. It was too painful. She forced herself to carry on.

"I don't know why I kept Alice's letters from my father at first. I was confused and frightened, frightened of change, of Winterbourne, frightened that we had drawn something evil out of Alice that could never be expelled. Perhaps the evil had always been inside her. What decay had we dragged to the surface? What had she done that she couldn't forget, and wouldn't forget her? I console myself with this, but there is little consolation to be found. By the end we were fearful of Alice and wished her gone, like children baiting an animal only to recoil when it bares its teeth. We'd had enough of the game, by then. It lost its fun. But it was our fault she ended up like that. We drove her to it. Did she really lose her mind? Or did we steal it from her?

"I was afraid that if Alice came back with her child then something bad would happen to them — to us all. Only now I understand my mistake. Father should have known sooner. It wasn't enough to tell him after Alice had died. I was punishing him for his distance, for the love he couldn't show. But it wasn't my deci-

sion to make and I regret it every day. What sadness it is that youth does not know wisdom.

"When I confessed, and he read the letters, he shut himself away for days. He would not eat, or sleep, or talk to anyone. I believed that part of him died then, too.

"When the baby, Sarah, was taken away to live with another family, Father said it was for the best. I didn't know then what he meant, but now I do. Of course I do. The further Sarah was from Winterbourne, the safer she'd be.

"But I'll never forget how he watched her grow, from afar, unwilling, though it saddened him, to intervene in her stable, happy life, wishing instead for her to be free. I even discovered after his death that he sent money to fund her learning, an anonymous donor. He found clippings from her school sports day, a poem she'd written for the local paper, a picture of her with her new family, and he pinned these up on his walls. By the time my father died, his study was covered. Affection for the daughter he never knew, yes — but also, though he never admitted it to me or to anyone, affection for Alice. I think he loved Alice. I think he loved her with his heart and soul and this was his way of making things right."

Rachel kept her finger over the final line until she was ready to read it.

"I hear Alice in my dreams, some nights. She is behind a locked door, calling for my help, begging to be released. She calls to me: 'Constance, I have a daughter, and my daughter has a daughter. Find that girl for me — and protect her.'"

Chapter 34
CORNWALL, 1947

I have discovered that if I peer close enough into the forest, I can see the women inside it. It has taken hours of solitude. I think it has taken days but I cannot be sure, because the light outside is so faded and drab that evening might just as well be the small hours of the dawn. Hours. Days. Weeks. Who cares for time passing? It has no bearing on me. Now I see their eyes, the curl of their fingers, and it is only a matter of time before one pushes through. Who will she be? Will she be like me? Laura painted the forest, I feel sure. Then she took one of the loops and she hanged herself with it.

I have the impression that other women have escaped the pattern. I feel them surround me. I hear them whisper when I lie on the boards, my cheek pressed against cold wood, wondering at the difference between that surface and the cool plump flesh that touches it. At the same time as they escape, they invite me in. The mural is not a flat pattern; it has depth, like a glass aperture breaking on to woods far darker and more plural than I know. New shoots grow from branches that are already there and I try to count them but I keep losing count. Why must they make themselves so innumerable? Repeat, repeat, they keep repeating, confusing me, trapping me, toying with me! Just as soon as I believe I am in control of it, it surprises me again, making me turn back to see the fresh buds that have caught me from behind.

It is like the seaweed on the beach below the Landogger Bluff. And the woman I see most, the woman who crawls from the pattern and cradles my head in her crooked arms is like the woman I saw on the sand, crawling and creeping toward the water. Her hair is black, matted and lank, and she reminds me of the little girl in my painting, moving by the day, made of oil and blood. She calls to me, *Come in, come in,* and I hear her, I do! I want to follow but I cannot risk my baby.

Whirls and spirals and coils and whorls, it is a miracle I hear anything above the din. Occasionally, though, I do. I hear the children, those devil-sent children, siding with my tormentor. Sometimes I cry over them. I failed them, just as I have failed my whole life, at love, at happiness, at becoming a mother. Laura tells me this is how she felt. The twins decided they did not like her. What was she to do?

I hear running footsteps and clattering laughter. I hear the hectic ringing of the bell box in the cellar. There are more children here than two. I attempt to reckon their steps and where or on what floor they hurry but it is just like the mural, just like that; it keeps multiplying until I meet myself again, not knowing which way is up and which is down. The horror of it! They are all around, these hurrying people, and I am at their center, cornered like a beast about to be drowned.

Do they knock? Sometimes they do. They knock and run, tittering or crying, and whispers like feathers come floating through the door, *Alice, oh, Alice, are you there, Alice?* Am I here? I am not sure. I think I am. Somebody is.

In a distant recess, he calls for me. The man I love calls for us both, Laura and me, and I sense him in another place, close by, far away, and I long for him to rescue me. My tears fall but often I get the better of them. I am stronger than this. My only rescue is here, in this room, with *them*. My only rescue watches me each day, and I it, contemplating which will move first. The life inside me is all that stops me climbing inside. You see, I think the women want it. I think they mean to take my child.

Come to us. You will be safe.

But my safety is with him.

Jonathan . . .

His name is a lost language, one I spoke for the shortest time. When I wonder at how he can keep me here, locked in this room, I tear my hair and batter the floor and howl like a dog. Do they hear my howls? They must, as I thrash the door, *stupid girl, silly girl,* thinking things that are not real. The creepers are real. The climbers are real. I could reach in and take one — there! I did it. It is heavier and greasier than I thought, wet as a snake and rough as rope. They would hear me if I did this.

They would hear you then. And I take the weed in my hands and close my eyes and let it wind around my throat. I am ready. I will do what I must.

In my mind I open the door that Mrs. Rackstile locked. Then I am crawling through this big, big house, crawling as swift as clouds across a wind-blown sky. I try to catch one, my feet and palms flat on the floor, try to bite it; it skitters into a corner. Why so secretive? That is what they say about me. They keep me inside, all day, behind windows, a prisoner. Sky is purple. Bats swoop. Outside, a lone star blinks.

In my mind I travel to the place where it happened, the place to which the girl Constance walks in her sleep, the hallway beneath the hook, and I look up at the hook and I see it clearly, as if it is real. I touch it, this special place. Where Laura died . . .

In my mind I feel them pull me back, pull my ankles, but I will not let them take me. My fingernails dig into wood, scratch until they bleed. I see the blood and struggle from the ones that went before, the marks they have made, and mine fit perfectly into those grooves, feeling my way through a space I know well. It is where I need to be, deep down there in the wood where they can't find me. And then I reach it. The dark spot, climbing up through the floor: it is beneath the floor, yet part of it, yet beyond it, all at once! It makes me spiral to think of it. I turn my head, winding it to the ceiling, like a cat with its neck twisted wrong. A storm is coming. I can tell by the sigh of the sea, its gray-green swell as it foams against the cliffs. It is a mad sea.

In my mind, I climb. Quiet. Quiet. Listen

again. They have gone. It is just you and me now. I had better hurry, before they catch me once more.

I attach the rope to the hook.

I stare down at my pale feet. The moon peers in. I am not in the hallway at all, but still inside my room as I always have been, bolted inside.

Now, I will escape. I tighten the loop. It was always going to come to this. Just as Laura let go of her life, for the next would surely be kinder. She kicked the stool from beneath her toes and choked and bucked and kicked to her death.

Years ago I wrote my fate — and now is the time to meet it.

CHAPTER 35

ALICE, WARWICK, 1936

He was Head of English. He had taught me my favorite poems. "Crossing the Bar." "The Raven." "Stopping by Woods on a Snowy Evening." It wasn't supposed to happen, although, as I supposed often in those days, it was inevitable that it had.

We lay in the music school on a Thursday night, his arms round me, his chest rising and falling and covered in the lightest sheen of sweat. We were surrounded by moon-bathed pianos and it seemed plausible that, against the drumbeat of my heart, they could start up together in chorus. Anything to drown out my thumping pulse, for that was what his proximity did to me: a seventeen-year-old virgin from Surrey who had only kissed one boy before and he was her second cousin.

"I hope to see my pilot face to face . . ."

That had been the moment. I had been sitting in English, gazing up at him reading

Tennyson. We had all been excited at the arrival of the handsome young substitute teacher, Robert Francis, with his wavy golden hair and soft, melodic voice that could easily have belonged to Romeo or Fitzwilliam Darcy. Ginny Pettifer had worn a faint coat of lipstick, and crossed her legs and re-crossed her legs.

He'd looked at me as he had spoken that last line. As if *I* was his pilot, and here we were, face to face, and the rest would happen whether we liked it or not.

"You're beautiful," Robert said now, kissing me.

For the first time, I believed him. I felt like a woman, not a girl. No more would I have to linger on the periphery of conversations between Ginny and her clique, listening to them sharing exploits of the boys they had sneaked out of Burstead to meet. Why did I know with certainty that I could never do such a thing — that, even if I dared, I would be discovered by the housemistress and hauled to judgment in my father's court? Girls like Ginny would never be caught. They had the magic.

Tonight, though, I had the magic. It was incredible to think of Ginny and her crowd in their dormitories, ignorant in sleep, while I lay naked next to Mr. Francis in Practice

Room 3, flushed and delirious after what we had done. The carpet was scratchy beneath my back. I kept thinking I heard a noise, a creak of steps or a tap at the window. Each time I startled, he stroked my hair. "What are you afraid of?" he asked.

"Aren't you afraid?"

"Not with you." His face was obscured by the night. Yet I felt his yearning like heat. He had so much more to lose than I did — his job, his reputation; he could go to prison for violating his position. But he *was* like Romeo, in that respect. He believed in love, as I did. Nothing could stand in the path of the real thing.

"I wish we weren't here," I whispered.

Robert raised himself on one elbow; he resembled a marble statue of a nude one might find in an Italian piazza. "I don't," he said. "It feels good to me."

"Have you done this before?"

There was humor in his voice. "Does it seem as if I haven't?"

"I don't mean that . . . I mean, with a student. A girl like me."

"There aren't any girls like you, Alice Miller. And no, as it happens, I haven't. Believe it or not, I've built my career on the utmost professionalism."

"I do believe it."

457

He stroked my knee with his thumb. "I'm not telling you off, Alice."

"I beg your pardon?"

"You sound contrite, as if I'm telling you off. I'm not."

"I know."

"I think you assume that everybody's telling you off. I'm not your father. I'm here to care for you, not to punish you."

"He would punish me if he found out."

"Nobody will find out."

"How can you know?"

"Because some things are divine, Alice. You're divine. We're divine."

"He'd kill me. He would. He'd sooner I was dead than this."

Robert's head bowed. "I could strangle him," he said, "for what he's put you through. Yet I must sit opposite him on parents' evening and shake his dirty hand — hands I know have caused you pain. I'd hope for him to find out about us, if only to give him the heart attack he deserves."

The thought churned my stomach. "It would be terrible. My life wouldn't be worth living. I — I'd have to leave. I'd have to run away."

"We could run away together. Shall we? After your exams are over?"

I pulled him toward me and met his lips

458

with mine. This was what love felt like, then, in a lifetime deprived of it. Burstead, for all its unhappiness, had at last delivered. All my hopes and imaginings weren't nonsense, as my father liked to tell me. Robert was my hero, my confidante, but he was also my protest against the institution of Burstead and the institution of my parents, inside neither of which I had flourished. My affair with my teacher was my secret and I protected it at all costs, enjoying the power it placed in my hands, power over my contemporaries and power over my weak mother and terrible father, with whom I was forced to reacquaint at exeats. When I was teased or taunted, I had only to think of being in Robert's arms, his kiss on my neck, open to him, adoring him, and none of it touched me.

What did he see in me? I tried not to wonder, tried not to ask, for I knew it made me unattractive. Robert said he was captivated by my flair for writing and invention, those very things my father had put down as the products of a nervous disposition, an ailment that needed to be cured. I shouldn't have told Robert about the misery of my life at home but I had no one else to confide in. And the more I told him, the more he seemed to love me and protect me, which was what I craved.

"I would like nothing more," I replied as he kissed me again. I was already dreaming of a train cabin in a far-flung mountain range, Robert at my side, thousands of miles from the house in Surrey or the clinical, corrective corridors of this austere boarding school. So long as we could keep our secret, the world could be ours.

I hated swimming. The stuffy, chlorinated pool was the scene of torturous galas, wicked clans of girls screaming from the sides with their polished ponytails and tightly clenched fists. Next week was the annual end-of-year swim race, an event I dreaded. I dreaded it more extremely this year because Robert would be watching, and I didn't want him to see me come in last again. In order to alleviate the usual humiliation, I had taken to racing lengths against the clock in my evenings. I found the exercise a distraction from thoughts of Robert, wondering about his home five miles from here and when I might have opportunity to visit, wondering what he was doing or who he was with, though he assured me his life was uneventful away from me: he would be marking papers and trying not to think about our time together.

I was so lost in these thoughts that it came as a shock when I surfaced at the deep end and saw Ginny Pettifer looking down at me from the poolside. Her arms were folded and she wore a triumphant smirk. I assumed she was anticipating my ritual embarrassment at the gala, and how her team would trounce mine ten to one.

"Hullo, Alice Miller," she said.

I felt vulnerable in my bathing costume. Now I had stopped, goose bumps appeared on my skin. The water lapped against the sides. Ginny's eyes gleamed.

Evening was creeping in outside. Normally I embraced the loneliness of having the pool to myself, everyone else in prep or gossiping in dorms, but with Ginny it felt ominous. I removed my swimming cap and waded to the metal ladder.

"I want to talk to you," said Ginny. She stood with her weight on one hip, playful, victorious. "And you'll want to hear what I have to say."

I climbed out and tried to move past her. But she grabbed my arm, hard.

"Could we speak in the changing rooms?" I said. "It's cold."

"We can speak here," said Ginny.

"At least — my towel —"

"I would have thought you were used to

being naked in public places."

"Excuse me?"

"Come along, Alice. I *know*. I *saw* you. With *him*."

Her expression was the very worst thing, utterly malignant. She tittered, let go of my arm because she knew I was rooted to the spot. She had me on a pin.

"The gold bracelet did it," Ginny said, her lips parting so I saw her pretty white teeth. "You've been hiding it under your pillow. But I saw it. I knew it was from a man; I could tell. And I thought, who'd be interested in plain old Alice? I have to say you astounded me. I don't know why he's attracted to *you*. He could have anyone."

I said nothing, conceded nothing. I was frozen, but feared that shivering would be an admission. I thought of the times we might have been careless, his fingers brushing mine in class or his voice when he acknowledged me in the corridor. I should have known that Ginny was the type to notice. I'd always assumed I was invisible to her, too ordinary to bother with. But I was her sport. Of course I was visible.

"Oh, Alice," she singsonged, "it's all going to end so very badly, don't you know? I'm going to tell *everyone*. I can't wait to see their reactions. I wonder what Mr.

Prendergast will say? Or Miss Holkham? Ooh — and what about your *parents*?"

"Ginny," I spluttered, "please —"

"Please what? Don't say anything? Well, I haven't so far, and let me tell you it's taken all I've got. I'm amazed I've been able to do it, in fact. It's been very tempting to blurt it to the girls and have a nice chinwag at your expense. But I wanted to see what you had to say first. Whether you admit it. You do admit it, don't you?"

"It's not what you think."

"What is it, then?" Her eyes widened. "He didn't *force* you, did he?"

"God, no, I love him!"

There it was: the consent. When Ginny said, "My, my, a love affair between a teacher and a student, what *will* everyone say?" I didn't have it in me to deny it.

"I must admit," said Ginny, "I've quite enjoyed carrying this scandal around with me, privately, as I'm sure you have too."

"It will be the end of him," I forced out. "And the end of me."

"Which do you care about more?"

"What?"

"Do you care about Mr. Francis more than yourself?" She sniggered. *"Mr. Francis, do you call him that? Or do you call him Robert? Oh, Robert!"* she trilled.

I charged toward the changing rooms. My vision was distorted and I felt as if I would fall. Ginny couldn't tell. I couldn't let her. Robert was the only thing in my life that was valuable. My father's anger was enough to make me vomit. I swallowed. I thought I would collapse. I put my hand out to one of the benches to steady myself.

"Come back here, Alice."

I stopped, turned to plead with her. "Ginny, I'm begging you. I'll do anything."

"Mmm," she smiled, "that does sound appealing. But listen, Alice, I've thought about all the things you could possibly do for me, and, well, there really isn't anything that pleases me so much as the prospect of sharing your secret."

"Ginny, please —"

"I've heard what a monster your daddy is. I wonder what he'll do? It'll be awfully fun finding out, won't it? Unless you'd rather tell him yourself, which I suppose is your only option. But you'd better be quick about it, Alice."

I watched her. She was close to the edge of the pool, her back to the water, that unbearable look of glee scratched across her face. *Your only option . . .*

Was it?

I stopped shivering; my teeth stopped

464

chattering. Perhaps Ginny sensed some change in me, some primitive part of her wise enough in all her stupidity to recognize that the authority in that moment had shifted. *You'd better be quick about it, Alice.*

I was quick. I closed the space between us in three steps and pushed her in.

I didn't know what I expected to happen. All I wanted was to hurt her and to give her a shock. But my strength surprised me. I shoved her hard — harder than I'd intended. Later, I would rationalize that I expected Ginny to splutter through the surface seconds later, damp and furious, and that even if it all came out afterward and my nightmares were realized, at least I had claimed my petty vengeance against the girl I detested. But it didn't happen like that. It didn't happen like that at all.

She must have fallen wrong. She must have slipped, maybe in trying to resist me, because she didn't fall straight in. Instead her head hit the side of the pool, and it must have been hard because I heard a crack before she tumbled backward into the water. A fountain of red billowed from her head. She held one arm out for help, half-heartedly because she had lost command of it, and I did nothing. Her stunned eyes stared up at the ceiling, blinking slowly like someone trying not to fall asleep, until after a second they glazed over, like the milky eyes of a whole dead fish I once saw on a plate in a restaurant. Just like that, it was over. So quick, and even through my addled shock I thought this seemed unfeasibly easy, to kill someone by accident.

"Ginny," I whispered, but I didn't do anything. I didn't do what I ought to have done. I didn't crouch down and put my hand out and help her. It was too late, anyway.

I watched, transfixed. The clock above the pool continued turning. The ceiling lights continued their harsh buzz. I was dripping; I could feel cold water snaking down my back between my shoulder blades. My mind was blank. If I jumped in now, made an attempt, at least, to repent, it would work out better for me in the long run.

But I didn't. I couldn't.

I can get away with this, I thought instead. Pretend I was never here. I had told no one I was at the pool, and my unpopularity ensured that no one would ask. I turned my back and went to the changing rooms and dried myself off slowly, thinking about how, tomorrow morning, when this shocking accident was revealed, I'd pretend to be as sad and scared and confused as everyone

466

else. *Poor Ginny.* But she'd always been wayward, hadn't she? Drinking with boys at exeat, stealing from her parents, defying the teachers . . . It had been only a matter of time before she came undone. Already I anticipated the discourse that would come out of her tragic demise. I was good at pretending, always had been. I returned to my dormitory and slept soundly that night.

CHAPTER 36

LONDON, PRESENT DAY

Paddington Station was busy, teeming with commuters and tourists. Rachel moved through like a swimmer against the tide, not quite in sync with the usual pulse and rhythm of things after her Polcreath quarantine. It seemed years ago, not weeks, since she had last been here. Travelers scrolled their tablets, watching the ever-flickering departure boards; echoey messages were read out over an announcement system; queues lined up at the ticket office; people babbled into phones or browsed card stalls.

She took the Underground to King's Cross and headed to the British Library. Inside it was quietly studious, with the lovely old smell of books and concentration, the richness of learning for learning's sake. She hoped she would be learning today.

Rachel spoke to an assistant, who showed her how the county archives worked and how to access family papers. She settled into a booth and opened the system. First, she searched for "Winterbourne Hall, Corn-wall." Up came reams of intelligence about the house, newspaper items from the turn of the last century, surveys marked with the park boundary, photographs detailing the south face and chapel, the stables and the crenellations that soared against the skyline — and it was strange to see Winterbourne like this, available to anyone, and in that availability the house became less exotic and interesting, more ordinary, more like any privately owned mansion. The photos didn't convey any of the house's sheer extraordinariness. Rachel supposed that unless you could hear the gulls and smell the sea you were nowhere near.

She tried "Winterbourne Hall" and "de Grey family," which brought up information on her ancestors' genealogy, eventually arriving at Jonathan, his wife and twins, but only touching the surface of what she already knew. Rachel needed to go further back, right to Winterbourne's beginning, the forging of its bricks and mortar, and find out how the house had come into this world and by whom.

Finally, she met her answer. She leaned in, absorbed.

She read that a man named Ivan Randolph de Grey had built Winterbourne in 1810, favoring, quite evidently, the Gothic Revival style. It seemed that Ivan had spent time in France admiring the gargoyles and buttresses of its grander cathedrals, and, wishing to stake his ownership over that part of Cornwall (he was reportedly the richest man in the region thanks to his plumbing business, something about lead pipes and drainage systems that she skimmed over), he chose "the most extreme outcrop" Cornwall had to offer: the renowned Landogger Bluff at Polcreath.

"De Grey had his mind set from the moment he saw it," claimed the biographer, *"desiring, as he put it, 'a dramatic sort of place, where in winter thunder strikes with the fist of God and in summer the sun shines brighter than anywhere in England.'"* She learned that the project took four years and three months to complete and had resided in the de Grey family ever since. *"It became an obsession for Ivan de Grey,"* the item alleged, *"and remained the apple of his eye until his death in 1851."*

So a megalomaniac had built the house: Rachel could well imagine that. But there was more. Some piece was missing, if only she dared look.

Checking about her, nervous in case

470

anyone should see but needing to rule it out, needing to read the words "no results found," Rachel typed in "Winterbourne curse." *"Did you mean **Winterbourne witch**"?* the system shot back. She paused over the keyboard for a moment then thought, *yes; perhaps I did,* and clicked on the link.

And there it was. She knew immediately that she had stumbled across classified information. This wasn't contained in the annals of Winterbourne's acceptable, above-board history. This was something else. *"Legend of the Polcreath Witch Hunt,"* she read, *"December 1806. Winterbourne Hall site of Unlawful Witch Trial! Body of Mary Catherine Sinnett found drowned at Polcreath Point."*

Mary Catherine Sinnett.

Rachel sat back, bewildered. She joined the dots immediately.

M. C. Sinnett.

The signature on the little painting of the cottage . . . The initials on the back of that horrible mirror, hiding all that time underground . . . The name struck her with clarity and conviction, sending a liquid shiver from her neck to the base of her spine.

"It's how she got me," Constance had written. *"Winterbourne is hers."*

Rachel scanned dozens of pieces, as she slowly and disbelievingly assembled the

471

story. It went that Ivan de Grey had coveted the site where Winterbourne now stood — that remote, craggy outpost — so deeply that he couldn't get the land out of his mind, even when he learned that it was already occupied, namely by a spinster called Mary Catherine Sinnett. Mary Catherine had lived alone in her cottage for years, minding her own business away from the rest of the community, with a small livestock to sustain her modest needs. Rachel could picture it perfectly. After all, she had seen it herself. All she had to do was think of the little picture in her bedroom, the house surrounded by dark firs, the brown cow chewing and the upturned milk pails.

"Local witch took own life to escape punishment! Mob takes law into own hands! Mary Catherine Sinnett GUILTY of witchcraft!"

Rachel closed her eyes to better picture the woman. Mary Sinnett would have been plain, perhaps even ugly. Lank hair: a solemn expression. She might have been stained in some way, a birthmark on her cheek, or else an innocent skin complaint that might today be understood as eczema. Rachel imagined Ivan de Grey approaching poor Ms. Sinnett's cottage, conceding to knock on her door, this strange, lonely woman who possessed what he craved — and he wasn't a man used to hearing no. *"After Ms. Sinnett's death,"* the article continued, *"it was alleged that Ivan and Mary Catherine had enjoyed a brief affair, although this was commonly believed to be a subterfuge on de Grey's part, enticing Ms. Sinnett to invest in their union as a way of extracting her land. When he was refused his reward, de Grey severed contact with Ms. Sinnett and led a campaign against her that resulted in her death."*

Rachel was aware of the library going on around her, but it was as if she had entered another world. She pictured Mary Catherine and felt solidarity with her, this unfortunate woman who had stuck to her principles and been pursued to her end.

Of course they had all believed she was a witch. Even without the great Ivan de Grey's assurance, the evidence was clear. Mary was unmarried, she had no children; allegedly she concocted remedies using the herbs she grew in her garden. Once, Rachel read, a local man had crossed her path, only to develop a poison cough weeks later. The village's crops failed two summers in a row. It didn't matter that laws against witchcraft had been repealed decades before: communities like this continued long after to

473

enact vengeance against suspected felons.

And all along Mary Catherine had believed that Ivan had loved her.

"Occasionally I would hear her," Constance had said in her diaries. *"I would hear her singing, quiet and sad, of a man she'd loved and a broken heart . . ."*

Rachel sat back in her booth. Part of her recoiled at the absurdity of what she was prepared to accept. It was one thing for this woman to have existed, to have endured a broken heart and a terrible persecution and to have died in the Landogger waters — but to still be residing at Winterbourne? To have haunted the family all this time, as, what, revenge for the duplicity she suffered? Another part couldn't dismiss it. The theory was extreme, and yet it was the first thing that made any sense at all.

"It has always been here, this thing, at Winterbourne . . .

"Tempting the women into horrible games then destroying them one by one . . ."

Rachel had studied the injustices of witch hunts at school — in America, Salem and Hartford, but the principles were the same. *It became an obsession . . .* De Grey would have stopped at nothing to secure his land for Winterbourne, and thus the very foundations of the place, where Mary Catherine's home had once stood, were damned from the outset. Mary had quite reasonably defended her position. She had lived there a long time and so had her family. She loved her home and wished to remain in it.

Ivan de Grey was forced to conjure a plan. If this troublesome woman would not award him his prize, he would be sure to take it from her by some other means. Peering in one day at her spinster's house, the plate for one and the cup for one, the pathetic little stall where she'd done her rudimentary paintings, it was easy to settle. Ivan had smiled, and so their romance, too readily trusted by Mary, who was naïve in matters of the heart, began. When Ivan's cruel ploy failed to work, it wouldn't have taken much to make her pay up. Dig a little and it wasn't hard to find evidence, twist it this way and that: the ailing man, the failed crops, the birthmarks — women had burned for less. Whip round the villagers and secure their devotion — not a hard task for a man of his influence and standing — and settle on a date for her execution.

"On the night of 12 December 1806, Mary Catherine Sinnett was chased from Landogger Bluff and pursued down to the beach. Seeing no way to escape her fate, Sinnett herself entered the sea. Shortly after the New

Year, her body was found washed up on Pol-creath Beach, a little way down from where Winterbourne Hall now stands."

Rachel read the piece twice. All she felt was sadness. Sadness for a woman she had never met and who meant nothing to her, yet with whom she felt a strange attachment. She felt it for all those women who had been hounded to their ends in less enlightened times. Born of men's ignorance, men's misunderstanding and fear of what they could not control. Rachel could see Mary Catherine clearly in her mind, rushing into the hostile sea, knowing her death was inescapable but that she had to claim it on her own terms: she could not be killed at the hands of another. The whole village united against her, united in their confusion and hopes for a better life, for surely this witch was responsible for every unhappy thing they had endured.

The truth was here. The curse the de Greys had feared, whether it was true or not, here was why they feared it. But something was missing.

Then she saw it.

"Ivan Randolph de Grey moved quickly in building Winterbourne Hall, but during its construction he faced criticism over his handling of Mary Sinnett's belongings. Glad at

the freeing of the land, and failing to locate her kin, de Grey had dispensed with the contents of Sinnett's home at a church auction, selling mainly to passing travelers with no knowledge of local legend. Instead of donating the gains to the community, de Grey channeled them into his project, maintaining that Sinnett's assets, including the land she had lived on, belonged to him. De Grey preserved one item from the cache for his private possession: a Gothic, elaborately framed mirror . . ."

The mirror in the cellar, hiding in the dark . . .

The mirror in the hall, throwing back a reflection she barely knew . . .

Rachel swallowed, fear slipping under her skin. The mirror had never been bestowed on Laura de Grey. It had never been given freely. It had belonged since the start to Mary Catherine Sinnett, the woman murdered by Laura's family, her memory sold with no more dignity or respect than a lamb to market. The mirror was it. It had been the mirror all along.

Rachel closed the archives and grabbed her bag.

CHAPTER 37

CORNWALL, 1947

"Alice . . ."

My name. Someone is calling my name.

It is very faint, as if it is coming from a great distance. Then, louder:

"Damn it, woman, what are you waiting for? Open the door!"

Someone else is with him, then. A key rattles in the lock; and at last, at last, there he is . . . Jonathan, my Jonathan, and I must be dead, I must be dreaming, I must have crept into the forest and found my love inside because it cannot be real, he cannot be with me, divinely perfect in every way! He tears the rope away. I cough and splutter, my neck red with pain and the air as tight as thread through a needle eye.

I look up at him. In one instant he is Captain Jonathan de Grey and in the next the man I used to love, my teacher, my friend; then he is decent, honorable Henry Marsh, then he is my tyrant father . . . I

478

want to tell him to put the rope back with the others, in the forest where it came from. Put it back where Laura put hers.

"What were you thinking?" he begs of me. "You meant to do it to me again?"

"I don't deserve to live," I say. "I killed her. I watched her die. I could have helped her but I didn't. I watched her die and they never suspected a thing."

"Mrs. Rackstile," he throws over his shoulder, "she's delirious. Fetch the pills."

His arms feel good. I could stay in them until the end of days. Perhaps he and I are already in the afterlife, and this is how it is. Heaven.

"Whom are you talking about, Alice?" he says. "Who died?"

"The girl in the water," I say. "She never left. She found me. I've seen her, on the cliffs, by the sea. The children have seen her too. She came back. She found me."

His expression is one of such heartfelt concern that I kiss him. Softly he parts from me. "No, Alice," he says. "You had nothing to do with that."

"It was a long time ago," I say, "before you knew me. And you are glad to have known me, aren't you, Jonathan?"

He strokes my brow. "Shh," he says, "quiet now. It will be all right. I won't let what

479

happened to Laura happen to you. You are not safe here; I understand that now. I'm going to make sure you're looked after, Alice. I promise."

His face shines gold like an angel's. His eyes are the bluest I can think of. He is young and perfect, before the war, before Laura, when we were both young and unmarked and we had yet to make our mistakes.

"I'm going to take you now," he says. "Where would you like to go?"

I smile. "Paris." I have always longed to go to Paris. Robert promised me once that we would go, walk the streets together, be free, be happy.

"Then we'll go to Paris." Jonathan lifts me from the floor. After that it is like flying, or like riding Storm; we fly from my prison, away from the forest, away from the picture of the girl kneeling in the soil, away from the curtains and the stopped clock, passages rushing past at speed and then down the stairs and out into the night.

Fresh air strikes me. I stare up at black, endless space, and the air is deliciously chill in my lungs, making them burn.

Winterbourne watches me from the shadows.

Jonathan puts me carefully in the back of

the car. He touches my face, kisses me deeply, and his kiss tastes of salt and the sea.

I close my eyes. And dream of Paris.

Chapter 38

CORNWALL, PRESENT DAY

Rachel returned to Winterbourne in the early evening. She was surprised to see Aaron's Porsche parked on the drive, and when she opened the door he was waiting for her by the fire, his head in his hands. When he heard her, he turned.

"What are you doing here?" she asked. It struck her that his appearance was changed: he looked worried, his face drawn. "What's happened?"

As Aaron explained that he hadn't been able to leave, in the end, not without her, she was only half listening. She had greater matters on her mind. Everywhere she turned, Winterbourne was tainted, every wall, every hanging, every chair and table, all of it steeped in wretched history, somehow bigger than the death of Mary Catherine Sinnett, somehow more sinister and widespread than just that. She had felt the bad thing. She'd felt it when she found the bats. She'd felt it down in the cellar.

"Fine," she said, "we leave tomorrow. But I need your help first."

Rachel went straight to it now — the monstrosity in the hall.

"What's going on?" Aaron followed.

They stopped in front of the mirror.

"What are you doing — ?" he asked, as she tried to lift the frame on her own. The glass was turned away, mercifully, for she could not bear to meet herself in it.

"I'm getting rid of it," she said.

"Why?"

"Just trust me. Help me carry it, would you?"

"What are you going to do?"

She considered the ways in which she could destroy the damned mirror — because she knew, intrinsically, that it had to be destroyed. It could not survive at Winterbourne. It could not be taken by anyone else; it could not be hung or admired or even hidden underground because it was dangerous, it was insidious; it would always find a way out. It had belonged to someone else, once, and no matter Rachel's beliefs in things unseen, she could not abide the thought of it in the world any longer.

It had to be returned. She might burn it. She might throw it from the cliffs.

Returned.

She looked out of the window. The sky was losing light. But they had enough time, maybe, to do it. "We're going out to sea," she said.

Among the junk in the stables was an upturned rowing boat, splintered and debatably seaworthy — but it was their only option. It took an hour to get both things down to the beach. "Careful," Rachel urged in the growing dark, as their muscles strained beneath the weight of the mirror, "don't drop it." Aaron asked why she cared if she wanted it demolished anyway. "We can't break it," she said. "We mustn't."

The water was scattered purple, the sky pinpricked with the gloaming's first stars. At first Aaron had argued about waiting until dawn: it was safer, surely, than this misguided outing by torchlight. But Rachel would not be deterred.

"Nothing happens until it's done," she said. "We don't sleep, we don't eat; we don't leave Winterbourne. Nothing happens until it's gone."

It was uncertain as to whether the boat could support the weight of the mirror. They heaved it in first, water splashing round Rachel's ankles, chased by the occasional shiver of seaweed. She squinted at the pale beach and hulking rock, and was amazed at how much she could pick out in the swollen night, details heightened through her determination to see them, not to be blind, and as she glanced up the way they'd come she thought of Mary Catherine being pursued down the cliffs. Had she come this way? Had she turned to the sea and thought, *This is the end*?

Rachel climbed in. Aaron followed with the torch.

"We don't need to go far," said Rachel, thinking about how far Mary Catherine had got before she surrendered to the waves. The water was calm, ripples lapping the prow as Aaron churned ahead. Below was ink. White glimmered where the moonlight caught the surface, and the glass in the mirror shone like a desolate lake, throwing the stars back to where they'd started. "Almost there," said Rachel, shivering but warmed by her will, as the pastel line of the shore inched further from sight.

She grabbed the oars and took over. They'd be two hundred meters out now, at least. Mary Catherine's mirror would sink and never be seen again. It would never wash up and never be found. She thought of the quiet of the deep, quiet and still, miles

and miles of it beneath her, more mysterious than space. And in between those two
things, the above and below, their little boat
danced insignificantly and alone.

"Here," said Rachel, throwing down the
oars. "Are you ready?"

They heaved the mirror with difficulty,
trying not to capsize because with every
movement the boat tipped perilously. The
mirror's ornate frame, those grasping loops
and swirls, seemed to hold her wrists and
arms as tightly as she held them, and she
was gripped momentarily by the panic that
it had her now, like a terrible weed, and she
would never be able to shake it off. But
then, with a final upsurge, the hulk of it
flipped over and dropped into the water
with an almighty splash.

The glass drifted down as gently as snow,
illuminated by the constant moon. Rachel
saw her reflection in it, her lips parted, her
hand reaching out, her eyes searching, until
the reflection and its host was engulfed by
the dark.

The water was still. How quickly and
quietly the mirror was swallowed, the surface calm again, just a gentle slop and slurp
against the flanks of their boat.

"Thank you," she said, and strangely she
felt the urge to weep. Lightness surrounded

her; the fog in her head cleared. "We can go now."

But Aaron was regarding her strangely.

He didn't blink, didn't answer. She touched his knee, and this seemed to prompt him to focus on her. "Aaron, I said we can go."

By the dim torchlight she saw his distorted features.

"No," he said, "we can't."

A strange feeling crept over her. "Aaron . . . ?"

"I tried, Rachel," he said. "I did try. I tried to make you see. But you still don't see, do you?"

There was a horrible quiet, leaden with some meaning she could not decipher. Rachel thought of the mirror sinking down, down, to its final, lonely bed.

"Why couldn't you have made it easier?" he said, in a weird, disembodied voice. "I came to Winterbourne to find you. I tried everything. I gave you so many chances, but you didn't take them."

"Aaron," she managed, "you're not making sense."

"I drove and drove and I thought about it so hard," he said. "And I even thought I should end it there, be killed on the road because it would easier, then, wouldn't it? It would be revealed afterward, of course, but there I am: a coward to the last. I wouldn't be around to see it. I wouldn't have to endure it." His eyes shone in the dark. "But then I saw that I could still have it, Rachel. I didn't have to go home without what I came for, after all. It could still be mine. And I was going to get it some other way, back at the house, make it look like an accident . . . but this is better. Out at sea, where no one can find us. Terrible things happen at sea, you know."

A knot of fear tightened in Rachel's windpipe.

"You're scaring me," she said.

"You're my solution, that's how it is. Or, rather, Winterbourne is. When you first told me about it, I had no idea what it was worth. But I know now."

The marble in her throat started to roll. Their boat bobbed its lonely dance. No one knew they were here, alone . . .

"What are you talking about?" she asked, her voice thick.

"I'm in trouble," he said.

"What kind of trouble?"

Stall him, was all she could think. *Buy yourself time.*

"My life is over." There was that quiet again, like a vibrating string. "I've run my company into the ground, Rachel. The business I've worked to build over twenty years — it's over. I've lost it all. There's nothing left. We're so far in debt I can't see daylight any more." Suddenly he laughed. It was thin, cold, entirely without humor. "Nobody knows. The people who work for me, they think everything's fine."

Rachel was trembling now, cold and afraid. This wasn't Aaron. This was somebody else, a dangerous stranger. She questioned if the person she'd known over the past two years had been real at all. Aaron had only ever shown her one version of himself, in business or on dates or on weekends away — not the real, everyday vulnerability of an ordinary human being. They'd never known each other like that.

"I've built a career on knowing how to multiply zeros," he said. "But these last months I lost my touch. A couple of negative investments . . . then everything I went for crumbled. Time and again it went wrong, and the more it went wrong, the more I had to make it right; and the more I failed, the deeper in I got. I've always been a fraud, haven't I? Just stolen from other people, that's been my trade. But I was *good* at this, Rachel, once upon a time. Good at gambling, because that's what it's been, the destruction, the addiction, the impulse to keep putting your hand in the fire even though you know you'll get burned. The higher the stakes, the better."

Rachel fought to twist her head around his admission. Aaron was a billionaire. His family had houses in the Hamptons and LA and Texas. He was from one of the finest dynasties in America and stood as one of the richest men in New York. But he couldn't go to his family: a man like him would never admit defeat.

She touched his arm. "It'll be OK," she forced out.

It was the wrong thing to say.

"How?" Aaron rasped; he was possessed by anger, a wild anger that knew no reason. "Aren't you listening? If this comes out I'm as good as dead. What will people say? What will they think? I'll be the joke of the century. I'll go to prison for what I've done: I've done things I can't tell you, things I'd never tell a soul. I won't do it, Rachel. I won't let it happen to me. I'm better than that. That's where you come in."

"I'm here for you," she told him. "We'll face this together."

But Aaron shook his head. "I'm sorry," he said. "It's not enough."

Then time seemed to creep out of kilter,

for the next few moments slipped and slid over each other so that she couldn't be sure what happened first or by whom. She went to take the oars but Aaron beat her to it. One toppled into the water and the other he clasped in his hands, raising it like a batsman ready to take a swing. Idiotically Rachel felt for the sides of the boat, as if such a thing would save her, and she thought, *No. Not now. Not this.* He said: "Oh, Rachel, I'm sorry. I really am."

"Aaron —"

"It's too late," he said, clutching the oar with frightening determination. "With you gone, I can sell on my own. I've talked with my people. You signed the document giving me power of attorney." He smiled at her incredulous expression. "Don't you remember all that paperwork? By the end you didn't know what you were looking at, or what you were signing. You trusted me with everything. It was easy."

Her tongue stuck to the roof of her mouth. It couldn't be true.

"Winterbourne might not solve everything," he said, "but it'll start me off. It'll be the injection I need to keep my head above water." He looked down at the glinting sea. "Which, I'm afraid, will be more than can be said for you. And I'll be depressed because of what happened, won't I? That'll work in my favor, buy some time and get some sympathy. And I will be sad, Rachel, you know. I will miss you. We've had fun and for a while I did have feelings for you; I thought you could be it for me."

"I still can, Aaron," she pleaded, "if you give me a chance."

"Sorry. I've given you enough chances."

Before he could act, she lunged for him, thinking if she could just kick him off balance she could grab the oar and knock him out with it. But it didn't happen that way. The boat rocked; she struck him to his knees and for an instant they were both going into the water, surely they were, but then something hard hit Rachel's head, a cracking, solid blow that sent her crashing to the deck, choking freezing air. Warm liquid trickled into her ear. She couldn't see. Then his arms were round her, cradling her, and she felt like a beached fish, all flesh and wetness, slippery, and just like that she hit the wetness of the water as he flipped her over the side and the depths consumed her whole. She was under for a moment before her legs dragged up a last vestige of strength and propelled her to the surface. She gulped air. It was bitter in her mouth, compact as ice. A hand pushed her down. All was black and green, roaring in her ears and eyes and throat, her body blazing with the effort of survival. She flailed and gasped, grasped at nothing and inhaled everything, salt, water, weed filling her lungs and every part of her. Her muscles drained. She was dizzy, and tired, so tired . . .

She thought of Seth, smiling at her over the breakfast table on the last day she'd known him. She thought of Jack Wyatt, his big hands and the gray above his ears. She thought of his dogs snoozing in his farmhouse, on rugs that smelled of corn.

She opened her eyes underwater, and let go.

A green-eyed woman took her hands and pulled her down.

CHAPTER 39

WESTWARD, CORNWALL, 1948

Jonathan never took me to Paris. For a while I thought we were there. I could see the Tour Eiffel glittering in the purple night. I could feel his hand in mine as we walked the Champs Elysées. We were far away from Winterbourne, in glorious Paris, but of course that was not true. I drifted in and out of reveries, punctuated by brutal, white-hot pain, needles, voices, fastenings, and my limbs flailed as I tried to fight them off.

I missed my foliage at Winterbourne and wanted to go back. I decided to imagine it on the wall in my new, empty room, painting it diligently in my mind.

They told me what had happened. I didn't believe it at first. *Jonathan drove you to us,* they explained. Not to Paris, never to Paris. We arrived at this place of doctors and medicines, a place where I am called "dear" and spoken to like a child.

The Priory of St. Josephine's is a hospital,

they say. I do not need a hospital. I need Jonathan. But when I protest, they think I am mad. When I cry, I am hysterical. I cannot win, happy or sad, frightened or resigned, once they have decided I am mad. Even when I tell them that I killed a girl, they say I am mad. I am too mad to confess, too mad to be trusted. I tell them that that is what brought me here: my guilt over Ginny Pettifer, my murderous heart that I tried to hide and tried to heal. I thought that if I loved enough, if I tried to do the right thing, then my heart would mend itself. But it wasn't to be. In the end, I am mad. And it is possible, of course, that they are right.

They try peculiar machines on me. Some of them hurt. The one I like best is a drug that floats me to faraway places, sideways, like driftwood on the sea. I used to see things floating from my bedroom window at Winterbourne, floating on the water.

In July, I give birth to a girl. She is the light of my life, the softest thing, the sweetest thing, and her head smells to me of the purest joy I have ever known. I call her Sarah. She has Jonathan's eyes, blue and bright. When I look at her, I see him and wonder.

I know I cannot keep her. They have told

me so. Each day I stare out of the window and wish for Jonathan to come and claim us. But he does not come.

She is the last person I will ever love. On the morning they come to take her away, I dress her carefully, gently, wrapping her in a blanket, touching her nose with mine and kissing her downy cheek. Her fingers are tiny and perfect. I hope she has a happy life. I hope she loves fiercely and is fiercely loved in return. I hope one day she has children of her own and she keeps them closer to her than her own skin.

After she is gone, I am only half alive.

I breathe, I sleep, but I am only half alive.

It won't be long now.

I am ready.

In dreams, I visit Winterbourne. I see a woman there, myself, Alice Miller, sitting on her bed and looking at the little painting of the cottage on the wall.

Beyond, through the window, just out of reach, is her daughter. Her daughter is waiting, her beginning and her end, a girl she knew for the shortest of times and yet also forever, a candlelit part of her that will never know the dark.

I touch the woman's neck and feel the life go out of her.

I feel her heart stop. I make it happen.

The heart that was mine, I stop; it goes cold, goes hard, no longer lives.

Chapter 40

CORNWALL, PRESENT DAY

She would always go back to Winterbourne.
Just as she had been drawn here for the first
time weeks ago, she would always go back
to Winterbourne. Just as from the moment
she'd been born their destinies had been
entwined, she would always go back to Winterbourne. Just as, tonight, she was scooped
from the water and carried to the beach,
gazing up at the shadow of the house on
high, she would always go back to Winterbourne. Night. Stars. Heaven. And warmth
on her lips . . .

Him.

His hands held her face. She knew those
hands, recognized them as integral to her;
she wanted to hold them for all time and to
have them hold her.

Jack.

How had he found her?

A man and a woman hovered above, kind
faces, saviors.

She was lifted, carried, weightless.

"Jack . . ." she whispered. But it hurt to speak.

"Shh," he said. "We'll be there soon."

CHAPTER 41

TWO MONTHS LATER

Nothing shone as brightly as a sun-soaked Cornish day. The sea dazzled and the sky shone. Gulls swooped. Sands were golden and the waves eased happily on to shore.

Rachel took delivery of the first lorry-load of exhibits. As the paintings were unloaded, carefully parceled and bound, she felt a homecoming more profound than a hundred return trips to America. It was the perfect solution. She had spoken to Paul last week and given him the promotion: he'd earned it. He would take over the New York space, she told him, while she set up a new gallery here. It meant she was able to expand at the same time as staying in England. She didn't know yet what the future held, but there was too much possibility here to turn her back on.

The orangery at Winterbourne was the ideal platform, light, bright, and with the incredible panorama of the Atlantic to offset the works. She was excited about the new direction, had already been in talks with upcoming artists and the draw of the house itself was enough to attract the more exciting names. Rachel hoped it would also be enough to entice visitors. Winterbourne had for a long time been a closed fortress, but now, at least in part, it would be open to the public. The chance to visit her gallery would be a chance to visit the grandest, and most elusive, house in the country. What's more, if she could make money from it, she could set about repairing those parts of the estate in need of improvement. Both her passions rolled into one.

Rachel waved the delivery guys off and set about unwrapping the frames. Immediately their colors and vibrancy filled the space. She had spent all week clearing and cleaning the orangery, and was gratified at the beautiful structure hidden beneath decades of dust and neglect. It felt good to breathe life back into Winterbourne, to polish it and feel proud of it, and to set it working again.

Already she was imagining how she would arrange the prints, and what visitors and reporters would say when Saturday's private viewing arrived. For Rachel's own part, this fresh start signified more than success and more than money. It signified change. From now, she would do things differently. She was no longer working at the expense of her personal life, canceling one out in favor of the other, and wondered why for so many years she had thought it necessary. Women had both the world over, not because it was easy but because it was what they did — because women were the strongest creatures alive. Rachel had come to Winterbourne to find her past, but in the end it had shown her that and more. It had shown her that she belonged to a triumphant, irrepressible sisterhood. And she could have it all.

At last, here at Winterbourne, she could be happy.

There was nothing like a brush with death to make life seem all the sweeter. Afterward they'd told her that she'd come back from the brink, and it was a miracle she had survived her ordeal at all. When they had found her she'd been drowned, carrying only the faintest pulse that might so easily have been missed had one man not insisted on striving on: just one more breath, one more resuscitation; Rachel had to come back, she wasn't leaving them yet . . . On an unconscious level she must have known that herself. She tried to remember what happened that night but events sprang up in puzzling order. Aaron and the water, the pain in her head, the fear, the pull of the mirror — and then the beach, cool and smooth on her back. And Jack.

Saved.

Her recovery, the hospital said, had been astonishing. Rachel recalled the ride in the ambulance, wrapped in a coarse blanket, and the sensation of her cold, sodden hair trickling down her back. In the ward she was treated for her head injury, shock and hypothermia. She must have fallen asleep because when she next woke she was somewhere else, cosseted in a plump, sweet-smelling bed, with a mug of hot tea at her side and the smell of burned toast seeping up from downstairs. She'd inched a hand out from under the duvet and a warm tongue licked it. Dogs. Blankets. Farmhouse.

Jack.

Rachel had turned to the man next to her and, as if it were the most natural thing in the world, as if they had been together and married for fifty years, knowing every inch and part of the other, he leaned in and kissed her. He tasted of open air and wild oceans. *Jack.* She could never find the words to thank him for saving her life. It sounded so dramatic, so unreal, but there it was, what happened.

You're lucky, she'd been told repeatedly over the past two months. It was odd to hear it after so long being affiliated with misfortune. But it was true. She was lucky that Jack had been in the Landogger Inn that night when a local had come in, saying he'd seen a pair of figures staggering down the bluff toward the sea. She was lucky that Jack had thought it unusual enough to investigate, and she was lucky that he cared enough about her, even in spite of their argument, to follow his instincts.

"I knew it was you," he'd said to her in the ambulance, tightly holding her hand. "Whatever had been said between us, you weren't getting rid of me. I'd have followed you across the ocean if I'd had to. I care about you so much, Rachel."

She was lucky that Jack was a strong swimmer. By the time he'd reached the beach, she and Aaron had been far out on the waves, and he'd had to dive in without a second thought. She was lucky that the tides were on their side — as Aaron had been making his confession the boat had already been drifting closer to shore. She was lucky that by the time she went under, Jack was mere seconds away.

Rachel left the orangery and stepped out into the sunshine. She looked toward the sea and it was hard to believe, so kindly it appeared now, that it had once held such menace. She didn't know what would happen to Aaron. She'd been told, after Jack's rescue, that he'd had no choice but to come ashore. The police had caught him, and he'd since been repatriated to America where the courts would serve his sentence.

She had been trying to avoid hearing about his plight. It upset her too much, it still astounded her, and she tried to rationalize it by remembering how desperate he'd been, and how in a moment of savagery had sought the only exit he could fathom.

But still his betrayal had the power to wind her.

How long had Aaron been machinating to get his hands on the Winterbourne fortune? Had it been from the instant she'd told him, in his penthouse on Central Park? Had it been afterward, when he'd tried to sell through Wanda Pearlman? Had it been when he'd said he'd had feelings for her, and she'd believed him, and had that all been a lie? The last she'd heard the case had had a brief moment on US news, reports of an attempted murder on a random English coastline by one of the country's leading entrepreneurs. Rachel had shut herself away from the noise, taking solace in

Jack's embrace. Aaron had been fearful, above all, of negative publicity surrounding his bankruptcy. What he'd wound up with was looking a great deal worse.

Jack.

She had only to think of him and their future together to feel brighter.

He'd be here any minute to help unpack, for she wasn't just taking delivery of the gallery but also her own possessions. Admittedly she hadn't much to bring over from New York, and she planned to hang on to the apartment as a toehold in the city: as much as she loved Cornwall, part of her would always belong to Manhattan.

Remembering something, she went inside the house.

Winterbourne felt lighter now. Even Jack agreed, in spite of his rather skeptical expression when she'd told him what she'd been doing on the boat with Aaron, and her belief that the mirror was in some way haunted. In the light of day, and with distance now from her discovery at the library, yes, it did seem, at times, unlikely. Yet something had held her in its grip that night, and had seemed to hold Winterbourne long before, and now the mirror had gone there *was* a change. The rooms seemed sunnier. Shadows crept more quickly back to their corners.

"It was a witch, then?" Jack had raised his eyebrow during one of the long afternoons they had shared since, strolling the beach. They'd made a habit of it: going for romantic dinners or picnics on the moors, paddling in the shallows, eating fish and chips on the rocks, cooking together and sleeping together and somewhere in between they'd fallen in love, unable to spend more than an hour apart. The kind of serenity she'd thought she'd never find again. "And you think the de Greys killed her . . ."

"More or less, yes," Rachel had said. "But it was more than that. This man — Ivan — showed her happiness, what she thought was love, and then he set about murdering her. She went straight from bliss to her grave. It's awful, don't you think?"

"And she's been at Winterbourne ever since."

"I know you think it's crazy," she'd teased, with a smile. "And maybe it is. But Ivan built Winterbourne right on her land, right where it happened. Now I'm not saying she's been a ghost all this time, maybe she's just been a bad energy. And the women that suffered here did so because they claimed the contentment that Mary was denied. Or, at least, they tried to. Mary couldn't accept that. Winterbourne is hers."

"But it isn't, presumably, any more, since you're here."

Rachel had turned to him, confident. "It's a different place now," she'd said, knowing it was true. "Trust me. I gave the mirror back to her. It's over."

She walked now to Jonathan de Grey's study, keen to find what she was looking for. She saw it straight away, on his desk, bathed in the calm sunlight that streamed in through the window. It was a black-and-white photograph of the captain and his governess, Alice Miller, outside Winterbourne, their hands on the shoulders of two children. When Rachel had first found the image, buried in the very bottom of his desk where it might never again have seen the light of day, she'd assumed it to be the captain and his wife. But written on the reverse, in pencil, were the words:

Alice, my darling, and I.

Rachel crossed the picture with her fingertips. She'd had it framed, so precious she understood it to be, and would hang it at the entrance to the orangery. It would be the first thing her visitors saw: Rachel's grandparents, together.

My darling . . . His choice of words had surprised her. But then, attached to the back of the photograph, she had found a folded note, written by the man himself.

She read it again now.

Dearest Alice,

You will never read this letter. You will never see it. And yet I cannot desist from writing to you. How can I make things right between us? How can I make it up to you? I cannot. If I could do it all again, I would, and do it differently.

But I did not know, my darling. I did not know until it was too late.

I thought it was for the best. You would be safe there, away from me and away from this place that had caused you so much damage. I wanted you to be well, and once you were well you could go anywhere you liked, you could be free. But I could not ignore my heart. My heart woke me in the night, it followed me around in the day; it knocked and tapped at my window, demanding to be heard. I realized what I had been hiding from, and it was simply this: that I loved you. After everything, and against the odds, I loved you. It seemed tremendously easy when I faced it. I should have seen it sooner, when you first arrived and I thought that yours were the kindest eyes I had ever seen; or when the children took to you so naturally, and you to them; or when I learned you had dined with my doctor and it caused me such pain. Alice, I couldn't bear to think of you with another man, and to my shame I tried to warn you away from him so I would not have to again.

It wounds me more than is possible to express that I realized all this too late. That I did not make it in time. And the worst wounding of all comes from the fact that you must have believed I turned my back on our baby.

That summer, Constance showed me your letters. She wept as she admitted her deceit, promising that she regretted concealing the letters from me and she only had because she'd been afraid — afraid, in part, of you, and what had become of you at St. Josephine's, and afraid of what the letters contained. Some of them, she had opened herself. To say I was angry with her is to do anger a disservice. But after the fire had calmed, I was seized by a terrible sadness.

There were months and months of letters . . . With each one, my heart dropped.

Nobody told me, Alice. I hope, wherever you are, that you believe it. If I had known, I would have run faster than the wind to your side. I telephoned the hospital and demanded that I should speak with you. Our baby, at that time, would have been a little over two months old. But the nurse told me the news that you had died. In childbirth? I asked, numb to my soul. No, the woman said — and these words will stay with me until my dying day, as terrible for their tragedy as they are for their truth. No, she said, Alice died of a broken heart.

Frequently I have imagined that I know how that feels. I have gone to bed at night with an ache in my chest so physical, so real, that I do not expect to wake.

But wake I do. Life goes on, just without as much color as before.

You changed my life, Alice Miller, from the day you came to Winterbourne. Your spirit and your laughter brought us joy, and I think of the joy we might have known together were circumstances on our side. I lied when I told you I had seen Laura in your eyes, and that was why we made love. I saw you, and only you. But even then I feared you would be drawn to the dark, as she was. I saw the marks on your body, marks that covered you, according to St. Josephine's, by the time of your death. I tried to protect you by denying my love. I yearn to have admitted it sooner.

So little I can do for you now, my darling, but I can do one thing. I vow to keep watch over your daughter, our daughter, and provide for her as best as I can. I vow to love her, if only from afar. I vow to spare her Winterbourne and its heartache. If she wishes to find it when she's grown, so be it and I wish her luck. Know that she is well and happy where she is, a long way from here, with a safe and loving family.

Trust me to protect her until my dying day, my darling Alice. And then, only then, if there is indeed a God, I hope to be reunited with you.

Yours, always,
Jonathan

As before, the letter made her cry. Rachel folded it and held it against her heart, feeling that organ beating steadily through the paper. Her mother, the child Jonathan wrote about, *had* discovered Winterbourne when she was grown, and it had cost her her life.

Now, with Rachel, things began again. Things were different. She could change her family's fate and break the spell at Winterbourne. She already had.

I'll do it for you, she thought, and she thought about Alice, and Jonathan, and most of all her mother, driving through the rain with a baby on the back seat.

"Hello?"

She heard his voice in the hall, just as she'd heard him the first time he'd come up to Winterbourne and frightened the life out of her. Rachel felt a rush of happiness and went to meet him, glad that of anyone to draw her from her grandparents' tragic love, it should be him, Jack Wyatt, with whom the dice would be cast anew. Their love would prevail. Their love had come through the storm and out the other side.

He kissed her deeply. "How's it going?" he asked. "The place looks good."

"We'll be ready for Saturday." She smiled. "You'll be here, won't you?"

"I wouldn't miss it."

They kissed again, and as Rachel felt his arms around her she realized she had loved Jack from the instant she'd met him, from the moment he'd challenged her, from the sheer and special difference of their worlds, from the morning she'd climbed into his

Land Rover and seen all those dog blankets strewn across the back seat.

Jack accepted her past and the complications of her future. Rachel had told him of her plans to trace her biological father. This man was the last piece and he was out there somewhere, the man who had known Sarah Thripps and the last vessel that carried Rachel's blood. Even if he were dead, even if he were a disappointment, she could handle it. At first Jack had worried such a journey would cause her pain. But when she explained, he understood. "I'm with you all the way," he'd said.

And supposing her father wasn't either of those things? Supposing he was alive, and well, and had been looking for her too? Stranger things had happened.

"Come with me," said Rachel. She took Jack's hand and they went outside into the welcome sunshine, walking across the gravel toward the orangery.

"Look at this place!" he exclaimed.

"Impressive, isn't it? It's just missing one last thing . . ."

Rachel lifted the framed image of Alice and Jonathan and rested it on the hook on the wall. "What do you think?" she asked, standing back. And at that moment, with the house serenely behind her and the warmth of summer bathing her skin, she felt that all was, at last, right and well in this little corner of the world.

"It's perfect," said Jack.

She squeezed his hand.

"That's what I thought."

Chapter 42

Days later, Rachel turned the pregnancy test over and looked at the result.

She smiled down at her stomach. Well. She hadn't seen that coming.

It was Saturday, the evening of the launch. Jack was downstairs; she watched him from the window carrying the last tray of drinks across to the gallery. She would tell him tonight, when the last of their guests had left. For now, it was her secret. Happiness filled her.

"Hello," she whispered to the tiny person inside.

Our child. Our baby. For now, though, it was time to get ready.

Before she left the room, Rachel glanced once more at the painting of Mary Sinnett's cottage. She had completely forgotten about it, having packed the painting up weeks ago in anticipation of returning to New York. Only last week had she found it, and, while her instinct had been to get rid of it, just as she had the mirror, it seemed sacrilege to destroy such a perfect work of art — and a harmless one at that. The curse was over. The mirror was gone. There was nothing to be afraid of any more. To prove it, she had found happiness at last with Jack, and now with the promise of her precious new family. Life was beginning again. Winterbourne rejoiced with her.

She'd thought about hanging the painting in the orangery along with the other works to be admired, but it hadn't felt right there. It felt right here, where it had always been, by the green drapes and alongside the view of the sea.

M. C. Sinnett. The little signature in the corner shone out at her. Mary's painting. Rachel touched the age-old oils cautiously, for a detail had troubled her these past days. It was that the cottage window, which had at first been flung open, was, she could swear, closing a fraction each hour. She examined it now to test if it had moved again, and it had, she thought, a little — but it had to be a trick of her mind.

Rachel put a protective hand over her stomach. She caught her reflection in the panes, one side of her face washed in light and the other coated in shadow.

There was a hard red mark on her neck, like a scratch, and sore, slightly, to touch. A black shape flitted across her mind but the sunlight chased it away.

EPILOGUE
WINTERBOURNE HALL, CORNWALL

Listen! Can you hear it?

There, right there. Listen.

Listen harder.

I hear them before I see them. Voices and shapes, a man laughing, footsteps: conversations that pull in and away as steadily as the sea. They congratulate the woman of the house. She talks about Winterbourne as if it is hers.

It is not hers. It is mine.

It will always be mine.

From my window, I look down as the people emerge, scattering like ants. They dress neatly and drink from tall glasses. Don't they know not to come here?

This house will always be mine.

My painting calls me, quietly, quietly, *Come back, come back; we are ready.*

I turn to it and lift my skirts over my ankles, for the grass in the garden has grown since I went last. The night summons me, a

519

full white moon. The wind kisses the firs. Can you hear? You might, if you listen. It is soft, naught but a whisper.

I step inside the painting, to meet the cool dark shell of the night.

ACKNOWLEDGMENTS

I'm grateful to the brilliant Madeleine Milburn — for bookish matters and so much more — and to her team at MMLA, especially Alice, Hayley, Anna, and Giles. Thank you to my editor, Clio Cornish, for her intuition, enthusiasm, and belief in the story. To Vanessa Neuling, for being a wise and generous first reader.

Love and thanks to Mum, Mark, and Jo, for enabling me to write with a young family. Also to my friends, whose kindness never ceases to amaze me, in particular Chloe, Jen, Kate, Caroline, Vanessa, Penny, Rosie, Gemma, Mel, Sam, and Emily.

Thank you to Victoria Fox, for the many things she taught me.

And to Charlotte and Eleanor: my candles in the dark.

ABOUT THE AUTHOR

Rebecca James worked in publishing for several years before leaving to write full-time, and is now the author of eight previous novels written under a pseudonym. Her favorite things are autumn walks, Argentinean red wine and curling up in the winter with a good old-fashioned ghost story. She lives in Bristol with her husband and two daughters.

The employees of Thorndike Press hope you have enjoyed this Large Print book. All our Thorndike, Wheeler, and Kennebec Large Print titles are designed for easy reading, and all our books are made to last. Other Thorndike Press Large Print books are available at your library, through selected bookstores, or directly from us.

For information about titles, please call:
(800) 223-1244

or visit our website at:
gale.com/thorndike

To share your comments, please write:
Publisher
Thorndike Press
10 Water St., Suite 310
Waterville, ME 04901

8|20